Meet Me in Ivy Falls

Meet Me in Ivy Falls

in

Ivy Falls

AMY TRUE

CAEZIK
ROMANCE
ARC MANOR
ROCKVILLE, MARYLAND

SHAHID MAHMUD
PUBLISHER

www.CaezikRomance.com

For Wendy…
Sister. Friend. Fighter.

Cover art by Diane Meacham.

ISBN: 978-1-64710-129-9

First Edition, First Printing, June 2024
1 2 3 4 5 6 7 8 9 10

CAEZIK
ROMANCE

An imprint of Arc Manor LLC

www.CaezikRomance.com

1

TORRAN

Being Front And Center Gives Me Hives.

I needed a win.

Wait, let me rephrase.

I needed a big freaking win.

It's all I could think about as I stood in the kitchen of my latest project: the historical renovation of a 1904 Craftsman bungalow that needed all the TLC it could get.

TLC. Tender loving care. That's all many of the old houses in Ivy Falls needed. But my business partner Manny swore the phrase meant "Tired, Laughable, and should be Condemned" when it came to the properties we bought.

Not this property though. This one was special. This one was going to change everything, and after the long months of grief I'd been wading through I needed this to go right.

Most days it was just me and Manny moving through the house along with a few contract workers who helped with plumbing, electrical, and drywall. Today, the kitchen was filled with cables and wires that resembled a tangle of black snakes. Those wires powering interrogation-bright lights and film cameras that sat in various corners of the newly renovated kitchen.

"Torran, we're almost ready for you," Lauren Gillroy, the producer for Hearth and Home Network, said to me before turning to the director of photography and discussing where they wanted me to stand for the one-on-one interview.

Manny walked in my direction, his fingers pinching the brim of his Tennessee Titans baseball cap. Like he was navigating around quicksand, he carefully moved his hulking body, taking care not to jostle any of the equipment that looked like it'd cost a year's worth of work to replace.

"Remember to say the countertops are quartz not marble. People always get that mixed up." He scrubbed at the black whiskers on his chin. "Also, the wall color is called 'Forest Flow' and plays nicely off the custom cabinets."

"I know I'm not as smooth as some supermodel strutting the catwalk, but I can give a simple description of the kitchen. If you happen to remember, the quartz was my choice. So was the paint color." I jokingly poked a finger into his thick shoulder. "I promise I have this under control."

Manny quirked a thick eyebrow at me. He wasn't my brother but he should have been by the way he could sense my moods, and today's mood screamed anxious with a good dash of terrified.

"You've got this, Tor. Pretend it's only you and me walking the house. As usual, you're trying to convince me that a rat hole with crumbling walls and hundred-year-old plumbing can be a shiny gem one day. You always have a vision. A focus for a house just like you did for this one. Talk about that and you'll be fine." He gave me a steady gaze like he was willing me his incredible strength.

"Okay, yes." I nodded like an idiot. "If I can live through repairing a broken sewer line, I can definitely handle a basic interview."

I wasn't sure who I was trying to convince more—him or me.

Several times I'd told Lauren that Manny should be doing the interview. That I was a behind-the-scenes, didn't-mind-getting-dirt-in-my-hair-and-drywall-on-my-skin kind of girl. Being front and center gave me hives, but Lauren insisted demographics showed female viewers connected more with a show when a woman was on camera. Lauren clearly knew this business. She spouted ratings data and advertising revenue numbers like she studied them day and night. The last thing I wanted was to upset her, because this TV pilot could change our lives.

The walls of the kitchen tightened in as more cameramen and assistants filled the small square space. Lauren swept across the room in three-inch heels. Her curtain of shiny black hair swung behind her. "Manny, I need you up on the ladder doing touch-ups to the wall with the green paint."

He gave me one last reassuring smile before moving past the wide picture window above the sink to the ladder set up in a corner near the creamy white cabinets with the nickel hardware.

"Torran, I want you next to the outer edge of the island. We'll start with you in the frame and then I'll need you to walk back and allow the camera to pan out as you speak." Lauren pointed to an X made with black electrical tape on the other side of the island. "Stop at that spot. When the director gives you the signal, begin with all the details needed to make this kitchen so stunning."

Warmth filled my cheeks at the compliment and I agreed to her direction.

Once I was in position in front of the island, a slate clapped down and the director pointed at me to start.

"When we first bought this house, the floor below us was crumbling." My voice came out shakier than a jackhammer against concrete. "Manny spent days under the house to ensure the foundation was stable."

A flash of my mom blazed through my head. What would she say about all this? Would she tell me to slow down? Speak clearly? Smile when I could?

Make it right, Torran.

It was the last thing she'd said as she was taking her final breaths. In that moment I didn't need her to explain. She knew about my goal to save the dying history of Ivy Falls. Had seen me visibly shudder as more than one historic house in town was taken down by a wrecking ball or a massive excavator. We were one step closer to that dream once we finished shooting this last scene in the house, and I had to do everything to make sure it went perfectly.

The camera tracked me as I walked behind the island. Blood pounded in my ears. The noises in my head, the ones that screamed I wasn't good enough, that I wasn't smart enough or lucky enough to pull this off, grew louder. I was supposed to stop at the mark on the floor, but my dark thoughts snowballed. If I couldn't get this pilot right, the show wouldn't get picked up. We'd lose our shot at getting the money we desperately needed to float our construction business. To buy more homes before the town council condemned them. To preserve the history of Ivy Falls for future generations. The last few months we'd been scraping by, always managing to give enough money to our creditors to keep them at bay for one more month.

I shook off the darkness. Forced myself to remember what we'd rehearsed. What Manny said about pretending I was only talking to him.

"We spent a week at town hall tracking down the blueprints for the house. Once we understood the original structure, we made every effort to keep the historical details in place including the beamed ceilings, shiplap walls, and turn-of-the-century fixtures lighting most of the house."

When I reached the corner of the island, edging closer to the ladder, a flicker of white caught my eye. Before I could correct my footing, I hit the corner of a rug someone had placed near the sink. Like a bad movie in slow motion, my boots skidded out beneath me. My brain knew what was happening but my body lagged behind. I tried to turn, avoid the ladder, but I rammed it with the corner of my shoulder.

Everything slid by like my body was in a *Matrix* glitch. The gallon can fell off the ladder and grazed the top of my head. A cold river of paint splashed over my hair and down my back. The chemical scent coated my nostrils. My mind went wild with images of green splashed across the soft white cabinets and dripping onto the heart pine floors we'd worked so hard to restore.

"Torran, *do not* move or open your eyes." The panic in Manny's voice pinned me in place.

Oh God, it was bad. So *so* bad.

Paint ran underneath my shirt and down the length of my overalls. My father had warned me that buying this property was a mistake. Half the town wanted this place torn down, and I'd ignored them all. A wave of grief, fear and rage swirled within me. I tried to tamp it all down, but—surprise, surprise!—the rage won out.

"What the actual fuck! Why can't one thing go right?" Panic climbed the walls of my throat and the air became too thin. "I don't know why we even bother to help Ivy Falls. No one gives a crap about what we're trying to do here. What we're trying to save. All they do is gossip behind our backs. Question whether or not we're doing right by the town, but are they doing anything besides sitting on their asses and complaining? No. And don't get me started on my father, who'd rather smile for the camera and the local papers than do his job and be a real mayor!"

As soon as the words were out, I regretted them. The town wasn't the issue—*I* was. I'd been so caught up in thinking about how everything had to go right that I hadn't bothered to survey the room.

"Stop rolling!" Lauren's shout vibrated in my ears. "And someone google how to safely remove paint from the face and hair!"

"I've got this." Manny's voice drew closer. "Tor, that can bumped your head pretty hard. Sure you're okay?"

"Yes, I'm fine. It barely hit me," I said in a trembling voice. "Please just get me out of here."

His warm hand landed on my shoulder. "I'm going to lead you out of the house and over to the shade of a tree so the heat of the sun doesn't dry out the paint." His fingers curled around my arm and a light autumn breeze brushed over my cheeks as we made our way outside. The wood on the restored front porch squeaked beneath my boots.

"Do we have a crowd?" I asked.

"No. It's quiet out here. Must be lunchtime."

Since we'd started filming, a regular crew of Ivy Falls characters including Silvio from the hardware store, Mrs. Vanderpool and her little dog, even my dad on some days, stood outside the rope blocking off the yard from the street. Their eyes set firmly on the house while a flurry of activity and filming happened. I sent a quick word of thanks to the karma gods that my screwup was not on display for the town gossips.

Once Manny had me down the steps, he barked out, "Get me some turpentine and dish soap. Haul the hose over this way too!"

The quick shuffle of feet said the crew was in frenzy mode. Manny stayed stoic helping to slow my racing heart which I was sure was about to rocket straight out of my chest.

Rivulets of paint continued to race over my skin. The weight of it dripped from my ponytail. All I could think of was my mom. How she was so much like Manny. She would have told me to stay calm. That this was the type of mistake that could be fixed. My stomach clenched at the thought that I couldn't go to her after this. Be soothed by her positive attitude that seemed to make any shitastic situation actually bearable.

Manny used turpentine and then soap and water to scrub the paint off my head and face. Besides the ache in my shoulder and slight throbbing at the back of my head, I was otherwise fine.

When Manny said it was okay, I opened my eyes. He tried to smile, cheer me up in his own small way. I could only manage a shrug, using all my willpower not to crumble in front of the entire crew who'd formed a semicircle around me. Their eyes clouded with worry. Lauren, on the other hand, refused to look at me.

Manny slung an arm around my shoulder. "When you screw up you go all in, don't you, Tor?"

He always did this. Teased me when I'd messed something up. It was meant to make me feel better. Let go of whatever stupid thing I'd done, but after what just happened in the kitchen that was impossible.

"I'm very sorry, Manny. How bad is it?"

"Don't worry. We'll clean up the mess. Get back to work like we always do." He gave me a reassuring glance that didn't quite reach his eyes.

I knew it. It was worse than he was admitting.

He walked in the direction of where Lauren stood next to one of the production assistants. The tight line of her shoulders warned she was at a breaking point. We were already over our production budget, and I didn't want to think how long we'd have to delay filming to clean up my mess.

I moved away from the camera crew and across the fresh sod we'd laid down in the front yard. The heat of the sun warmed my cheeks and I took a deep breath. Manny was right. It was an accident, plain and simple. Nothing we couldn't fix.

It wouldn't be until days later I'd learn the true fallout of my mistake thanks to a viral video uploaded to YouTube. A video that showed not only my hometown, but the entire world, what I really thought of Ivy Falls.

I'd wanted to be the town hero, but I turned into its villain in one click.

So much for my freaking win.

2

TORRAN

Another Link In The Gossip Chain.

Six months later...

WITH the chime of the clock tower ringing in my ears, I raced across the wide lawn in front of town hall, dodging kids playing freeze tag and mothers swapping local gossip.

Two more chimes.

Three o'clock.

Shit. Shit. Shit.

Being late was sort of my signature move. No matter how early I set my alarm, planned out my day, I was always about ten minutes behind. My mom claimed it was because I was always lost in my own world. Dreaming up designs for beautiful houses with big red doors and backyards large enough for family barbecues. I thought I was being creative. Everyone else thought I was being rude. Mom never pushed me on it because she said even in the womb I was taking my own sweet time, showing up two days past my due date.

God, I missed her.

Sometimes the grief was so powerful I wasn't sure I could get out of bed. But I'd let enough people down in my life and I had to push forward.

The scent of fresh cream and milk chocolate spilled out of the Dairy Dip as I raced past its wide glass doors facing the center of the square. My steel-toed boots pounded against the uneven brick sidewalk as I picked up my speed. A thin sheen of sawdust and colorful drops of paint covered the toes. Each mark a thrilling memory of the jobs I'd worked on. My younger sister, Tessa, groaned every time I wore them. I didn't care. They gave me confidence. And on a day like today when the future of my business hung in the balance, I'd take all the positive I could get.

I kept my gaze forward trying not to make eye contact with Old Mrs. Vanderpool who stood outside Ginny's candle shop. Her teacup Yorkie—Baby, who was dressed in a red and green Gucci sweater—barked at me. As I passed by, she whispered out a curse that was just loud enough for me to hear.

Not today. NOT. TODAY.

A few kids zipped past me on their scooters and I was grateful for their smiles. At least there were a few people in this town who didn't hate me.

My phone buzzed in the front pocket of my overalls. I was sure it was another text from Manny fuming that I wasn't on time. Again.

A car pulled through the only downtown stoplight. Once it passed, I rushed through the crosswalk, the bubble of the limestone fountain buzzing in my ears.

Every inch of Ivy Falls held a vivid memory for me. Skinned knees on brick paths as I learned to ride a bike. The warmth of my mother's hand as she led me to Val's Bakery to buy fresh bread. Even the heated thrill of my first kiss which happened in the tree-lined alley behind the Sugar Rush Café.

My phone buzzed again and this time I started to sprint. When I reached the far corner, I stopped in front of my destination: Ivy Falls Community Bank.

Open An Account With Us. It Makes Cents! was written on the stark white sign planted outside the two-story brick building my dad owned.

Since my father became mayor, he'd started a contest called "The Sign Says It All," encouraging local businesses to be clever with their signage. It was meant to build community spirit. Encourage tourism. But all it did was add to the fiery competition between the store owners who were always trying to one up each other.

If my father's staff thought this saying was going to earn them a win, they were in for a disappointment.

The scent of freshly waxed linoleum and old copper pennies hit me when I yanked open the wooden door. A few customers lingered in the teller line. When their stares landed on me, I looked away. I should be used to the angry glares by now. The way most people in town treated me like I was the walking plague. More than once my mom's voice rang in my head, telling me to be the bigger person, but it was hard when practically every resident of Ivy Falls saw me as the local pariah.

Should I have cursed out the town while on camera?

Probably not. But when your heart was breaking you did a lot of stupid things.

With my head tucked down, I made my way toward the corner of the wide square room. I was only steps from Isabel the bank manager's desk when Amos Tucker locked eyes on me.

From the time I was five, my dad's best friend and assistant would squat down next to me and ask about school. What kind of trouble I'd gotten into lately. In his regular uniform of a white button-down, khaki pants and bright red suspenders, Amos would plop me onto his desk chair with the squeaky wheels and spin me in a circle. My giggles filled the room until my father scolded us for our behavior. Amos would wait until my father shut his office door and then spin me a couple more times. Even now, twenty-two years after that first spin, he still had a mischievous sparkle in his eyes. He was one of the few people in Ivy Falls who didn't want me to burst into flames every time he saw me.

"Well, well, if it isn't Miss Torran Wright. How are you, darlin'?" He patted the sparse pieces of white hair clinging to his scalp before reaching into his desk and pulling out a butterscotch candy and offering it to me.

"No thank you," I said.

"You sure?" He frowned. "These used to be your favorite."

When I was five.

"Sorry, Amos, I'm in sort of a hurry. Isabel has my checks for the auction."

"Did you see my message on the sign?" His hearing had never been very good. "Pretty clever, right? I think we're going to win." His cheeks pinked up as he nudged my side with his elbow.

"It's cute," I offered.

He arched a wiry white brow at me. "Hmmm. Not impressed, huh? I've got funnier ones coming!"

I scanned the corners of the room, surprised by how few people shifted around the space. The bank was usually humming with people looking to talk to the loan officers or making deposits for their local businesses.

"Looking for your dad?" Amos followed my shifting gaze.

"No." The word burst from my lips too quickly.

This was the exact reason why I tried to avoid Amos every time I walked in the door. He and my dad grew up on the same street. Were on the town council together. He was like a beloved old uncle who told the same two stories over and over. By now I knew how to smile in the right places, laugh at the same jokes, because that was the sort of thing you did for the people you cared about. But being interrogated every time I stepped in the door had me rethinking my decision to have my business accounts here.

Not that I had a choice: my dad's bank was the only one within twenty square miles of Ivy Falls.

As if sensing my distress, Isabel appeared near the row of teller booths and waved in my direction.

"Gotta go, Amos."

"Sure. Good to see you, kid." He opened his mouth, hesitated like he wanted to say something but shook his head. I'd gotten that a lot in the last six months.

I rushed over the beautiful white oak floors toward Isabel's desk. It wasn't until I fell in love with architecture during my senior year of high school that I noticed the beauty of this old building. The stark white crown molding. The hand-carved cornices in every corner of the room. A true show of craftsmanship from Marcus Bosworth who'd built most of the early buildings in Ivy Falls after it was incorporated in the late eighteenth century. It was buildings like these that I was trying so hard to save.

I slid onto the chair and leaned in. "Can we make this quick, Isabel? I'm running late and I give Amos two minutes before he tells my dad I'm here."

"Of course, sweetie. I'll get you out of here lickety-split."

She slid open her desk drawer with a polished red fingernail. One of my dad's smarter decisions was to hire Isabel fifteen years ago. People were surprised when they learned she had a Harvard law degree but was working in such a small town. As she explained it, all the schooling in the world could get you places, but those places were worthless unless you loved being there.

It took one month, and a hot-off-the-press high school diploma, before I left Ivy Falls. Much to my father's chagrin, I'd picked the college with the most miles between me and the small Tennessee town where I grew up. But when my mom was diagnosed with colon cancer two years ago, and my little sister's husband left her with two small children right after, Ivy Falls yanked me back quicker than a sudden spring tornado.

"I made the checks out for the exact amounts you wanted. When you give Diego your winning bid," she winked, "fill in the payee info and you're good to go."

Her eyes narrowed and I braced for it. The quiet lecture about how I'd disappointed everyone. How it was sad that a hometown girl would say such awful things about the place she grew up, but the smile she trained on me was anything but bitter.

"Alabaster Cream?" She pointed to the white paint caked to the end of my ponytail.

"No," I said, reaching for the twisted bit of hair that hung over my shoulder. "It's called Winter Moonlight. I painted the inside of the house on Parkview in this color. It makes the dark wood accents look clean."

She leaned in, lowering her voice. "I know you miss Phoenix, but you're starting to make a real difference in this town." Her lips pinched together and her gaze went weary. Maybe I *was* going to get a lecture. Instead, she pulled in a heavy breath and said, "This place needs…" She broke off. Shook her head. "What I mean to say is that you should get a little recognition for taking on the hard projects. Making good changes in Ivy Falls."

I tried not to laugh. What this town really wanted was to string me up by my thumbs after what I'd done to embarrass them.

"All I need is to win the property at the auction today. Since Huckleberry Lane went into foreclosure, I've been dreaming about all the ways it can be beautiful again. How I can restore the intricate ironwork on the widow's walk. Rebuild that wraparound porch so the new owners can sit on it and have a cool glass of sweet tea on a summer afternoon. It'd be my first major project since I've been back."

"If Diego had any sense at all, he'd sell you the place outright. I know Huckleberry Lane was one of the first big houses that was built in Ivy Falls after it was incorporated. It's a darn shame it's gone to rot."

There was a tense roll to her words that was odd for the usually laid-back Isabel. I wondered if my dad was in one of his "moods" today.

I wished she was right about Diego and Huckleberry Lane but lately too many homes in town with decades of history were put on the market. I saw each one as a living, breathing manifestation of Ivy Falls' history. Through the grit and grime, I visualized the potential to turn each property back into beautiful showpieces again.

The renovation vultures who attended the auctions were another story. As soon as they saw the listings, they descended like soulless ghouls with visions of bland, cream-colored duplexes that'd turn Ivy Falls into just another plain and charmless town. I couldn't let that happen, especially to the house on Huckleberry Lane.

It was a bad idea to get attached to any home with sentimental value because it messed with your business brain, but I didn't care. Huckleberry Lane was my last shot at redemption. A chance to earn back the town's respect, as well as re-establish my reputation, after I'd become a one-hit wonder on the internet.

13

I'd worked hard to erase that terrible day from my mind. To forget about the half-million (and growing) online views, and the contemptible glances I got whenever I walked into Minnie's Market to buy a box of cereal or check out the paint samples at Hendrix's hardware store.

Isabel sat back and fluffed her silver bob. "No one has so much as blinked at that house in two years. I'd say it was as good as yours." Her gaze darted around the bank. "Everyone knows you're the right person to restore it whether they'll admit it or not. Once you get a hold of that place it's going to be a beauty."

"Unfortunately, it doesn't work that way. If you have the money, you have a shot to bid," I said, pulling the checks across the desk. "Just hope this is enough to scare off any other buyers."

The lines of zeroes made my head spin. Manny had questioned if we needed this house. If it was the right project for us. After showing him the numbers, the kind of profit we could make, he'd been convinced—but we both knew it was a risk. The money we'd put out was the last of our company's savings and our credit cards were maxed out. If this didn't go well, no connection to the family bank would save us from our looming creditors.

Like Amos a minute ago, Isabel hesitated before a slow smile crossed her lips. "It doesn't matter what happened in the past, you've got skills, young lady, and this town is darn lucky to have you."

"Thanks. Can you spread the word around?" I joked.

She returned the laugh. "I'm working on it. You and Manny go and do your thing. People will get over themselves soon enough."

"I hope so," I said, pushing my chair back. "Still, keep your fingers crossed for me."

She gave me a wink. "Don't need to, honey. It's in the bag."

The creak of a door sounded behind me. I pushed in the chair and tried to make it to the side exit.

"Torran!" My father stalked across the room and customers scuttled out of his way. The sharp, unforgiving creases in his blue pinstriped pants matched his demeanor. His thick head of silver hair was combed into its perfect white helmet and his mouth drooped into its regular perma-frown. "Were you even going to say hello?" he said, planting himself in front of me.

"I'm in a hurry today. Auction and all." My heart pounded in an unsteady rhythm as I waved the checks in my hand. One interaction with him was all it took to turn me into a wobbly-kneed little girl again.

Several sets of eyes fixed on us and he pulled me into a corner. My phone made its annoying buzz again.

"I'd like to have dinner soon with you and Tessa and the girls. Can you break away from all your leaky plumbing and termite-infested hovels to join us?"

The snark in his tone stung. Too many times he'd questioned why he'd paid for an engineering degree if all I was going to do was "crawl around old houses" (his words, not mine). I'd tried a dozen times over the last year to explain why I loved my job but he never listened.

Story of my life.

"I'm busy and things aren't great with Tessa and the girls."

"You should make time. Family matters most." His voice went up an octave like he was performing for the crowd. He was in what my sister liked to call "mayor mode." I took a breath, trying my best to be cordial, aware of the audience watching, but just looking at him made a cavern split open in my chest. Mom always said he was a bear on the outside but inside his heart was soft like a lamb's. For years I'd tried to see it, give him chance after chance, but after what he'd pulled the day she died all I saw was a man minus a heart.

"Like I said, I'm busy."

"Please." His voice dropped low, his gaze landing on the customers who were still watching us. "Let's not do this today. Come into my office where we can talk in private."

A mix of raw emotion scrambled my brain. I heard my mother's voice, begging me to figure things out with him, but then flashes of that empty hospital hallway filled my head. It'd been almost a year since we'd lost her and now he wanted to talk?

I couldn't do this. No matter how bitter my memories were, I wouldn't cause a scene. There were already enough whispers flying around town about me, and I refused to add another link to the Ivy Falls gossip chain.

"I'm already late. I have to go." I spun away and pushed out the exit door.

With the warm spring sun beating against my head, I raced past the old post office and the spot that used to be Olga's antique store. She unexpectedly closed the business a few months ago and went to live with her daughter in Georgia, leaving yet another storefront empty in the square.

When I reached the door to my truck, I leaned my head against the window and pulled in a full, yet shaky, breath. Nothing could rattle me today, not even my own father. My single focus had to be winning Huckleberry Lane. Keeping my promise to my mother and showing everyone in Ivy Falls that I was worthy of their trust again. That no matter what I'd said in a flash of anger, I really did care about this town.

3

BECK

Run And Never Look Back.

THE speedometer raced over thirty as I drove past the town's carved wooden sign welcoming me to Ivy Falls: *Home to 10,032 smiling faces and award-winning berry cobbler.*

I expected memories, but nothing could have prepared me for the knot tightening in my gut as I sped through the center of town, past the park where I played Little League, and my old high school.

When my friend Diego reached out to tell me his company was auctioning off my childhood home on Huckleberry Lane, he'd told me that unless another interested party bought it, it'd probably get leveled to build condos. I'd brushed him off at first because I had zero interest in returning to the place that held so many memories for me. A day later, he sent me another text with the listing and I couldn't believe my eyes. It seemed impossible that the once beautiful house was now in a state of rot. If my parents had still been alive, it would've pained them to see the place in such bad shape.

All week long I'd tried to forget about the text, the house, but it was like a fucking siren pulling me back for one last look. Forcing

17

me to remember all the good times I'd had with my family before my life went dark in one blazing moment.

A line of stores including the Dairy Dip and Minnie's Market slid past my window. I kept an eye out for one of my favorite spots. As I turned the corner, my stomach knotted. The storefront for Robert's Hobby Shop was empty. Just like everything else in my life, the spot where my dad and I had spent hours mulling over which model car sets to buy was now pitch-black.

After a few more turns, I pulled into the driveway of 2227 Huckleberry Lane. Built in 1895, the once stunning two-story Colonial Revival home now had a gabled roof that sagged like a frail old man. Cream-colored paint flaked off the wide center pillars. Inky-black oil stains dotted the cracked concrete driveway. The lawn my dad had mowed with precision every weekend was now a rocky pile of dirt and weeds.

I didn't blame my grandpa for selling it after my parents died, but it would've been nice if someone had cared for the house the way my mom and dad did when we lived here. Diego told me the house had had several owners over the last few years until a property management company bought it and began renting it out. When the company defaulted on their loan, the bank contacted him about selling it at the auction today.

Wet, sticky heat clung to my forehead and dripped down the back of my neck. I shrugged off my suit jacket and laid it across the back seat. Forcing my feet forward, I climbed the rotting wood stairs until I stopped on the wraparound porch. The old swing my parents loved hung on by a single rusty chain. I cupped my hands around my eyes and looked through the big bay window. Piles of empty beer cans and fast-food wrappers littered the living room floor. Like some avant-garde art show, swaths of colorful graffiti covered every inch of the walls.

The place was a mess. All the floors would have to be replaced, as well as the windows and front door. I could only imagine what kind of shape the rest of the house was in if the living room was that big of a disaster. Maybe someone should put a wrecking ball to it.

"No," I said more to myself than the house. I'd been back in Tennessee two years and had managed to stay away from Ivy Falls. I couldn't reopen that chapter of my life no matter how much it killed me that the home my parents had taken such loving care of now looked like the scene of a bad horror movie.

The porch groaned under my feet. Another warning sign to run and never look back.

I sped down the crumbling stairs and back to my car. Once I was behind the wheel, I floored it out of the driveway. My condo was only forty-five minutes away. Forty, if I pushed the speed limit. I pictured a cold beer defrosting in my hand as I reviewed the proposal for the new account my team was pitching in eight short weeks.

I did a quick U-turn and headed back through town. A flash of my little sister, Piper, running in the front yard filled my head. She'd loved that house. The way she could dance around the wide-open kitchen. Play her beloved piano in the front room with the natural light streaming in through the big bay window. She cried all the way to the state line when we left.

What if I bought it? Restored it and brought her home? It could be a reminder of how things could be good and simple again.

Thankfully reality took hold of my muddied brain. I knew nothing about restoring a house, and with everything else I had going on in my life buying it would be a supremely bad idea.

I stopped at the next light and an old Ford truck with sky-blue paint rumbled up beside me. In the driver's seat a woman belted out a Moon Taxi song at the top of her lungs. Her blonde ponytail swung behind her as she tapped the wheel in rhythm to the beat. The windows of my car vibrated as the music grew louder. Her sweet voice moved through my car like it'd found a way in through the air vents.

There was only one person who loved the soulful beats of the Nashville indie band as much as I did.

Torran.

It felt like a sign—if you believed in that shit.

Panic quickly filled my chest.

Should I ease down the window?

19

Call to her?

Give a casual wave hello?

No. I wasn't supposed to be here. I'd already decided I was going back to Nashville because there was nothing left for me in Ivy Falls.

The truck's engine revved. When the light turned green, she sped through the intersection.

My foot stayed on the brake. There was too much pain here. Too much of my parents in every corner of this town. But I hadn't seen Torran in a decade, and as much as I did not want to admit it, things hadn't changed since we were kids. She was the sun and I was the Earth unable to resist her gravitational pull.

I hit the gas and was quickly behind her. A burst of laughter escaped my lips as her truck (which I'd nicknamed Sally Mae because it matched Torran's sassy personality) hugged the curve near the Dairy Dip like she was gunning for Turn 4 at Daytona.

I stayed on her tail as she sped past the Pool and Brew on the corner of Main Street, its rickety steel sign declaring: *Serving Drinks Colder Than Your Ex's Last Text.*

Ouch.

Further down the road, the sign for Mimi's Pizza read: *We'll Give You A Cheesy Grin.*

What was going on with the signs in this town?

Torran took one too many sharp turns. The back passenger wheel careened over several curbs. The truck finally slowed and bumped into the parking lot of Diego's business, Gold Star Properties.

I pulled into an empty spot across the street. Torran hopped out of her truck and raced to the line forming in front of the door. There was still the same bounce in her step—like she heard one of her favorite alternative songs on repeat in her head. She rushed up to a guy standing on the sidewalk who could have been The Rock's body double.

A sudden ache whipped through me. Was he her boyfriend? Husband?

My hand hovered over the gearshift. All I had to do was put the car in drive and go. But this was where the auction was being held. I could go inside and casually watch as someone bought my old house. If I did run into her, I could say a simple hello. No big deal.

I waited another beat and then another until the sharp rise in my pulse forced my legs out of the car.

What the hell was I doing? Things ended for Torran and me years ago, but I could never get her out of my head. Forget the way she smelled, kissed, stood on tiptoe to whisper in my ear. No matter how many women I dated, they never quite measured up to her, which wasn't fair. I mean, who really gets over their childhood sweetheart?

4

TORRAN

My Best Dream And Worst Nightmare.

"RIGHT on time as usual," Manny teased even as the lines around his eyes deepened. "Did you get the checks?"

"Yep, right here." I patted at my front pocket.

"Good." His broad linebacker shoulders relaxed as he gazed at a sea of worn John Deere hats, paint-splattered coveralls and skin worn brown by the late spring sun. "Man, there are at least thirty people here." He tilted his chin toward the cracked sidewalk leading up to a small yellow bungalow that housed Gold Star Properties, the site of today's auction.

I stood on my tiptoes counting. "Twenty-nine," I huffed out.

He gave a good yank on the brim of his Titans baseball cap. "Where'd they all come from?"

"I don't know but I wish half of them would go home."

Ferris Johnson turned around and gave me an irritated glare. Around town "Fixer Ferris," as the ladies in the knitting circle liked to call him, was known as a jack of all trades. Helping out widows with overflowing toilets and front doors that squeaked. It was only in the last year he'd turned his interests into renovating houses. He shuffled forward as the line moved, grumbling under his breath about the evils of the internet and green paint.

No matter how much time passed, the locals still gave me trouble about my disastrous TV debut. They could shoot me dark looks, whisper unkind things under their breath as much as they wanted, but I wasn't going to run away. I wanted this property and no one was going to shame me into giving up.

As the line grew, I recognized a few other contractors who'd challenged me at these auctions over the past year. The rest were out-of-towners whom I guessed wanted a quick turnkey place to make a little cash.

It was hard not to laugh. Had they *seen* any of the houses listed today?

When the renters moved out of Huckleberry Lane, I might have done a little trespassing. At dusk one evening, I shimmied inside an open window. The putrid stench hit me first. Two steps inside the kitchen and I had to hold my T-shirt up to my nose to breathe. The place was a complete disaster. All the appliances were gone. Sledgehammers had destroyed anything the past tenants couldn't steal. All the sinks and tub drains were filled with cement. They'd even left gross little surprises in all the toilets which explained the smell.

I'd seen some horrific properties since I first started working with a small construction company back in Phoenix several years ago, but Huckleberry Lane was by far the worst. None of that mattered. I'd loved the house for a long time even if the memories of it made me slightly nauseous.

"Folks, sign in, grab a numbered paddle, and then follow me to the courtyard outside. We'll start the auction in five minutes," Diego Morales, my old classmate, and local real estate magnate, called from the doorway.

People scooted in through the entrance and took their turn scratching their name on a clipboard. When I made it inside, I showed Diego's assistant, Brittany, my cashier's check for ten thousand dollars, a requirement to be part of the auction, and a second check showing proof of funds. Once she confirmed my signature, she handed me a bright yellow auction paddle. Manny took it from my shaky hand.

"What's going on with you?" he said, guiding me down a set of brick steps. Magnolia trees flush with bright white blooms circled the cobblestone courtyard providing some much-needed shade. Manny chewed on the corner of his lip. His gaze flicking to me every few seconds. "Did you get into it again with your dad?"

"No," I lied. "I'm fine."

His lips formed into a thin line but he didn't say any more. He knew by the tone of my voice that I didn't want to talk about it.

The courtyard filled up quickly and I steadied my feet like I was readying for battle. Although I hated it, construction was still a man's game. Like at every other auction, I had to prove I could stand toe to toe with the men who treated me like a fly who'd dive-bombed into their grits. I'd already renovated several historic homes in town that nobody else wanted, and I'd keep buying and restoring each one until the history of Ivy Falls came alive again.

Even though I'd put on a brave face, I couldn't help the nervous tap of my foot. The way I knocked the plastic paddle against my leg. I needed this house. If I could bring the property back to its original state, it would shout to every busybody in Ivy Falls that I was committed to this town no matter what I'd said on that video clip.

My mother's voice floated through my head.

Make it right, Torran.

One of her last wishes was for me to help Ivy Falls, and I'd screwed that up with the video. This house was my final chance to set things right.

The last of the crowd filled the tight space. Ernie Fields, who always wore the same faded brown Carhartt jacket, passed by and said, "You don't belong here."

Brad Fulton sneered at me from under a thick mop of dark hair, adding, "Go back to Phoenix." He'd only had his contractor's license for a year and already gained a reputation for whining about the price of lumber and choosing cheap finishes.

They could grumble all they wanted, but nobody would be sneering or laughing when I outbid them on the best house on Diego's list today.

The final bidder, a guy in a dark blue suit and black sunglasses, was the last to enter the courtyard. Great. Another outsider. Probably a proxy here to bid for a real estate developer who wanted to tear down the beautiful home and build a bunch of cookie-cutter condos that had about as much appeal as a glass of warm milk. He moved into the shade of the magnolia like he didn't want to be seen.

"Let's go over the rules before we get started." Diego's deep brown eyes lit up as he began to list each address for sale. "All these homes are sold as is. There are no warranties or returns. The winning bid will assume any liens or back property taxes. If you secure any of these houses, you will be expected to sign on the dotted line and take ownership today. If you can't pay for your final bid with a cashier's check, you forfeit your ten-thousand-dollar deposit. Are we clear?"

The crowd bobbed their heads in agreement. I glanced at the man in the suit. There was something familiar about the set of his shoulders. The way his light brown hair swept over his forehead.

"Good. Let's begin." Diego raced through the first five houses on the list. I hoped as people made their bids, and lost, they'd trickle away, but the crowd still stood shoulder to shoulder in the courtyard when Diego announced, "Our final property today is 2227 Huckleberry Lane. It's three thousand four hundred square feet. Four bedrooms, two baths, located on a corner lot. We'll open up at two hundred thousand dollars and take bids in one-thousand-dollar increments."

Manny leaned in. "What's our max for this place?"

"Two sixty-five," I said. "Comps in the neighborhood are coming in right at around three eighty to four hundred."

"And what's our reno budget?" he asked.

"Around a hundred thousand."

The key was to take the auction slow. See who the anxious bidders were. The ones who came in with a number first and had the least money to spend. The people to watch out for were the quiet bidders. They took their time. Waited on the auctioneer to call for last bids and then swooped in and offered a ridiculous amount that knocked out the rest of the competition.

My gaze veered back to the guy in the dark suit. Most of his face was blocked by the tree's wide branches, but I could make out a small tick of a smile. It could have been a friendly gesture, but there was something about it that was unnerving. He was trying to intimidate me. I may not have looked serious with sawdust covering

25

my ratty, loose ponytail and paint splattered across my overalls, but I played this game better than any suit from Nashville.

Cam Willoughby, an old-timer with a reputation for high finishes and taking forever to turn a house, chimed in with the minimum opening bid. Lucas Pride, the newest contractor in town who was known to cut corners, choosing cheap laminate over hardwood floors and prefab cabinets over custom, followed up with another bid, a thousand dollars higher. They went back and forth like old biddies arguing over whose pie was better at the church potluck.

Manny elbowed my side. "You better get in there."

I lifted the paddle as high as I could to get Diego's attention, and damn if it didn't shake even though I did my best to hold still. "Two hundred ten thousand."

Cam and Lucas went at it again until they neared the two twenty-five mark. Diego swung his hand between the two over and over until a deep, low voice behind me called out, "Two hundred and fifty thousand."

The two men's mouths dropped open. Manny's hand tightened around my arm. "You better start bidding again or that suit is gonna run away with it."

Before he could finish the sentence, my hand shot up. "Two hundred and fifty-five thousand."

Cam and Lucas shook their heads when Diego pointed in their direction. He repeated the number, and they both dropped back into the crowd mumbling that it was too much.

"We're at two fifty-five," Diego announced. "Two fifty-five. Do I hear two fifty-six?"

The crowd went quiet. I tried not to show any emotion, though I felt like bouncing on my toes in glee. Ten thousand dollars under my max budget was an incredible buy. With that extra cash, we could fix up the front yard. Add a few perennials. Maybe a sprinkler system. Give the house real curb appeal. All I needed was for Diego to confirm my final bid and Huckleberry Lane would be mine.

"Two hundred and seventy thousand dollars." The voice boomed behind me.

"That's the proxy in the suit," Manny said, his voice tighter than piano wire.

Oh, hell no. A corporate stooge was not outbidding me. I didn't want to imagine what a developer would do to it. Visions of wrecking balls made me fume. This was *my house*. I wasn't going to walk away, not when it could mean so much to the community. My arm got halfway up to bid again when Manny stopped me.

"Don't do it, Torran. I know you want the house, but we're gonna go bankrupt if you bid any higher. I love this job and I need to put food on the table for Louisa. Let this one go. Please."

I wanted the place so bad I was willing to go over budget even if it meant having to beg my dad for the cash. I envisioned painting the eaves a soft white, the perfect contrast to onyx-black shutters. How a custom hand-carved oak door from my favorite carpenter in Franklin would add to its charm. Restoring it to its original beauty would prove to everyone in Ivy Falls that these houses were worth saving.

I wanted to argue until I saw the fear in Manny's eyes. He'd gone right for the jugular when he mentioned Louisa. He knew how much I adored his young daughter.

I took a shuddering breath and lowered my paddle.

Diego called out the suit's bid again. It echoed inside my head like an agonizing scream. I clutched Manny's arm. All eyes watched me, waiting to see if I'd jump back in. I lifted my chin and waited until Diego's voice called out, "Sold." With that single word, small fissures found their way into my heart. Huckleberry Lane was gone and there wasn't a damn thing I could do about it.

"Let's get out of here," Manny said. "We need to look at paint for the master bath at Parkview."

I barely heard him as I turned to get a good look at the man who'd stolen my dream. He stepped out of the shade and when we locked eyes, his grin faded. He slid off his sunglasses and a chill went through me. I knew that tilt to the head. The small scar etched beneath his bottom lip that would be easy to miss if you didn't know it was there.

The left side of his mouth lifted, showing a deep dimple.

It was really him.

My best dream and worst nightmare come to life.

The man who'd taken my house, who'd smirked as he outbid me, was its past owner and the only man to ever break my heart. Beck Townsend.

5

BECK

Armor Fully In Place.

I'D always pictured this moment between Torran and me as some kind of soft reunion where I'd confess my past. Explain why I'd stayed away from Ivy Falls for so long, and that despite everything, she'd forgive me. But with her glaring at me like I was the devil returning to haunt the town, I'd clearly misjudged the situation.

I should have gone home, stayed out of the auction, but I couldn't do it. The idea of someone else owning a piece of what was my history, Piper's history, forced my paddle up time and time again. There was no choice now. I had to tell her why I was here. Why I'd bid against her, but before I could put together a coherent sentence, she fled out of the courtyard with the Rock's stunt double trailing behind her.

Over the years, I'd done a little online snooping. Seen the article in *The Tennessean* about her business. Even watched that horrible clip on YouTube a few times. Anger cramping in my chest as the paint slid over her beautiful head.

I'd considered picking up the phone and calling her. Apologizing for how I'd left her *and* Ivy Falls, but I never found the right words to tell her I was sorry about how things ended for us. That if she knew the truth, she wouldn't want me anyway.

A familiar ache burned in my arms and inched up my chest. I tugged down the cuffs of my suit jacket to hide the reality of what my life looked like now.

My phone pinged with a text from my business partner, Pete. After a few meetings this morning, I'd left the office to come to Ivy Falls. An itch in my brain telling me I had to see the house one last time. Pete never hovered even though I was a few years younger than him. Lately though, he'd been on edge.

In the last month our advertising agency had lost two major accounts, and we were readying a pitch for a new client we desperately needed. Me going MIA I'm sure was not helping with his anxiety, and I didn't want to think about how he'd take it when I told him I'd just bought a house in a town forty-five minutes away from work.

Voices in the courtyard grew as bidders moved toward the tables to make their payments. I skirted past them and up the brick steps. With every step I thought about what I'd say to Torran, but I knew nothing would erase the decade we'd been apart. The way I'd disappeared from her life without a word. Honesty would have been the right approach, but I wasn't ready to share why I'd been absent from her life for so long.

What I wanted to know was why she wanted Huckleberry Lane? Was it because it meant some kind of connection to me? The question made me walk faster to the door.

When I finally stepped outside I was relieved to see Sally Mae still idling at the curb. Leaning in the window was the same big guy I'd seen whispering in Torran's ear at the auction.

I lingered at the edge of the stairs until the Rock dashed across the street to his own truck. Once he pulled away, I raced toward Sally Mae, sliding behind the tailgate as Torran started to back up. As soon as she saw me in the rearview mirror, she slammed on the brakes.

"Seriously? Don't you know better than to walk behind a truck with its engine revving?" she shouted out the window.

Ten years apart and the sound of her voice still shot a thrill through me. I took a thick, uncomfortable swallow before strolling up to the side of the truck.

"And don't you know better than to back up without looking?"

Her mossy-green eyes narrowed into a deadly stare.

Yeah, I'd seen that video clip, and I was a fucking idiot to tease her about it.

The air sparked between us as I put my arms up on the roof and leaned in closer. "I'm sorry. Guess I was in a rush to see you before you sped off."

Her face stayed a hard mask. "Maybe you should think twice before walking into a spot you're not wanted."

The slow and deliberate way she spoke said she meant more than me just walking behind her truck. I'd forgotten how cutting her words could be when she wanted.

I knew she had a tougher side. As kids, whenever her dad would appear, she'd throw up this wall like she could guard herself from whatever snide comment he'd fling her way. After a while I started referring to it as her "armor." In all the time we'd known each other, she'd never used that side of herself against me. Until now.

"Okay, I deserved that. But seriously, how are you, Tor?"

"No," she snapped. "Only my friends get to call me that name."

Yeah. Armor fully in place.

"And I take it after what just happened in the courtyard we're not friends anymore?"

"I haven't seen or talked to you in a decade, Beck. What makes you think we'd be friends?"

Since I'd moved back to Tennessee, I'd imagined this moment so many times. How her eyes would flare when she saw me again, but this was not the kind of spark I wanted.

It was hard not to spill everything pinging around inside my head. How Ivy Falls was always on my mind. That even though I'd had to walk away from her, that choice haunted my every waking moment. But this wasn't the time for confession. What I needed was an act of contrition.

"I'm sorry about the auction. It looked like you wanted the house. Well, *my* old house. Why?"

She jammed the truck into park and cut the engine. "Really? It *looked like* I wanted the house? What gave you that idea? Was it me outbidding everyone else until you swooped in like a jackass and made it impossible for me to counter?"

Her voice grew rougher and panic built in my chest. This was not how I wanted this to go. I was screwing it up like every other relationship in my life.

"The house, I bought it because…" I wavered. What could I say about Piper? That since the day we'd lost our parents, she'd descended into a black hole she could never climb her way out of. "I did it for Piper. It'll be good for her to see the place restored. And my parents, they…" I hesitated trying to find the right words. "Well, they loved the house. If they were alive, they'd be sad to see the way it is now."

Her shoulders gave a little and she said, "I'm sorry they're gone."

Even though it'd been years since I'd lost my mom and dad, I still hadn't gotten over the ache that gripped my heart whenever people offered their condolences.

"Thanks," I said quietly.

"What happened? Why did you never come back to Ivy Falls, Beck?" Her gaze searched mine, begging for an answer I wasn't ready to share.

"I was sad to hear about your mom," I said, desperate to change the subject. "Diego told me she passed a little while ago."

Her distant stare swiveled to the front window like she couldn't bear to look at me. "Yeah. It'll be a year in June."

A quiet intensity hung in the air. Hints of her jasmine perfume wafted toward me. The scent memory took me back to days when the only things we worried about were high school grades and how her notoriously early curfew made our make-out sessions frenzied.

"How is Piper?" she finally asked.

"She's hanging in there," I mumbled.

Hasn't been in jail for a while.

Sober again after another stint in rehab. I think.

All the responses flew through my head, but I replied, "She lives in New York City. Waitressing and auditioning for TV shows and small theater productions."

"That's good. I remember how much she loved the Ivy Falls theater. Miss Cheri still runs it. I'd bet she'd love to know about Piper."

31

I expected the tension in her shoulders to ease a little as we talked about my sister whom she'd always adored, but her fingers stayed gripped to the edges of the steering wheel.

"How is Tessa?"

Like I'd said the absolute wrong thing, the tight lines around her mouth went firm again.

"She's okay."

There were subtle things about her that had changed over the years. Her hair was a darker shade of gold now. Instead of one, three earrings now decorated her lobe. There was a small tattoo of the number eight behind her left ear. A raw instinct inside of me ached to reach out and trace the shape. I pushed down the urge, curling my fingers into fists.

"I don't know why you're here, Beck, but I'm going to ask one thing of you." Her voice went cold like I was no better than some stranger she'd met on the street. "Don't screw up the house. Too many places in Ivy Falls have had their historical bones stripped away, and the town is slowly losing important pieces of its legacy. A few months ago an independent contractor gutted the Sorenson place that was built in 1890. Then a developer came in and leveled the Sandersons' early-twentieth-century Folk Victorian to build a few townhouses," she said, gritting her teeth. "In one fucking fell swoop, over a hundred years of Ivy Falls history was gone."

As kids when she wanted to make a point she always gave a dead-eye stare, refusing to blink, or give any indication that she cared, even though she really did. She was giving me that same look right now and it made me sweat.

"I'll restore it right. Make it beautiful again."

"No, I need a promise because I've worked my ass off to breathe life back into the important houses in this town, and I don't want you messing it up. Tessa has two daughters. I want them to know and see the history of their hometown. I want you to assure me that you'll hire qualified people. Make the right choices in renovating the house, because I swear to God, if I see another French Country knockoff I might just lose my damn mind."

This was no joke to her and I wanted her to know I'd heard every word. I leaned in closer hoping she could see the truth in my eyes, but I quickly got lost in the curves of her soft pink lips. The way she could still perfectly arch her right eyebrow when she was irritated.

"You have my word," I finally sputtered out.

"Good. Maybe you can keep *that* promise."

The hurt and anger in her voice was like a dagger straight to the heart. I had known coming back here would be filled with memories, but I had never anticipated the ache that would fill my chest as I witnessed how clearly she hated me.

"I have to go." She cranked the engine over. It roared once and then sputtered out. The lines in her forehead multiplied as she turned the key again. This time all that filled the air was a sharp click like the engine wouldn't catch.

"Dammit." She flung her hand out and I quickly stepped back. Her thick boots hit the pavement and she stalked to the tailgate, pulling out a plastic step-stool. Stomping around to the hood, she set down the stool and then climbed up. A barrage of curse words flew from her mouth before she pushed up the hood.

When she'd first bought Sally Mae, I may have teased her once or twice about being so tiny she couldn't see over the steering wheel. That joke, or any other kind of teasing, wasn't going to fly now so I stayed quiet and moved in to stand beside her.

God, she smelled good. And the way her ponytail swung over her shoulder sent me back to the days when we'd ride our bikes around Ivy Falls in the summer. Try to trap fireflies in glass canning jars at night. From a young age, even before we started dating when we were fifteen, we never left each other's side. Now she could barely stand to look at me.

"Carburetor again?" I managed to push out over the catch in my throat.

"No. It's the damn spark plugs."

She turned a few knobs, her fingers going slick with dirt and grease. Every move she made she did with confidence and it was hard not to smile. I'd forgotten how much she loved this old truck. How she'd worked every summer, saved every single bit of birthday and Christmas money to buy it from Mr. Lathan's widow after he passed away. The day it clunked and sputtered into the driveway of Huckleberry Lane she wore a smile brighter than any sun I'd ever seen.

"I can't believe you still have Sally Mae," I said.

She continued to push and prod more wires. "Some of us can't throw away the past so easily."

Another zinger I totally deserved.

She kept huffing and cursing as she worked around the engine. I felt like a useless ass standing next to her with my hands shoved into my pockets.

"What can I do to help?" I said, even though I didn't know a damn thing about cars.

She snorted like she remembered that fact too. "Climb inside the cab and wait until I tell you to turn over the engine."

"Okay. Yeah. I can do that."

I rushed around to the open door and crammed my body inside. The floor carpet was a muted black. An aftermarket radio took up a small part of the dashboard. The blue two-toned bench seat still had a split down the middle. The memory of Torran and I making out in that exact spot in a secluded area by Lake Rainer shot a lick of heat through me.

"Try it now," she said.

I gripped the key and cranked it right. That faint click moved through the air.

"Stop," she ordered and I eased back into the seat. Sitting inside the truck was like being in a time machine. Every gouge in the upholstery, small crack in the windshield, was a reminder of the days we'd jump in Sally Mae and go anywhere just to be alone.

The truck bed was still a faded baby blue with flaky paint hanging off the sides. My eyes scanned for the old purple sleeping bag she kept in the back for when we went stargazing. All that was there now was a ladder hitched to one side and a faded red toolbox. Another reminder that she'd grown up. Moved beyond our time together.

"Try it again," she said.

I turned the key. There was a low clunk followed by a guttural sputter before the engine roared to life.

Torran pushed down the hood, threw the stool in the back, and returned to the door. A thin stripe of oil covered the edge of her jaw. I started to tell her about it when she motioned for me to get out of the truck.

"Sally Mae hasn't changed, has she?" I said, taking my time to slide out. Do anything to delay her. Make her stay and talk to me for a while longer.

"Nope." She climbed back behind the wheel and slammed the door with a heavy clunk. "A lot of things in Ivy Falls refuse to change."

"Wait." I panicked and gripped the edge of the door again. "Will I see you around town?"

"It's a small place. I'll do my best to stay out of your way."

"That's not what I meant. Maybe you and I, we could have coffee? Talk? There's a few things I'd like to say to you."

"I'm busy and you've got your hands full with the house—if you even know what you're doing."

"I swear I can handle it, Torran."

She flinched like my saying her name caused her physical pain. After pulling in a thin breath, her narrow gaze traveled down the length of my tailored suit. "Yeah, right. Goodbye, Beck."

She revved the engine and peeled down the street. I waited for her to look back, give any sign that my reappearance meant something, but she'd made it clear that she was done with both the conversation and me.

6

TORRAN

Worse Than Bad Gas Station Sushi.

DISEMBODIED. *Disemboweled.* As a seventeen-year-old kid, I'd dug through the dictionary trying to figure out the right word for what it felt like to have my heart ripped out.

After Beck and I ended, I wandered around Ivy Falls like a part of me was missing. A hole settled deep in my chest that no one could fill. Not my parents, sister, or my friends. Little did I know that only the threads of time: days, weeks, months, years would sew me back together. But it only took one short interaction with Beck today to yank out those carefully fixed stitches.

I gripped the steering wheel, praying Deputy Ben wasn't hanging out in that little alley between the Dairy Dip and Mimi's Pizza. The last thing I needed was a speeding ticket as I floored it through the town square and took the corner near Park's Pharmacy at too quick of a clip, my wheels squealing as I turned.

Who the hell did Beck think he was? He couldn't just waltz into Ivy Falls after a ten-year disappearing act and pretend things were fine between us. And how had he acted so cool when

36

I spoke about his parents' death? Their passing had become sort of a town mystery.

When their obituary showed up in the *Ivy Falls Gazette,* all it listed was their bios and Beck and Piper as their next of kin. Town rumors swirled but no one could get the real story. I'd tried to hunt down more information. Googled his last name for months, but nothing came up. When I finally found Beck's maternal grandparents in Oregon, they'd asked for privacy and hung up on me. Two days later Beck's email arrived. In a few brief sentences, he said he was staying in Portland and that we were over.

Discarded.

That was the right word for how I felt. After years of being inseparable, he'd simply cut me off.

That fury I felt at the auction rose in me again.

I hated the way he'd bid on the house like money was no object. How he thought he was so cute sidling up to my truck, looking too damn beautiful in that expensive suit. When he called me Tor I had to suck in a quick breath because the sound of my name on his lips lit a freaking match inside my chest.

He'd claimed he'd bought the house for his sister, but that twitch in his left eyebrow warned it wasn't the whole truth. Another thought sent ice through my veins. Did that mean he was going to live there too?

My pulse raced as I imagined him walking around the town square, bumping into him casually at Sugar Rush or Minnie's Market and not having a clue what to say. Or, in my typical way, saying the absolute wrong thing.

Why was this happening? I was just getting things back on track. And what the hell did Beck know about renovation? Just by the soft sheen of his hands (which I may have caught when I was checking him out) it was obvious he'd never picked up a hammer in his life.

A pissed-off growl spilled past my lips and I pressed harder on the gas pedal. Manny had tried to calm me down after the auction. He knew something was off, but he was good at reading my cues. And today my cues had warned that he shouldn't push.

I'd promised him I'd look at paint samples for the little ranch house we were working on over on Parkview. But that would have to wait because I needed to vent to someone who would understand my fury over Beck's unexpected homecoming.

I took one more sharp turn and pulled into the parking lot of the Pen & Prose bookstore. All of my favorite memories were tied up in the ivy-covered brick building nestled at the edge of the town square. The P&P, as my mother loved to call her store, is where I'd spent a major part of my childhood.

Shoving my shoulder against the heavy wood door, I pushed my way inside. At first it was hard to come here after we'd lost her. Now it gave me comfort to see her elegant touches around the store. The rich wood-paneled walls that matched the mahogany checkout counter she'd had custom-made so she could lean over and share whispers with customers about her favorite books. How the children's section looked like a rainbow explosion with bright prints on the wall featuring her favorite illustrators like Vashti Harrison, Ian Falconer, and André Ceolin.

Across the space she'd set out oversized chairs and love seats in muted colors of crimson and charcoal, inviting customers to stay and relax. She'd wanted it to feel like an old English study, a place where people could come and get lost in a good book. Judging by the success of the store over the years, she'd more than achieved that goal.

All the P&P regulars sat in their typical places this afternoon. Susan and Barb, who owned my favorite café, the Sugar Rush, looked cozy as they thumbed through the latest issue of *Bon Appétit* on a small couch near the romance section. Maisey Bedford sat with her twins near the board books using an animated voice to tell the story about a pug with too much attitude.

I pushed away the shock of seeing Beck again and let the scent of paper and hard-bound leather loosen the tension in my neck and arms. Let the thud of my solid steps across the walnut floors tame my speeding heart. Allowed myself to remember all the wonderful times I'd spent in the shop with Mom.

She'd been my inspiration for starting my own business. Since Tess and I were young, she'd spoken of wanting to own a little independent bookstore where the people of Ivy Falls could come and hide from the worries of their day. It'd taken years, but when

Miss Betty's tea shop went out of business and the space became available, my mother worked her magic on Dad.

At dinner one evening when I was seven, she supplied him with a business plan. As usual, he could not deny her. Less than a year later the P&P was up and running. Between the monthly book clubs, and the weekly children's story hour, the bookstore cemented itself as a cornerstone of the Ivy Falls community. My dad may have been elected mayor, but it was my mom who was the town's beating heart.

My sister peeked her head out from behind a bookshelf where she stocked non-fiction. "Hey, Tor," she said with that easy smile that had mercifully returned after months of pain. "Did you see my new sign for the contest?"

"Yeah." I leaned back to get a look at the sign outside. "I don't think *If Art Doesn't Make You Think, Question, Contemplate, Then It's Not Doing Its Job* is going to bring home that goofy trophy Dad has made every year."

"It's the truth. That's what matters." She shrugged like she could care less about the contest, but, as always, she'd do whatever she thought would make our dad happy.

When I reached the end of the aisle, Tessa was rearranging shelves. As she tucked back her long auburn braid, a sweep of grief rushed through me. Every day she looked more like our mother. Long, elegant nose. Full lips. High cheekbones. She was my opposite in every way and yet in the last year I'd never felt closer to my little sister.

"You're staring," she said while her focus remained on the shelf.

"It's okay if they aren't perfectly straight, you know," I teased.

She huffed out a sigh and went back to making sure the covers were aligned. "It has to be neat. Easy for customers to find what they want."

I was thrilled my mother willed the shop to Tessa. She'd worked here through most of her teen years and, just like me, she used the bookstore as a refuge from the world. Besides her girls, it was the only thing that kept her grounded after Billy, her slimy, worthless, piece-of-crap husband ran off almost two years ago with Trini, a waitress from the Pool and Brew.

"How are you feeling today?" I asked.

She pulled at the end of her braid, a nervous tic that said she didn't want to answer.

"Tess, on a scale of one to ten?"

This was our code for how we were feeling about our grief. We'd adopted it from our time in the hospital with Mom. Nurses would ask about her pain on a scale from one to ten. Now all we had to say was a number, one for deep in darkness, ten for actual happiness, and we'd know where we were at for the day. How often we needed to check in with each other.

"Five," she whispered before moving to the end of the section and pulling a bunch of heavy tomes from the shelves that also looked a little sparse.

I moved in closer and set a hand on her shoulder. "I'm here, you know. We can talk about anything. The girls. How Barb's hair is an interesting shade of lavender this week. Even how 'Fixer Ferris' gave me a furious look at the auction today like I'd driven Sally Mae over the award-winning roses in his front yard."

How the asshole who'd broken my heart, and done a ten-year disappearing act, was back in town.

She arched a brow at me. "That bad, huh?"

"Yep. I'd say my number is hovering right around a four today."

She straightened the shelf one last time before stretching out her arms and pulling me into a hug. She even smelled like our mother—hints of rose water wafting off her sweater. Every inch of me ached. I missed our mother so much it was like half my heart had disappeared.

"You need to ignore all those people who can't get over the video," she said gently.

I held on to her for another minute wanting to forget all of today's horrors for just one more set of breaths.

Of all the people I hated to disappoint, it was Tessa. When her husband left, she'd gone into a deep depression. I'd moved in to help out with her girls. She still didn't eat or sleep enough, but slowly she was blooming back to life. My problems were the last thing she needed to worry about right now.

"Does your number also have something to do with Huckleberry Lane?"

"I'm going to throttle Manny. Does he call you the second he leaves my side?" I said, pulling away abruptly.

Manny and Tessa never moved in the same circles until she became a single parent which forged an ironclad bond between them. Which meant every time something happened with our business, Manny told Tessa before I could even dial the phone.

"Don't be mad. He's worried about you. Said something about a stranger buying the house. That you were pretty upset about it."

I shook my head, trying to rid my mind of how damn good Beck looked in that suit.

"Tor, tell me what happened," she coaxed in her gentlest voice.

"The stranger who bought the house was Beck Townsend."

Her eyes went wide as I sank into a thick red chair and spilled the entire tale about the auction. How Beck's sudden reappearance, and the way he outbid me for Huckleberry Lane, sat in my stomach like bad gas station sushi.

She arched a brow, pursed her lips, but remained quiet as I let the rest of the story about his half-apology, and Sally Mae's refusal to start, unravel. When I had finally finished rambling she squeezed my hand.

"I'm sure it hurt to see him after all this time but you'll get through it. You're the strongest person I know." Her voice went calm like she knew I was at a breaking point.

A part of me wanted to tell her about what Mom had said on that final day. Why Huckleberry Lane and all the other houses I wanted to save were such an important part of honoring Mom's last wish, but Tessa already had so many worries and I refused to add to them.

"Just by your short interaction, you're sure Beck won't be able to fix the house properly?" she said, pulling me back to the conversation.

"Last I'd heard, he owned part of an advertising agency in Nashville. When does he have time to work on renovating a house?" A sick feeling oozed through me. "What if he passes it off to some contractor who knows nothing about historic renovation? What if they demolish the mahogany railings? Or replace the hardwood floors with some type of laminate?" I hunched forward as my stomach tumbled.

Yeah. Worse than bad gas-station sushi.

She played with her skirt. The edge of her mouth ticking. "Okay, I have to ask. How does he look after all these years? Is he like Ryan Reynolds cute or Chris Evans rugged?"

"Tess!" I groaned. "That is so *not* the point."

"Hey, inquiring minds and all that because word of him being back is going to spread around town quicker than the stomach bug we all had last year."

Even though I didn't want to answer, I loved the fact that a teasing edge had finally returned to her voice.

"Chris Evans," I mumbled before dropping my head in my hands.

Tessa kneeled in front of me and ran a finger along my jaw, showing me a thin line of oil. "I thought you fixed Sally Mae's alternator?"

"It's her spark plugs now, but don't tell Dad. It'll be one more thing he can give me grief about."

"Hey," she said, her voice sobering. "Beck has memories of the house too. Didn't you say he bought it for Piper?"

I only managed a nod.

"Why don't you talk to him? Offer some advice. At least then you'd know what he was planning."

"Hell no! The last thing I'm going to do is offer my services to him just so he can turn me down."

I wished I hadn't inherited my father's quick temper. When I saw a problem in front of me I wanted to slay it like I was a fire-breathing dragon defending its castle. Unfortunately, I'd learned over the last few months that when you overreacted you got burned. The fiasco with Hearth and Home had taught me that hard lesson.

"Do you love that house?" she asked with a steady tone that reminded me so much of our mom.

"Yes, but I can't deal with the other baggage that goes along with it."

"I remember how badly he hurt you, but it's been a long time, Tor. Maybe you should forgive him. Let him off the hook, not because he deserves it but because you need to move on."

"Watching him drive away with his family when I was seventeen was like having that stupid RV drive straight over my young heart. The only thing that made me hold on was the fact that I knew he'd be back in a year. That he was excited about being homeschooled and exploring the US with his family. But then…" I pulled in an achy breath. "After his parents' sudden death, I couldn't get any real information besides that obituary that appeared in the paper. Don't you remember the hell I went through?"

She nodded, her mouth going grim. "Yes, I remember it all. Mom was so worried about you. You wouldn't eat or sleep."

"I spent months waiting for any communication from him. Then out of the blue he sent me that email breaking up with me. A fucking *email*, Tess."

She gripped my hands tighter like she could sense I was unraveling again.

"A few months later, Maisey Bedford showed me that picture of him with that pretty brunette looking all cozy."

I hated the way my voice cracked on the final word. It'd been ten years since it happened. I should be over it. But while his callous breakup was rough, what I couldn't understand was how carelessly he'd thrown away our years of friendship. The fact that there was no easy deceleration to our conversations. After he sent that email, there was nothing but radio silence and that hurt more than anything else.

"What I need to do is work on what I can control. That's getting Parkview finished and sold. Then Manny and I can decide what to do next."

She pulled me into another gentle hug. "I know you'll figure it out."

"What do you think Mom would say if she was here?" I whispered.

She sat back. Gave me a determined look that said she was about to dole out a hard truth. "She'd say talk to Beck. That there's probably more to the story than you know."

"Ugh," I groaned. "I hate it when you're so damn reasonable."

She cackled out a laugh. "No, I just don't have a temper like yours that goes from one to a hundred in less than a heartbeat."

"Gee, wonder where I get that from."

"Uh, while we are on that topic of Dad." She hesitated. "I should probably tell you something. He is…"

"Coming through the door," I finished.

He had his "mayor face" on. A simple smile. An easy lilt to his voice as he greeted Maisey and her twins. When he had to perform, he was always this stalwart, kind man. Sadly when it was just the two of us it was like storm clouds bashing into each other.

Tessa stepped back, making room for him near my chair.

"Did you tell her about dinner tonight?" he barked.

The tips of her cheeks went pink. "I was getting to that."

Her stare flicked back to the shelves, and I was surprised by how bare they looked. Maybe she hadn't had time to unpack her new orders. Another thing that had fallen to the side as she tried to juggle so many things in her life.

"I'm making chicken Parmigiana which I know is your favorite, Tor. The girls are planning to make cookies after school too. It'll be... fun," she mumbled.

Now he'd lassoed Tessa into his plan after I'd said no at the bank. That was pretty low.

"Tonight isn't good for me. I need to go look at paint samples for Parkview. Manny is meeting me at the house later to test swatches."

He bristled. "Can't you do that another time?"

"No, I can't. I'm trying to run a business."

"You should make time for family. That little hobby of yours can wait."

"Really? You're going to lecture me about family?" I tried to keep my voice level even as my temper grew. "Forget it. I know exactly how the night will go."

"Don't, Torran," Tessa pleaded quietly.

I should have stopped, but I was tired of my dad ignoring the past, like if he pretended that last day at the hospital with Mom never happened, we would too. That moment was burned into my brain, and no matter how many dinners we had I'd never forgive what he'd done to Tessa and me. And most of all to our mother.

"You'll blast into Tessa's little place and without even as much as a 'hello,' you'll start complaining about the drafts whispering through the old windows. Before we can take a single bite, you'll yank on the Windsor knot in your conservative tie and question Tessa about her monthly sales numbers and grumble that she isn't doing enough to promote the store."

Barb and Susan swiveled their heads in our direction. Tessa's face went pale as I railed on. It was either yell at Dad or fall to pieces, and I refused to do that in front of him because he'd only use it against me later.

With stares from the regulars growing around us, I jumped up from the chair.

"I need to go."

Dad shoved his hands into the pockets of his dress pants and shook his head. "Stop being so dramatic. We should be able to have a damn meal together. It's what your mother would have wanted."

I froze and bit the corner of my lip. A hint of copper coated my tongue. Over the years I'd tried endless times to connect with my father on some level. I played sports, ran the finance club in high school, all in an effort to have some link with him. But no matter how hard I'd tried, he'd found fault with what I'd done. When my mom was alive I did my best to placate him, act nice, but now I was broken and tired and couldn't forget the past.

Ignoring my dad, I said to Tessa, "Tell the girls I'll see them for baths and bedtime stories later on."

Tessa's shoulders sagged as her gaze whipped between me and Dad. The last thing I wanted to do was hurt her but getting into a full-fledged fight with my father in front of her girls would be a thousand times worse than my absence from a meal.

I walked to the door and pushed it open. Before I was completely through, I turned to find my father had gone to talk to Barb and Susan but Tessa stayed in place. I caught her eye and mouthed, *I'm sorry*.

She gave a sad smile. Mouthed back, *It's okay*, but I knew deep down that the hostility between me and my dad, the way it pained Tessa, was anything but okay.

When I walked in the store my mood may have been a four, but between Beck's reappearance and my dad's continued disappointment in my choices it'd now definitely dropped to a two.

7

BECK

Turning A Corner Onto A Much Darker Street.

EVER since the accident, sleep had become my enemy. When I closed my eyes and drifted into that blurry state between wake and rest, the sounds of the explosion, the phantom heat of the fire, jarred me out of bed. This morning, for once, it wasn't the fiery hiss of the explosion that rocked me from an uneasy sleep but the vision of Torran's pained gaze as she looked at me for the first time in ten years.

Knowing sleep would not come again, I took a shower, dressed, and made my way down the elevator to the underground garage. Once I was in my car, I slowly pulled out of my condo complex. This morning I had to go back to Ivy Falls. Take another look at the house and convince myself that I hadn't just made one of the biggest mistakes of my life. That this plan would make things better for Piper.

Deciding to take the scenic route, I drove the two-lane highway that led out of town and wound past miles of open grassy fields covered in white dandelions. The road was like an old rollercoaster.

46

Ebbing and falling every few feet until it smoothed out into a flat straightaway. In the distance sat sprawling red farmhouses. Horses in colors of chestnut and raven-black dotted the landscape.

The more I drove, the quicker my blood pressure dropped. I rolled down the windows and let the cool morning breeze blow across my cheeks.

This will all be okay, I kept repeating like I could somehow hypnotize myself into believing it was true, but the hurt in Torran's eyes kept flashing in my head.

I reached for the radio dial and scrolled to my favorite music station, needing something to calm my nerves. Only two bars into one of Paramore's greatest hits, the music faded and was replaced by a familiar ringtone. As soon as I answered, the hair on my arms stood on end. The rapid-fire voice blazing through the car could only belong to one person.

"Morning, Piper, what's going on?"

She sighed and all the muscles in my neck and jaw tensed. My little sister didn't have to utter a word for me to know something was wrong.

"Can you send me more money?" Her gravelly voice said sleep was eluding her too.

"What happened to the grand I sent you last week?"

"I used it for… stuff."

I bit back the other questions in my head like how much "stuff" included weed and her favorite companion, Jose Cuervo.

"How's the job hunt going? Didn't you say you had an interview last week?"

Another sigh. "It didn't work out. The guy was a total perv. I didn't like the way he ogled me when he asked about my *past experience.*"

I loved my sister but she had an excuse for everything. She couldn't make it to her therapist appointments because she'd lost her MetroCard. Her prescriptions couldn't be filled because it was too long of a walk to the pharmacy. The auditions she was being offered were for parts that were beneath her. She couldn't find a job because nobody in her Greenwich Village neighborhood was hiring.

I pressed a finger to my temple where a headache was beginning to throb. "It's serving coffee and pastries. How much experience do you need?"

"Beck," she moaned. "The place is three subway stops away, and then another fifteen-minute walk."

I swallowed down all my frustration. For years I'd been trying to get Piper to move closer to me, but every time I mentioned it, she chose to live somewhere farther away. When I was in California for college, she stayed with our grandparents in Oregon. After she graduated from high school, and I moved to Atlanta, I begged her to come live with me. Take classes at a local community college and give us a chance to get close again.

She refused, choosing to go to school in Las Vegas. She lasted a year until she dropped out. Only months later, both our grandparents passed quickly, leaving me to control our family trust. She traveled across the country over the next two years, couch-surfing at various friends' apartments and taking waitress jobs where she could find them. She'd go months without calling until she needed money. I went out of my mind with worry, imagining all sorts of bad shit happening to her. Last year she finally landed in New York, claiming she'd gotten her life together and wanted to be an actress.

"Okay, let's make a deal. I'll send you another five hundred, but you need to line up two more interviews."

"Why are you being such an asshole? This is New York City. It's not that easy to find a good job without a college degree," she huffed. "That money is mine. Mom and Dad left it to me."

"They did but Grandpa and Grandma changed your access due to your…" I broke off, not wanting to bring up her rocky past. "Just prove to me you can get and keep a job and I'll continue sending money for rent, food, and acting classes. If you can't handle that, I've got a second bedroom at my condo waiting for you."

"I'm not coming to Nashville. It's too much for me, you know it, and I hate that you keep pushing."

The wobble in her voice opened a crevice in my heart. Ever since we'd buried our parents, Piper had gone off the deep end. She'd stopped playing piano. Skipped so many days of school our grandparents lost count. Already in and out of rehab once, I had to plead with her to finish high school. When she'd received her diploma, she'd beamed at me. I'd thought we'd turned a corner at that moment, but I didn't know it was on to a much darker street.

"Make the interview appointments," I said, giving in. "The money will be in your account by the end of the day."

"Thanks, big brother. You're the best."

The truth about Huckleberry Lane burned on my lips. How I'd bought the house for her in hopes it would make up for all the times I'd failed her, but the softness in her voice stopped me.

For once, I wanted our conversation to end on a pleasant note even though I wanted to warn her to be safe. To make good decisions. But she was twenty-four years old, living in a huge city with all kinds of temptation. Temptation that kept me awake at night.

No matter my pleas, or promises that things would get better, she had to want to stay clean. I'd learned over the years, and two stints of inpatient rehab, that she wasn't going to listen to me no matter how hard I tried.

※ ※ ※

I drove into town and took a turn at the only stoplight. It surprised me that the once bustling square now had a few empty storefronts. As I continued to drive toward Huckleberry Lane, I laughed again at how odd the business signs were.

The one outside Followes Music read, *Do We Sell Sheet Music? Of Chorus We Do!* At the corner, the sign for Minnie's Market said, *Cheese Is Always A Gouda Choice.*

Another laugh exploded from my lips, releasing all the tension I'd been holding in my body since my run-in with Torran. The way she'd stared at me like she thought I was a total idiot made me even more determined to make the house beautiful again despite the fact that I had no idea where to find a contractor. I did have Diego, though. I was sure he had some connections in the community.

A few more turns and I pulled into the driveway of Huckleberry Lane. Again I was shocked by the sad state it was in. It reminded me of a pair of beat-up loafers I'd had as a kid. They were scuffed, worn down in places, but the soles were still sturdy enough to carry you all the way to the state line. All it would take was some work, a little polish, and the house would be better than new.

Determination shot through me. I was going to do this by the book and prove Torran wrong. Hell, if it turned out nice enough maybe I'd sell my condo and move in, although I was sure that'd be quite the negotiation with Piper, especially since she was always accusing me of acting like a helicopter brother.

Heat from the early morning sun warmed my head as I climbed out of my car and walked across the weed-riddled front lawn. When I reached the front door, I planted my feet and braced for what I might find inside.

The knob wouldn't budge.

Crap.

When I dropped off the checks to Diego he'd warned me it would be my job to figure out how to get inside. The last renters had disappeared in the night taking the only set of keys with them.

The back of the house was in even worse shape. Broken lawn chairs littered the charred grass. And I meant charred. Someone had doused the ground with gasoline and set half the backyard on fire. The scent of burnt metal and plastic made my heart race.

Flickers of the explosion that took my parents' lives filled my ears. The skin on my arms and chest ached. I gulped down the acid coating my throat as my knees buckled beneath me.

I never knew when the memories would be triggered. Sometimes I'd be sitting alone in my office and a jarring sound like the slamming of a door would send me down a dark spiral. Other times I could be at a restaurant or a bar and the whoosh from a lit grill would make the terrifying fragments of that day come alive in my mind.

My hands continued to shake. The rise and fall of my chest stuttered until I reminded myself that I was safe. That all of it was over. In the past.

If only my brain would get the message.

Coming back to Ivy Falls was a mistake. There were too many memories here. Reminders of what I'd lost. It was simply brick and wood but if I stood still, let the air go quiet, I could almost hear my parents' laughter inside as my father stumbled and dropped the cake he'd made for Mom's fortieth birthday. How Piper's tap shoes clicked on the stairs as she made her way down in some frilly pink costume for a dance recital.

50

It all was a reminder of why I'd been pulled back here. Why I needed to restore the house. Once I'd put it back right, made it the way my parents loved it, Piper would realize that we could start a new chapter. That her life could be vibrant and happy again.

I shook out the pain in my arms and made slow steps over dozens of smashed beer bottles and cigarette butts. At the back of the house, I found another row of broken windows, the jagged edges reminding me of sharp monster teeth. The last thing I wanted to do was crawl over shattered glass, but at this point it was that or kick down a door.

I pulled a pair of old gloves from my back pocket and used a dismembered chair leg to smash out the window over the sink. After clearing away most of the glass, I slid an old towel over the opening and climbed through like a snake on its belly.

The smell of shit hit me first. I threw an arm over my nose and raced to shove open the rest of the windows in the back part of the house.

As soon as light flooded the space, blood left my head and drained to my toes. It was worse than I could have ever imagined. The kitchen was nothing but a shell of broken cabinets and cracked tile countertops. Deep gouges, like hammer marks, covered most of the hardwood floors. I walked the rest of the house, finding new horrors in every room.

I trudged up the creaky staircase and took in a full breath before I pushed open the door to the master bedroom. Black wires hung from the ceiling where a light fixture used to be. Wide gashes made by a sledgehammer left chunks of drywall scattered over the floor. I turned in a slow circle taking in the damage. Diego said the last renters were angry about being kicked out, but why would anyone do this to a house?

A faint dripping sound filled the room. Water rings covered the ceiling in what resembled yellow piss stains.

Out in the hall, a red nylon cord hung from the ceiling. I yanked on it and the door to the attic released, revealing a narrow set of rickety wood stairs. Once the steps were locked, I climbed into the narrow crawl space. Spindly pink insulation hugged the walls. The rotting smell of wet wood filled the air.

With the punch of a button on my phone, the flashlight illuminated the space. I hunched down and moved across the ceiling searching for the source of the leak. The wood creaked below me but I kept inching forward. I only got two more steps when the floor beneath me released a low groan. Before I could react, my right leg and then my left went through the ceiling.

Wood and plaster crashed to the hallway floor below. I flung out my arms, stopping my body from following. The hem of my sleeves inched back. A patch of mottled and scarred skin stared back at me. I tried to heave myself up and lost hold of my phone. Around me the remaining wood started to buckle. If I moved another inch, the whole floor would go.

Torran's words about making the right choices pinged inside my head. She'd been dead on about everything, and I was stupid enough not to listen.

Stretching out my fingers as far as they'd go, I managed to press a contact number on my phone. On the fourth ring, Diego's voice burst through the line.

"Hey, Beck! What's going on?"

All I muttered was, "I totally fucked up."

8

TORRAN

Thanks For The Heads-Up, Captain Obvious.

THE song blaring from my phone almost knocked me out of bed. A burst of laughter followed by singsong children's voices bounced off the walls of the small guest room. I understood now why my nieces had acted so guilty when they handed back my phone the other day.

They'd changed my ringtone to the theme song of their favorite cartoon, and now a chorus of young voices chirping about playing in a magic garden and defeating an old witch knocked around inside my skull. In their small and clever little minds, they'd considered this payback for missing dinner the other night.

Thankfully the song quieted and I rolled over. Not two seconds later, it started again. This time I swiped the phone off the bedside table and growled, "Hello."

Diego's strangled tone made me sit up. There was only one reason he'd call on a Saturday morning. The house was going to be mine. I knew Beck would flake.

"Tor, there's been an accident at Huckleberry Lane. My kids and wife are sick and I can't head over there…"

Before he could say anything else, I hopped out of bed and yanked on a rumpled T-shirt and a pair of semi-clean jeans. I tucked my hair under a baseball hat, grabbed my keys off the table near the front door and raced out to my truck. My head filled with visions of Beck. His body bloody or twisted at odd angles. I shouldn't have cared about him, but the tether to our past, the way my heart beat out an unsteady rhythm when I saw him again, made me push Sally Mae's gas pedal to the floor.

It took all of five minutes to get to Huckleberry Lane from Tessa's house. I parked in the driveway and sprinted to the front door. After twisting the knob several times, the lock wouldn't give. I jumped off the porch and sprinted to my truck for my tools. When I was back in front of the door, I used a small flathead screwdriver to depress the notch under the knob and worked it back and forth until it came free. Once the internal screws came loose, I pushed my way inside.

The house still reeked like a combination of shit, warm garbage and rotten eggs. I tried not to gag as I climbed the creaky staircase to the second floor. A chunk of ceiling coated the moldy brown carpet. Little white dusts of drywall hung in the air like a thick fog. His legs dangled from the ceiling like one of those string puppets.

"Who's there?" Beck's muffled voice rang out.

A part of me wanted to shout up at him. Tell him what an idiot he was for not paying attention to the aging state of the house. How every part of it was practically a wall-to-wall tetanus shot. But if I said anything, he'd hear the tremble in my voice. How I was terrified that the rest of the ceiling was going to give way and send him crashing to the floor.

I quietly climbed the attic stairs. Once inside the damp space, my gaze landed on Beck. His arms were splayed out on either side of the hole. Sweat trickled down through the light stubble on his chin. Even in his precarious position, he was still the hottest man I'd ever seen.

And a total fucking idiot.

"What the hell do you think you're doing, Beck? Climbing around a clearly unstable ceiling is dangerous."

His eyes widened. "Thanks for the heads-up, Captain Obvious. I was trying to check out the state of the place, when this"—he nodded to the open hole surrounding him—"gave way."

54

"How long have you been hanging there?" I asked.

"About four or five minutes."

His arms shook beneath his long-sleeve black T-shirt. A shiny patch of skin covered a small part of his wrist. I was about to ask how he got the scar, but by the way his entire upper body trembled it was clear he couldn't hold on for much longer.

In all the times I'd thought about him over the years, I never imagined him being in this position. Him needing me. When we eventually crossed paths at something like our high school reunion, I'd expected we'd mumble through small talk and lie about how good it was to see each other. We'd linger a few seconds too long. Let the past wash over us before we realized we were strangers who could do nothing more than discuss the bad decorations and the state of the weather.

"Torran! A little help please," Beck yelped.

The vulnerability in his voice melted my defensive armor. If I didn't fix this fast, he was going to get hurt. No matter how twisted my feelings were, I couldn't let that happen.

I inched into the narrow space with spindly pink insulation crawling over the floor and walls. There was hardly enough space for one body, much less two.

My mind raced with panic. I couldn't lift him out on my own. He weighed twice what I did, and there was a chance if I moved even an inch more, the floor would go out from under me too. A half-dozen options flew through my head until an idea hit me.

"I need you to hold on for two more minutes. Can you do that?"

He shifted his body an inch and grunted out an answer that sounded like yes.

I took the attic steps two at a time, sprinted down the stairs and out the front door. Untethering the tall ladder from the back of Sally Mae, I carried it inside. Once I was in position below Beck's legs, I climbed up.

"Beck, there's a ladder about a foot below you. I'm going to grab your legs and guide them to the top step. When you feel your shoe hit metal, you need to start lowering yourself down. Slowly. You got it?"

"Can your weight steady us both?"

I bit back the harsh words running through my head. So tired of people underestimating me just because I was small.

"Yes, I've got you," I shot back.

"Let's do this quick then. My hands are slipping."

I steadied my legs on the second step from the top and grabbed Beck's calves. Pulling down, his muscles writhed under my grip. Heat moved up my arms. Now was not the time to think about Beck's body, or what was underneath those track pants dangling above my head.

With a thud, Beck's tennis shoes hit the top step. I inched down a step at a time, balancing my weight to keep the ladder from tipping while Beck lowered his body. When his feet hit the second step, all the air whooshed out of my lungs, my anger fading as soon as I knew he was safe.

Once back on solid ground, I held the ladder steady as Beck climbed down. Not a second after his feet landed on the dirty carpet, he pulled me into a tight hug.

"Holy crap. That was a close one."

The soapy scent of his skin, and the warmth of his touch, made me relax in his arms. It sent me back to the last night we spent in the tailgate of Sally Mae, watching the stars, kissing, undressing each other. His hands shook as he lifted my T-shirt over my head. Small gasps fled his lips as I pulled off his jeans. With the sounds of the lake lapping behind us, we crossed an intimate line both of us had been dancing around for a while. He whispered so many promises about our future. How after he returned home in a year nothing would keep us apart. I held on to those promises like people held on to their most prized possessions.

He placed his hands on my cheeks like he'd done when we were seventeen. Those same small gasps returned as he leaned in closer. Close enough to kiss.

"Guess I should have known better than to climb up there," he whispered.

His words were like ice water being poured down my back and I shoved him away.

"Why are you here by yourself? Only a dumbass would walk through this disaster zone without a licensed contractor!"

His eyes darkened. "Oh, so now I'm a dumbass?"

"Damn right you are. Do you know how dangerous a house like this can be? Faulty wiring. Possible asbestos. Squatters. Tons of bad things, which of course, I'm sure you're aware of now that you've taken out half the fucking ceiling!"

"I didn't think about any of that. All I wanted was to see the shape of the place. Know that it wasn't some writhing pit of shit!"

"Couldn't you tell that the moment you came in here? The stench alone should have warned you. Not to mention the gouges in the floor and the holes in the walls."

His eyebrows shot up. "You've been here before?"

"Yes." I kicked at a piece of ragged ceiling near my left boot. "I needed to see it before the auction."

"How? I had to pretty much *Mission Impossible* my way inside."

"That doesn't matter," I said, punching up the sides of the ladder and carrying it back downstairs.

Regret filled every inch of my bones. How had I gotten pulled back here again? I should have just told Diego to call the police or fire department to help Beck. But no, I had to step back into this living, breathing reminder of what I'd lost. How I'd failed my mom. Beck's stupidity only served as a caustic reminder that he was out of his depth and going to screw this up.

"You knew this place was a dump and you still wanted to buy it? Why?" He was on my heels down the stairs and then raced past me blocking the bottom step.

"Move," I gritted out.

"No. I need to know the reason why you wanted this house." His arms stayed taut against the banister. "Please, Torran, tell me the truth."

That single promise I'd made to my mom reverberated in my head but I pushed it away.

"The house has great bones." I jabbed the top of the ladder against his arm, forcing him to move. Once I was out the busted front door, he caught up and met me stride for stride.

"It would be a shame to let someone who knows nothing about its history come in and totally screw it up."

I gave him a hard look as I stopped at the tailgate of the truck. "Don't forget your promise, Beck."

He sank down onto the curb. The droop to his shoulders said all I needed to know. Now that he'd been inside the house, he'd figured out what a big job it was. That he'd been dumb, reckless to buy it. But I wasn't about to save him no matter how much it dug under my skin that he'd made such a stupid decision.

"I'm sorry, Torran," he whispered. "Like everything else between us, I'm not sure that's a promise I can keep."

9

BECK

A True Force of Nature.

IT was hard not to laugh at what a fool I'd been. For the few minutes I'd been inside the house reality had taken hold, and now I fully understood why Torran had wanted to rip my head off after the auction. She knew how much work, time, and money it would take to get the house back to its former state.

Watching her move so confidently around the space, an idea began to form in my head, but I was positive no matter how much I groveled she'd still say no. But what was I going to do? She was the only solution to my problem. Somehow I had to figure out a way to get through her armor.

Torran shoved a toolbox to the back of her truck before wrestling the ladder into the bed. I didn't offer to lend a hand because I knew better. She was a tornado of determination. Never letting anyone set her path. Or tell her what to do. A true force of nature.

The twinge in my chest reminded me how much I'd missed having her in my life. The little way she twirled the ends of her hair when she was nervous. The tick in her cheek when she got annoyed.

Convincing her to work with me would take more than a wink and a wicked grin. If she was going to agree to my plan, it had to be more about restoring the house, helping her business, rather than saving me. Plus after the damage I'd left in my wake, I owed her this one.

She jumped down from the truck and made her way to the driver's side. She climbed inside the cab and I jumped up and raced to the passenger door. A song from The Dead Weather blasted out of the speakers. Before she could peel away from the curb, I slid inside.

"What are you doing?" she demanded.

"I want to keep talking."

"No. I have to go to work." To make her point, she reached across my lap and pushed open the passenger door. Her hand skimmed across my thighs and I loved the sudden flush in her cheeks.

"But it's Saturday."

She rolled her eyes.

Yep. Battle shield firmly in place.

"Every day a house isn't on the market, you lose money. In this business there's no such thing as a day off. You'd know that if you had a clue what you were doing."

I stayed glued to Sally Mae's worn seat even as Torran's shoulders tensed up around her ears.

"What do you want from me, Beck? I just saved your ass from a potential trip to the hospital. I warned you about the house." Her eyes narrowed as she caught on. "There is no way I'm helping you out of this mess!"

"But you were bidding on the house. I know you want it."

"Yes, I was bidding on the house until you buzzed in like a stray bullet and took it. Then you start poking around things you don't understand and make it a complete disaster zone."

"What happened in the attic was an accident. If anyone should get that, it's you."

Heat burned at her cheeks and shame washed over me. Poking fun at her video mishap was only going to make things worse.

"We are not talking about me," she ground out. "You got yourself into this mess. Don't expect me to jump in and save you."

"I'm not asking you to save me. I don't need anyone to save me!"

I'd forgotten how she could burrow down into my skin like a splinter and cause so much pain. She knew me too well. Could push all the right buttons to drive me mad.

"Fine," I said, climbing out. "I'll ask Diego for help because it's clear you don't give a crap."

"Good luck with that! And while you're at it, tell him to call the fire department, not me, the next time you do something stupid."

She gunned Sally Mae and tore down the street. Her taillights faded into the distance. Once again, I'd screwed everything up and I only had myself to blame.

"Dammit!" I yelled up into the bright blue sky. By now I should have realized that she wasn't going to make this easy for me. That I deserved every bit of anger she tossed my way.

I began to pace the lawn. Kicking at dry weeds and dirt clods and cursing under my breath, which earned me a few dark looks from the guy mowing his lawn across the street. Even the house made an accusing creak like it thought I'd acted like a total asshole.

Part of me ached to get in the car and drive straight to Diego's. Tell him that I wanted to get rid of the house no matter how much it cost me. But my commitment to Piper wouldn't let me give up that easily. She needed this house.

I looked at my watch.

Nine a.m.

If Torran was the same creature of habit, I knew exactly where she was headed. I jogged to my car and sped away from the house, hoping my intuition was right.

10

TORRAN

You Wanna Piece Of Me? Well, I Wanna Piece Of Cake.

THE scent of cinnamon, sugar, and rising dough hit me the minute I walked inside the Sugar Rush Café. Blood still boiled in my veins, and the only thing that could calm me down was a combination of my two favorite things: caffeine and carbs.

Two little boys scanned the long glass case near the cash register. Pastries and donuts lined each of the six shelves. The boys argued over which was better: rainbow or chocolate sprinkles. It was the same argument my nieces had every time I brought them here.

Once the boys made up their minds, and their mother ordered an extra-large coffee (amen), it was my turn.

"Hey, Barb. Love the sign outside."

This week her hair was piled up in a beehive and colored a deep shade of peach. She smirked. "The credit has to go to Susan on that one. You know how she loves her cakes."

When Miss Pat, who'd owned Sugar Rush for over two decades, retired last year, Barb and her wife, Susan, roared into town on their Harleys and bought the place. At first people were a little resistant to them being outsiders, but once they started serving up the best donuts, cakes and practically sinful pastries, people warmed to them quickly. Because they did not bleed loyalty to Ivy Falls, they were practically the only people in town who didn't sneer when I came in close proximity.

"Burn yourself on the fryer again?" I said, pointing to the white bandage covering most of her forearm.

"No. New tattoo. This one is a mermaid with shimmering scales." Her eyes scanned me for a long minute. "Want your regular order?" she asked.

"Yep," I said, readjusting the khaki satchel on my shoulder. Once I had left Beck behind, I turned up the radio and screamed out all my fury along with the pounding beats of the Foo Fighters. I was a damn grown woman but he still could make me act, and feel, like I was seventeen again. And did he really think he could sweet talk me into helping him with the house? Just thinking about it made my blood pressure spike again.

"You okay, sweetie?" Barb narrowed her kohl-rimmed eyes.

"I'm fine," I said, plastering a smile on my face. If Tessa was here, asked me about my number, I'd probably say minus-two and dropping at this point.

"Well, then a large coffee and two crullers are coming right up."

"Thanks," I managed to breathe out.

The small café with its black metal tables, white penny tile, and bright pink wallpaper was usually the hub of the town. A place where people gathered to have small talk, read the paper, enjoy a cup of coffee, but it was surprisingly quiet for a Saturday morning.

"Hey, Torran." Susan appeared at the counter and handed me my food. Her short bob was raven-black and she was barely tall enough to hand the paper bag over the counter to me. Her eyes darted around the room before she leaned in. "Heard you didn't get the house on Huckleberry Lane. Sorry 'bout that."

Ah yes. Small-town gossip. Faster than a bullet train.

"It's okay. There are other houses," I said with a little too much acid in my voice. Even in one of my favorite spots in town, I couldn't get away from Beck.

63

The bell on the front door jingled and both Barb and Susan's eyes narrowed into the you're-a-stranger-to Ivy-Falls stare.

"Here, let me pay for her food."

Beck stepped up behind me and pushed a twenty across the counter.

"Tor, you know this guy?" Barb eyed Beck like he was a stray puppy who might need a home.

"Unfortunately," I said, spinning around and practically slamming into Beck's wide chest. "What the hell are you doing here?"

"Getting donuts and coffee," he said in that smooth-as-honey voice that used to win me over.

"I can pay for my own damn donuts!" I said, snatching the twenty off the counter and shoving it back at him.

Barb and Susan watched us with wide eyes.

"I know you can, but after what just happened I'd say I owe you breakfast." He reached around me and set the twenty back on the counter.

His fingers skimmed my sides as he pulled away, and I felt his gentle brush all the way to my toes. God, it was no more than a five-second touch and already my body was aflame.

"Better idea," I said, pushing away the heat. Letting the fury take back over. "Use the twenty for the house because you're going to need every penny."

I slammed the money back against his chest. We stood in a stalemate for at least two full breaths before Barb cleared her throat.

"Tor, honey, would you like to make introductions?"

Susan tipped her chin at Beck and I swear she was about to grin at him.

"Barb and Susan, this is Beck Townsend," I huffed.

He reached over the counter and shook their hands.

"It's so nice to meet you. Did you just move to Ivy Falls?" Susan's warm brown cheeks did turn into a full-on smile.

"I grew up here. Moved away," he mumbled. "But I'm back. Recently bought the place on Huckleberry Lane where I used to live."

Barb's thick, penciled-in brows shot up. "Oh." Her stare veered back to me. "I get it now."

Beck gave a knowing smile and I yanked him over to a corner near the fridge filled with custom-made cakes.

"Are you following me now?" I snapped.

"Maybe." He gave a playful grin like he thought I'd be amused. When he didn't get the reaction he wanted, that grin faded. "I remembered this used to be your weekend tradition with your mom. Thought I'd take a chance and maybe catch you here, even though you said you were going to work."

I tried not to show any shock that he'd remembered my mom's Saturday routine with us even when we were in high school.

"You're not going to change my mind. I said everything I needed to at the house."

"Give me a chance, Tor. All I need is five minutes."

Before I could give him another irritated look, beg him to leave me alone, the echoes of my own voice rang through the restaurant. My blood went cold at the sound of that YouTube video playing at full volume.

"Manny spent days under the house to ensure the foundation was stable…"

Mabel Lynne Parker and Suzanne Fitzpatrick, who were two years behind me at Ivy Falls High, glared in my direction. Their eyes shifted between their phones and me.

"Once we understood the original structure, we made every effort to keep the historical details in place…"

The weight of every stare in the restaurant made me curl my hands into fists. I could recite every line of the video clip by heart as I was sure most of the town could by now. Some idiots had even turned my WTF line into a meme.

Barb stomped out from behind the counter, nostrils flaring. "Mabel Lynne and Suzanne, don't you have better things to do? Stop hiding out here from your families and watching that damn YouTube."

All the color drained from the women's cheeks as they slid their phones into their purses and rushed out the door. Once they were gone, she leveled an inferno-level stare at her few patrons and everyone quickly went back to their food.

"Damn busybodies," Barb growled and returned to the counter. "If it wasn't for *TMZ* and *People* magazine, those women would be ten times worse about the local gossip."

Susan shot me a sympathetic look before rushing off in the direction of the coffee machine.

I couldn't move. Couldn't think. It was bad enough that the whole damn town hated me, but now Beck had a front-row seat to my living shitshow.

"Torran." He gently touched my shoulder. "Let's get out of here."

"And go where?" God, I hated the way my voice shook. "It's like this all over Ivy Falls." I planted my feet and steadied my shoulders. "No. My mom said the only way out is through and that's what I'm going to do."

"Are you sure? I'll take you anywhere."

The way his eyes filled with worry, the firm set of his lower lip, was how he'd always acted when we were children. Like he thought he could shield me from the jagged-edged parts of the world, but we weren't children anymore and I wasn't about to run away.

Barb placed our drinks on the counter and went back to the kitchen. I grabbed mine and moved to the now free table where the women had been sitting. After sinking into a metal chair, I did my best to ignore Beck, even though I knew he'd probably take the chair next to me.

When we were kids, we'd spent hours sitting at these tables talking about our dreams for the future. We'd been friends since his family moved to Ivy Falls the summer before sixth grade. It was here he'd first held my hand on my fifteenth birthday. That day I was convinced I'd never worn a smile so big. Back then I'd have never thought we would become total strangers as adults.

I focused on my caffeine and carbs, trying to ignore the heat of Beck's stare. The pity that lingered in his whiskey-brown eyes. There were too many things going on in my life right now. Why wouldn't he listen and go away?

As I expected, he slid out the chair across from me. He lowered his voice and said, "Give me five minutes. Let me tell you about my ideas for the house."

The rumble of his voice sent a zip of heat through me. It was the voice of a man, not the boy who'd left me behind so many years ago. I did still see hints of the young Beck I knew back then. It showed in the way he chewed on his lower lip when he was nervous. How he scraped a hand through his hair when he was deep in thought. I'd tried so hard to forget those things about him, but memories had a sneaky way of hiding away until they decided to appear when you least expected, or wanted, them.

There was one other thing I remembered about him. He was determined to always get his way. Tessa's words in the bookstore about not knowing the full story, about forgiving him, banged around loudly inside my head.

"Fine," I grumbled. "Your five minutes start now."

11

BECK

Nothing's A Secret In Ivy Falls.

AS Torran dumped half a carafe of creamer and three packs of sugar into her coffee, I examined the curve of her lips. The way her mouth pursed in concentration. It was hard not to reach for her. Offer her some comfort as people glared like she was a black storm cloud threatening their otherwise sunny day.

"Enough with the staring," she huffed. "Yes, I did crawl out of bed this morning. No, I haven't brushed my teeth or combed my hair." She yanked down her baseball cap a little too roughly. "That's what happens when you race out of your house to save some jackass who thinks he wants to play contractor for the day."

"So we're back to jackass again?" I teased. "Want to be a little more creative?"

Her gaze moved to the army of small boys in soccer uniforms scrambling in the door. "Oh, I have much better words for you," she said in a low grumble. "Things like dumbshit and asshat come to mind, but contrary to public opinion I do have some self-control."

68

I swallowed down a laugh. I'd forgotten how quick she could be with a comeback.

Two teenage girls rushed in the door giggling over the funny message on the sign outside.

She glanced at her watch. "You now have four minutes."

"What's the deal with all the weird signs around town?"

"That's what you want to ask with your remaining time?"

I refused to break eye contact with her.

"Since my dad's become mayor, he's wanted to bolster town spirit and tourism." She huffed and pushed away her bag of donuts. "He figured he could do that by creating a contest for the funniest, or most clever message put on signs for the local businesses."

"Your dad is the mayor? I can't picture him being the type to shake hands and kiss babies."

"That's where you're wrong. He loves all the fawning because, you know, his ego wasn't already big enough."

I chuckled and a hint of a grin tugged at her lips.

A chink in the armor. I'd take it.

"Do they win a cash prize or something for the funny sayings? Seems like people take it pretty seriously around here."

"You've been gone for ten years. Have you forgotten how competitive this town can be?"

Okay. Armor fully back in place.

"The winner is announced at the Fourth of July picnic. All they get is a trophy and bragging rights."

I nodded and went back to gripping my warm cup. A few older guys wearing Carhartt jackets and worn trucker hats sat at a back table staring daggers at Torran.

"Go ahead. Ask me about my viral screwup. I know you're dying to." I hated the way her voice dipped down into a tone of defeat.

I'd watched the video more often than I'd like to admit. Every single time I fought back my anger that someone hadn't warned her. Stopped her from hitting that ladder.

"That's not necessary," I said.

"By the comment you made after the auction, I figured you already knew," she said on a rough exhale. "How'd you find out?"

69

"Diego may have said something to me."

"Of course," she muttered. "Nothing's a secret in Ivy Falls."

I paused. Held her gaze, wanting her to know I wasn't judging her. "Tell me what happened that day. I'm sure there's a lot more to the story."

Her eyes went soft and she focused on the crumpled napkin in her lap like she couldn't bear to look at me.

"It started out as a good thing," she spoke quietly. "After college, I lived in Phoenix for a while. There was some buzz around the company I was working with at the time. We were renovating historical homes in the downtown area and Lauren, a producer from Hearth and Home, reached out to me. Asked about a meeting. Talked about the possibility of doing a pilot episode for a new renovation show."

She sat back and curled the napkin between her fingers.

"But then my mom was diagnosed with colon cancer. She got sick very quickly and right after that Tessa's piece-of-crap husband, Billy, left her with two small kids. Poor Tessa was a mess and asked me to come home. I couldn't sit around here doing nothing, so I started looking at old houses."

She ran a shaky finger around the rim of her cup. The pain of what she'd been through etched into the beautiful lines around her mouth.

"I bought a bungalow on Westfort just behind the Dairy Dip," she went on. "It was a nightmare. Termites everywhere. The foundation was a mess. Diego recommended Manny to come and look at it. Right after that we started working together. After we finished the house, an article about us appeared in *The Tennessean* and Lauren got back in contact. She said the network wanted to give us a pilot. That they liked how dedicated we were to Ivy Falls, and that if we did well it could possibly turn into our own show."

I hated the way her voice trembled. How reliving the memories made her shake. My fingers twitched at my sides aching to touch her but I gripped the side of the chair instead.

"The accident happened on the last day of shooting. The bungalow we'd bought on Fable Lane was worse than the one on Westfort. When we were finished it was absolutely period accurate. Manny and I were sure the network was going to love it because we'd done everything right." Her lower lip quivered and she bit into it. "I was doing a one-on-one interview walking backward to where Manny was on a ladder doing touch-ups in the kitchen. Someone laid down a rug and before I could change course, my feet went out from under me and I hit the ladder."

Her eyes shuttered closed like they had in the video when paint dripped down over her head and back.

"That house was the only thing that kept me upright after my mom passed. I said those awful things about Ivy Falls because I was angry and scared that I'd ruined everything. The minute after my tirade, I wanted to take all of it back."

She opened her eyes. Shook her head. "It wasn't until a few days later that our Instagram blew up. Commenters tagged us and Hearth and Home with the link from YouTube. It didn't take long for the bad publicity to swell, and the network canceled the pilot. It took a while to sell that house and it didn't put Manny and I in a great financial position."

"I don't get it. If everyone was awful to you after that, why did you stay in Ivy Falls? You could have gone back to Phoenix or anywhere else with your skills."

"Tessa and her girls need me. Being here keeps me close to my mom too," she gulped. "Reminds me that no matter what people think of me, I want to help this town. Save its history from being lost to a strip mall or a set of cheaply made condos. When I first started working, I saw how renovating one house on a block in Phoenix made the street come alive. Made people want to invest in a home that was built at a time when people appreciated craftsmanship. How a house was more about who you were as a family rather than just a place you laid your head at night. My mom…"

She quickly snapped her mouth shut like I wasn't worthy of whatever secret she was about to share.

"Now you know why I'm the town pariah." She let out a brittle laugh.

"It was a mistake you made months ago. Why is everyone still worked up about it?"

"If you ask my father, he'll say I brought shame to Ivy Falls. To add to that, the town council claims our tourism numbers are down and it's my fault. But mostly, I think people are disappointed that a hometown girl spoke so badly about where she grew up. Can't say I blame them. But I thought the house, your house…"

"What about the house?" I pressed.

She shook her head, refusing to make eye contact. Keeping that secret still locked deep inside.

"Torran, why were you bidding on my house? It's about more than restoring it, right?"

I couldn't handle the pain in her eyes, and I reached out and placed my hand over hers.

She slowly slid her hand away. It hurt but I understood how hard this was for her. I'd been fighting my own demons for most of my adult life.

"It's important to me. That's all."

There was definitely more to the story but I wasn't going to push her. I'd learned over the years that she would only share the most intimate pieces of herself when she was ready.

"You wouldn't listen to me before about working together but hear me out."

She sat back like she wasn't convinced but gave me a small nod. "You've got about a minute."

"It's true what I said about wanting to buy the house, renovate it for Piper, but what if we could make both of our dreams a reality?"

Her left brow went up. "Go on."

"Let me contract you and Manny to historically renovate the house. I need someone to do it right, and you two need another project to work on. It makes sense that we pair up. I know that once you get it done it will be so beautiful that all of Ivy Falls will see that you really do care about this town."

The lines of her shoulders went tight like she could still feel the weight of the stares around us. "I'm not agreeing to anything, but go ahead and tell me your ideas for the house."

It wasn't a yes, but it was a start.

"First, I want to repaint the eaves and the house a warm shade of soft yellow." I kept my voice all business, not wanting to spook her. "Open up the walls between the living room and dining area and build a gourmet kitchen. Lay new sod in both the front and backyard. And, of course, fix the damn roof," I said, holding her gaze. "You may believe I went into this without a plan, and I'll admit I wasn't thinking straight when I outbid you, but now that

I've had time to see the house, there's a dozen ideas forming in my head."

"Opening up the walls, changing the kitchen, messes with the history of the house," she flung back.

"Right. Okay. Tell me what you'd do."

There was a question in her eyes. Like she was worried that if this didn't work out I'd take her ideas. Her gaze darted around the room. Most people had gone back to their conversations and meals, thankfully.

Slowly she twisted her coffee cup in her hands before letting out a ragged breath. "I'd start by looking at the old building blueprints if they're still available at town hall. Figure out how to reframe the crumbling part of the structure to keep it period accurate. Ask Manny to either salvage or recreate the mahogany staircase."

As she talked, her voice became more animated and it was hard not to smile. She'd always had a designer's eye. Even when we were kids riding our bikes around the streets of Ivy Falls she'd stop at some of the old houses and tell me about the style, Georgian or Colonial. I'd stare at her in fascination as she talked and eventually she'd punch me in the arm, tell me to stop being weird.

I set my hands on the table and leaned in, getting lost in her voice. The edge of my long-sleeve T-shirt inched up, showing a sliver of rough skin.

Torran's gaze zeroed in on the spot. "I saw that at the house. How did you get it?"

I quickly yanked down the material. No matter how much I wanted to tell her the truth, I wasn't ready to explain all the things that had happened to me after my parents died.

"It's nothing. Got it while I was cooking one day."

She tightened her lips like she didn't buy it, and I quickly changed the subject.

"After what happened today at the house, it's obvious to both of us that I can't do this without help. I'll pay you and Manny whatever you want if you'll do the renovation."

Her face stayed emotionless as she sat back and crossed her arms over her chest.

"I have to do this for Piper, Tor. She needs this."

"Why? What's wrong with her, Beck?"

"It's too long a story to tell," I said.

"Sounds familiar," she shot back.

"One day soon I promise I'll tell you everything. But for now, can we agree to this? Please, if you won't do it for me or my sister, then do it for Ivy Falls."

I went straight for the tender part of her heart because it'd become clear after my accident today that without her help I was totally screwed.

12

TORRAN

Am I Boring You?

THERE was a chasm of ten years between us and in that time he'd changed more than I'd imagined. The Beck I'd known as a kid had confidence. A swagger to his walk. When he'd appear, everyone in the room would notice. Even when he was troubled, he'd managed to hide it, but I saw it in the way his voice trembled. The crease that popped up between his brows. Something was off now. Like he'd put up a wall between the world and his feelings.

Why was this house such a big deal? What did it mean to him and Piper?

Every warning signal in my head screamed I should walk away right now. Refuse to help him. Let the past go like Tessa advised. But a small part of my heart still remembered the warmth of his touch. How his goofy, lopsided grin always calmed my frantic heart. How no other man had ever been able to see inside my head the way he had.

I also wanted answers. Needed to know why after all this time he was back here. Why he'd so carelessly thrown away what we had.

But I held back because I knew deep down that if I opened that door, he'd expect me to share things about my life too and I couldn't go there. It was true that I wanted the house fixed properly. That it would help fulfill my promise to Mom, but agreeing to work with him meant casting aside all my pain. Years of beating myself up, wondering what I'd done to push him away.

Rather than look at his determined gaze, my eyes went to the quiet square outside. The way the morning sun made all the maple trees lining Main Street shimmer. How the brick-paved sidewalks welcomed you to our quaint little town with hidden treasures waiting for customers behind every shop door. How in the summer the baskets hanging from light poles were covered in blooming pink and red flowers. The way the town became a cozy autumn hideaway when the leaves turned copper and gold. How the scent of wood-burning fires and freshly made hot chocolate coated the air.

The sad truth was I knew all of that history and charm would be lost if I let developers, and people who had no clue about historical renovation, come in and ruin Ivy Falls. If I let Beck work with another contractor, I'd have to drive by Huckleberry Lane every day and live with whatever he'd decided to do. I knew I wasn't strong enough to handle it if the project turned into a total mess.

"If Manny and I agree, we'll require fifty percent of our fee upfront." I tried to keep my voice level and all business. There was no way I could let Beck think this was a done deal. That he'd swayed me so easily.

"I knew you'd help…" he started to gush.

"Quiet," I said like a stern schoolteacher. "Once we start the project, you have to listen to what we say. You can have input on the design, but when it comes to the bones of the house, its structure, plumbing, electrical, you have to defer to our knowledge, even if it means spending more money. I've seen way too many shitty renovations in this town, and I won't put my name on it unless it's done right."

"Okay. Anything you want, Tor."

I hated the way my body heated at the sound of my name on his lips. How every inch of me wanted to reach out and swipe back that loose sandy-brown hair that hung over his forehead.

"I'm not done," I ground out.

His shoulders went tense as he squirmed in his chair. I reached for my satchel sitting at my feet and pulled out a small leather-bound notebook. The pages flew through my fingers until I stopped on a specific, well-worn, page.

"By my estimation, it's going to cost close to two hundred thousand to fix all the problems. That's not firm until Manny does a full inspection. If he says something must be repaired or replaced, there's no argument. And I'll warn you now, even if we estimate a cost, there's always contingencies."

"Contingencies?" he echoed.

"Yes. Rats in the walls eating through wiring. Termites. The house most likely has old pipes which could be corroded in places, and we don't know how much damage was done when those idiots poured that damn cement into the drains."

His phone pinged once and then twice more. He typed out a quick text and set it down.

"These are things we won't know until we can get in there and see what's going on," I told him. "Our fee on top of that is twenty percent of the final overall budget. Are you ready for that kind of expense?"

His phone dinged twice more. He glanced at the screen and then picked it up and typed again.

"Am I boring you?"

His face paled. "No. Of course not. I don't mean to be distracted. It's just when Piper texts, I need to answer."

I more than anyone else understood the need to keep tabs on a sibling. After Tessa's husband left, I cranked up the volume on my phone so I would never miss a call from her.

"Do you need a minute?" I said, softening my voice.

"No. I'll answer and then put my phone away."

He typed out another message. When he was finished, he slid his phone into his pocket with a shaky hand. What was it about his sister that made him so off-kilter?

"Have you told Piper about any of this? Are you sure she wants to come back here?"

"It's, well…" He hesitated. Drummed his fingers nervously on the table. "It's kind of a surprise. I know she'll love it once she sees it."

"That's a big risk, Beck. What if she wants no part of it? Refuses to come back. What will you do with the house? Will you move here from Nashville? Sell it?"

The way he refused to meet my eyes warned again that he'd not thought any of this through.

"She'll want to be here," he finally breathed out. "The house meant a lot to her and my parents. I know this is the right thing to do."

So many questions were on the tip of my tongue. I wanted to know what happened to his parents. What had him so shaken up about Piper. But a part of me didn't want to crack open that wound. To hear why it'd been so easy for him to walk away from me.

"Let's get back to the terms. I know you work in Nashville, but you'll need to make yourself available to us any time if we have questions."

A thin smile pulled at his lips. "Have you been googling me?"

I rolled my eyes and bulldozed forward, refusing to answer because I may have done a lot of sleuthing after he outbid me.

"On the weekends you'll need to come down and look at the work, but know that once we get going it's hard to change things unless you want to spend more money. None of this is going to be easy. Or cheap."

I meant for my words to be sharp. Caustic. He needed to understand this wasn't a game or some weekend hobby he could mess around with for years.

"Please don't sugarcoat it for my benefit," he joked.

"Huckleberry Lane is going to take everything we have to restore it properly. I'm not going to wait around while you decide whether or not you have the stomach for this kind of project. If it's all too much, you can sell it to Manny and me right now. Walk away free and clear."

"No," he bit out too quickly. "I'll follow all your rules."

"All right. I'll talk to Manny and we'll see what happens next."

"Thank you, Torran. I promise you won't regret this." He gave me a slow smile, which when I was younger would have melted me to the core.

"Just so we're clear," I said roughly. "I'm not going to allow you to turn every interaction into a walk down memory lane. You and me"—I wiggled a finger between us—"totally, one hundred percent professional."

"Deal."

He popped out his hand and I pressed my palm to his. An ache dead center in my chest warned that I couldn't let my heart rule any of this decision. This agreement could be life-changing for Manny and me and I wouldn't let anything—my fears, or my past with Beck—overshadow what could finally make things right for me in Ivy Falls.

13

BECK

It's A Kitchen For Fuck's Sake.

TORRAN made me sweat for three full days before she called to say Manny had agreed to the terms she'd set out. Now as we all walked the house a week later, I felt like a third wheel as they swapped a series of nods and grumbles, communicating in a language all their own. Manny would point a muscled arm to a wall, comment about whether it was load-bearing, and Torran would practically finish his sentence like they shared a brain.

Or were a couple.

Since the day I'd sent that horrible email to Torran ten years ago, I'd tried everything I could to get her out of my head. My focus had to be on my own recuperation and looking after Piper. More than once Piper tried to talk me into getting in touch with her again, but my mind was too messed up. Grief had stripped away the elements of my life that I'd relied on to stay grounded. My parents. My sister. My body. All of it was gone. I'd become a shell of my former self and that was a person I was convinced Torran couldn't love anymore.

"Nope. Don't even think about it," Manny barked out in a deep voice, shaking me from my thoughts.

"Come on, I'd be saving us a ton of money if you let me refinish the original cabinets," Torran argued.

Manny propped his mitt-sized fists on his hips. His deep black hair, muscles, and six-foot-four frame reminded me of some being who'd sit on Mount Olympus.

For at least three full heartbeats, he and Torran stared each other down. She looked like Jack compared to the Giant from one of my favorite fairy tales. When I couldn't handle the tension anymore, I said, "Do you mind telling me what the problem is?"

They both turned on me like I was breaking up some important moment.

Or knew I was jealous.

"I'm part of this project and I'd like to know why you two keep eyeing each other like you're trying to negotiate a peace treaty. It's a kitchen, for fuck's sake."

Torran's face softened. "Sorry. We get like this on all our projects. I want to restore. Manny wants to replace. It's a little dance we do with every job."

"And no matter my protests, she always seems to get her damn way," Manny grumbled, knocking her arm.

There was a silent system of communication between them that made my gut clench. That made me remember at one time Torran and I had shared the same kind of secret language. Now she shared that connection with another man and it was my own damn fault.

"I'd like to restore," I said, coming up alongside Torran and brushing her side. Heat raced through me as my hand found a place beside hers on the crumbling countertop. Not so subtly, she inched away. "My mom loved these cabinets. I'd like to see them stay if it's possible."

Manny grumbled, "Fine," and Torran let out a small cheer. She rushed into the next room and Manny tracked her movement until she was out of earshot. "So Tor told me you two went to high school together?" His deep voice was more like a growl. "That you had to move away before your senior year. Why?"

"My dad was a tech whiz. He owned a business that invented several different processors that made computers run faster. It was acquired by a major company for a pretty nice price. He used the money to buy a huge RV. After I finished my junior year of high school, our family left Ivy Falls to travel the US for a year. Dad drove most of the time while my mom homeschooled me and my sister."

"Are you planning to live here once the reno is done?" His gaze flicked to the living room where Torran lingered.

"Uh, no," I hedged. "My sister Piper will." My stare moved to Torran too. "But I will be visiting a lot."

He must have heard the throaty change in my tone, because he gave me a dead-eyed stare. "You have history here. I get it, but you and I need to be clear about something." His voice went rough, bordering on fierce like he wanted me to remember this moment. "This is business for me and Torran. It's taken a lot of work to get people in Ivy Falls to respect what we do. It hasn't always been easy, especially in the last few months because of what Tor said about the town in the heat of the moment."

He stopped and shook his head.

"But we've made it this far, and I won't let one project screw it up for us. This renovation needs to go as smooth as the Cumberland River. No more accidents or problems." Manny's gaze moved to the second-floor ceiling. "Get my point?"

"Of course."

The low clop of Torran's footsteps moving up the stairs echoed through the house. Manny tried to walk away but I grabbed his arm. My fingers barely fit halfway around his bicep. His pointed stare moved to my hand and I quickly stepped back.

"Tell me the truth. How bad was it after the video went viral?"

He huffed under his breath as if weighing whether he should say anything. Like his loyalty was always to Torran.

That twinge of jealousy sparked again. I used to be the loyal one in her life. The person who'd do anything to protect her, but I'd lost all that when I walked away without a word.

"It was awful," he grumbled. "Everyone in town wanted her to leave. And her words weren't exactly a rousing push for local tourism." He grimaced. "We had problems at the houses after it too.

We'd lay sod and a day later someone had driven over it. A new coat of paint would go on the exterior and it'd get egged sometime in the night." He cursed in a low voice. "Even Tor's dad has given her all kinds of trouble. And don't get me started on all the cruel on-line comments we've gotten on our website. It's only in the last few weeks that she's finally started to come out of a funk, and I swear to heaven and earth if you screw this up for her, send her back to that dark place, I'll make you regret you ever crossed the city line back into Ivy Falls. Got me?"

"I'd never do anything to hurt her." The edges around his mouth went firm. Of course, he knew about my past with Torran. "I mean I'd never hurt her again."

"Guys, let's go!" Torran called from the second floor. "We still need to walk through the rest of the bedrooms."

Manny took a long look at me and shot out his hand. "I believe you're doing this for the right reasons, Beck. Don't make me regret trusting you."

After I shook his hand, he rushed up the stairs to the second floor. I hesitated, swallowing down the knot crowding my throat.

There was no way I was letting Torran down. Not this time.

14

TORRAN

Fraternizing With The Enemy.

AT the edge of town behind Bud's Meat-and-Three and Cady's Ice and Water, sat a little park tucked into a hidden cul-de-sac. It was my nieces' favorite spot with a few swings, three yellow twisty slides, and a single ramada with two picnic tables.

This morning it was filled with a few families enjoying the cool May morning. I'd tried to avoid eye contact, but more than a few people shot nasty glances in my direction.

Yeah, it was going to take a bit more than fixing Beck's house to get this town to forgive me.

"Faster! Faster!" Iris and Rose yelled.

My head started to spin as I pushed the cold metal of the merry-go-round over and over. My nieces held on tightly, cheering and shouting at me. The muscles in my arms burned but I continued to spin them. Their happy squeals filled me with joy. It'd taken two weeks of apologizing, and two strawberry-banana smoothies, to finally get the girls to smile after I'd missed the dinner with their grandpa.

84

Rose jumped off the spinning orb at its fastest turn. Her hair billowed out in a light blonde wave as she sprinted toward the tallest twisty slide. Iris hesitated at the corner of the merry-go-round. Even though she was eighteen months older than Rose, she was more cautious, like Tessa had been when she was young.

"Hold on, sweetie," I said. "I'll slow it down."

"No! If Rosie can do it, so can I."

Her bright blue eyes flickered as I caught the edges of the wheel, trying to slow it down without her noticing. She took a deep breath and jumped. A victory cry left her lips as she hit the ground and peeled off in the direction of her younger sister.

I held back my own cheer. It was hard not to push Iris like I'd pushed Tessa. Always trying to get her to be more adventurous, move outside her comfort zone. It never worked. Tessa preferred the quiet reading nook in her bedroom to the games of hide-and-seek I played with the neighborhood kids outside.

For years I urged her to come and play, but Tessa never budged. She was content in her own world of make-believe. She didn't need the company of other kids to feel complete. Her books and her own imagination were enough. Even now as an adult she was quiet. Reserved. Never asking for help even when she needed it most.

It was that knowledge that led me to move in with her. She'd never asked me outright to stay in her small guest room, but anyone with eyes could see she was drowning in her own misery. That the sudden shock of her husband's infidelity and flight from their lives was too much. Neither of us said it, but his actions were a painful reminder of all the times our own father had chosen his own interests over us.

A steaming cup of coffee appeared in front of my face.

"Thought you might need a little pick-me-up this morning."

Tessa gave a half-smile and moved to one of the porch-style swings that were anchored around the edge of the park. The entire time her gaze never moved from Iris as she tried to cross the swinging bridge.

"Hold on with both hands, honey."

"It's fine," I said, plopping down beside her. "She's six years old, Tess, and she's already been across at least a dozen times this morning."

"Should have known." Tessa snorted. "That little girl would do anything to impress you."

Her gaze veered to two women near the slides who sneered in my direction. My sweet, calm Tessa stared right back as I sighed and leaned back against the bench waiting for the caffeine to kick in.

"Number?" she asked without looking at me.

I took a long sip and caffeinated goodness hummed through my veins. "Low five. How about you?"

"Four. I got a text from Billy this morning." She teared up as she watched Rose chase Iris across the woodchip-covered ground and up to the top of the yellow twisty slide.

"What did he want?" I asked, trying my best to keep venom from my voice.

"One guess," she replied, clutching her fingers around her cup.

"Money?" I hissed.

All she did was nod.

"You're not going to give him any, right?"

This subject always made my stomach bunch into knots.

For most of their marriage Tessa worked to pay their mortgage, put food on the table, while her good-for-nothing husband floated from job to job. Sometimes bartending at local restaurants. Taking on the occasional catering gig.

"No," she sighed. "I'm not. But he did ask about the girls."

"Is he going to see them? Spend time with them like he should?"

"He's in Atlanta…" She gulped, her lower lip trembling. "With *her*. But he did say he wanted to come back in a couple of weeks to see them."

"What about the divorce? Did he agree to it?"

She looked at her sandals.

"Tessa, you have to push him on it. The quicker it's over, the faster you can move on."

"I know." Her watery eyes focused on her girls. "The truth is I don't understand any of it. If he's not in love with me anymore, that's fine. But to leave the girls behind? How does any human, any parent, do such a thing?"

My heart ached for her. She was a beautiful, kind woman. Any man would be lucky to be her partner, but for some reason Billy couldn't see that.

Sadly, I wasn't surprised. He'd always been a selfish creature, putting his own interests before Tessa and the girls. I bit my tongue over what I wanted to say. That he'd always taken advantage of her gentle nature, but her love and devotion refused to see it.

The last thing she needed was an "I told you so," so I snuggled in closer, intent on being her rock that refused to move even when she leaned on me the heaviest.

"It's hard, Tor," she sniffled. "It may have not been ideal, but at least our parents lived under one roof. Worked as a team." She sucked in a rattling breath. "I don't think I'm strong enough, brave enough, to do it alone."

"Alone?" I said, wrapping an arm around her shoulders. "You are not alone. You have me and Manny and all the people in this town who adore you."

"Dad too. He's really been there for me and the girls."

I wasn't going to speak up against that. He may have not been around much for us as kids, but he was doing a few after-school pickups and the occasional drive to soccer practice for the girls.

We sat in silence, the chains from the swing rattling as we swung back and forth. In the distance, Iris' laugh drifted toward us.

"The girls forgive you for missing dinner yet?" Tessa finally said.

"Yes. It only took two weeks of groveling and a large smoothie."

"They're letting you off easy," she said, kicking off her sandals. "Pity. It was my best chicken Parmigiana yet."

My stomach grumbled in reply. Tessa's cooking rivaled some of the best local chefs, and I hated the fact that I'd missed out on one of my favorite dishes, but I refused to make things uncomfortable for her or my nieces. They'd had enough heartache over the last year. I didn't want to add to that tension by arguing with my dad in front of them.

"We'll have a special dessert after dinner tonight. That'll get them to truly forgive me."

"Store-bought, right?" Her lips twitched as she blew on her own cup. "Or maybe something from Sugar Rush?"

I couldn't help but laugh. I'd tried my best in the kitchen, but no matter how closely I followed a recipe, my cooking was a total disaster. A few months ago, I'd tried to make a cake for Iris' sixth birthday. It was going well until I pulled it out of the oven to discover a flat, burned mess. I reread the recipe and realized I'd forgotten to add the eggs.

A flash of red scarf caught my eye. With her long legs, and silver hair floating behind her, Isabel walked in our direction.

"Good morning," she said cheerfully.

We echoed our hellos.

"What are y'all doing here?" she asked.

"Just a little sisterly chat," Tessa said, swiping at her cheeks. "What brings you here?"

"The ladies are holding our monthly book club outside today. Getting in a breath of that fresh spring air before the suffocating, wet heat, and mosquitos, take over."

Tessa suddenly found her coffee very interesting. The hairs on my neck went straight up. Book club was usually at the P&P.

"So," Isabel said slowly. "I was over at Sugar Rush early this morning getting some donuts." She shook the white bag in her hand. "And Barb mentioned that you have a new project, Torran?"

Her gaze flashed over to one of the benches under the ramada. Miss Cheri, who ran the town's small theater, sat with Old Mrs. Vanderpool, who stared like she expected me to shout out obscenities at the children. Over the last six months, I'd tried to do everything to get her to soften up. Apologized, sent her a coffee and a donut at the café, but the town's oldest matron was immovable when it came to holding a grudge.

"Yes," I sighed, turning back to Isabel. "Manny and I agreed to help out with the Huckleberry Lane property."

A smile ticked in the corner of Tessa's mouth. "When you and Manny are done with it, it's going to be beautiful."

"Hope so," was all I could offer as two more ladies entered the park and stared absolute daggers at me. "You better go meet your group," I said. "Don't want to be seen fraternizing with the enemy."

She ignored her friends and gave me a full-watt smile. "You, honey, will never be the enemy."

A small part of my heart tugged at the softness in her voice. She reminded me so much of my mom.

"See you two around." Isabel flounced off in the direction of the ramada and the heat of Tessa's stare burned into my back.

Taking another large gulp of coffee, I said, "You knew already, didn't you?"

Tessa returned her focus to the girls, but the corner of her mouth gave a betraying twitch.

"Manny can't keep a secret to save his life. I bet I wasn't out of the house for two seconds after our walk-through before he called you."

"Not true." She took a dainty sip of her tea. "While you were working late at the Parkview house last night, he brought Louisa over for dessert. I practically had to pry the truth out of him." Her gaze flicked back to the girls hurtling down one of the circular slides. "He's worried about this deal. How it will affect the short ninety-day time frame you've put in place. How he's going to have to split his days between that project and the finishing touches on Parkview."

"We juggle projects well," I said. "It'll be fine."

"You can't blame him for worrying. Money is always a concern with a small business."

Tension wafted off Tessa in heavy waves. A question about why the ladies were meeting at the park instead of the P&P hung on my lips but I couldn't quite push it out.

"Iris, be careful!" Tess called out as her oldest pumped her legs to go higher on the swings. The lines around her mouth were deeper. Small purple shadows lingered below her thick black lashes. She was too damn young to look so tired and broken. "Tell me more about this agreement with Beck," she said while still keeping an eagle eye on her girls.

"Beck's paying us to do the reno but I told him he has to be available for questions. That he can't be a silent partner. He has to be all in if we're going to do it right."

"I know what I said at the store, but do you think you can trust him after..." Tessa tugged on the end of her braid. Just like our mother, she wasn't good with confrontation.

"There are a dozen reasons I can list why this is a bad idea," I admitted, "but the thought that some other contractor could screw up the property is a more tangible pain. I need to restore the house and make everyone see that I have a serious stake in this town. That I care. Show them all I'm not a total screwup no matter what that video shows."

My sister reached over and squeezed my hand. "No one thinks you're a screwup, Tor."

"I love that you can lie to me with a straight face, especially with half this park shooting me death stares."

She huffed out a laugh. "Tell me the truth. How weird was it to see Beck dangling from the ceiling?"

"God. What else did Manny tell you while you were having this 'surprise' dessert?"

"Don't do that," she whispered. "We're just friends."

Every time I teased Tessa about Manny her entire body went tense like she'd been zapped by a live wire. She deserved to have love, companionship again, but she insisted that her only focus could be on the P&P and the girls.

"I know. Sorry."

She shook it off like she wanted to change the subject. "How much damage did he do?"

"A lot. He took out half the ceiling in the second-floor hallway."

"Wow," she whispered. "That much?"

"Yeah. It's proof he's completely clueless about what to do with the house."

"So, this is *all* business?"

Tessa gave me her patented mom stare that warned she'd know if I was lying.

I wasn't going to tell her that when I'd brushed Beck's leg in my truck, I almost hit the roof. That it was practically illegal how good he smelled. That I had visions of pressing my mouth to his full lips to see if his kissing had improved in ten years.

"Of course. We're partners—that's all."

"Does Beck agree?" she pushed.

The way he'd softly asked if I wanted to leave the Sugar Rush, gone out of his way to make me feel comfortable when we sat at the table, proved there was still a spark between us. But I was smart enough to know how it would end.

A tumble with Beck would be glorious. It was very hard to ignore the way he filled out an old pair of Levi's. The way his day-old scruff had a hint of red in it. It'd been too long since I'd been skin to skin with someone I cared about, but going down that road with him was filled with caution signs I had to obey.

"What happened between us was long ago. He's got his shiny life in Nashville, and I'm needed here," I said with a little too much force. "And didn't you say at the P&P that I should act like an adult? That's what I'm doing here. My feelings for him are complete and total ash. Once the job is done, we'll go our separate ways."

Tessa pursed her lips but didn't say another word. I was glad because I wasn't sure how much longer I could lie to her about all the mixed-up and complicated feelings I had about Beck coming home.

15

BECK

A Gray Void In My Head.

I'D tried calling Piper twice but both times it went straight to voice-mail. For an hour I paced the floor of my condo, letting my mind go to all the wild places it shouldn't. When I couldn't handle all the dark scenarios trolling through my head, I grabbed my keys off the counter.

For the entire forty-five-minute drive to Ivy Falls, I concentrated on how I could carve out time on weekends to come back to the house. The more I thought about the work it would take to get it back to a decent state, the more my mind went to my recent conversation with Manny.

The serious set of his massive shoulders as he swore he'd make me regret screwing up things for them if I stepped a toe out of line. It felt a bit protective. Like he'd do anything to keep Torran safe. An ache built in the center of my chest. I used to be that guy for her, but my choices stripped away that important connection. Now we were just two strangers in an unlikely alliance, which made the pain in my chest flare even more.

After I drove past the town sign, I took the long way around. The old limestone fountain sparkled in the early morning light. Various joggers and small families on bikes moved around the brick-paved square. Colorful flowers draped out of moss-covered hanging baskets hooked to every light pole.

It'd been too long since I'd felt a sweeping kind of peace. Not the kind that reminds you of being a child, but more like a sense of hope that allows you to take a full cleansing breath. Reminding you that life can be simpler if you take the time to appreciate the smaller things, like the waft of fresh donuts coating the air, or the sounds of kids playing on the wide lawn in front of the Ivy Falls courthouse.

Once I got to Huckleberry Lane both sides of the street were lined with cars. *Happy Birthday* balloons billowed from one of the mailboxes. I parked a block away and walked to the house.

Since the walk-through, we'd had new locks installed and Manny and Torran gave me a new key. The front door creaked open with a low moan, and I was reminded once again what a challenge the house would be. Even though we'd cleaned the last time we were here, the place still reeked like week-old garbage. Colorful graffiti tattooed the walls and I couldn't even imagine how many coats of paint it was going to take to get them back to normal.

I climbed the stairs and stopped. The sound of a scrape echoed through the house. An ooze of uneasiness swept through me. Was Torran right? Should I not be here alone? Who knew what other things might give way beneath my weight or, God forbid, climb out of the walls.

A tree outside the window swayed in the breeze, its branches pressing against the glass. I let out a chuckle before heading to the first bedroom, which once belonged to Piper. Long gone was the white wicker furniture and pink wallpaper with unicorns. One entire wall had been painted black with chalkboard paint. The last renters had left behind a long list of swear words that would make a long-haul trucker blush.

I pulled work gloves from the back pocket of my jeans. Beneath me was a sea of what used to be brown shag carpet. I knew Torran wanted to try and restore the original floors. Pulling up carpet seemed like the best place to start. I put on my headphones, cranked up a playlist and went to work.

I'd picked this room on purpose. Once I got Piper here, I'd show her how this could be her safe space. A spot to relax and figure out the next steps of her life. Sure, she'd said too many times to count how New York was her home now, but the defeat in her voice was clear every time we talked. The carousel of audition rejections was obviously wearing her down.

She could find creative outlets here if she tried. Ivy Falls had a local theater, and between the fashion scene and the budding array of new restaurants popping up in Nashville, there were ample opportunities for her to work. It'd been coined "Nashvegas" for a reason.

For over a half-hour, I tugged and pulled at the carpet. The ragged and sharp edges of it bit through the cheap gloves I'd bought at Hendrix's hardware store. A sea of dust and dirt spit up into the air as I worked piece by piece. Sweat beaded my hairline and ran down the side of my face. I'd opened a window but the late spring heat still managed to make the room feel like a sauna. I should have worn short sleeves but my scars had been aching a lot lately and I did not want a constant reminder of them while I worked.

The scars were just one more reason why I wanted Piper here. After our parents' accident, things became a blur. I don't remember the ambulance ride or being airlifted to the hospital. Later, I was told I'd been put into a medically induced coma so doctors could treat the burns on my chest, torso and arms.

That time period is a gray void in my head. A series of fractured images, voices, and movement that now seem like an old movie that's spent too long in a vault. The aged images too fuzzy to recognize.

After they reduced my meds and I came out of the coma, I spent many more weeks in the burn unit. There was no real way to describe the pain. I tried to verbalize it once for my grandmother when she asked. I could only tell her to picture having an animal slowly tear the flesh from your limbs but add fire to the sting of the bites. The pain was a thousand times worse than that, but it put enough of a picture in her head that all she could do was wrap a bony hand around my fingers and quietly sob.

It was the same thing with Piper. When she'd visit me at the rehab hospital, she could only stay for a minute or two at first, not being able to handle my screams as physical therapists stretched out my arms, forced me to bend my back. But she kept returning, eventually helping me when I needed to use stability balls or work with a foam roller. In those excruciating months, she'd held my hand. Stared at me with fiery eyes and told me to work harder, to focus on getting better.

I was so immersed in my own recuperation that I didn't see her falling apart. One of just many ways I'd failed her over the years.

My muscles ached as I rolled the grimy old carpet into thick cylinders. Once I had half the room completed, I went to grab the water bottle I'd left downstairs.

In the hallway the hole in the ceiling mocked me. I stepped toward the stairs, the childhood memories coming back in a thick wave. Piper and I chasing each other with Nerf guns. The sound of the music our parents loved: Supertramp and Fleetwood Mac, floating in the air. How my mother loved experimental Italian cooking, our house always smelling like a mix of oregano and minced garlic.

When Diego first contacted me, he explained how the auction worked. That anyone could buy the houses on his list. What they did with the homes after was up to the buyer. He'd said the town council had discussed rezoning the area to be multipurpose use, which meant it could be bought by a developer and knocked down or turned into some kind of business. Torran's words about the town losing its heritage rang in my ears. This may have started as a plan to save my own history, but it felt good to know that the work done here was about something bigger than me trying to recapture my own past. It didn't hurt that it also gave me an excuse to see Torran regularly. To slowly try and rebuild what I'd broken years ago.

As I gazed at the paint-splashed walls, I considered all the things Torran and Manny had said about the house. The way he could restore the beautiful banister. How she wanted to resurface the original cabinets. All the things my parents would have loved. My throat went prickly dry. I tugged off my gloves, blisters already forming on my fingertips, and headed back to the stairs intent on finding my water bottle.

Barely down the first few steps, a small creak came from the master bedroom. I went still. Waited. It had to be the house settling. After another beat, the distinct sound of footsteps made me go cold. I wasn't here alone.

I crept back up to the landing and grabbed a large piece of broken ceiling tile. Not a great weapon, but it'd work in a pinch. With slow, measured steps I approached the master bedroom, not sure what, or who, I'd find.

16

TORRAN

Climb Your Ass Down From Mount Arrogance.

I wasn't supposed to be in the house. I'd promised Manny I'd wait before doing any demo, but after I'd said goodbye to Tessa and the girls at the park, I'd headed here to start working.

The truth was I needed to keep busy because the more I thought about the agreement we'd made with Beck, the more I worried I'd made a colossal mistake.

I pulled a screwdriver from my tool belt and went to work on the cabinets in the master bathroom, working the screws out of the hinges and setting the doors in a pile on the floor. The steady pace of the work helped me forget the ugly stares from the ladies in the park. I knew I deserved their ire, but it still cut into me that they were angry, especially since most of them had been so close to Mom. But that was why I was here. Why I'd essentially made a deal with the devil. If I could fix this house, I could keep my promise to Mom, and hopefully win back the town's trust.

I reached for the sledgehammer I'd brought in from my truck, eager to release all my pent-up anger and nervous energy on the ancient cabinets. I curled my fingers around the handle and swung the hammer back when the sound of shuffling feet made me stop dead.

I gripped the sledgehammer and stepped out of the bathroom. Slowly I inched to the closed bedroom door. When it creaked open, my heart filled my throat and I unleashed the full force of a swing. A hand quickly moved out and caught the steel head, stopping its forward motion.

"Holy shit! You could have taken off my head." Beck yanked the hammer toward him, and I stumbled into his chest.

"What the hell are you doing here?" I roared.

"I'm here to work. Isn't that why you're here?" he snapped.

"You are such an ass, Beck! Did you think maybe you could call my name? Give me some warning you were here?" I spun around and charged back to the bathroom.

"First, I didn't see Sally Mae in the driveway. Second, I didn't know I had to announce my presence," he said, following behind me.

"The truck is parked farther up the street because of the neighbor's birthday party, and she keeps leaking oil that I don't want on the driveway. And announcing your presence would have been damn helpful considering I almost bashed your head in!"

"Something tells me you'd get pleasure out of that," he said, dropping the sledgehammer and a flimsy piece of ceiling tile on the floor.

"Yep. Someone needs to knock some sense into that thoughtless brain of yours."

"Thoughtless brain? Who's the one swinging heavy equipment without looking first?"

"Only because I thought you were a fucking burglar!"

"Obviously you can see that I'm not."

His eyes flared and a surge of need zapped through me. I couldn't do this. Be this close to him and not remember how deep brown his eyes were. The faint scent of soap that always lingered on his skin.

"This isn't going to work," I said, tugging off my gloves.

"What isn't going to work?"

"You. Me. This house." I flailed my hands out to my sides. "It's all a very bad idea."

He inched in and heat burned behind his eyes. "What's bad about it, Torran? Is it that it's hard to be this close to me?"

God, yes, I wanted to say but instead I planted my feet. Glared right back at him. "You can climb your ass right back down Mount Arrogance because I'm perfectly fine around you."

I prayed he didn't hear the tremble in my voice. Notice the fire burning in my cheeks. See the twitch in my fingers because I ached to touch him.

He reached forward and swept back a hair from my face. We stood not speaking, barely breathing. He leaned in and with a honeyed voice whispered, "You sure about that?"

I knew that look. A combination of hunger and desire I hadn't seen since we were in high school. He slid his hand behind my neck, and without any hesitation, pulled me in. The warmth of his breath tickled my cheeks. My mind screamed not to let him closer, give in to the heat careening through my veins, but the protest died in my throat as he swept his mouth over mine.

He tasted like coffee and peppermint as he sucked on my bottom lip. A small whimper sprang from my mouth and I melted under his touch. He gripped the back of my shirt like he knew I'd puddle to the floor without him holding me up. This shouldn't be happening. I hated him. What he did to my heart all those years ago. But I still held on to him with every bit of strength I had.

We stumbled back into the crumbling sink. He ran a line of kisses down my neck and I arched into him. Ten years had passed, but our bodies had no trouble recognizing each other. I'd sworn we could only be business partners, but the ache between my legs screamed for much more.

Beck threaded his fingers through my ponytail, inching down the tie. The grip of his fingers sent another shock through me. My hair spilled across my back as he wound me in closer.

"You don't know how long I've dreamed about this," he sighed into my mouth. His fingers slid down the front of my shirt, expertly releasing the first set of buttons.

With every movement the rational part of me screamed to stop, but the heat of his stare, the weight of his body against mine, felt too good. I tightened my arms around his neck and he lifted me onto what was left of the counter. Another small scar peeked out from underneath his right sleeve. I wanted to ask about it, but he distracted me with the desperation in his kisses.

After years of thinking about him, wondering what he looked like, how he'd changed, I needed to feel the warmth of him to prove he wasn't some fantasy. I eased my fingers beneath the hem of his shirt, but he gripped my hands and tugged me closer. I pressed my breasts into him, my lips seeking the sensitive spot under his chin, hoping it was still his weak point. His low moan said I'd met my target.

His fingers slid around the edge of my jeans and then down the side of the zipper to the spot that ached for him. I arched into his touch and he smothered my mouth with another hungry kiss.

"Excuse me for interrupting."

My father's broad body filled most of the doorway. His face was set in its usual hard mask. It only took a single look for him to turn me into a fumbling seventeen-year-old again.

I pushed away from Beck and clutched at my open shirt.

"Dad, what are you doing here?"

He glanced around the chaos of the bathroom, focusing anywhere but on me in my half-state of dress. "I was on the ninth tee at the club yesterday when I heard you'd be working on this place." The edges of his jaw worked as he stepped further into the bathroom. "For the life of me, I don't get why you do this job. It smells like the inside of a porta-john."

I swallowed the urge to scream at him and his judgment. Sick of the way he glared at me like I was hawking my body on Main Street rather than trying to preserve Ivy Falls' rich history.

Once he'd surveyed the space, he turned his irritated gaze on me. "Can I speak to you out in the hall, please?"

Beck stood frozen and I wanted the floor to open up and swallow me.

Dammit. How had I let this happen?

With shaky hands, I buttoned up my shirt and brushed past him. In the hall Dad gave me that look of disappointment I was used to by now.

"Your sister was upset you didn't join us for dinner the other evening." He stared at the crumbling wallpaper like he couldn't bear to look at me. "Your nieces hardly ate a thing because they were too sad that you weren't there."

He knew just what to say to hurt me. Tessa and the girls meant everything to me and I already knew how upset they'd been by the way they'd treated me when I got home later that night. Still, it galled me that he thought he could shame me when it came to them.

I'd stayed on the phone with Tessa for hours after she got the seven-word text from her husband saying he'd run off with Trini from the Pool and Brew. After I moved back to Ivy Falls a few weeks later, there were more than a few nights where I held her shaking body as she sobbed. Cared for her girls when she couldn't get out of bed.

"I find it ironic that you're lecturing me about not showing up for one dinner when you spent half my childhood in other states. Hell, you couldn't even be there for Mom when she needed you most."

I knew how to hit where it hurt too.

"I didn't come here to fight," he said with surprising calm. The act was for Beck's benefit—I was sure he could hear us from inside the bedroom.

"Why did you come here?"

"I know your finances are tight." He lowered his voice. "Why are you taking on another project when Parkview isn't finished?"

I couldn't believe he was here, getting into this with me right now. For the last year, he'd watched me and Manny at town council meetings. Fighting to keep the history of this town alive. Why couldn't he see that the work I was doing was important? That if Mom was here she'd be supporting me through all of this?

"I'm paying Torran and Manny to help me on this project." Beck stepped into the hall and stopped next to me. The heat of him burned into my side. "I need their expertise and intelligence to make sure the house is renovated the right way. As you may remember, I used to live here."

My father's lips thinned into an unhappy line. "Yes, I remember."

Beck glanced at my father's starched khakis and blue polo. "Were you here to help, sir? I can put you to work. There's an extra pair of gloves in my car and a sewer line out back that needs fixing." A wicked grin ticked up the corner of Beck's mouth. I loved that one line from him could make my dad flinch.

"That will not be necessary." Dad's gaze moved to the hole in the ceiling. "Looks like there is a lot of work here. I hope it will be done to code."

Another zinger shot my way. He'd morphed into Mr. Mayor now.

"Of course," I volleyed back. "You know Manny has a great working relationship with the city."

He humphed under his breath. "This is a valuable piece of property. At one time we were considering having it rezoned for business."

"It's a good thing I bought it then," Beck flung back. "It's important that we save and respect the town's history. Don't you agree, mayor?"

My father gave one last glance at the crumbling walls and finally mumbled, "We'll see."

"Did you need something else?" I said, trying to keep the venom from my voice.

"No, we're done here."

"Yes, I think we are," I shot back.

He gave a firm nod like he had to have the final word. "I'm sure I'll be seeing more of you, Beck."

"Only if you come back to help. The sewer lines will be waiting."

My father gave a tense laugh and fled down the stairs.

Once the front door slammed shut, I slumped back against the wall.

"Are you okay?" Beck asked, soft and low.

"I had things under control with him."

"I know you did, but it can't hurt to have backup." He slouched next to me. "At least we're consistent," he teased. "You know, with your dad catching us in a compromising position."

He waggled both his eyebrows and I let loose a roaring laugh. The scene was so ridiculous, my luck so bad, that all I could do was cry or laugh. Laughing was a much better option.

"It could have been worse," he chuckled. "Remember the time the button on my jeans popped off and we were late for curfew? Your dad stood on your front porch and kept staring at the fact that my pants were barely hanging on to my waist."

"Yeah, I heard about that for weeks." My throat went dry as I continued to howl. "He mentioned more than once that I should buy you a belt for your birthday."

Beck laughed louder. "Or what about the time Sally Mae got stuck in the mud near the lake?" he gasped. "We tried to get her back wheels out and at one point you pinned me down with a kiss and then I flipped you over. By the time we were done, we were covered head to toe in muck."

"Yeah, that was fun trying to explain to my parents why I had gravel in my hair and, well, other places."

His laugh filled the hallway and my cheeks ached from smiling so hard.

"Thanks for saying what you did about needing my expertise."

"And intelligence," he said with another grin.

"Yes, that too," I whispered.

We swapped a few more stories about our childhood adventures. The frogs we caught in the creek. Forts we made in the dense woods behind my house. The hours we'd hid in my treehouse eating too much candy (SweeTARTS for him; Hot Tamales for me) and reading every book we could convince my mom to give us.

We kept talking until a loud creak from the gaping hole in the ceiling brought me back to reality. That familiar buzz in my chest warned me again that this deal between us was probably a very bad idea.

We stood in an uncomfortable silence, neither of us wanting to acknowledge the kiss.

"I think we should get back to work."

"Yeah, right," he said, his smile fading.

He strode away and I couldn't keep my eyes from wandering to the way his butt still fit perfectly into those damn Levi's, and that it'd taken absolutely no time for us to break the rule about walking down memory lane.

17

BECK

A Slow Kind Of Torture.

I sank onto the dirty brown carpet, grateful Torran couldn't read my mind. Before her father interrupted us, I had visions of pressing her into the wall. Doing all sorts of wicked things to coax that sweet whimper out of her again. Stripping away at her armor bit by bit with every kiss and panting sigh I placed against her skin. But, as usual, Miles Wright had crappy timing.

I pulled the patches of carpet away from the wall trying to figure out what Torran meant when she'd said her father hadn't been there when her mom needed him most. His icy demeanor only ever thawed around Mrs. Wright. She'd had a special type of kindness that drew people to her like flies to sweet tea.

During the summers when Ivy Falls was cloaked in a wet, suffocating heat, her bookstore became my secret hideout. I'd search the shelves of the Pen & Prose for some new adventure until I'd run into Mrs. Wright who always had an armful of suggestions. She'd lead me to the aisle where Torran was camped out and we'd read for hours, caught up in whatever new world we'd discovered.

The scent of cat piss, dirt, and dust brought me back to the present. Sweat rolled down my face and my skin itched and ached. I hated that I had to wear long sleeves, but I wasn't ready to share that part of me with Torran yet. It's why I'd stopped her when she'd reached for the hem of my shirt.

Trying to take my mind off Torran's blazing touch, I rolled up another length of carpet until it was settled in a corner of the room. Like Manny had predicted, there was a layer of hardwood underneath painted a stark white.

"Why the hell would people do that?" I mumbled.

"It's a sign of the times," Torran said from the doorway.

I loved how the scratch from my stubble still colored the arch of her neck. The way the white plaster dust covered her arms and face in a thin sheen. How her hair was tugged back up into a tight ponytail. Looking at her filled my body with a need, an ache, I couldn't describe. Even through the grit and grime, she was beautiful.

"New owners come in and they want to update. I can't tell you the number of 1970s banana-yellow kitchens I've torn apart." She cocked her head back to the master bedroom. "Or early Eighties bathrooms I've encountered with hideous floral wallpaper."

"That's true. My mom always hated the wallpaper in there."

She moved to the corner and unrolled the carpet.

"What are you doing? It took me ten minutes to wrestle that bad boy into a tight roll."

She huffed and walked out the door. Two minutes later she reappeared clutching a small utility knife and a roll of duct tape. "The key to this job is to work smarter not harder."

The muscles in her arms flexed as she cut down the carpet roll into three foot sections. Her hair swung behind her as she yanked the silver tape around each of the pieces.

"Manny would be mad if he saw the way you rolled the carpet. Do you know how much it weighs? Cutting it down into manageable sections makes it easier to discard, and it doesn't strain your back." She paused staring at my hands. "Those gloves are meant for gardening. You need ones made of thicker material or you're going to get blisters."

Too late for that.

Her gaze moved across the dirty floor and she shook her head once she saw the series of curse words written across the black wall.

"How'd you learn all this?" I asked. "When we were kids you had a small interest in architecture, but construction, that's a little bit of a leap."

"When you want to pull your head out of your nineteenth-century ass, I'll explain it." She kicked a carpet roll into the corner and started to walk out of the room.

I reached for her arm. The heat of her sparking through me again. She gave a pointed stare to where my hand met her skin and I released her. "Sorry, I didn't mean that the way it came out. You're perfectly capable of doing this job. I've seen that firsthand." I glanced at the knife still clutched in her hand. "I'm only curious about how you got into this line of work."

Torran leaned against the doorjamb. I hated the hesitation in her eyes. There was a time when I could ask her anything and she'd pipe right up with an answer, but I was an ass, and that armor of hers was fully in place.

"During senior year, my history class went to Franklin to tour an old Civil War house. The minute I walked into the foyer something hit me. It was like taking a trip back in time. The arched entrance. The heart pine floors. Even the wallpaper. It was all preserved. If I closed my eyes, I could picture the family descending the staircase. Going into the parlor for late-afternoon tea."

The far-off look in her eyes made me step closer. My hands twitched at my sides aching to touch her again. She noticed how I moved in and took a step back.

"When we went to tour the outside, the guide pointed out holes in the wall from bullets exchanged during a battle on the back lawn. He took us downstairs into the cellar where the family hid from the fighting. The original chairs they sat on were still there. Preserved for all to see."

Her voice had that sweet lilt that I loved. When we'd sat wrapped in a blanket near our favorite lake as kids, the same tone would ring in her words as she talked about our future. In those moments it was like nothing else existed in the world except the two of us. I'd often thought of those times after I'd buried my parents, needing to hold on to that light so the darkness didn't swallow me whole.

"It might sound weird, but a sense of comfort washed over me," she went on. "Like all our history was being saved for future generations. We didn't have to read about it in a textbook because it was alive and in front of us in living color."

She picked at the white pieces of drywall stuck to her arm before walking to a corner and unrolling another carpet remnant.

"The guide told us that in the late 1960s the house was close to being condemned until a few investors stepped in and saved it. The fact that a piece of history almost went to rubble hit me hard."

"And Manny? Have you always worked together?"

She stopped halfway through taping the roll of carpet. Her shoulders went up to her ears, that flicker of armor returning.

"Manny and I are a long story. Let's just say we have a good relationship. We balance each other out."

Yeah, but did Manny feel the same way?

I pushed away the thought and went back to work, trying not to picture how his arms could easily circle her small waist. How he could wrap her up like a giant to keep her safe. Hell, she probably didn't even need to cut up the carpet. I bet The Rock himself could haul the whole thing out without even breaking a sweat.

"That's good," I mumbled. "You deserve someone you can rely on. Who believes in what you're doing."

She rolled up the last bit of carpet and turned to face me. The lines around her eyes pinched into cute little Vs.

"Not that it's any of your business, but Manny and I are *friends*. That's all." She shoved the utility knife back into her tool belt. "When I bought my first project on Westfort, I discovered it had foundation issues. Diego recommended Manny and he came to look at the property. He wasn't out of his car ten minutes when he found the problem."

Torran pointed to the corner of the room and started to roll up the yellowed carpet pad, motioning for me to do the same.

"When he gave me his estimate, he didn't ask to talk to my husband, brother, or boyfriend. He knew I ran the worksite and treated me like an equal. I gave him the job on the spot. We worked together a few more times and then Lauren approached us about that episode for Hearth and Home. Partnering with him is the best decision I've ever made. In this business when problems can pop up every day, it's handy to have someone like him around."

She continued to roll back the pad, huffing along as she went. "I'm not deluded. I know I can't work on these sites all by myself, conquer every problem. It helps to have a second set of eyes. A partner with whom I can share ideas and dreams. My dad even respects Manny, which is saying something."

Her voice caught on the mention of her father. She was an amazing woman. Why couldn't Miles Wright see that?

"I know your dad's always been tough on you, but he must be proud of what you're doing with all these houses."

"You saw him today." Her gorgeous mouth puckered. "Not sure ' proud' would be the word he'd use, especially since he caught his adult daughter making out like a teenager."

I smiled but refused to apologize. If I could get her to look at me that way again, like she wanted to see, touch, every inch of me, I'd do it in a heartbeat.

"Since Mom's been gone, it's gotten worse between us. She's not here to be the buffer. Tessa tries but…" She broke off and went back to focusing on the carpet, ripping up an edge in the corner of the room.

I could never figure out Torran's dad. When she ran hurdles in high school and tore past the other girls, the crowd cheered but her dad always had a criticism. When she made honor roll, her mom would beam at her while her dad mumbled under his breath about taking harder classes. It pained me to see that so many years later she was still fighting the same damn battles with him.

"So tell me more about Tessa," I said, sensing she needed a change of subject. "You said you're living with her right now?"

"Yes, just until things can get back to normal for her and her girls."

"What happened between her and Billy?"

She quirked an eyebrow.

"Yes, Diego may have said something to me about it. But to his credit, he didn't give me many details."

"He broke her heart. The girls' too." Her words came out clipped and rough. "He's an asshole, who not only abandoned his wife but his two children, all while our mother was dying."

"I'm sorry. Tessa doesn't deserve to be treated like that."

"No one does," she snapped.

Her comeback struck again at how much I'd hurt her. There'd never be a good time to tell her the truth, but we were alone now and I saw my opening.

"Torran, I—"

"About earlier," she spoke over me. "It shouldn't have happened." She kept her focus on rolling up the carpet. "We had a weak moment and it's over. Let's focus on what needs to be done here. No more distractions. No more…"

"Touching," I laughed, trying to get her to loosen up. She gave me a stony look in return.

"Beck, you agreed," she started.

"To be totally professional," I said quickly because I didn't want to give her another reason to push me away. Or call off our agreement. I needed her too much.

Her focus returned to cutting up and rolling the carpet into small pieces. We worked in silence for a while until she yelled, "Shit!" and wrenched a thick metal staple from her hand. A gush of blood slid down her thumb. I jumped up and pressed the edge of my T-shirt to her hand.

She gave me a slight shove and covered the puncture with her own shirt. "I should have my gloves on. First lesson in renovation: always make sure you wear the right equipment to protect yourself."

Her warning was laced with meaning.

If we were going to keep working this closely, I'd have to arm myself from a lot more than sharp things. I was going to have to protect my heart, because the more I saw her, talked to her, the more I wanted to confess the truth. Convince her I was a guy worth trusting again.

Now that I'd kissed her and remembered the sweet taste of her mouth, it was clear that working together was going to be a slow kind of torture. A torture I absolutely wanted.

18

TORRAN

Popping Up Like A Whac-A-Mole.

I walked a path across the floor doing everything I could to push away the smell of Beck on my clothes and skin. Dammit. How had I slipped under his spell again?

I'd sworn I wouldn't let his presence cloud my judgment, but all it took was him pulling me close and I'd turned into fucking Jell-O. And I hated to admit it, but laughing with him in the hallway had felt good. Like I could finally shake off the darkness my father always seemed to leave in his wake.

Beck wasn't subtle in the way his gaze tracked me through the house. How he wanted to follow me into every room. But this part of the job was sacred to me. I wanted to be alone when the property was torn down to the studs. I loved the quiet silence of wandering the old hallways. It let me size up each of the rooms. Allowed me to dream about how each space could be designed. How the light played against the walls and what paint colors would make the room come alive. It was like a blank canvas waiting for me to create a picture that would make the buyer feel like they'd finally found their home.

Manny understood how important this part of the process was to me. He respected my methods and hung back until I was ready to share my ideas.

Beck was different. He'd made it clear he wanted to be part of every detail. Have a say on what finishes and fixtures we used. It was part of my demands when we talked about this partnership, but now I had to figure out how I was going to deal with his constant presence, and all my old feelings that kept popping up like a Whac-a-Mole.

Beck hefted a carpet roll onto his shoulder.

"Here, let me help."

I moved to his side and set my hands on his waist. He sucked in a quick breath as I shifted his body so his legs were shoulder-width apart. Slowly, I inched my hand up his back and over his muscled shoulder, shifting the roll so it was perfectly balanced. The heat of him sent a shock through me. That kiss, the way he slid his hands over my body, rolled around in my head again.

"You need to learn to lift with your legs or you're going to screw up your back," I said, quickly stepping away. "And next time, wear short sleeves. It's got to be at least ninety in here without air conditioning."

"Don't worry. I've got this," he said as he shuffled out the door.

This kind of job wasn't for everyone. I'd seen lesser men crumble under the work required to fix a house this size. Whether he knew it or not, the next months would be a test for him. I'd felt the soft skin on his hands. He'd never done real manual labor. Punched through walls as a thick layer of Sheetrock dust covered his hair. Crawled across floors until his knees were raw and bruised.

Manny wouldn't let him off easy either. I'd noticed the way he'd watched Beck the day of our walk-through. He'd push him to the edge to see if he'd break, and if Beck was still the same guy he was ten years ago, he'd push right back.

A tiny giggle from the doorway made me spin around.

"How'd you get in here?" I said.

Manny's daughter looked at me with big brown eyes. "I walked through the door."

"This is a construction zone, Lou. It's not safe for kids. Go back outside."

111

As usual she ignored me and stalked across the room, her pink tennis shoes thudding across the floor. In the back corner, she bounced up and down like I'd done earlier.

"You missed a spot." She tapped her shoe against the floor. "You need a T-nail right here."

I moved to her side and placed my boot to the spot and sighed as the floor bounced beneath me.

"You are some sort of house whisperer. Just like your dad." Lou giggled as I poked her belly.

"Yeah, it's a gift," she said with more attitude than a nine-year-old should have.

I picked up her hand and twirled her in a circle. The first time I met Lou, Manny and I had just agreed to work on a project together. When she walked into the house with an empty front room she twirled from the door all the way to the far wall. Now it was tradition for her to do her little ballerina moves in each of our empty houses.

"Where's your pop?" I asked.

"Outside talking to that man. He was telling him he was carrying the carpet wrong."

While I could be assertive, Manny was outright tough. At a worksite a few months ago, he fired a subcontractor after he tried to convince Manny he should sell the old cabinets instead of donating them to the Ivy Falls Community Church that was renovating its kitchen.

I steered Lou out the door. Beck appeared at the top of the stairs, blinked, glanced down the hall and blinked again. "Isn't she a little young to be a squatter?"

Lou jutted out her lower lip. "I'm not a squatter!"

"Well, you're too big to be a mouse," he teased. "Exactly what are you then? A panda bear?" He tapped his chin. "No." He glanced at her pink shoes. "I've got it. You're definitely a rabbit."

"No, I'm a girl," she giggled.

I loved the way Beck got her to smile. How she scrunched up her little cheeks.

"I know lots about animals," Lou said. "We've got a doggie named Fergus at my house. Plus, a ferret and a parrot." She lowered her voice. "My daddy rescued Mr. Peepers from a man who taught him the F-word."

Beck trained an amused look on me, and I pressed a hand to my lips to keep from laughing. But Lou was right, that bird was a handful.

"Louisa Marie Parks!" Manny's voice carried up the stairs. "You know better than to sneak onto a job site without my permission."

Lou squeezed her little fingers against mine. I loved when she did this—acted like I was the only one who could protect her from her dad who was all bark and no bite.

"I kept an eye on her, Manny," I said as he stopped at the top step.

"Lou Lou, you know better." He tapped his foot like he was irritated, but the way he arched his brow said he knew she was in good hands with me.

"She's definitely your daughter," I said. "I walked the entire second bedroom after we pulled up the carpet. Didn't find a single problem with the floor. But this one…" I cocked my head in Lou's direction. "She's inside for ten seconds and finds a spot that needs a T-nail."

"See," Lou huffed. "Told you it was important to bring me."

Manny gave her a reluctant smile. "All right, it's true. You do have a knack for these things, but it was still wrong for you to come inside without an adult. There's glass and a broken ceiling which makes this a dangerous place." His gaze swung to Beck, who refused to wilt under Manny's sharp stare. "I'm going to walk the rest of the house and start my notes. You plan on being here all the time?"

"When I can," Beck answered. "I have to work in Nashville during the week, but you can definitely count on me on weekends."

"We only have a crew on Saturday. Sunday's a rest day."

Manny glanced at me and his eyes narrowed on my neck. Shit. Could he see the red marks caused by Beck's stubble?

"Well, Sunday is a rest day for most people," he grumbled, his eyes still lingering on me too long.

"Hey." I nudged his shoulder trying to ignore his steady gaze. "You're here too."

Manny said something under his breath about "work ethic and sanity."

Early on in our partnership we'd agreed not to work Sundays. Being home with Lou was important to him. When we first became partners, he'd made it clear his daughter was his first priority. That one statement told me all I needed to know about him.

"Pop, are you gonna tell Miss Torran about the lady outside?"

Manny tugged off his baseball cap and scratched at his dark hair. "I was getting to that." I didn't like the way his entire body tensed. "Lou, go into the bedroom and do not move. Tor, we need to talk privately."

Beck got the hint and followed Lou into the bedroom as she lectured him about new flooring.

Manny took a few steps back down the hall and stopped before hitting the stairs. He refused to meet my eye and goosebumps flooded my skin. Crap. He'd figured it out about Beck and me.

"All right, spill it. What's going on? Who's outside?" I said too quickly. "My dad already made an unwanted appearance today. Is it Old Mrs. Vanderpool? She was giving me the stink eye at the park earlier today."

Before he could answer, a familiar cadence of clicking heels echoed against the concrete walkway outside. A second later, Lauren Gillroy from Hearth and Home walked through the door.

"What the hell is she doing here?" I said, tugging Manny back against the wall and out of sight.

"I caught her lurking outside when I drove up. She's here to see us. And, well, the house."

"The house? How does she even know about this place?"

"Why don't you come down here and I'll be happy to tell you?" Lauren's high-pitched voice floated upstairs.

Manny shrugged and I shouldered my way around him. When I vaulted off the last step and into the entry, Lauren gave a quick wave like we were old friends. Hardly.

"Hello, Torran. It's good to see you again."

Several responses played through my head, most of them words that were worse than what was written on the walls upstairs. The last time I'd seen Lauren I'd said quite a few things that would've gotten me a long censoring beep on television.

When we'd first signed the contract with Hearth and Home, Lauren promised she'd take care of us, look out for our best interests, but when push came to shove, and my video went viral, she didn't lift a finger to help us.

"Why are you here?" was the most civil thing I could say.

"Well," she hedged, her eyes darting around the chaos of the house. "I was wondering if we could talk for a minute?"

"About what?"

It took every ounce of control for me to not totally lose it in front of the woman who'd made me the laughingstock of my entire town, not to mention the whole damn country.

Lauren shifted uncomfortably back and forth on her four-inch heels. "First, I wanted to apologize for the video being released on YouTube. After doing some digging, the network was mortified to learn one of our cameramen uploaded it without permission. He was promptly fired."

"Huh, that's funny," I shot back. "The video is still up and has over a half a million views the last time I checked."

"Yes," she gulped. "But you did sign a release."

If I stood still long enough, I could feel the weight of that green paint as it swerved down my back. The raw scent of it as it dripped onto the lovingly restored floors.

"This conversation is over," I said, jamming my finger toward the front door. "You can leave now."

Lauren huffed but straightened her shoulders. "Please, let me explain why I'm here."

"Go back to Atlanta, Lauren." Manny sauntered down the stairs, his grip whitening on the crumbling banister.

"I'm here to offer you a new deal," she blurted out. "My boss heard about this house and wants to film its transformation. Have Torran go on camera narrating the changes you've made. He'd like her to talk about the importance of preserving old homes like this one and the value it adds back to the community."

"Heard from who?" Manny said.

"We got an anonymous email. The person gushed about the kind of renovations that were planned for this house. How you're both so talented. That the network would be dumb not to give you another chance to showcase your work. That's all I know."

Manny and I swapped the same irritated look. If she thought she could waltz in here and sweet-talk us, she was dead wrong. And exactly who in town would brag about us? It didn't sound legit.

"Torran, everything all right?" Beck leaned over the banister with Lou standing right next to him.

"Just a small miscommunication," I said unconvincingly. "Can you take Lou back to the room where we were working? She can give you some pointers about the rest of the carpet."

Beck let out a low chuckle at the way Lou propped her hands on her hips and gave him a firm nod.

Once they were out of earshot, I took a step toward Lauren and lowered my voice. "That video ruined our reputation in this town. No one told me they'd laid down that rug. You and the cameraman were standing there the whole time. It would have taken one word of warning to prevent it. But no, you let me crash into the ladder and be doused by a can of green paint. And then no one told us the camera was still running," I fumed. "Do you have any idea how mortifying it is to get tagged in an Instagram post with over a thousand people snarking about what an idiot you are? Not to mention the damage it did to my relationship with practically everyone in my hometown!"

Lauren yanked the collar of her pink blouse away from her throat before squeaking out a reply. "It all happened so fast. If I had a chance to do it over, I would. Please believe me, I ordered that part of the episode to be deleted but Roy, the cameraman, has always been shady. He uploaded it without the network's permission but then…" She searched the ground for firm footing and huffed out a heavy breath. "It went viral. Our ratings went up and the network let it go. We do feel bad about it and because of that my boss is prepared to offer you this deal."

She pulled down the edges of her suit jacket looking entirely out of place amidst the graffiti and ragged grooves in the beat-up floor.

"If we film this renovation, Hearth and Home will give you ten thousand dollars per episode. We will listen and follow your every direction with a promise to stay out of the workers' way. When the house is finished"—she nodded at me—"Torran will do a complete voice-over. Explain in detail everything you've done to bring the house back to its historic state. It will be a five-show package with a rider stating that if the shows earn the appropriate viewership, we'll open negotiations for a full season next year. The payment will go up to twenty thousand dollars per show with a guaranteed total of ten episodes."

Manny tugged on his cap but didn't show any emotion. He was so much better with the poker face than I was.

I took a rough gulp and did the math in my head. Fifty grand plus an additional two hundred thousand dollars for one full season. With that money we could pay off some of our debt and consider new projects. The offer was tempting, but Hearth and Home had burned us once and I wasn't about to jump in again without some serious thought.

"That's an interesting offer but it doesn't erase the damage you've already done to our reputation," Manny said. "You haven't exactly proven yourself to be trustworthy, Lauren. We'll need time to think it over."

"I expected that response so let me give you one more thing to consider. If you agree to this project, we'll take down the video immediately and sue anyone who reposts it without our permission."

Manny and I swapped a knowing look. For days after the video went live, we went to every lawyer in Ivy Falls for help. The entire town was so angry with me no one would take our case. We went to several lawyers in Nashville hoping to find a way to force Hearth and Home to take it down. Unfortunately, those lawyers told us what we already knew: the contract we'd signed was ironclad.

If we wanted the video to disappear, Lauren's offer might be the only way.

"Like Manny said, we need some time to think." I stepped back so she had a clear exit to the door.

She rolled back her shoulders. "Considering what's happening in this town, how much you both claim to love it, I thought you'd jump at this chance."

"What do you mean by what's happening in this town?" I said.

Her eyes went wide. "The email we received said your little town was dying. That by the end of the year half the businesses on Main Street would be shuttered. Whoever wrote that email claimed that a show like ours could create new interest in Ivy Falls. We win. You win. The whole town wins."

By the pale color of Manny's cheeks it was clear he knew nothing about this either. People said it was my fault tourism was down, but I had no idea things were this bad. The empty shelves in the P&P flashed through my head.

Oh my God, was Mom's bookstore in trouble too?

"Again, we can't give you our answer now," I said shakily. "We're contracted through the owner. He'll need to give us permission."

She clucked her tongue. "You have a week. This is going to be a short production schedule and we'll need to start shooting soon." She glanced between me and Manny. "I hope you'll give Hearth and Home a second chance to prove we're a good partner. You two have something special and we want to share that with our audience." Lauren's gaze moved to the high ceilings and crown molding. "And if this house turns out the way I think it will, you may just be the saving grace of this town too." She swung her dark hair over her shoulders before walking out the door.

"Did you know about the town?" Manny said only seconds after she was gone.

"No. There were fewer people in Sugar Rush when I went in to get my coffee the other day." I sunk down onto the bottom step, all the air fleeing my lungs. "And now that I think about it, many of the storefronts around the square are vacant." Acid began to coat my throat. "What everyone has been saying is true. I ruined tourism for Ivy Falls. This is all my fault."

"This isn't your fault, Tor. My guess is that Ivy Falls has been in trouble a long time."

I dropped my head in my hands and groaned. "Well, my video didn't help matters."

Manny slid down next to me but remained uncomfortably quiet.

"I can sense the wheels in your head spinning," I said. "Tell me what you're thinking."

"We could use that money. Beck may be paying us to do the work here, but we're still over budget on Parkview. If we want to keep working on other houses…" He stopped. Curled his hands around the brim of his hat.

"We need the money, plain and simple. And if we agreed to do the show, brought more people to town, I could get Ivy Falls to finally forgive my F-bomb tirade and put us on solid ground financially. Like Lauren said, win-win."

He gave me a reluctant nod.

With a house this big, it was likely that we could have some major issues. One bad A/C pump, or broken water pipe, and this project would be in a world of hurt, but the risk didn't scare me. It made me want to take on the challenge even more. But there was Manny too. My viral mistake hadn't only affected me but his livelihood too. If we couldn't make this work, he'd also be out of a job. It broke my heart when I thought about the horrible situation I'd created for him and Lou.

"We have to talk to Beck," I said.

"I'll leave that up to you seeing as you're working so closely now." His stare returned to my neck and heat flared at my cheeks. I could never hide anything from him.

"Shut up." I tossed an old beer can at him. "I'm not sure how he'll feel about getting this all on camera, especially since this is part of his own private history being resurrected."

"Don't know until you ask," he said with a huff.

The creak of footsteps upstairs had us automatically looking up to where the remnants of Beck's crash through the ceiling still covered the hallway floor.

Manny shoved his hands in his pockets, trying not to look worried. It didn't work.

"We *can* do this without the show. If it doesn't feel right, I can call Lauren right now and tell her no."

This was what I loved about Manny. He didn't want a slick deal. A big payout. This was more about the love of the work than earning a quick buck.

"The money would help a lot, but I'm not sure my pride, or our business, could take another hit if things went sideways on this house."

"Go over everything with Beck. Maybe an outsider will have better perspective. Plus, he gets the whole media world." He gave my head a firm pat before turning back to the stairs.

"Hey, I'm not your faithful dog."

"Nope. A dog would actually listen to me." He laughed as he climbed his way back to his daughter, her small but firm voice ordering Beck around the room.

119

19

BECK

A Biography Of A Long And Complicated Life.

MOST employees didn't cross the threshold of Rowe and Townsend Advertising until at least seven a.m. That was why I always showed up at six. I liked moving through the hallways, letting the hum of the computers and quiet drip of the coffee maker calm my mind before starting an endless day of meetings and phone calls.

There was no calm this morning thanks to the consistent throbbing in my hands and knees. Torran had warned me about my gloves, and Manny offered his worn knee pads, but I had refused to show any signs of weakness last weekend. Now, almost five days later, I was still aching in places I didn't know I could ache.

My mind kept flickering back to Torran standing in the hall with Lou at her side. How when she and Manny volleyed back and forth, I couldn't help but think that the three of them looked like a family. That dull ache that was always hiding in my chest flared again.

More than once I'd seen the way they acted like partners, friends, but that small hint of worry still lingered in my mind. With him around did I stand a chance with her?

I forced my mind to the way she'd cornered me in the hall and asked my opinion about the TV show like I mattered. After listening to her, hearing the pros and cons of the deal, I told her I was behind any decision she and Manny made. The way she smiled at my response had me reliving our kiss.

That was real. The way she held on to me for dear life, leaned into my touch, said it meant something to her. She'd warned me we had to be professional, but that was going to be hard when every time I looked at her all I saw was the soft pink tint of her lips and the delicious curves of her body. The way her eyes crinkled at the edges when she laughed.

I walked to the wide picture window that was the back wall of my office and tried to focus back on work. The sweeping landscape of Green Hills greeted me. The "Batman" Building in downtown Nashville was a deep-gray silhouette in the distance.

"Hey, Beck." Pete leaned against the doorjamb. I tried not to smile at the way he was dressed. He insisted on business casual in the office and always put his own unique twist on it. The staff was going to love today's outfit. Dark jeans and a short-sleeve button-down covered in illustrations of French bulldogs.

I tipped my chin in the direction of his shirt. "Are we honoring Bogart today?"

Pete often brought his dog to the office, insisting it kept morale up and stress down. The staff agreed, often bringing treats for Bogie and buying him his own sheepskin bed for Pete's office.

"Of course! Always gotta be thinking about the man."

He walked in and plopped himself into the brown leather chair in front of my desk. Along his arms were colorful and intricate tattoos that he claimed were a biography of his long and complicated life.

"Where have you been? I didn't see your face around here once this weekend, which is rare."

"I, uh, had a bunch of errands and things to do." I avoided his stare and tried walking easily to my desk, which was hard because every muscle in my legs protested.

"Everything okay with Piper?" He searched my face like it might give a hint that something was wrong.

"As far as I know." I sighed.

"Oldest kids like us are always the caretakers." A grimace crossed his face. "I've gotten my little brother out of too many scrapes to count."

From the start, I'd been honest with Pete about my sister's issues. It was only fair to put all my cards on the table in case I had to fly off to take care of her.

Pete, who was four years older, had risen through the ranks at our Atlanta firm, bringing in three multimillion-dollar accounts in a year. When he was ready to move on and start his own agency he took me to lunch, told me he was moving to Nashville and wanted me as a partner. I gaped at him for at least five minutes before I quickly said yes.

Pete followed my gaze out the window. "I've always thought picking this space for an office was a good choice. It's cool to be able to see Music Row and downtown Nashville from here."

"Not to mention we're close to clients and we don't have to pay downtown rent," I added.

"I think we've really started to build something here. We've got some of the best account executives, graphic designers, and art directors in town."

"That's because practically everyone around here knows you, Pete."

"Yeah, I have pals from Vanderbilt undergrad. Ties to people in the local advertising community." He let out a low breath. "That still hasn't helped us get to where we need to be, Beck. Our creative should be tighter. Your accounts division needs to be hungrier."

"We're getting there. Things will be better when we land Brinkley as a client."

Pete dragged a hand over his cropped black hair. "It's not going to be easy. Teddy Ray Jones is a tough businessman. I heard he made the CEO over at Allied Design cry before he fired the agency."

"The CEO *and* the creative director is what I heard."

He pointed to a thick cream folder on my desk. "That the research?"

"Yes." I handed him the file and couldn't hide my wince as every muscle in my back screamed.

"You okay?" he asked, studying me intently.

"Yeah. Fine. Might just be lifting things a little too heavy." It wasn't a lie. That damn carpet weighed a ton.

He sank back down into the chair near my desk and flipped through the mounds of intel we'd gathered on Brinkley Food Group. Picture after picture showed the interior of each of their restaurants. Every single one was a rebuild of an old home or historic business.

Torran would've loved the way the company sought out ancient, condemned buildings and brought them back to life. It was what made Brinkley stand out in the overcrowded restaurant market, and why I saw it as a great opportunity to bring them into the Rowe and Townsend family. No other major firm could give them the attention they needed, build their brand like we could, which was why I was determined to impress the hotheaded CEO, Teddy Ray Jones, at our pitch meeting in six weeks.

"Why all the pictures of their storefronts?" he asked.

"I've been researching how they pick their locations. Think it might be to our advantage to show them we can increase their brand visibility by highlighting all the ways they're different from the chain restaurants flooding the market."

"That's a good idea. Talk to Marissa about it."

"Will do," I said, making a mental note to send an email to the VP of Account Services.

Pete leaned forward, hands on his knees. "This would be a major score for us, Beck. I don't think I need to impress upon you how seriously we need it. You have to focus one hundred percent of your time on this pitch. No other distractions or problems. Adding Brinkley to our roster could give us access to a lot of other clients. We need to reel them in and get Teddy Ray to sign on the dotted line."

"I promise landing this account is priority one. The pitch will be spot on. In fact, I can picture you and Teddy Ray having beers at a Titans game right now, discussing how Rowe and Townsend is going to help them own the restaurant market."

"Now that's what I like to hear!" Pete jumped to his feet as the sounds of the office started to come to life. He took two steps toward the door and stopped. "You said you were doing errands, but were you also working on your condo this weekend?"

"Uh," I mumbled. "Why do you ask?"

"There are three Band-Aids on your fingertips. I always look like that when I'm working on a project at home."

Quickly, I slid my hands into my pockets trying not to look guilty. I'd just promised my partner the only thing on my mind was work. That I was determined to bring in a new million-dollar account. Explaining that I'd bought a run-down house in Ivy Falls, or fallen back in deep with my high-school ex, wouldn't scream I was one hundred percent all in.

"Oh yeah, you know, always trying to improve the place."

I hated lying to him but at this point I had no choice. Thankfully, before he could ask another question, my phone rang with a familiar ringtone.

"That Piper?" he asked.

"Yep."

"I'll let you get to it then. Tell her I said hello."

Once he was out the door, I answered the FaceTime call.

"You're up early." I smiled at my little sister whose long hair hung down around her face like a black curtain.

"That's what happens when your ogre of a brother insists you take the subway halfway across Manhattan for a job interview."

Purple shadows rimmed the lower parts of her eyes. Small creases carved into the skin around her mouth. She was only twenty-four, but the way she'd been living these last years had aged her quickly.

I gulped down all my fear and worry and plastered on a hopeful smile. "And did you get the job?"

"You are now talking to the newest waitress at the Midtown Café," she huffed.

"Great job," I gushed.

"Whatever." She pulled a rubber band from her wrist and knotted up her hair. "The job doesn't start for a little while. Training and all. I'm low on cash. Will you transfer more to me?"

My head screamed with about a dozen questions. What was she doing with all the money? Was she spending it on alcohol? Drugs?

I couldn't let my mind go there.

"How much do you need?" I asked.

"About two grand."

"To cover what?" My voice leapt up an octave.

"God, Beck. Food. Rent. Other necessities. I also have something special I want to buy."

124

"What is it?"

"None of your business. It's my money, dammit. Stop giving me a hard time."

I let out an aggravated breath and forced my voice to be even. "Okay. I'll send you the money on one condition."

"You are treading on my last nerve."

"You have to agree to check in with me at least twice a week from now on."

"I'm not a child," she grumbled. "There's no need for you to constantly keep tabs on me. If Mom and Dad were alive, they wouldn't be this annoying." As soon as the words left her mouth her face drained of color.

I knew she hadn't said it to hurt me. This was always her knee-jerk reaction when I pushed too hard. It made me worry about how I was going to ease into telling her about Huckleberry Lane. After Torran and Manny spoke to me about the Hearth and Home proposal, I'd agreed they could film the house, so it wasn't a secret I could hold on to for much longer.

After an uncomfortable pause, she said, "Beck, I'm sorry. You know I love you."

"The money will be in your account before the end of the day," I said, doing my best not to let any of the stress I was feeling cloud my voice.

"Thanks." She gave me a sad smile and the call disconnected.

Every instinct in me said I should call her back. Tell her I loved her. Confess that I'd bought our childhood home. That things would be so much better when it was finished and she could move back to Tennessee. But I held back because I knew Piper. For years she'd sworn she'd never return to Ivy Falls.

Buying the house was an obvious risk, maybe a totally reckless choice, but she'd been dancing on the razor's edge of life for too long. A pull deep inside of me, part fear, part worry, warned that the house might be my final chance to reach her.

20

TORRAN

It Should Be Illegal For A Guy To Look That Hot In A Suit.

IT'D taken a week of negotiations, and one too many breakfasts with Lauren at Sugar Rush, before we'd all agreed to Hearth and Home's offer. Ten days later the preproduction team descended on the house. Lauren and her slew of assistants photographed every room. They wanted before and after shots for social media and to use as transition segments at the end of each episode.

The camera crew couldn't start filming until the permit was approved by the town council, which Lauren assured me would only take about two weeks.

In the meantime, we'd agreed to continue with small renovations in the house. This morning my plan was to tackle the wallpaper in one of the smaller bedrooms that featured a cast of dancing bears and multicolored trees that reminded me of some kind of weird psychedelic forest.

For the first two hours, I sprayed the walls with a mix of liquid fabric softener and water to break down the glue. I'd just started to pull down the edges in the corner of the ceiling when a voice said, "Wow! Someone must have had an odd Goldilocks fantasy."

"I was thinking more like Hansel and Gretel on drugs," I said, smiling at Tessa.

She moved around the room touching walls and counting out the square footage. I'd taught her a few things about construction. While she had no interest in joining my business, she was always curious to learn.

"Nice size for a bedroom but there's no closet."

"It happens a lot in these old homes," I said, climbing down the ladder. "Back in the late nineteenth century, closets were rarely part of the design. They had old wardrobes where they hung their clothes." I patted a portion of a side wall. "I'll have to cut into here to create one. Some codes in the state say you can't call it a bedroom without a closet."

A dozen questions bubbled on my lips as she walked around the room. I wanted to know about the bookstore. Was it in trouble like the rest of Ivy Falls? Had she talked to our dad about it? Hell, had she talked to anyone about it?

"Number?" I asked quietly.

"A solid five. What about you?"

"It was a six until I started thinking about how much work it's going to take to get this paper down."

She gave me a half-smile and turned back to surveying the room. "I got another text from Billy this morning."

"What did he say?" I forced the words to be emotionless because she'd shut down if I showed any sign of anger. Even though he was an asshole, she still wanted to protect him.

"He confirmed he's coming to see the girls right after Fourth of July."

"Is he going to bring *her*?"

"No. At least he didn't mention it," she said, her cheeks going too pale.

"What about the divorce?"

"I've brought it up several times but he always dodges the subject."

"Maybe when he shows up, you can press him on it."

Her shoulders gave a little and all I wanted was to wrap her in my arms. Protect her from all the pain her piece-of-crap husband was causing. Instead of ranting on about what an asshole he was, I reached for an extra scoring tool. "Want to help?"

"I can't. My lunch break is almost over. I only came by to remind you about story time and a certain promise you made to two little girls."

Last night during bath time, I'd promised I'd sit with the girls at the P&P's story hour while Penny, a long-time employee, read their favorite book, *Harold and the Purple Crayon*.

"Four o'clock?"

"Yes. I'm reading today because Penny's out sick." I hated the way her voice trembled again.

Tessa avoided story hour like vampires hid from sunlight. She'd settle the girls on the rainbow-colored carpet and then make some excuse about work in the office. Story time had been our mother's favorite event at the store. Tessa still couldn't bear to pick a book from the shelves and take over our mother's place in the fire-engine-red chair set in the center of the children's section.

She'd been through so much in a short time. Now she was tackling an ache so heartbreaking I could practically taste her pain. I couldn't be at the house when Billy showed up because I wasn't sure I could keep all my rage bottled up inside.

"Come to get a little dirt under those nails?"

Manny stood in the doorway, his adoring gaze fixed on Tessa. I loved that he harbored a small crush on her. That he treated her like the queen she really was. But no matter how he felt, he'd never act on it. He understood the pain of losing someone you loved, and he was too good a man to ever do anything that would make Tessa uncomfortable.

"Not today. I'm only here to remind my sister she has a date later this afternoon with two little angels."

"Friday story hour?" he said with a laugh.

"That's right. You should bring Lou." I loved how he could bring the light back to her eyes.

"What do you say, boss?" Manny asked. "Can I leave a little early?"

I held back a laugh. I'd never been his boss, but he liked to say it around the new guys so they'd know I was the one in charge of the site.

"Will your work be done by then?" I teased.

"Of course!" He mock saluted me and Tessa giggled.

"Then I order you to leave at three to go get your daughter."

He winked at Tessa before he practically danced out the door. For a big guy, he could really move.

"Dad said he might come by too." Tessa pulled at a loose bit of wallpaper to avoid my stare.

"He's actually going to leave the office early? Alert the media. It might be a miracle."

"Come on, Tor. He's trying. The other day he went out of his way to bring me lunch. And I had a late vendor meeting yesterday, so he offered to pick up the girls from the babysitter's."

"I could have helped out. You don't need him." I returned to the wall, scoring the paper a little harder than needed.

"It's only the three of us now. I think Mom would want us to spend more time together." She sighed. "You didn't even go to the cemetery with us a couple of weeks ago."

I gulped over the raw scratch in my throat. Every month since we'd lost her, I'd gone to visit Mom with Dad, Tessa, and the girls.

On that day, the loss of her ached deeply and I needed to be alone. I'd waited until they drove away before I'd laid my own flowers on her grave.

In the fading afternoon light, I talked to her like I always did, filling her in on Beck's return and details about the house. Promising I'd do everything I could to honor her last wish.

"It's too hard, Tessa. My anger runs deep and it's hard to let go."

"Please." The ache in her voice mirrored mine. "Can't you give a little?"

"No. When she was gasping for her last breath, it was only the two of us there to witness it. He should have been there."

Tessa pulled me into a hug. "You have to move on. We both do."

I held on to her and blinked back tears. "I miss her so much it aches."

"I know but staying angry at Dad doesn't help matters."

"You have to understand that every time I see his face, I remember that day. It cuts into me like a sharp knife, opening a wound that should be healed by now."

She pulled back. Gave me that steady stare. "Forgiveness is the greatest act of kindness."

It was one of our mother's favorite lines and I wasn't sure if she was saying it about our dad or Beck or both of them.

"Not there yet," I said on a whisper.

"Okay. But promise me you'll at least try."

"For you I will."

She patted my cheek and turned for the door, bumping straight into Beck.

"Hey, Beck, it's been a while." She gave me a grin that said she agreed with my Chris Evans comparison.

"Good to see you, Tessa."

"You too. I hear you own a business in Nashville."

"Yes. Advertising."

"Do you like it?"

"Sure. It allows me to be both creative and use my business degree."

"And I take it being the boss allows you to take off early on a Friday?"

"It has its perks. Thought I'd stop in and see if Manny or Torran needed a hand."

Tessa's gaze ran up and down his expensive suit which didn't exactly scream he was here to work.

"Okay then. I'm headed to the bookstore. And Tor," her tone went serious, "do not be late or it will be way more than two smoothies you owe the girls."

"I'll be there."

I went back to work on the wall, cursing under my breath that I'd just made a promise to Tessa about our father that I wasn't sure I could keep.

"If you push hard enough, do you think you'll hit drywall?" Beck teased.

"I know what I'm doing," I huffed.

He stood inches away. The scent of his spicy aftershave cascaded over me. Slowly, he eased off his dark blue suit jacket.

Are you fucking kidding me? It should be illegal for a guy to look that hot in a suit.

"What did you say?"

"Nothing. I didn't say a thing."

A smirk appeared like he'd heard every word.

Once he laid his jacket across the tarp covering the floor, he slid the tool out of my hand and went to work. That flicker of shiny skin peeked out from under his starched cuff. I was still curious how he got the scar, but before I could ask he turned his back to me.

His dress pants clung nicely to his butt just like his Levi's. The tight muscles in his back flexed and moved beneath his tailored blue shirt.

My mouth went dry. I fought the urge to move toward him. Reach out and place a hand across his back so I could feel the sharp planes of his shoulder blades shifting up and down as he worked.

I'd be lying if I'd said my recent dreams weren't filled with Beck fantasies. It was hard to think of anything else when I'd spent the last few days in the same space that used to be his childhood bedroom.

Every time I let my mind wander, I saw Beck in the shower. Beck in nothing but a towel. Said towel falling to the floor. I cursed at my body, my brain, for getting all hot and bothered for no reason.

We were partners. Nothing more. But obviously, my lady parts weren't listening.

"Want to talk about what's bothering you?" he asked, the muscles in his arms stretching against the thin cotton fabric.

Hello fantasy number four—Beck busting out of his shirt.

"No," I said, unable to look away from the sweat starting to bead on his upper lip. "It can get warm in here. You can roll up your sleeves."

"I'm fine," he said too quickly. "This way I won't get wallpaper all over my skin like you."

There was something stiff and tightly coiled about his voice and movements. Like he was ready to burst out of his skin at any moment.

To ease the tension, I placed my hand over his and changed the motion to move in a circle. "It works better this way. Provides more nicks so the fabric softener can seep in and loosen the glue."

Beck followed my motion. His hip bumped mine as we worked our way across the room. Heat scorched through my skin with each small step. My mind was a jumble of emotions. Anger at my father. Sadness over disappointing my sister. Need pushed past both those feelings as I looked at Beck.

I hated the way my heart did a little dance every time he appeared. How the sound of his voice sent warmth through my core.

The way his smile forced me to cross my legs, the ache in my lower body almost too much to bear. Even now, I wanted to reach out and brush a hand across his forehead to push back a wayward piece of light brown hair.

Before I did anything idiotic, I stumbled across the tarp needing space. He reached out and caught me around the waist before I fell on my ass.

"Careful. You okay?"

He held on to me and I swore I could feel the rapid beat of his heart. The lines around his mouth softened. It would be so easy to lean in and press my mouth to his again. Shove my chest against his tight body and soak up every part of him.

When we were teenagers, a subtle glance or touch from Beck would send an electric zap through every single one of my veins. I'd been with other men in college and while I worked in Phoenix, but no one could ever make my body sing the way Beck could.

We stood in a breathless pause until the grind of a tile saw brought me to my senses.

"I'm fine," I said, quickly moving to the far side of the room. "I'll, uh, work over here for a bit."

The wicked grin that slid across his lips said he knew he'd gotten to me.

I forced myself to focus back on the wallpaper in hopes it would make both my body and mind forget how much I wanted him.

21

BECK

Crossed Over Some Invisible Line.

THE sun shifted across the room as we worked. I asked Torran about the progress on the roof and the filming schedule, purposely avoiding tricky topics like her father and the way she'd reacted to my touch.

I knew working with her would be difficult, but I never imagined the way my body would ache when I looked at her. How all I wanted was the warmth of her skin to slide under my fingers. Have her arch into me. Hear her pant and moan my name.

Every inch of me was trying to be good. To keep my promise that we'd stay professional. But it was hard when I looked at her standing on the ladder. Her hair turning a molten gold in the light. How her faded Goodbye June T-shirt inched up from the side of her denim overalls showing luscious pale skin. Her body taunting me from six feet in the air.

Torran's phone chimed, snapping me back to reality.

"I'm going to head out for a bit. There's a story time at the P&P. I promised my nieces I'd be there, and I can't be late or Tessa will give me that motherly stare that will make me feel guilty for weeks."

133

"Ah, story time. I loved when your mom would gather everyone into a circle on the rainbow rug. She was so good at making all the different character voices, especially when she read stories like *Where the Wild Things Are*."

"Yeah, she loved to do the roar and talk about the way the monsters gnashed their teeth."

It was hard for me not to think about how my own mother would tuck me into bed when I was little. The way I'd beg her to read some of my favorites like *Goodnight Moon* and *The Cat in the Hat*. My mom did an awesome impression of the cat that made me howl with laughter.

"Which book is being read today?" I asked, trying to forget the searing pain of the memory.

"*Harold and the Purple Crayon*," she said.

"That's a great one. I bet your nieces will love it."

She toed at a worn piece of tarp covering the floor. "Removing this wallpaper is going to take some time, and it's easier to do when there's more natural light."

"I can keep working for a while. Nothing waiting for me at home but cold pizza and a pile of bills."

"Okay. See you tomorrow?"

"I'll be here bright and early."

She walked to the door and hesitated. "This will only take an hour or so. I can come back and help you later."

Her voice hitched like something was bothering her.

"Go and have fun with your family. I promise I won't screw this up."

"It's not that I think you'll do something wrong." She chewed on her bottom lip and shook her head. "Never mind."

I slid the tool into my pocket and approached her. Her shoulders shifted. Her eyes focused on the ground. She was holding something back. Were there problems with the house? Was her dad giving her shit about her finances again?

"Torran," I whispered. "What's going on?"

She finally looked up. I sucked in a sharp breath, struck by the intensity of her bright green eyes. When we were kids hanging out at our favorite spot at the lake, I would try to count all the different flecks of color around her pupils. Sometimes my gaze was so intense,

Torran would shove me away by the shoulder, her cheeks pink with embarrassment. I'd told her over and over how beautiful she was, but she never believed me. Another thing that made me want to kick her father in the nuts.

"Want to come to the bookstore? I know you probably haven't been there since you came back to town." She shoved her hands into the pockets of those sexy overalls like she was nervous.

As soon as the words were out of her mouth, her skin went pale like she realized she'd crossed over some invisible line. I was sure if I turned her down, she'd never offer up an opportunity like this again. And hell, it'd be nice to see the P&P again. Wander through the aisles where I'd spent much of my childhood reading.

"That sounds great. Let me grab my coat."

"This isn't a formal affair, Beck. We'll be sitting on an old rug littered with smashed Goldfish and Cheerios. Think you can leave the jacket here."

I rubbed my hands up and down my arms.

"Second thoughts?"

She searched my face trying to see if I wanted an out. There was no way I was turning down a chance to spend more time with her.

"No. Absolutely not. Let's go."

⅔ ⅔ ⅔

It was crazy how smells could smack you in the face and transport you back to another time. I hadn't set foot inside the Pen & Prose since I was seventeen, but the place still carried the scent of old paper and the chemical-lemon smell of furniture polish.

Torran walked down the center walkway past the non-fiction and romance sections toward the children's area. I followed her carefully, navigating my way around hip-high bookshelves crowded with dozens of board and chapter books. A sense of ease filled my bones as I found a spot on the rainbow-shaped rug next to her.

If I closed my eyes, I could remember the first time my mom brought me to the P&P. How she'd held on to Piper's hand as we explored the cozy space. The way Torran's mom quickly introduced

135

herself as the owner. The bright lift of Mrs. Wright's lips when my mom explained how we'd just moved to town.

Mrs. Wright didn't hesitate to steer me toward the children's section where her daughter with the golden hair sat with an open book in her lap. With soft light streaming in through the window, I thought Torran was an angel. I was only twelve at the time, but I swore that was the moment I fell in love with her. It would take four more years before that truth slid past my lips.

To my surprise the P&P was packed. I had no idea story time attracted such a big crowd.

"Are there always so many people here?" I asked.

"It is a little more crowded today." Torran's gaze moved around the room. "There's Diego with his wife and kids. And do you see Old Mrs. Vanderpool? She's standing near the picture books."

I recognized the small woman holding a bag with a mesh front where a tiny brown dog poked out its head. When we were younger she'd yell at us when we jumped our bikes off the curbs in the square calling us "hooligans" at the top of her voice.

"Is that Baby?" I whispered.

"Yep."

"That dog has to be at least fourteen."

"Fifteen. That's why he's in the case. Can't walk much now."

Torran tipped her chin to a nearby bookshelf where a woman with silver hair was standing next to her father. "That's Isabel. Do you remember her? She manages the bank for my dad?"

I searched my memories but came up with a blank. Another side effect of the accident. Sometimes I couldn't remember names or faces.

"And you remember Barb and Susan from Sugar Rush."

Just as she spoke, the two women waved in our direction. Barb's hair was a distinct shade of cranberry today.

"So why are they all here?" I asked as the room continued to fill up.

"My gut says the Ivy Falls gossip train let everyone know that my sister was doing story time for the first time today."

"That's nice, isn't it?"

"Yes. I'm happy their anger with me hasn't rubbed off on Tessa. She doesn't deserve that."

The heartbreak in her voice had me inching closer to her on the carpet. Part of me wanted to stand up and call out everyone in the room who was not subtle about giving her the evil eye. She was working her ass off to make this town better. Yes, she'd made a mistake, but the hard work and sacrifices she was making in Ivy Falls showed her loyalty to every single person who cared about her.

Torran had that special knack like her mom. In her presence she made you feel strong, nearly invincible at times. It made my blood boil that none of them could see her love and commitment to this community.

I pulled in a low breath, calming the angry thud of my heart. Her hand was laid out flat on the rug and every inch of me ached to reach out and touch her. I'd finally got up the nerve when two little girls buzzed across the carpet toward us.

"We're so glad you're here, Auntie Torran," said the littlest one with blonde pigtails.

The other little girl, who had hair the same reddish shade as Tessa's, nudged her sister out of the way. "We agreed in the car I could sit next to her."

"How about I move back and you can sit on either side of her?" The two girls stared at me with wide eyes.

"Who are you?" The blonde little girl placed her hands on her hips, demanding an answer.

"This is Beck. He's helping me with the new house." Torran scrubbed the blonde one's head. "This ball of energy is Rose." She turned warm eyes on the other little girl. "And this beauty is her older sister, Iris."

Rose still eyed me like I was an uninvited guest at this party. "I thought Mr. Manny was your helper?"

"He is but Beck grew up in the new house. He wants to make sure it's pretty again."

The explanation seemed to be enough for the girls because they forgot all about me and asked Torran a dozen questions about the house, including if she was going to put a pool in the backyard.

"A pool? I don't think so," she replied.

Iris turned her big blue eyes on me. "You need a pool. It's hot here in the summer."

"I'll definitely keep it in mind."

She gave me a wide smile that mirrored Torran's and I swore I could feel my heart swell in my chest.

Since my parents passed, I'd never given much thought to my own future. With Piper in and out of rehab, I couldn't allow myself to think beyond the next day or week. But with these two girls snuggled up against Torran's side, it was easy to consider what my life might be like if she gave me a second chance.

Tessa sank into an oversized red chair at the front of the room. In a corner, hovering in the shadows, Miles Wright watched his youngest daughter read about Harold and his walk in the moonlight. His lower lip quivered and his watery stare darted between his daughters. Torran focused on her sister like she was willing her to get through the reading.

To most people this would have seemed like any other story time, but beneath the surface all three of the Wrights were struggling with this moment. I gazed around the room seeing touches of Torran's mom everywhere. I couldn't help but wonder if it pained Tessa to come here every day and be constantly reminded of her grief.

Manny's daughter, Lou, snuck in and found a place on the carpet next to the little girls. Torran's gaze never moved from her sister as she inched back next to me. Manny stood near the fiction bookshelves. His attention was locked firmly on Tessa. Every move she made, how she slowly turned the pages, or leaned down close to speak to the kids circled around her feet, made him grin from ear to ear. There was something else too. It was as though the firm way he held his hulking body was suddenly relaxed and calm.

He certainly had feelings for a Wright sister, I'd just stupidly guessed the wrong one.

As Tessa's voice continued to explain Harold's journey, Rose crawled into Torran's lap. The little girl popped a thumb into her mouth and eased back into the warmth of her aunt's arms.

This life suited Torran. Having her own business. Taking care of her family.

It made me question if she'd ever let me back into her life. What could I offer her anyway? I was married to my work and in a constant state of panic when it came to my sister. I lived off frozen dinners, beer, and sports when I wasn't at the office until the late evening.

Torran, on the other hand, had proven she could take care of herself. She had a business and a solid group of family and friends supporting her. Of course she'd had some missteps like the video, but in typical Torran fashion she'd come back stronger than ever.

Everything inside me screamed that I should walk away, not screw with her life, but I was tired of being alone. I wanted a partner to fight with and make love to. Someone who'd call me on my shit and not be afraid to upend my world. I didn't have to look far to know who that girl was. She was sitting right next to me smelling like fabric softener and tangerine shampoo.

Tessa finished the story and the crowd gave an appreciative clap. We stood and the girls ran toward the shelves with all the picture books. Torran's dad made a beeline for her and I took a quick step back.

"It was nice of you to come and support your sister today," he said to Torran like he was trying his best to keep his voice soft.

"Tessa and the girls know I will always be here for them. That I won't disappear when they need me most."

"I'm trying to do the same."

"Actions not words, Dad. That's what matters."

"I know." He gulped once and asked, "How is everything with Huckleberry Lane?"

I stepped away, giving them space as their conversation turned to details about the house and the filming permits the Hearth and Home crew needed.

Tessa hadn't changed a single thing about the store and I quickly found my way to the non-fiction section. There were memoirs and biographies settled on the shelves, but a thin layer of dust warned that many titles had never been replaced.

While I was thumbing through a book on World War II, a woman with short brown hair and a baby balanced on each hip approached me.

"Beck Townsend, is that you?" The young woman readjusted the babies and gave me a broad smile. "It's me, Maisey Bedford. I used to be friends with Piper."

It took a moment for my brain to kick in and recognize this woman as the same tiny girl who'd played dress-up and did small local plays with my sister.

"Wow, Maisey. Good to see you."

Her eyes darted around the store. "Is your sister here? I haven't seen or heard from her in years." She gave me a sad smile. "We all read the obituary in the paper about your folks after they passed. A lot of us hoped you'd move back."

I took a dry gulp and refused to let myself think about how different things would have been if my grandparents had brought me back here. How life could have changed for Piper. Seeing Maisey all grown-up was like picturing all the opportunities Piper had blown over the years. What I would have given for my sister to be in a solid relationship with someone who didn't steal from her while she slept. Someone who would encourage her sobriety. Prove to her she could have a life beyond partying and chasing the next high.

"No. She's living in New York. Auditioning for acting jobs."

"Does she still play the piano? When we were kids, she'd play and I'd dance. It was always so much fun."

"Sadly, she stopped a while ago," I said, trying to not let her hear the ache in my voice.

She gave me a wistful smile until the baby boy on her right hip began to cry. She shifted him and rearranged the pacifier in his mouth. "That's too bad. Piper was always better at performing. Her life sounds exciting and glamorous compared to living in Ivy Falls." The little girl on her hip started to fidget and Maisey bounced up and down to keep her quiet. "Not much has changed here. Still the same quiet town where everyone knows each other's business." Her stare shifted to where Torran was standing. "And, you know, the local shops are slowly dying one by one." She leaned in and lowered her voice. "Rumors are even this beloved store is having financial difficulties."

I glanced in Torran's direction, still hearing the tremble in her voice when she talked about Hearth and Home's offer and the email stating the town was in trouble. She'd confessed that everyone blamed her for the drop in tourism. It made sense why she was so worked up about the house. If the town was struggling, she felt even more of a responsibility now to set things right.

140

"Did you marry someone local?" I asked.

"No. I met their daddy at UT in Knoxville. We got married a few years back and I convinced him to come back here. He's practicing law over on Silverlake Street and I'm staying at home with these two."

"Sounds like a good life."

The two babies started to cry and all her shifting and bouncing couldn't make them stop.

"Guess it's time to go," she said with a tired sigh. "Please tell your sister hello and to call me if she's ever back in town. I'd love to see her."

Maisey shuffled off toward a big stroller parked near a series of low bookshelves. As she clipped each baby into their seats, I couldn't help but look away. No matter how hard I tried with Piper, she'd never have a normal life. The memories of our parents' deaths, even with years of therapy, wore on her soul like a festering wound, and no matter how hard I tried to make it better, easier for her, she fought me at every turn.

I stalked toward the front of the store as my need to escape took over. My breathing sped up. Sweat beaded on my upper lip. Every inch of my skin ached. I raced to the exit and pushed out the door.

I put my hands on top of my head and turned in circles, dragging the thick, moist air into my lungs. For a few minutes, I paced the parking lot trying to forget how I'd failed Piper, Torran, even my parents. If I'd only been a second quicker, heard my mother's scream sooner, maybe they'd both be alive now. How if I hadn't been so afraid of Torran seeing me broken, we wouldn't have lost so much time.

The erratic beat of my heart made it hard to pull in enough air. Coming back to Ivy Falls. Walking through the P&P. All of it was a reminder of what I'd lost. I leaned against the rusty tailgate of Torran's truck and waited for the familiar pain to pass.

A shuffle of feet forced me to look up. Torran approached the truck. Her eyebrows knitted together with worry.

"Hey, what's going on? You took off like a rocket after you saw Maisey."

"It's nothing. Let's go back to the house. There's a lot of work to be done."

She searched my face for a minute and I kept it fixed in an unemotional mask. It was an easy feat because I'd been hiding my pain for years.

22

TORRAN

Melted Me Open Like Hot Water Poured Over Ice.

SINCE we'd come back from the bookstore, Beck's once pleasant mood grew darker. I wasn't sure what Maisey had said to him, but for the last hour he'd stalked around the room like he'd just lost the biggest account of his life.

I tried to make small talk as I brought in a set of work lights. Danced around the room. Even sang a medley of my favorite COIN songs off-key, but his pissy mood never lifted. He pretended he was fine, but his shoulders bunched up as he picked and pulled at a tricky piece of wallpaper in the corner that refused to budge.

He'd changed in so many ways in the last ten years, but there were other parts of him that were just the same. The lazy tilt to his head when he was thinking. How a small bit of his pink tongue poked out of the side of his mouth when he was focused on something important. In some ways he was a complete stranger and in other ways he was still my beautiful Beck.

"Are you going to ever tell me why you're so pissed at your dad?" he said more to the wall than me.

"It's a long and brutal story," I confessed. "One I'm sure you do not want to hear."

He stopped working and with long strides he crossed the room until he was standing below me.

"If you want to tell me, I'm here." The gentle tone of his voice sent a deep ache through me.

Nope. This wasn't supposed to happen. I swore I wouldn't allow him to get to me, but deep down I knew that was a lie. The moment he'd kissed me I felt it. My heart opening up again.

I stepped down and one of the straps of my overalls fell from my shoulder. When my feet hit the floor, he reached forward and slid it back up. A tense stare passed between us before I mumbled out a shaky thank you.

"You and your dad have never had it easy. I know he's been hard on you over the years."

They were simple words but the calm lull to Beck's voice melted me open like hot water poured over ice. Suddenly I wanted to tell him everything. About college. About how broken I felt when he left me. How I wasn't sure I'd ever love anyone the way I'd loved him.

"It was my mom's last day," I said, setting my tools down on the khaki-colored tarp that spread across the room. "The nurses called Tessa and me to say she was fading in and out. That we should come and say our goodbyes. On our way to the hospital, I left voicemails for my dad. Sent him text messages. He didn't respond to a single one."

"That's weird. I know your dad's a hard-ass but he was always attentive to your mom."

"I know but it was like, *poof*, he was gone like some bad magic trick."

"What happened next?"

"Tessa went in first to see her. I needed to gather my thoughts. Figure out what I wanted to say." My voice broke and I looked away.

"Hey," he said in that low, careful voice. "It's okay. Take your time."

I sucked in a breath and forced out the next words. "Mom was so fragile. Pale. A skeleton lying in that bed. All I wanted to do was scoop her into my arms and ask her to stay. I couldn't do that though. Tessa and I agreed that we needed to tell her it was time to let go. To be free."

I brushed away a tear tumbling down my cheek.

"The monitors continued to beep and chime for an hour. Her breaths grew ragged with each passing minute. Tessa and I constantly checked our phones. Waiting on some word from him. When my mom slipped away, my father was nowhere to be found."

This time the tears came in one crashing wave. Beck pulled me into his arms and rocked me back and forth. With anyone else, I might have felt childish losing it so quickly, but Beck had lost both his parents. I knew he understood my grief.

"After she was gone, did he show up?" he asked.

"Yeah." I swiped at my eyes again. "He was waiting in the hallway. When we asked why he didn't come in, he only shrugged and told us he'd already said his goodbyes. Even now," I gasped, "his behavior, it just feels so callous."

Beck chewed on the corner of his lip and didn't say a word.

"What are you thinking?"

"While I know your dad can be a jerk, it seems off that he'd behave like that. Maybe he had a reason?"

Anger bubbled in my chest and I pushed away from him. "You've been gone a long time, Beck. There are a lot of things you don't understand."

It was a dig and I shouldn't have said it. But I couldn't have him defending my dad even a little. Not after what he'd done to Tessa and me.

I climbed the ladder and went back to work, needing to keep my hands busy. Beck stood below me on the tarp watching me fixate on the wall. The room was at least ninety degrees even with the windows open, but his shirt was still buttoned at the neck and collar. I couldn't figure out why he insisted on being so formal. If he was going to stay and sweat, he could at least roll up his sleeves.

"What did you think of the P&P?" I finally said to break the silence between us.

"It looks the same. Feels the same. Which is comforting."

"You didn't answer me before. Did Maisey say something that upset you?"

He bit into his lower lip. "She asked about Piper. What she was doing with her life."

"And did you tell her?"

He looked down and shook his head. "I lied. Said she was doing fine."

"Are you ever going to tell me what's going on with her? What happened to your parents?"

"I…" His gaze dropped to the floor. "It's too hard."

He spun around and moved to the window. The edges of his shoulders heaved up and down. I'd seen tht posture too many times when Tessa was overwhelmed. At a breaking point with either the store or her own life.

Grief was a hard thing to navigate. I understood that better than anyone, but it burned me to the core that he still couldn't be honest with me about how his parents died.

I followed him to the window and planted myself right beside him. "Don't you think it was excruciating for me to reveal what my dad did? To have you witness after all these years that with a single look, one terse word, my father can turn me into a frightened child again?"

"You just stood toe to toe with him at the P&P. I wouldn't call that frightened. I'm not even sure you understand the meaning of the word."

His words were so sharp, I took a step back. "What the hell is that supposed to mean?"

"It means that you have a parent who is still living and breathing. Things may be rocky between the two of you, but he is still *here*."

"You've been gone a long time, Beck. My dad and I are complicated and you are the last fucking person in the world who gets to pass judgment on me, especially after how carelessly you broke my heart."

"There are a thousand things you do not understand, Torran. That you will never understand about me or my life."

"You're right—because you made the choice to walk away."

He stood with a firm chin not saying a word.

"Go home, Beck. I'm tired of doing this with you."

"Doing what?" he snapped.

"I share every single part of my life with you and in return you give me crumbs. If you want to suffer in silence that's your choice, but I don't have to stand by and watch it."

"I'm not asking you to."

"Good, because I'm sick of your angsty shit. Don't let the door hit you in the ass on the way out."

I climbed up the ladder again, swallowing the sob building in my chest. Just when I thought things were getting better between us, that he was actually opening up, that door slammed shut tightly again.

"You can't order me out of my own goddamn house," he fumed.

"Fine, but you can get out of this room," I tossed back.

He stalked to the corner of the room and snatched his suit jacket from the floor. His untucked shirt inched up revealing a large swath of scarred skin.

I tried but couldn't stifle my gasp. "Beck, what happened to your back?"

His shoulders tightened and he stood painfully still. I wasn't even sure he was breathing.

I climbed down the ladder and crossed the room, gently setting a hand on his arm. "Please, I'm begging you. Talk to me."

"Torran. Stop."

His voice shook with an ache I knew too well. For the days and weeks after Mom was gone, none of it felt real. I went through the motions. Thanked people for coming to the funeral. Wrapped up the dozens of casseroles delivered. Helped read stories to the girls and make cocoa late into the night when I'd find Tessa crying at the kitchen table. In our own way we had to figure out a way to deal with the solitary journey ahead of us. Face the incredible loss in our lives. I'd thought I was getting through it fine until I had to deal with my dad over and over, stirring up my grief every single time.

"If I tell you about my mom and dad, Piper... the accident... it makes it all real again."

The pain in his whisper made me step closer. He needed to know that he was safe here. That the grief he carried like a heavy coat didn't have to hurt him so much if he just shared a little bit of it with me.

"Please, Beck. Tell me what happened the day your parents died."

23

BECK

A Genie You Can't Shove Back Into The Bottle.

WHY I bothered to hide anything from Torran was beyond me. She was like an emotional psychic—able to instantly sense when something was off. I'd purposefully picked a fight with her knowing she'd kick me out, and then I wouldn't have to talk about my encounter with Maisey and all the bad shit it stirred up inside me.

I turned around and the hurt etched into her face, the raw ache in her stare, almost brought me to my knees.

"That last night before I left with my parents, we drove to our favorite spot at the lake. You knew right away something was wrong," I said over the knot growing slowly in my throat. "In amongst the chirping crickets and low bellows of the bullfrogs, you begged me to tell the truth. It is eerily reminiscent of this moment."

The same ripple of pain that swept over her cheeks that night now drew down the corners of her beautiful mouth.

"Over the years, I've become an expert at keeping my feelings bottled up inside to protect Piper. Make her think our lives are under control. She's needed that steadiness."

"I'm sure you've been a rock for her," she said.

"No, I haven't. I've never been enough for her." The words were knives stabbing at my chest. "She's a recovering alcoholic and drug addict who tears through jobs and men like she goes through tequila and opiates. I jump every time the damn phone rings, worried it's the police calling to tell me she's in jail, or even worse"—I sucked in an unsteady breath—"in the morgue."

"Oh, Beck," she said quietly. "I'm sorry for you both."

Even now, I couldn't help but think about Piper. Was she in her small apartment eating dinner, or in some club letting yet another douchebag take advantage of her so she could score one more drink or pill? Was that the special thing she wanted to buy? The thought shot ice through my veins.

"We've been through rehab so many times I can recite the entire intake procedure. One suitcase. Few personal belongings. No phone. No shoelaces. Limited contact with the outside world."

Even though every instinct in me said to get up and run, not relive those horrible days again, I owed her the truth about what happened ten years ago at a campsite near the Truckee River in northern California the day my parents died.

I closed my eyes and took another shaky breath. If I wanted her to believe in me, trust me again, this was the only way.

Slowly, one button at a time, I undid my shirt. With each movement, every breath, the memories of that night spilled over me: the ear-splitting boom and the roar of a heat so intense that it yanked all the air from my lungs.

My trembling hands moved to my cuffs. Once they were undone, I hesitated. This wasn't some kind of genie you could shove back in a bottle. When she saw what I looked like, what I'd become, there was no going back.

After one more full breath, I shrugged off my shirt and dropped it onto the floor.

A few agonizingly long beats passed while I waited for her to gasp in shock again.

Race out the door and never look back.

Instead, with the softest touch, she tracked her fingers over the crisscross pattern of burned and mottled skin that hugged my shoulders, covered both arms, and snaked down a large portion of my chest before ending in a huge swath across my back.

Plenty of women had seen my ravaged arms and chest. As I'd lain naked in bed with them I'd made up stories about car crashes or motorcycle accidents, never able to tell anyone that the mottled skin that tattooed my upper body came from a failed attempt to save my parents' lives.

Her caress moved over the planes of my chest and every inch of me ached for her. I waited for reality to set in. For her to flinch. Curl away in horror.

Because I couldn't bear for that to happen, I stepped back from her touch.

"Don't." The soft sweep of her voice nearly did me in.

"Maybe this was a mistake," I said, reaching for my shirt.

Her determined voice stopped me. "You're wrong if you think I'm scared."

Torran's soft hands moved back to my jagged edges and raised, shiny skin.

"This doesn't change a thing, Beck. I still think you're beautiful."

Her sweet words slackened the ache in my jaw. The knots in my neck. I'd longed to tell her about this. To bare every part of me and know that she had the entire truth. To understand that the boy who had left in that RV with his parents was long gone. Every single one of my muscles twitched under the caress of her touch, and I reached up and spread my hands over where her hand had stopped over my heart.

"How did you get the scars?" Her voice was as soft as the wind in the trees outside.

I bent my head and started to speak but she reached out and tipped my chin up like she wanted me to know she wasn't afraid. That just by looking into my eyes she could give me the courage to push out the words.

"I can't imagine the weight of grief you've been carrying, but if you share the truth with me I promise you won't carry it alone anymore."

Her voice loosened the tight knot in my chest. I stepped in, needing to be closer. As soon as I'd returned to Ivy Falls, I'd seen flickers of that young girl who'd become my first love. Even with those years between us, she was still that person who could smooth out my rough edges. With just a few words, ease the pain in my troubled heart.

"We'd just finished skiing at a place called Northstar in Lake Tahoe." I tried to keep my voice steady but it was impossible with Torran staring at me with such abandon that it hurt to look at her. "The temperature outside was long past freezing. My parents went into the RV to change while Piper and I were battling it out with snowballs. I chased her with my arsenal all the way down to the river when a loud explosion shook the ground beneath us."

My voice cracked and she gripped my hands like she knew I needed her strength.

"Piper and I sprinted back to the campground. The propane tank had exploded and our RV was engulfed in flames. Without thinking, I tore open the door and jumped inside. The heat bit at my arms and back but I didn't feel any of it." The story spilled out of me in rough, painful spurts. "All I wanted was to find my mom and dad and pull them out. The roar of the blaze filled my ears. I climbed over charred seats and burning curtains, screaming for them until a hand grabbed the back of my jacket and yanked me from the flames."

I paused, seeing it all over again in my head.

"An older couple smothered me in a blanket to put out the fire. My skin was burning, Piper was screaming, and all I could think was that if I could get back inside I could save them." I gasped and held on to Torran with everything I had. "If I hadn't chased Piper, I could have been there to help them. Get them out."

"If you'd been there when it exploded, you and Piper could be gone too." Her voice was as thick as mine. "Under the circumstances, you did the best you could. Your parents wouldn't have wanted you to die saving them."

She pulled me into a hug as my body trembled.

"I still don't understand. Why wouldn't you answer my calls? Did you think I couldn't handle this? What the accident had done to you? Because if that's the case, I have to ask if you really knew me at all."

I thought being apart from Torran was painful, but what cut me to the core was the sound of utter grief that clung to her voice.

"I couldn't talk to anyone at first. They put me in a coma for the first few days so I could heal. When I woke, it was agony. The doctors promised over and over that 'after one more surgery' I'd be better, but the pain endured for months. After three skin grafts, they finally released me to my grandparents' care. By then, all I could do was concentrate on my rehab and navigating what my life, Piper's life, was going to look like with our parents gone."

"Oh, Beck." Her voice was wracked with pain.

"It wasn't that I didn't have faith in you, but I was broken. Life-less. I didn't want to drag you into that. Not when you had such a bright future."

Her face went from pained to angry in a flash. "A future I wanted to spend with you, you idiot—no matter what your body looked like. That last night together at the lake we promised we'd go to college together. Find jobs in the same city. Share our lives through thick and thin. Good or bad. But you walked away like you thought I wasn't strong enough to stand by your side. You took away my choice to decide." She stopped and her cheeks drained of color. "That girl in the picture. The one you posted online after you sent the email. Were you together?"

I dropped my head. "No. She was the daughter of one of my physical therapists. I asked her to take a picture with me. I knew it'd eventually get back to you. I thought it was the only way you'd let me go."

"Dammit, Beck!" She pushed me away, tears sparkling in her eyes. "All this time I thought you'd fallen out of love with me. That you wanted to move on. Do you have any idea how much that fucking destroyed me?"

I reached for her and this time she let me pull her into my chest.

"We could have gotten through anything, if you'd just believed in me," she cried, and I buckled, bringing her down to the ground with me. "That last night we had at the lake, I gave you my whole heart. Tangled up in a blanket, skin to skin, we made so many promises to each other. When you left with your family, I thought time would pass quickly. I'd finish my junior year and then you'd be home again. We'd go back to being us." A disgusted chuckle escaped her lips. "I was such a naïve little girl."

"No, Tor. You believed in us, and I did too until everything went so fucking wrong."

"It was easy to be mad at you, make you the villain, when I didn't know the whole truth. Blame you for why I've never trusted my heart to another man." She let out a heartbreaking sigh. "When you disappeared, you not only broke the bridge connecting us but doused the damn thing in gasoline and set it ablaze."

Slowly I ran my hand over the messy ponytail she loved. "I deserve every bit of that anger, but at the time I could barely figure out who I was without my parents, much less be a guy who could be there for you."

"I get now why I had to be your last priority. If anything happened to my family, Tessa would be the first person I'd protect—but knowing all that doesn't make the memories hurt any less."

She melted into my arms, and I let all the pain and anguish of the last years melt over the top of our bodies.

"I picked a college over a thousand miles from Ivy Falls and I stayed away," she whispered into my chest. "Not only because of my father, but because every corner, every shop, reminded me of you. I couldn't drive near the lake without my heart aching. Walk past the movie theater without remembering how you'd drape your arm over my shoulders, pull me in close and place a soft kiss to my forehead."

"I'm sorry I made everything such a mess."

"When I first saw you at the auction, I hoped you were a ghost—a figment of my imagination. The reality of you reappearing in my life felt like a cruel joke much like that damn video. But…" Her whole body shook and I held on to her like I'd never let her go again. "The truth is all those old feelings, no matter how much I've fought them, they've resurfaced again."

She leaned in and ran a gentle finger over the scar beneath my lower lip. A reminder of the time we jumped into the lake as kids and I scraped my mouth against a thick branch floating in the water.

When she was done tracing its edge, she pressed her mouth to the thick, patchy scar above my heart and I nearly sprang straight out of my skin.

"Can I touch you?" I whispered.

She gave me a small smile and I unlatched her overalls, letting one strap and then the other fall. Once her shirt was gone, I undid her bra and let it fall to the floor. She was the most stunning woman I'd ever seen. As a kid, she'd been all sharp curves and angles, but this woman next to me was no longer a girl. She was a shining light. Every inch of her long neck and soft breasts a vivid symbol of all I needed in my life.

"Tell me what you want." My words were meant to be a statement but they tumbled out of my mouth more like a plea. She'd pushed me away time after time, and I needed to know she was sure of this choice.

"You," she rasped. "It's always been you."

Her admission was all I needed. I pressed my lips to her forehead, cheeks, the open skin at her neck, my mouth eager to brand every part of her skin as mine.

Our tongues swirled in a dance that had my blood humming. My brain screamed to move faster, but I'd waited for this moment too long. Dreamed of it for years. I was going to take it painstakingly slow. Memorize every inch and freckle as I explored this beautiful woman who'd held my heart since I was twelve.

I loved the way she moaned and sighed beneath me as I lowered my mouth to slowly caress her nipple with my tongue. Her body rocked and moved like my touch was something she craved. My hand palmed her back until my fingers found the top of her lace underwear. My body strained against the wool fabric of my pants. I'd been hard since the moment she'd confessed she wanted me.

"The last time I touched you like this we were kids fumbling on a blanket, not quite sure where our hands and lips should go. Hell, it'd taken me at least two minutes to figure out how to open the shiny silver condom package."

"I remember," she said, pressing another hot, wet kiss to my chest.

"But now, here in what used to be my childhood bedroom, a place where I've had dozens of fantasies about you, I plan to touch you in all the right places. Make you ache so badly that my name rips from your throat."

Her kisses became more insistent as she used her tongue to trace a line down to the spot where my waistband began. I bucked under her touch as she skimmed her hands down the front of my pants. Knowing I wouldn't last long if she kept going, I pulled her back to me.

"This isn't going to be a quick and fast roll in the sheets." I sucked and kissed all the places on her neck I knew she loved. A sensitive spot beneath her chin. The deep hollow of her throat. She whimpered as I continued the exploration of her body. "I'm going to take my time. Trace the red outline of your lips. The hard peaks of your nipples. The sweet wet spot between your legs."

She grabbed my hands and placed them where her overalls hung on her waist. "Take them off," she ordered.

"Yes, ma'am." I shoved the material down until it puddled around her feet. With the lightest touch, I slid my fingers down along her side, over her delicious hipbone, and then past the small strip of lace between her legs.

She grasped my fingers and placed them on her wet center. Slowly I used my fingers to taunt and tease the outside of her. I bent down and used my teeth to pull off the small slip of fabric. My fingers slid back up her legs. I touched her again, letting her quiver on the knife's edge of bliss. She bit the corner of her lip and reached out for me like she wasn't quite ready to go over that edge yet.

She clawed at my pants and I grabbed hold of her hands and slowly inched her down onto the khaki-colored tarp, shoving tools and paintbrushes out of the way. After tugging down my pants and then my boxer briefs, her hands moved to my chest, gently touching as she kissed every bump and jagged scar. Her hands lingered lower and I had to suck in a breath not to lose it right in that moment.

"Wait," I groaned.

My gaze ran the length of her from head to toe. I couldn't believe I was here. Getting to touch and taste her again. I sat back on my heels and slowly took my time running my fingertips along her ankles, up past her calves, and onto her gorgeous thighs. Gently I pushed her legs wide and bent down, eager to taste her. To take her to that edge another time.

She writhed beneath my mouth. Her body arched into me for more until she took a heavy breath and shoved me back.

"Condom," she demanded.

I reached for my pants and pulled the foil package out of my wallet.

"What? Are you still seventeen?" she teased breathlessly.

Heat filled my cheeks and all I could do was shrug as I slid it on.

"Come here already," she said.

I crawled forward and bent over her. The light in her eyes was more radiant than the setting summer sun. I reached up for her neck and pulled her to me. We never took our eyes off each other as our mouths and bodies became one.

I eased into her slowly and then out again, over and over. Our slow rhythm became a pounding force. We clung to each other like if I let go we could be easily parted again. Torran's cries of passion and the way she clawed at my back said she wanted me deeper. I slid my hands through her hair and she kept moving, rocking against me, begging for more. I drove into her again, finding the spot that made her eyes shutter close.

"Look at me," I whispered, needing to watch her fall apart beneath me.

She opened her eyes and pinned that beautiful mossy gaze on me. We continued to move and I slid my fingers through hers, holding on until we went over that edge together.

With her body still shaking beneath me, I rolled over and pulled her to my chest. She unleashed that smile I'd been waiting for. The one that meant real joy. True happiness. I pushed back another loose golden hair and our lips met again. This time it was softer. Sweeter. We laid together for a breathless minute until I looked into her eyes and said, "You really are the most gorgeous woman I've ever seen."

"Stop," she joked and punched my shoulder, quickly replacing the jab with another molten kiss to the scar that covered most of my right shoulder.

"Now that I've seen you naked, you know that is the only way I'm going to picture you from now on. Not that those little overalls didn't already make me hot..."

She quieted me with another scorching kiss, and I tugged her in close, making a solemn vow that I'd never let her go again.

155

24

TORRAN

This Isn't Your Own Private Love Shack

THE sharp clank of metal hitting metal forced me to peel open my eyes. Beck slept peacefully, the early morning sun lingering along the curve of his full mouth. A mouth that was... amazing.

He sighed and rolled toward me, his arm flopping onto my stomach. The heat of him sent a thrill through me I'd been missing for years. I'd been angry and confused about his silence, but his confession about his surgeries and rehab, how he was wracked with guilt about Piper, dug into my soul.

I reached over to smooth back a hair from his forehead and it was hard not to smile at his sleeping form. He looked so peaceful. Like for the first time in years he was finally happy. I wondered if my face wore the same expression.

The sharp ping of metal rang out again. I pulled my shirt over my head and walked to the window. Outside, a big black truck backed into the driveway. Workers paced on the lawn, ready to mount ladders to put on a new roof.

"Torran, you here?" Manny's voice rang out from the bottom floor.

"Isn't that her truck out front?" Lauren's voice followed.

Shit. Shit. Shit.

I bent down and shook Beck's arm. He inched open one eye.

"Get up," I whispered. "Manny and Lauren are here and they can't see you."

I tossed him his clothes, his shirt hitting him squarely in the face. I couldn't help but laugh. This whole scenario was ridiculous. The two of us trying to pull on our clothes like two teenagers afraid of getting caught by our parents.

"This wasn't how I was planning this morning would go," he said, yanking on his pants. "After a long snuggle, I was going to get you coffee and donuts." A lopsided grin covered his still sleepy face.

"That's sweet but the last thing I need right now is Manny catching us in here." I glanced at his open fly. "And I seriously don't want Lauren seeing that." Another giggle escaped as we crept to the door.

When it was clear, we hurried down the back stairs that led into the kitchen. We got a few surprised stares from the plumbing crew as we rushed through the back door. Once outside, we sprinted through the tall grass, stopping behind a neighbor's fence.

Beck heaved in big breaths. "Nothing like an early morning sprint to wake you up."

I fell back into the grass and started to cackle. "Are you kidding me! That was like the time your mom came home early from the grocery store and caught us half-dressed on the blanket in your backyard. I couldn't look her in the eye for a solid month after that."

It was his turn to let out a snort. "Ah, come on, this was fun. And you know Ivy Falls needs something new to gossip about." He gave me a quick wink.

At any other time a reference to my video would have pissed me off, but with him grinning at me like we were still hormonal teenagers it was hard to muster up any anger.

He swiped a hand over his tangled mop of hair and fell back into the grass next to me. "I don't regret a single thing." Slowly he threaded his fingers through mine. "We agreed to keep our relationship strictly professional, but last night I had to touch you. I've been dreaming about it for years."

It was criminal how his stare could make my entire body snap to attention with a hungry ache. "It was unexpected, but I don't regret it either. But Manny, he'll know in a second when he looks at us so we have to do our best to stay professional."

"I'll do anything you want."

He reached out and grazed my cheek with the tips of his fingers and I felt heat all the way to my toes. It was like no time had passed between us. His touch was like a sense memory sending me back to the days when we couldn't stand to be away from each other for a minute. Our hearts aching whenever we had to be apart.

"Let me take you to dinner so we can talk. There are so many more things I want to tell you."

"Tor?" Manny's voice filtered out the upstairs window.

"Dinner. Please," Beck pressed.

Damn. It was hard to resist when he asked so sweetly. "Okay. Call me later."

I leapt to my feet and swiped the dirt from my overalls. Beck wound his arm around my waist and pulled me back into the grass, peppering my neck and lips with gentle kisses. For a moment I let myself get caught up in the moment. Sank back into the thrill of his touch, forgetting the men climbing on the roof and the frenzied tone of Manny's voice calling my name. His hand slid under my overalls and stopped at the top of my breast, his finger teasing the edge of my hard peaks. A small whimper escaped my mouth when he pulled away.

"I've missed that sound," he whispered in my ear, his hand moving to the other breast.

Warmth blazed between my legs.

How could he do that to me with a single kiss?

"Beck, you have to stop," I groaned.

He gave one last peck to the side of my cheek, that wicked grin pulling up his lips. He pulled me to my feet and tipped his chin back to the house. "Go on. I'll call you later."

With wide strides he made his way to his car parked at the curb. I should have started back in the direction of the house but my feet stayed planted. Even after sleeping on a hard floor, his hair tousled in five different directions, he was still hotter than any guy on the cover of *GQ*. And for a few brief hours, he'd been all mine.

❧ ❧ ❧

I darted back inside the house, the taste of Beck lingering on my lips. Rushing to the bedroom, I straightened out the tarp and pretended I didn't look like a woman who'd been up half the night having mind-blowing sex with my ex whom I'd vowed to hate forever.

"There you are. Didn't you hear me calling you?" Manny stood inside the threshold; his usual Titans hat pushed back on his head.

"What?" I yanked the headphones out of my ears. "Did you say something? You know I can't hear anything when I have Goodbye June cranked up."

His head tilted like he didn't believe me. "Have you been here all night?"

"Yep," I said, focusing back on the wall.

"Were you alone?"

I ignored the question as I pressed a putty knife to a loose edge of wallpaper. "I'm determined to remove all this before lunch. The mosaic tile was delivered for the master bathroom floor. My plan is to start that later today. Get us back on schedule."

He moved around the side of me. I held my breath, hoping he wouldn't recognize the telltale signs of sex. My kiss-swollen lips and very apparent case of bedhead. His eyes surveyed the room and landed on a condom wrapper balled up in a corner.

Oh crap.

He let out a deep grumble and tugged me to the corner of the room. "Tor, what are you doing?"

"I don't know," I whispered. "Beck and I were here working late, and we got to talking. One thing led to another..."

He held up a hand. "I don't need the gory details. And you don't have to lie to me. All I want to know is if you're okay?"

Manny came into my life when I'd needed a real friend. The bungalow on Westfort shook my confidence. Bad contractors. Shoddy plumbers. Even the electrical work I'd used most of my savings to

159

pay for wasn't done to code. At the brink of a total breakdown, I'd met Manny and we agreed to be partners. Since that moment, we'd always had each other's back. When the anniversary of his wife's death came around, I supported him and Lou in all the ways I could. After the YouTube video went live, he'd returned the favor, pulling me out of a self-imposed month-long exile. Kicking my butt out of bed. Forcing me to face life again.

"Yes, I'm good," I said, reassuring him.

He placed a big mitt of a hand on my shoulder. "I'm glad you're happy, but this guy hurt you once. I want to make sure there's not a repeat performance."

"He explained what happened when we were kids. It's made it easier to forgive him. Think about giving him another chance."

The frown lines pinching between his brows said he wasn't convinced.

"It's okay, Manny. It felt right to be with Beck again."

He scrubbed a hand over his mouth and leaned back against the wall. "I can see how he feels about you. The way his eyes track your every move. I was the same way with Gina."

I never had a chance to meet Manny's wife. She died of a brain aneurysm two years after Lou was born. Manny didn't talk about her often, but when he did his voice was tinged with a kind of pain that only comes from losing the love of your life.

The sharp tap of hammers floated in through the open windows. "Fix that hair before Lauren comes up here. She has some questions about that double basin sink we're putting in the kitchen."

Shouts came from the men working on the roof.

"I better get outside and make sure those fools know what they're doing." He walked to the doorway and stopped. "Hey, Tor, next time go to his place. This isn't your own private love shack," he chuckled.

"If there is a next time," I shot back.

"It'll happen again. You can see that by the way you look at each other."

"And what way is that?"

"Like two starving lions who spy their first meal in days."

"Oh, please. Don't go all Animal Planet on me."

"Sorry." He shrugged. "I just call 'em like I see 'em."

25

BECK

No Room For Awkward Small Talk.

HAVING Torran in my arms last night was the first time in years I'd let go of all my worries. The upcoming pitch. My sister's sobriety. Both were overshadowed by the smell and feel of her.

I'd heard her stirring this morning but refused to move. Afraid to wake and find regret shining in her eyes. I'd never stopped dreaming about touching her soft skin, feeling every inch of her body move under me. We'd lived separate lives for ten years, but when we kissed it was like we'd never been apart.

Thankfully with Manny's surprise appearance there was no room for awkward small talk. Things were never simple or easy with Torran—and I wanted more.

She'd agreed to dinner, and I was determined to make it the first step in winning her back. After I parked, I rode the elevator up to my condo, my mind racing with all the ways I could sweep her off her feet.

A romantic dinner.

Flowers.

No. She deserved something better. Unique. An overture that said I was trying. That I wanted and believed in her.

Once I reached my floor, I stepped out into the hallway and almost tripped over a young woman curled up a few inches from my neighbor's door. He was a budding singer-songwriter and had a revolving door of women and parties. The hallway was always littered with beer bottles and trash, and I worried this girl might be one of the asshole's castoffs.

I stalked past her and a part of me thought I should check on her. It was what I would have wanted if someone had encountered Piper that way. After a few more seconds of overthinking it, I walked toward the sleeping girl. A heavy black coat covered most of her face.

"Hey. You can't be here." I touched the girl's shoulder to make sure she was breathing. She shifted and finally sat up. Dark brown eyes the same color as mine stared back at me.

"Hi, big brother. Surprise."

I double-blinked and shook my head, making sure she was real. "Piper? What are you doing here?"

After so many years of begging her to come home, it didn't seem possible that she was right in front of me.

"Well, that's a shitty hello, especially for someone who took a red-eye from New York just to see you."

I did my regular preliminary scan of her. Her eyes were clear. There wasn't even a whiff of booze on her breath. "Why didn't you tell me you were coming?"

"I sort of did. Remember when I told you I wanted to buy something special? It was a plane ticket."

"Fine, but why keep it a secret?"

She was acting sober but a low swirling in my gut said this was much more than a surprise visit.

"I thought it'd be fun. And…" She hesitated before looking down at the beat-up Doc Martens on her feet.

Okay, here we go. The real truth.

"To be honest, I wasn't sure I'd be able to get on the plane and come. Too much history, you know." Her voice wobbled and the heavy wool coat she pulled over her bony shoulders swallowed her much too thin frame.

"I'm glad you're here," I said, pulling her into a hug.

"Where have you been?" She wiggled her eyebrows. "I've been here since three in the morning. Knocked on the door at least a dozen times."

"Why didn't you call me?" I asked.

She scratched at her black hair which hung in tangles around her pale face. "I fell asleep."

"Have you eaten?" I asked.

"No and it's been a while since I've had blueberry pancakes."

My heart stuttered at the mention of our mother's specialty. "Of course it has. Come inside and let's get you settled."

I wrapped her into another hug even though that small tug of worry warned this was much more than an out-of-the-blue visit.

26

TORRAN

Like A Starry-Eyed Teenager.

THINGS moved in a hurry once Hearth and Home secured the filming permit. A crew of people descended on the house along with a truckload of equipment. I hadn't heard from Beck about dinner, but I figured he was as caught up in his work as I was. Even though I was busy answering Lauren's constant questions, and following Manny's directions on what project needed attention next, flickers of that night with Beck filled my head. The way he seemed to know exactly where to touch me. How we moved in a rhythm that said we'd never been apart.

The questions that buzzed in my head for years were finally answered, and it felt like for the first time a heavy weight was lifted off my chest. That a full breath could finally fill my lungs. Seeing Beck, his bare chest covered in a patchwork of jagged skin like an embattled warrior, it was impossible not to forgive him. Fold him into my arms and offer comfort when his whole body quaked as he spoke about Piper, the fire and his parents' deaths.

A sudden thud on the roof brought me back to the moment. Manny had been supervising the crew for days and finally there wasn't a giant hole in the hallway ceiling. I forced myself to focus back on work, pushing away the thought and scent of Beck.

Even with an entire crew at the house, we were days behind schedule. We needed to get back on track if we were going to make our July deadline.

My phone buzzed and I pulled it out of my pocket hoping it was Beck, but it was only a reminder from Tessa that I'd promised the girls I'd be home for dinner tonight.

I released a low breath and headed for the master bathroom. From the doorway, I surveyed the floor and began constructing a pattern in my head for the white mosaic tile. It wasn't original to the house, but it was as close to the time period as I could get.

Rechecking my measurements for the space, I went to work laying down a chalk line in front of the spot where we planned to put a claw-foot tub. My plan was to work outwards toward the toilet, stopping to cut specific pieces to fit around its base.

Once I was convinced everything was done right, I positioned the tile in a perfect pattern until thoughts of Beck crept back into my head again. The way he'd hissed my name as I touched the scars etched into his chest. How he'd moved over me, taking his time to kiss every inch of my heated skin. The agonizing moments he'd slowly worshipped my body until he brought me to a high I never thought possible.

My skin flushed and I shook away the memory. This wasn't the time to be distracted. The tile had to be laid right or it would screw up the entire layout for the bathroom.

After a few minutes of sketching out a plan, I went to work. With an electric drill, I mixed fortified thin-set mortar in a bucket with water. When it was the right consistency, I applied the mortar to the subfloor using a notched trowel. Spreading the mixture in a wide swath, I made sure not to obscure my chalk line. Once I was satisfied with the application, I laid down the first sheet of mosaic tiles flush with the line. I pressed down the tile with a rubber float and then repeated the process, making sure to maintain consistent joints between tile sheets.

Two hours later my back throbbed, and even though I wore knee pads, the ache in my shins warned of tight muscles tomorrow. I surveyed the room and couldn't help but smile at the finished product.

My phone beeped and I hated that my heart picked up rhythm once I recognized Beck's number.

"Hey," I said, trying to sound as casual as possible.

"Hi, yourself. What are you doing?"

"I finished laying the tile in the master bathroom. It looks pretty close to the original."

"How long did that take?"

"Not too long. It needs to set before I can finish it up with the grout."

"You're amazing. Do you know that?"

My cheeks heated like a starry-eyed teenager. "Thanks, but this is just what I do."

"Well, I think you're pretty damn special. You're not only restoring part of Ivy Falls' history, but my history too. That means more to me than words can say."

My insides lit up like a damn Christmas tree. He saw that I loved what I did. How hard I'd worked to prove myself in this town. That was more respect than a lot of people had shown me lately.

"Listen, about dinner." The downturn in his voice quickly extinguished my good mood. "I've had a little hiccup here and need to push it to next week. And I may not be able to come by the site for a while."

A small throb started at the back of my head and worked its way toward my temples. Why was he being secretive again?

"Whatever, Beck." I couldn't keep the hurt from my voice. "It's not like I have time for dinner right now anyway."

"I'm not blowing you off. It's…"

A female voice spoke in the background and I dropped the tool in my hand. He was with another woman. I could be one of many in his life. It wasn't like us having sex was a promise of fidelity, but that didn't make it hurt any less.

Dammit. Why was I letting him do this to me again?

"I need to go," I said, my voice too damn shaky.

"Torran, I'll make it up to you. I promise."

"We'll talk later," I said before hanging up.

I forced my mind to focus back on work even though that cavern in my chest I thought was closed now began to crack open again. All my instincts that had screamed we should keep things professional were right. This project could be the only focus of my life. I needed to keep my mind on that and not worry about all the promises Beck made to me about this deal. Whether he'd up and disappear one day again.

That familiar heat of anger buzzed through me and I chucked my phone out the bathroom door. It skipped twice before crashing into the bedroom wall. It should have given me a sense of satisfaction, but all that raced through me was a swirl of nausea and a sick sense that I'd already lived this moment once before.

27

BECK

Make Sure You Seriously Grovel.

I dialed Torran's number over and over. Each time it went directly to voicemail. I pocketed my phone and sped around the condo, opening cabinets in the family room and then moving to my bedroom.

"Problem?" Piper said from the threshold.

"I fucked up."

"Again?" she teased as I searched the top of my dresser and then knelt to check under the bed.

"What are you looking for?"

"My car keys," I said rushing past her.

"Who or what have you fucked up?" She moved to the counter and sat on a stool as I checked every nook and crevice in the small galley kitchen. Opening and closing more cabinets with a loud bang. "Beck, stop! What is going on? How can I help?"

She settled her hands on the marble counter and focused clear eyes on me. I loved that she finally looked like her old self. Healthy pink skin. Soft round cheeks. It was surprising what not flooding your body with alcohol and drugs, and getting more than three hours of sleep, could do for someone.

I stopped my frantic search and faced her. The only way to explain was to finally tell her the truth.

"It's Torran," I said.

"Torran Wright?" she yelped. "Was that her on the phone? The one you fucked up?"

"I didn't fuck up entirely. We were supposed to go to dinner…"

"And you bailed because I'm here." Her shoulders sank in the defeated way I hated. "You've already taken time off of work for me, and now you're flaking out on a date?"

I moved around the counter and sat on the barstool next to her. "It's important to me that I spend time with you. Torran will understand once I explain it to her."

"What exactly is going on with you two?" She glanced at the Band-Aids covering two of my fingers.

"Besides the new pitch at work I was telling you about earlier, I've also been working on another project. It's something that means a lot to me, and I hope it'll mean a lot to you too."

She twirled a lock of dark hair around her finger. A nervous tic she still had from when we were kids. I hoped I wasn't making a mistake by telling her about the house.

"I'm not sure if you remember Diego Morales. He was a year older than me at Ivy Falls High. Anyway, he owns a property management and auction business. He's a great guy. Married and has twins."

"You're stalling, Beck." She waved her hand in the air, encouraging me to move on.

"Diego sent me an email saying our old house was going into foreclosure. That it'd be sold at auction." The glow in her cheeks faded, but she nodded for me to continue. "Believe me, I had no intention of making a bid. All I'd planned was to go and look at it. Then I ended up at the auction and Torran was there bidding against me." I hesitated, unable to spill the last bit of truth to her. "It would have bothered Mom and Dad to see it in such bad shape and…" An unsteady breath filled my chest. "I bought it as an investment."

Her eyes narrowed. "How long has this been going on?"

"Since April."

"Shit, Beck. That's some secret to keep."

I stayed frozen, waiting for her to celebrate, or curse me out, but she went painfully silent, which was the worst reaction of all.

"I should have told you…"

"Yeah, I'm not happy that you kept this from me, but it's done now, I guess," she sighed. "Explain to me more about this situation with you and Torran."

"She's a contractor in Ivy Falls. She's been buying historic places like our old house and returning them to their original state. Or as close to it as possible."

"Let me get this straight, she wanted to fix our house? Make it as pretty as Mom and Dad had it and you stepped in and screwed that up?"

"Yes, well, no." I tugged my hands through my hair. "I did buy it, yes, but then when I went to inspect it, I almost fell through the ceiling and Torran had to come and save me."

A loud snort erupted and she slapped her hand over her mouth. Once she stopped laughing, she said, "She white-knighted your ass?"

"Pretty much." I laughed too. "It was clear to me in that moment I was in over my head. I knew if I was ever going to get the house back to its rightful state, I needed Torran's help. After a lot of coaxing, she agreed we could be partners and restore the house together."

Piper turned to me, hands on her hips. "And why did you not tell me any of this?"

"Because I wanted to wait until it was done."

"Why?"

The fact that I wanted her to live there danced on the edge of my tongue, but she was still so fragile and I didn't want to freak her out with that expectation.

"It wasn't in great shape, Pipe. I was worried that if you saw it, it might bring back too many memories. Stir up old feelings you weren't ready to face."

Her lips thinned into a somber line. "Listen, Beck, I know I haven't exactly been the pillar of responsibility most of my life but you can talk to me. Be honest. Restoring the house does bring up a ton of memories, but it's also like giving a gift to our parents."

Her words flooded through me, releasing a heavy burden I'd been carrying for weeks.

"Do you want to go see it? I can take you with me right now."

She dipped her chin and looked away. "Maybe another day. I'm tired and I want to be mentally ready to go there. To relive the memories of Mom and Dad."

"I understand."

She placed her hand on top of mine. "Go and apologize." She stood and walked into the kitchen.

"But I feel guilty leaving you here."

Plus, I had Jack Daniels and Jose Cuervo stashed in a cabinet near the sink that I was too afraid she might find. She still hadn't given me a good reason for her visit and leaving her alone felt like opening a door to trouble.

"Stop it," she bit out. "You can't keep hovering. When we were downtown last night, I thought you were going to freak out every time we passed a bar. I know I haven't given you a lot of reason to, but you have to start trusting me."

"I'm trying," I confessed.

She rolled back her shoulders. Gave me a steady stare. "I've got my ninety-day AA chip. It took a long time to get there and I'm not about to screw up my life again."

"I'm proud of you," I said, reaching out to grip her fingers.

"Good. Now will you please leave."

There was something in the way she looked away. Like she was still afraid to open up certain parts of her life to me. "You're sure?"

Her head snapped up. "I swear to God, Beck, you better leave right now or I'm going to pull out a cast-iron skillet and whack some sense into you."

It was impossible to hold back a laugh. Damn, it was good to have her here.

"I'll have dinner ready when you get back," she said.

"You can cook?"

She gave me an eye roll to end all eye rolls. "I *am* capable of taking care of myself. Give me a little credit, okay?" She stopped and placed her hand behind a cabinet door. A second later she tossed me my keys.

"Thanks and, of course, you're welcome to anything in the fridge."

"I'm not saying I'm like that Giada chick on the Food Network, but I will have some pasta ready when you get back."

She was right. I needed to start trusting her.

"I'll only be gone a little while."

"Go already!"

I rushed out the door and hit redial on my phone. The call went straight to Torran's voicemail again. She wouldn't be expecting me, but I couldn't let this day end without letting her know I could, in fact, keep my promises to her.

❧ ❧ ❧

I edged my car to the curb. The tight knot in my chest released when I saw Sally Mae still parked in the driveway. Before I could get out of the car, my phone dinged with a picture from Piper. It showed a line of bell peppers and onions cut up by the sink. Her message read, "Don't screw it up. Make sure you seriously grovel."

I laughed and for the first time I thought maybe I could convince her to stay. That I'd made the right choice in buying the house.

Workers climbed down from the roof as the last rays of sunlight dipped below the purple-pink horizon. I moved up the path to the house trying to sort out all the things I needed to say to Torran.

When I walked in the house, Manny was at the top of the stairs with a sander. I tiptoed past him and followed the low hum of a Kings of Leon song coming from inside the gutted kitchen. So much had changed in ten years, but not Torran's love of indie bands from Nashville. Although KOL wasn't really indie anymore, not after their hit "Sex on Fire" blasted through every radio in the country the year I turned thirteen.

I followed the music and stopped at the entrance. My hand flew to my mouth as I muffled a laugh. Torran's body was half under the sink, her ass in perfect view. I took a long moment to admire it.

"That's a beautiful sight," I finally said.

Her body vaulted up and she smacked her head against the top of the cabinet. "Shit!" She backed out of the space, rubbing her head.

172

I quickly rushed to her side and knelt down. "Sorry. I didn't mean to startle you."

"What the hell are you doing here, Beck? You said you wouldn't be back for a while."

I knew that tone. She'd already given up on me. Again.

"I needed to come here and tell you in person that I'm not letting you down. Backing out of our dinner."

I held out a hand to help her up. She knocked it away and snorted out a cruel laugh like she didn't believe a word I said.

"Can you chill with the attitude for a second and let me explain?"

Her eyes narrowed and it was like I'd lit a fuse on a bomb.

"It's that *attitude* that has kept my business alive for the last couple of months. It's that *attitude*"—the word slipped out of her mouth with a sharp venom—"that is going to save this house. *Your house*. So don't you give me crap about how I work, what my focus is, when I'm trying to save your ass!"

I took a step back as her fury filled the entire room. Her armor solid as a rock.

"Tell me what this is really about? Are you regretting the other night?" I asked even though I wasn't sure I wanted to know the answer.

A flicker of sadness moved across her face before she leveled her shoulders. "I'm not some naïve little girl, Beck. It's possible for me to have a one-night stand and not get attached."

Her frigid response knocked the wind out of me.

"Go back to Nashville. I have everything under control." She turned her back to me but I wouldn't let her push me away.

"I never said you didn't have things under control."

"Like I said." She bent down, ready to crawl back under the sink. "Go home. I'll take care of the job here. I'm sure you have other things to do. People to see."

"What the hell is that supposed to mean?"

She ignored me and reached for a wrench set on a paint-splattered tarp next to the open cabinet. I went through our last phone call in my head. How I'd danced around the topic of Piper being here.

Piper.

She must have heard her voice in the background. *Fuck.* I was already on shaky ground with her, and by not being honest about my sister I was blowing it again.

"I know what you're thinking and you're wrong. I'm not running away from you. From our agreement."

"You don't have a damn clue what I'm thinking," she said more to the old pipes under the sink than to me.

I shoved my hands into the pockets of my jeans and kicked at the ragged edge of the tarp. "When I got home after the other night, I found Piper sleeping in front of my door."

She stopped working but still refused to look at me. "I thought you said your sister was in New York?"

"She was but I've been trying to talk her into coming to visit. The last time I spoke to her she wasn't interested."

Torran inched back from the cabinet. Her bright green eyes bored into me. "What changed?"

"She finally got a job, and an important audition, and flew all the way here to tell me about it. We've spent the last two days catching up."

Torran stayed quiet but I recognized her hesitation. Jumping on a plane and showing up unannounced at your brother's apartment didn't exactly sound like something a sober person would do.

"Is she okay?" she asked.

"Yeah, I was worried she might be high too. But besides looking a little tired, her eyes are clear, and she doesn't reek of booze. Her timing is weird though and I get a sense that something else is going on."

"Give her space. If she needs to talk, she will. I've learned that over the last year with Tessa." She chewed on her bottom lip. "You should bring Piper here. Show her all the work we're doing."

"I did ask her before I drove here. She's not ready, but she said soon."

She nodded and let out a heavy breath. "I apologize for being so shrill. It's just this." She waved a hand between the two of us. "I'm still trying to wrap my head around it, especially after all these years."

"I get it. There are a lot of reasons why you're still leery of me. *Of us.* But I promise I'm not stepping back from our agreement. I just need some time with her."

She leaned back against the counter, hesitancy heavy in her eyes. I couldn't blame her. I'd done a real number on her heart and one intimate, and very hot, night of sex was not going to change that.

"What are we doing, Beck?" she said quietly.

"Last time I looked we were having an honest conversation."

"No, I mean *us*. We said we weren't going to walk down memory lane, yet here we are complicating things." Her voice went tight. "Doing things without thinking them through."

She took a step back like she needed to clear her head.

"That last night between us at the lake when we lost our virginity, said our goodbyes, I believed you'd come back. That'd you keep all your promises to me. When you disappeared, it crushed everything I believed in. It's hard for me to let it go. Move on so easily."

That armor of hers was back up and it killed me.

"What can I do to earn back your trust?"

"I need to take a breath. Be convinced you're not going to disappear on me again."

A familiar ache filled my body. All I wanted was to get closer to her and here she was pushing me away. I shouldn't be surprised. I'd broken her heart, and it was going to take more than an intense roll in the sheets to undo all the damage I'd caused.

"Okay. I'll do whatever you want but please don't shut me out."

"For now, let's focus on the house. Go back to being partners in this. We can talk about what's happening between you and me after everything is finished."

"Fine, but just so you know, I'm not going anywhere. I want to take things slow. Learn about each other as adults, not as kids who can't keep their hands off each other."

She arched a brow. "Yeah, we're older now and still can't control that part of ourselves."

The low grind of the sander filled the air as Manny continued to restore the staircase.

"Slow," she said like she was mulling it over.

"Think about it," I said with a desperate plea.

She crossed her arms over her chest. "Like I said, let's finish the house first."

"That's not a no," I said with a little too much glee.

"It's not a yes either," she said wearily. "It's a pause until we finish what we started here."

She turned away and went back to the sink. I understood her hesitancy, why my explanation about the past wasn't enough for her. If I had to prove to her day after day for the next forty years that she could trust me, I'd do it. I only hoped she'd give me that chance.

28

TORRAN

How Do We Get To An Eight?

A week later Piper climbed the front steps with Beck hovering behind her. Slowly, she ran a hand over the front door, which was painted her mother's favorite shade of ruby red. She moved into the front hallway and gasped as her gaze wandered over the restored staircase leading to the second floor.

"Do you like it?" I asked, taking soft steps into the entryway behind her.

Piper gave one sharp nod and then launched herself into my arms. "It's so good to see you," she gushed.

Under her blue gingham sundress, Piper's shoulder bones popped through the material. I pulled back to look at her face. While dark shadows shaded the space under her eyes, there were still hints of that curious fourteen-year-old I'd said goodbye to many years ago.

"It's good to see you too," I said. "Thanks for coming by and checking things out."

Piper glanced at the scaffolding crisscrossing up to the ceiling and the sawhorses scattered throughout the room. "It took a little bit of arm-twisting from Beck, but I'm glad I'm here now. Is it safe to walk around?"

"Sure. Both the production team and our construction crew took off an hour ago, so the house is ours."

After I introduced Piper to Manny, we spent the next twenty minutes walking through the house. Piper blinked away tears when Beck showed her the way we were restoring the cabinets in the kitchen. Her hand ran along the carved railing as we walked up the new set of stairs and she complimented Manny on his craftsmanship.

Beck stayed behind me, and before we reached the second floor he leaned in and whispered, "Do you know how hot you look with that tool belt hanging low around your waist?"

"Uhhh," I mumbled. *Dammit.* All he had to do was talk in that low, rough voice and words evaporated from my brain.

I'd told him no more walks down memory lane. That we had to focus on the house, and I was sticking to it even if the lower parts of my body protested.

"Any chance we could let Manny finish the tour?" His warm breath against my neck sent a lick of heat through my core.

He said we'd take things slow, I repeated in my head before turning to face him and that stupidly gorgeous face of his.

"First, tell me how Piper is," I said, nudging him away. "This seems like a big step for her."

"She seems good. We've taken long walks, spent some time exploring downtown Nashville. I was a little anxious walking around all the bars and she kind of let me have it. Told me she wasn't a breakable doll and that I had to stop treating her like one."

"Good for her."

He grimaced. "Yeah, she talks a good game. I've heard it all before and still nothing changes."

Piper and Manny's voices moved to another room, and he cocked his head toward the first floor. He moved into the living room and took a minute to survey the space. We were making slow progress. Drywall now covered most of the walls, and the wiring for all the lighting fixtures was up to code. We'd kept the windows open while we were working and thankfully the putrid scent of rot and waste was now replaced by the thick, heavy scent of fresh paint and concrete.

"What else is bothering you?" I asked as his shoulders tensed.

"Piper chose to come here on her own even if she claims I goaded her into it."

"That's good, right?"

"Yes, but I worry that maybe I should have waited. Brought her back when everything was finished. You saw her blink back tears in the kitchen. There are so many memories of our parents here and seeing it in this shape may be too much."

"You have to listen to her, Beck. If she says she's ready, then you have to believe her."

"She told me that part of her AA journey is making amends. Accepting the choices she's made. Facing the demons of the past. That being here can help her move on. I was worried how she'd react when I told her you knew all about the accident, but she understood. That she was glad you knew the history and wanted to make this house right for our parents."

"You're a really good brother. Keep listening and following her cues."

He moved in close and slid a hand around my waist. "Is this okay?" he asked as his fingertips inched their way under my T-shirt. The heat of his touch ignited every element in my body. Hunger filled his eyes as he held me, the unsaid question lingering in the press of his hands to my skin. "Can I kiss you?" The words pressed against my neck like a soft and aching caress.

I'd told him we needed to go back to being partners. That I couldn't let go of our past so easily, but deep down I understood that I craved his presence, his touch, the low way he whispered my name like it was a precious vow.

My brain might have been throwing up warning signals but my body said fuck it as I leaned in and pressed a smoldering kiss to his lips and then dragged my teeth down his neck.

"We have to keep things professional while we're here," I stuttered as he pulled aside the collar of my shirt and slid his wet mouth over my shoulder. He pressed me back against the wall. His perfect lips finding my collarbone and then working their way up to the tingly spot behind my ear.

"Professional? We can stay professional during the day, but what about when we're alone? Can we be more?" he said against my heated cheek.

The tips of his fingers skimmed over my hairline and then down behind my ear.

"Eight," he whispered right at the spot where I had my tattoo, sending a shiver through my entire body. "What does it mean?"

"It's my number for a nearly perfect day," I panted as his hand inched higher up my waist.

I should stop him. Push him away again but my body ached for him.

"Nearly perfect?" he said in between kisses.

"It's a code Tessa and I have. Every day we give a rating to how our day is going. For me, a close to perfect day would be an eight on a scale of one to ten."

"And what's your number today?" he said against the hollow of my neck before planting a scorching kiss there.

"Six, maybe six and a half," I gulped out as heat licked through me.

"How do we get to an eight?" His voice turned husky.

I sucked in a breath as he slid a finger through my belt loop and tugged me in closer, the hard edge of him pressing into me.

"Does this get us there?"

"Close," I moaned and he sucked on my bottom lip until I opened for him. Our tongues did their regular dance, swirling and searching, each movement more insistent. It was a sin the way he could flip a sexual switch inside me. One minute I was sure we could only be partners, and then with a single swipe of his tongue I couldn't remember why I'd protested his touch in the first place.

His hand slid up my chest until it reached the outside of my bra. He took his time slowly rubbing my aching nipples and I wrapped my leg around his and arched into him.

"What about now?" he moaned in my ear.

"Seven and a half," I teased.

He pushed me harder against the wall. While one hand slid inside my bra, the other moved down to stroke the front of my jeans. I swallowed back a moan and leaned against him needing more.

180

All of this was crazy. We were standing in a partially finished room in our half-renovated house with his sister and my partner only steps away. Footsteps moved on the landing above us and Piper's voice echoed through the house.

"Stop pawing each other down there. We need to finish the tour."

Beck's laugh filled my ears as his forehead landed on my shoulder. "Twenty-four years old and she's still cock-blocking me."

"See, she's doing okay." My words came out fast and punctured. I thought I could handle a single touch from him, but nothing with Beck was simple. All he had to do was glance my way and the lower half of my body lit up like a fricking neon beer sign.

"Yes, it's good to see." He moved aside my ponytail and pressed his lips to my shoulder, sucking on the tender skin.

"Don't make me come down there, you two," Piper yelled. "There's plenty of time for you to screw around later."

I pushed Beck away and he got a determined look in his eyes. "To be continued, because now it's my mission to get to an eight."

I tilted my head up and gave him a pointed look.

He threw his hands up. "I know. I promised slow."

For a minute he took a walk around the room until the part of him that needed calming finally listened. When he was ready he tipped his chin to the stairs. "Let's go look at the rest of this masterpiece."

I followed him up the stairs and toward the sound of his sister's voice. When we found Piper and Manny, they were standing in her old bedroom. All signs of the hideous pink wallpaper were gone. She walked across the floor and ran her hand over the wood framing against one wall.

"A closet?" she cried. "I always wanted one in here!"

Beck gave me a heated grin, and neither of us could escape Manny's knowing stare. I glanced at Beck and wondered if his lips were as kiss-swollen as mine. Manny's face went dark, confirming my suspicions.

We were so busted.

After touring the rest of the house, we ended back on the wrap-around porch outside.

Manny said his goodbyes quickly in a rush to get home to Lou.

"It's beautiful. My parents would have been so happy," Piper gushed, her eyes moving over the house. "It looks like there's still a lot of work to be done, but it's exciting to hear that a TV show is filming it all."

"So far so good, but there can always be hiccups. Right now we are shooting for it to be done right after Fourth of July."

"My audition in New York isn't until next week. And I have some time before I start at the restaurant. Do you think we can talk over dinner about some ways I can help? Paint or something?"

I glanced at Beck and he gave me an enthusiastic nod.

"We can always use an extra set of hands," I said.

Piper bounced on her toes and pulled Beck down onto the grass as she talked a mile a minute about all the things she loved about the kitchen.

Watching the two of them connect over their shared memories sent a wave of pride over me. Saving this house was not only a spark of hope for the town, but it was reviving a dream for the two of them who deserved something good after all their years of pain.

29

BECK

A Time For Work And A Time For Play.

"LET'S hear it again."

I paced around the conference room as the sounds of a country melody echoed off the walls. Last week, I'd given Sienna, one of the newest members of our creative team, permission to go to Music Row and record a jingle for the Brinkley Food pitch. The sharp twang at the beginning sounded a little too loud to my ears, but I let the music continue. As Sienna's lyrics about mouthwatering ribs swelled into the chorus about crispy fries and tangy barbecue sauce, the entire room buzzed with excitement.

When the final note played, the room exploded into applause.

"Great work, everyone. I think Teddy Ray is going to love it. Now where are we at with the media plan?"

The room went painfully silent. My team leads averted their eyes to the paperwork spread out across the conference table.

"Please tell me someone has thought about how we're going to introduce the jingle into the market. Picked stations? Contacted media reps about cost?"

The head account executive, Marissa, clutched at the pink scarf tied around her neck. "We wanted to make sure you liked the song first before we proceeded."

My arms and chest started to ache. Stress always made my scars burn with pain.

"Okay. What about the point of sale examples? The tent cards and miniature menus we were going to put in the peanut stands on all the tables?"

"Uh, well, they're still in the prototype stage," Karl, the creative director, answered like he'd rather be in any other meeting than this one.

"And why is that? You've had four weeks to work on it!"

I'd never been the type of boss to raise my voice, but the clock was ticking on this pitch and we weren't anywhere near prepared—which was in large part my fault. I'd been so wrapped up in Torran, the house, Piper's surprise visit, that I'd been ignoring the one thing I should have been paying attention to.

"We have other clients, Beck. Pauly's Pet Supply needed banners for their new store openings. Rainbow Paints is introducing their spring color line and wanted new brochures." Karl's voice faded on his final words.

With losing two accounts so close together we couldn't afford to hire new staff, which pushed everyone to capacity. Most of the art and accounts department were already coming in early, skipping lunch, and staying way past sundown.

The silence in the room was deafening. I'd promised Pete my best work, and I wasn't about to let him down. Teddy Ray was known for being tough and outspoken during pitches. He'd smell blood in the water if we went in unprepared.

I walked to the white board covering one side of the wall. After popping off the cap of a dry erase marker, I said, "Okay, let's start from the beginning. Karl, tell me what you need and I'll get you extra help."

Karl sat up straighter in his chair and started his long list. I may have been distracted, but my focus was laser sharp now. From this point on, things would run smoothly, even if it meant sleeping at the office until the day of the final pitch.

⁂ ⁂ ⁂

I worked through lunch and dinner outlining every detail of our presentation. My sources in the ad community told me there were three other agencies pitching the account. My old firm in Atlanta, as well as two out of Knoxville.

Both those companies had twice the number of billable accounts as Rowe and Townsend, not to mention huge leverage when it came to media buying. At every other agency, Brinkley would be just another company on a huge roster of clients. With us, they'd get the highest priority. I planned on capitalizing on that aspect in our pitch, but we needed something more.

A quick knock pulled me from my thoughts. Pete stood in the doorway with Bogie slobbering near his feet. "You still working at it?"

I leaned back in my chair, rubbing at my tired eyes. "Yep. I'll be done in about an hour as soon as I tie up a few loose ends on the Brinkley pitch."

Pete swiped a hand over his mouth. The lines in his forehead pinched together. "About the pitch," he began. "I'm hearing talk around the office that things aren't going well. People are grumbling about a lack of leadership."

He took the seat in front of my desk, resting his hands on his knees. Bogie plopped down beside him and seconds later was snoring louder than a freight train.

"I know you took that time off to be with your sister." He let out a slow breath. "But when you're here, you don't seem engaged. I guess what I'm asking is do I need to step in, Beck?"

Pete's weighted words hit hard and I knew I had to confess everything that was going on.

"Having Piper here has been a little difficult lately."

His brows shot up. "Why? Is she okay?"

"Yesterday was rough. Her agent called to say her audition was postponed for another month due to a recasting issue on the soap opera. After the call, she retreated to her room for too long and it took a lot of pleading to get her to come out and eat dinner."

"That world of entertainment can be rough."

"She seems better today. The last time I called she told me to get a life and hung up."

He cracked a smile. "I like that she's always had fire."

185

"There are a few other distractions going on in my life, but I promise it's all under control. I swore when I agreed to be your partner that I wouldn't let you down and I meant that."

"What kind of distractions are we talking about?"

"There's a project I've got going on in a little town about forty miles from here called Ivy Falls."

Pete's lips tightened. "What kind of project?"

"A house."

"You bought a house?" His voice went sharp.

"It's more than a house. It's where I grew up."

Pete sat back, dropping his hands in his lap. "What about your condo?"

"This is more of an investment. The house is in pretty rough shape, and I've hired a good team to restore it to its original historic state. They're even filming a TV pilot about it for the Hearth and Home Network."

"Shit, Beck. That sounds like a lot of work. No wonder things are falling through the cracks."

I jumped to my feet and started to pace in front of the window.

"I know that look," Pete said. "There's something else going on."

Crap. How did I tell my partner that I'd almost dropped the ball because I'd been spending all my time trying to win back my high school sweetheart? Even to my own ears it sounded like a lame excuse, but I didn't regret a thing.

The agency used to be my whole life. It filled my days, nights, weekends. But with Torran back in my world, I'd realized how lonely I'd been. For the first time in years, a life that had been dark without my parents was suddenly full of light and it was all because of her.

Pete's mouth flattened. "Okay, Beck, spill it. You look like a man who is about to jump out of his skin."

"The team who is helping with the house. One of them is my high school ex."

"I knew it had to be something like that."

"Why?"

"Call it experience. You used to always answer your phone on the first ring. Now it goes straight to voicemail. Your body may be in meetings, but your mind is somewhere else. I get it. A new romance can be awesome, especially if mind-blowing sex is involved. And you've got that satisfied vibe going on."

"Her name is Torran and she's a genius when it comes to historic renovation. When she's around I feel alive. I screwed it up once with her and I don't want to do it again."

"I'm happy for you, Beck. You deserve some good in your life after all the shit you've been through, but Brinkley is important if we want to keep the agency going."

He paused and I didn't like the dark look that crossed his face.

"I got a phone call today from an old friend who recently left Mercury Advertising in Knoxville. He told me they're also pitching a jingle to Brinkley."

"Fuck." I tore my hands through my hair. "This can't be happening. That was our ace in the hole."

His mouth went grim. "You know the stakes. If we can't bring in this account, things will have to change. Do you get what I'm saying?"

Get my head screwed on straight or our partnership was in jeopardy.

"This will be the best pitch Teddy Ray has ever seen. We'll add a new idea. I just need time to go back through the research again."

"That's what I like to hear. After we get this account, you'll have plenty of time for your girl. Hell, I'll even give you a vacation so you can spend as much time with her and the house as you need."

The house. My head spun and I grabbed the Brinkley file off my desk.

I thumbed through the pages and pulled out a single sheet of paper and handed it to Pete. It was a newspaper article from last year heralding how Brinkley had taken a condemned building in a small town in southern Mississippi and turned it into one of their highest-earning restaurants.

"What if I ask Torran if there's a property available in Ivy Falls that we could pitch to Teddy Ray? Even get her to draw up a preliminary design?"

Pete paused. Tented his hands in front of him. He looked at the article and then back at me. "I think it's a good idea. Talk to her and see what she says."

That pool of dread in my stomach began to subside. "If she agrees, we can sweeten the idea by telling Teddy Ray about the show being filmed for Hearth and Home. How it could bring more visibility to the Brinkley brand."

"But didn't you say it was a pilot? Don't those things need approval before being picked up?"

"You don't know Torran and her partner, Manny. They are incredible at what they do. The show is definitely getting picked up."

"Good." He moved to the doorway and then turned to look at me. "You've always worked your ass off, Beck. But there's a time for work and a time for play. You need both if you're going to have a decent life." He scrubbed a hand over the dark whiskers on his chin. "I've spent way too much time chasing the next career goal. Thinking I needed to be richer. More accomplished. It's gotten me a nice ride and a decent house, but *a lot* of ex-girlfriends. Be smart. Don't screw things up the way I have. You'll regret it."

Every once in a while I'd catch Pete in a quiet moment staring at the family photos on our art director's desk. A sad smile lifting his lips when the head account executive's kids came in to join her for lunch. He'd told me about his rough childhood with his single mom and brother, but he'd never outright said he'd wanted a family. But now, watching the steady line of his shoulders fall, it was clear he'd been hiding a lot behind his steely façade.

He walked out the door with little Bogie trotting behind him.

All the air went out of my lungs as I crashed into my chair.

I did need balance and that would come after we scored the Brinkley account. The key was convincing Torran and Manny that this would be good for their business. It could also prove to Torran that I was serious about earning back her trust. That no matter how slow she wanted to take things between us, I was never leaving her side again.

30

TORRAN

Me And Paint, We're Practically Synonymous These Days.

PIPER jerked the paint roller over her head in short, rough strokes. "Am I doing this right?"

"Here, let me help." I guided her roller up and down in long swaths. "If you want to get the color on evenly, you need to drag the roller from ceiling to floor. It takes a little bit longer but the color goes on better if you use this approach."

Piper's shoulders shifted up and down underneath her black tank top. She was painfully thin, but color flushed her cheeks and a wide smile lifted her lips. There'd been a few wobbly moments over the last week, but her eyes were clear and her attention to detail was painfully accurate.

When the camera crew arrived yesterday, she stood back and watched with intensity. During a break she asked Maggie, our gaffer, about the lighting set up in one of the bedrooms. How she lit the shots in the kitchen as we loaded in the appliances and then the custom quartz countertops.

Today the crew spent most of the day trailing me as I discussed how I was using a bone-colored paint to add more light to the house. How one wall in the dining room was getting an antique wallpaper with a deep rust and sage green floral pattern that would become the focal point of the space. In between painting breaks, Piper snuck out of the room to watch the crew film each portion of the slowly transforming house.

"Tell me about the audition in New York," I said, picking up a roller and going to work beside her.

"It's for a small part on a soap opera. My agent says if I do a good job it could become a recurring role."

"That sounds exciting. Do you know what the character is like? Have they sent you a script?"

"It's for the sister of one of the main characters."

She pressed the roller into the pan with a little too much force and splashed paint across the khaki tarp. Her eyes flicked up like she was waiting for me to scold her.

"It's okay. Happens all the time. That's why we have the floor covered."

Relief flooded her face. "All the same, I'll be more careful."

I patted her hand. "It's fine, and you know me and paint, we're practically synonymous these days."

Piper let out a low snort but went back to work like she was too polite to bring up a touchy subject. She covered the last part of the wall and a few quiet moments passed until she spoke again.

"The character's a drug addict." Her mouth thinned and she looked everywhere but at me.

I gave the corner one final layer of color before I set the roller down. "I'm not going to lie, Piper. Beck told me about what you've been through over the last couple of years."

"Great. Should I leave now?"

"Of course not. Who's going to climb the ladder and do the corner touch-ups?" I teased and the tight set of her mouth softened. "There's no reason for me to judge you. What you and Beck have been through is a horror no young kid should have to face. He said you've had some rough patches but you're putting it behind you. We're all stumbling through this life. Asking for help is what makes us human. It's what we do with our next chance that matters."

"Yeah, I guess you've been knocked down lately too." The lines in her forehead pinched. "I'll be honest, I did laugh at the video and I feel kind of bad about it."

I pointed to the tarp and she sank down next to me. "Don't. It happened and if I let it define me and my career then I may as well give up right now. Am I still hurting over the video and the sting of all the horrible comments? Yes. But I can't let it stop me from moving forward."

"At first, wasn't your instinct to run away? Leave it all behind?" Her childlike tone begged for an honest answer.

"The day I got the call from Manny telling me about the video, I was leaving flowers at my mom's grave. It didn't take long to search the internet on my phone and see it in living color. Yes, at first, the whole thing did knock the wind out of me. I'd worked hard on building up this business and it took ten seconds of film to make me look like an incompetent ass."

"Didn't you want to do something to make the pain go away?" The anguish in her eyes was palpable.

"I did want to disappear under the covers, but Manny wouldn't let it happen. He yanked me out of the house. Forced me to go to work because we still had a job to finish."

She scratched at a drop of dry paint on her arm. Her gaze floated to the golden light streaming in through the window. "What did Beck tell you about the day the RV exploded?"

"Not a lot. Only that you two were having a snowball fight when it happened and that he tried to save your parents."

"The early months of the trip were amazing. We stopped in places like Hot Springs National Park in Arkansas, and the Blue Hole of Santa Rosa, which is this cool little swimming spot in New Mexico. Dad insisted we go to a spot in Tucumcari called Tee Pee Curios. It was like being transported back to 1950. It was a little weird with all these old-fashioned cars and actual teepees. Mom loved it though."

Her far-off look said she was completely immersed in her memories.

"Beck took pictures everywhere. He said he wanted to share the trip with you when we got back home."

My stomach curled into a knot, but I didn't say a word.

"Then we got to California and drove over the Golden Gate Bridge at sunset. The trip felt magical. Like we were these four explorers on a great adventure." She shifted back on her arms, the color leaving her cheeks. "When we got to Lake Tahoe the snow was coming down in these lacy quarter-sized flakes, and Beck and I wanted to take snowboarding lessons. My parents agreed and we spent the entire day on the mountain." Her lower lip started to quiver. "Things went bad after that. After the explosion, our mom's screams tore through the icy air. Without any thought for his own life, Beck tried to save them."

She scratched harder at her skin, the paint chipping off in her hands.

"Want to know what I did? I watched. It was like I was paralyzed. My brother risked his life to save them and I stood still as a statue. Some daughter I am, right?" Her hands shook and she clutched them in her lap. "It's times like these that my body screams for a drink or a pill. As if it knows I want to be numb."

I slid a hand over the top of her arm. She clutched my fingers as if desperate to hold on to something real.

"All you can do is live your best life and honor your folks. That's what they'd want for you."

She shrugged. "It's harder than it looks."

I pulled her up and pointed at an empty wall. After dunking my roller in the pan of paint, I encouraged Piper to do the same.

"My mom used to say that every new day is a fresh start. A chance to make the time we're alive count. When I see the number of views inch up on that video, I try to remember I can only control this moment. Not what happened yesterday or could happen tomorrow. Only today."

A quick breath rushed out of my lungs as I worked the paint down the wall.

"If I think about it in those terms, it helps me move on. Whether it's demolishing a kitchen, or laying on a fresh coat of paint, *I'm* the one deciding what happens next."

A single tear rolled down her cheek. "I wake up every day hoping I can be that strong."

"You can do it. And you have lots of people around to support you."

"Beck's lucky he found you again. It's been a long time since I've seen my brother smile. Not a grin, or a smirk, but a real, full-blown smile." She glanced around the room at everything we'd accomplished. "One more thing I have to thank you for."

"I'm lucky too. He's helping me make a dream come true by renovating this house and he's also asked for help on another project too."

"Uh-oh," she groaned. "What else has my brother dragged you into?"

I laughed. "It's nothing bad. Manny and I are going to help his team find a house in town that could be the potential site of a future client's restaurant chain. Put together a proposal of what it would cost to revive another part of Ivy Fall's history."

"Ugh, restaurants," she moaned dramatically. "That only reminds me of what I have waiting back in New York." She pushed the roller dramatically against the wall and went back to work.

She was just like Beck in so many ways. On the outside she could put up a good front, but inside she was a mass of tangled and complicated feelings. I understood her confusion and pain. Grief was a difficult road to navigate. One minute you thought you were breaking out of the dark tunnel you felt like you'd been traveling for days, and then the walls inched in, making the shadows loom larger. It took time but if you kept moving, eventually you'd see the light.

There were days I thought I was close to seeing that flare but then the scent of rose water, or a picture of Iris, who looked so much like my mom as a child, would remind me that she was gone and that black spiral would grab me by the ankle and drag me down. Working on the house though, doing small things to honor her in each room, was pushing me back to the light again.

"He's proud of you, you know. All the progress you've made to get better."

Piper made herself a little smaller. "I know. Just hope I don't screw it up."

"You won't."

She tilted her head like she didn't quite believe me. "How do you know?"

"Because I see how hard you've worked to get here. You won't let it slip away."

She was about to add something when Lauren swept into the room, her long dark hair bouncing loosely around her shoulders.

"Torran, can I have a minute?" Her gaze darted between me and Piper. "Alone?"

"Sure," I said. "Piper, want to take a break?"

"Yeah. It'll be good to stretch my legs a bit." She gave a small smile to Lauren and left the room.

As soon as she was gone, Lauren's shoulders went tight and her hands twitched at her sides. "We have a problem."

Those four words were like a bomb exploding in my head. "What kind of problem?"

She fidgeted again, swaying back and forth, which only made my anxiety spiral.

"Is it the network? Do they not like the house? What we're doing?"

"It's not the network. It's a problem here."

"Here? You mean Ivy Falls?"

"Yes. I just got a call from the network. A hold has been put on our filming permit until we can meet with the town council and settle some issues."

"What kind of issues?" I said coolly. "Can they just stop production like that?"

She nodded and it was like the earth spun out beneath my feet. This was about that damn video. I couldn't do this to Manny again. Ruin this great opportunity.

"Hey." Lauren waved her hand in front of my face. "You're not going to freak out on me are you?"

Passing out on her would not look professional. I steadied my feet. Looked her in the eye and said, "Tell me more."

"According to your town council, they've received numerous complaints about the production. How it's causing traffic congestion."

"Traffic congestion? There are like only ten thousand people in this entire town."

She shrugged. "That's what they're saying, along with us breaking noise ordinances and leaving out too much trash. The written complaint says we have to address all the issues at their next council meeting which is in two days. For now, they've put a hold on any and all filming so I had to send the crew home."

I tried not to implode in front of the woman who held the future of our business in the palm of her hands.

"Did you tell Manny?"

"I informed him before he left to get his daughter. He wanted to tell you himself but I thought it was best for me to deliver the news."

"Why?"

"Because, more than any other person, you understand how this town operates." She shifted back on her heels. "I need you to tell me what the weak spots are here. How we can get the council to lay off. Your father *is* the mayor. What do you think is the one thing that will turn the tide for us? Get them off our back so we can keep filming?"

My mind went blank. I needed to get out of my own head for a minute. Forget about the town's anger with me and find the true root of the problem. Flashes of the empty shelves at the P&P, vacant seats at the Sugar Rush, flew through my head. The complaint was a smoke screen. They thought I was going to embarrass them again.

I pulled out my phone and a minute later Beck's honeyed voice came through the receiver. Before he could say more than hello, I gave him the full story and told him it was going to take a lot more than money to fix the problem facing us now.

31

BECK

I'm Pretty Sure They Think They're Gonna See A Show.

THE last time I was in the town council's meeting chambers it was to receive an academic award alongside Torran when we were fifteen. It was still the same claustrophobic box with a large ten-foot wooden desk built in a semicircle at the front of the room. In one corner hung the town flag alongside the one for Tennessee. Twelve rows of chairs took up most of the space, which was filling up quickly with half the town.

Quietly each of the five council members filed into the room and took their seats behind the desk. Miles Wright sat dead center. The knot in his red-and-blue tie as stiff as he was.

Lauren took the seat on the aisle. A pile of papers sat nestled on top of her lap. Our game plan to fight the complaint. I sat beside her while Torran took the chair next to me with Manny flanking her other side. Tessa, who sat beside Manny, kept swiveling her head from side to side.

"What's the matter?" Torran asked.

"Do you smell popcorn?" Her sister's eyes narrowed like she was trying to find the source of the smell.

Manny's mouth went firm. "Two rows behind us. I think the culprits are Ernie Fields and Brad Fulton."

Sure enough the two of them sat, looking like twins in their matching John Deere hats, passing an oily paper bag back and forth. When they caught us staring they gave taunting smiles.

"What the hell? Do they think this is the movies?" Torran gaped at the men who then pulled out sodas and cracked them open.

"No," Manny grumbled. "But I'm pretty sure they think they're gonna see a show."

Torran's leg began to bounce. I wanted so badly to pull her in close. Press a soft kiss to her lips. Whisper reassurances in her ear, but I'd promised that we'd be friends, partners, so kissing her in front of most of the town was out of the question.

I leaned back and locked eyes with Tessa, silently pleading for her to do something. She gripped Torran's hand and leaned in. They swapped quiet whispers. The only thing I could hear was Torran quietly saying the word "three." Tessa gave her an empathetic smile and replied, "four."

Three. That was too far from eight for my liking.

The room quickly filled. Torran and Tessa whispered about Isabel from the bank who sat in the front row. Miss Cheri, Piper's old acting teacher, stood near the back of the room. Her hair was the same cloud of big black curls as it had been ten years ago. Mrs. Vanderpool sat primly in the back row with Baby tucked under her arm.

Lauren leaned in close to me. "Is that dog wearing a Gucci sweater?"

"Do they make those for dogs?" I asked.

She gave an emphatic nod as the last of the remaining seats were taken.

"This isn't normal, is it? All these people here for a small council meeting?" Lauren said.

Manny and Tessa shook their heads at the same time and that small knot in my stomach grew into a large, uncomfortable fist. This was all about Torran.

After her panicked phone call, we agreed to meet with Manny and Lauren at Sugar Rush a few hours before the meeting and go over the council's complaints. Allegations of work trucks parked too far from the curb, excessive trash, and noise after five p.m. were laughable. Most towns would have welcomed the national attention. The potential for their little spot to get some airtime. But this was Ivy Falls. After watching the way they'd treated Torran, I'd learned this was more about pride than publicity.

Torran's father rose from his desk and knocked a gavel down, bringing the meeting to order. Before we got to our permit issue, the council heard from the town on a variety of other matters.

Mrs. Vanderpool complained about the increased cost of dog licenses and how they'd gone up only a dollar for cats while it was two dollars for dogs. She huffed that it was "doggie discrimination," which got a chuckle from the crowd. She went on to complain about there not being enough "poo-poo" stations around the square and that she was sure she'd stepped in excrement left behind by Doctor Lowe's poodle, who liked the grass near the courthouse. That caused a firm and emphatic reply from the doctor, who swore he always picked up after his sweet Phoebe.

"Is this meeting odd or is it just me?" Lauren whispered.

"You don't know the half of it," Tessa replied. "Once there was an hour-long discussion over Milton Parke's new hot dog business that he wanted to call 'Weenie World.'" Half of the women in town spoke up, complaining that it sounded like a place of pornography and should not be allowed a business license until the name was changed. The argument went on and on about the various euphemisms for penis until Wally Murphy, the mayor at the time, ended the conversation by saying 'Weenies are welcome in Ivy Falls.' That got an interesting response."

Lauren let out a low snort which earned us more than a few irritated glares.

Once Mrs. Vanderpool finished her speech about the lax responsibilities of the town's dog owners, Minnie Winslow, who owned the market, started in about how the flowers planted around the old limestone fountain were hideous and needed to be changed. Ginny Deveraux, who owned the candle shop, stood and claimed she liked them. They went back and forth about the difference between zinnias and mums until Mr. Wright interrupted with numbers about budgeting and the cost to replace them.

When the topic turned to zoning, Torran clenched her hands together in her lap.

"What's the matter?" I whispered.

"They're talking about the abandoned properties near the Dairy Dip. All Craftsman bungalows. By the way Amos is talking, they want to rezone for commercial. More of the town's history gone if someone comes in and bulldozes the houses to make way for a strip mall or a parking lot."

Her cheeks went a little pale and I wanted to reassure her that things were going to swing in our favor today, but I wasn't so sure. By the way everyone deferred to her father, it was clear his opinion held sway with the council. If we couldn't use our plan to convince him, Hearth and Home may never get back to filming.

"Now we get to the matter of local permits." Susan Lewis, who I was told was the newest member of the council, read off the complaint against Hearth and Home. As we expected, it listed out the issues with noise, trash, and parking. The final claim was a zinger: potential damage to local reputation.

Torran's shoulders inched up to her ears and Manny shot her a look that begged for calm. At the Sugar Rush earlier, we'd all agreed it was best if Manny spoke. He rose to his feet and delivered all the rebuttals to the complaint. How they'd stagger the trucks along the street, park some in the driveway to limit congestion. The way they could take most of the production inside after five p.m. to control the noise. That he'd already given the crew a strong lecture about cleaning up. How he'd be personally responsible for any debris left in the yard.

During his entire speech the council remained stone-faced, not acknowledging any of our solutions. Lauren took the floor next. She spoke of how Hearth and Home was honored to feature such a beautiful town as Ivy Falls. That the show would have a high production value. Bring a ton of exposure to the town. When she was finished, the council requested a moment to confer but Mrs. Vanderpool interrupted.

"I don't know why we're giving this company another chance to feature our beloved town. No matter what that fancy girl says, I'd guess that it's going to put us in a bad light again."

Silvio from the hardware store jumped to his feet. "We don't need to give people a reason to make us the laughingstock of the internet again." He turned to Torran and sneered before sitting back down. The crowd began to mumble, their voices growing to a crescendo.

"Maybe I should tell them about the viewing numbers and impressions. How it could increase tourism," Lauren whispered.

"No," Torran said. "This isn't about the production at all. It's about me."

Her lower lip trembled as she stood. Every part of me wanted to curl her into my arms and protect her, but the way she tipped up her chin, planted her feet, said this was something she had to do on her own.

"Before you make a decision, may I speak?" she said.

There were more snickers in the crowd. Low whispers grew to a fever pitch as she locked eyes with her father.

"You have the floor," he said with a brittle tone as if he was in just as much pain as she was.

The crowd went quiet as Torran took a thick gulp. Tessa gave her a look so fierce it was like she was trying to will her sister all her strength. Again that protective feeling swept over me, but I sat back and let Torran take the lead. She'd more than proven not only to me, but to everyone in this town, that she had something important to say.

32

TORRAN

The Toughest Nut To Crack In Town.

MAKE *it right, Torran.*

My mother's words steadied me even as half the town leveled tense stares in my direction.

"Although she wasn't born here, my mother was devoted to this town. As a child I walked these streets hand in hand with her. I remember the comforting feel of the brick and stone under my feet. How everywhere we went people had a smile for me and my sister."

I gave a pained smile to Tessa before turning back to the council.

"I have fond memories of the roar of the crowds at football games, track meets, soccer tournaments. People in Ivy Falls always ready to be there any time a child from this town needed an inch of support."

Dad took a heavy gulp. Pulled at the stiff knot in his tie like it was choking him.

"When my mother grew ill and I came home, there was never a day we went without food, flowers, or a note of kindness. That meant a lot to her. To me. To our entire family." My voice broke and

I heaved in a full breath. "It's in this place that I first learned how to ride a bike, went to school, fell in love for the first time."

I paused and glanced at Beck.

"All of my best memories, and some sad ones too, were made within the boundaries of Main Street and the town limits at the edge of the Buckley's farm."

People shifted in their chairs. Some dabbed at their eyes.

"What I said that day on the video had nothing to do with my true feelings for Ivy Falls. I was scared, angry, and still truly grieving. Many of you, I'm sure, have made the same kind of mistake in the height of fear. I'm not excusing what I did. How it reflected badly on this town. What I'm asking is that you allow me to earn back your trust. Let Manny and I do the show and return some interest to this town."

I clasped my shaky hands together and forced out the next words.

"Someone in Ivy Falls, I don't know if they're here or not, believed enough in us to reach out to Hearth and Home. Asked them to give us another chance. I'm hoping that all of you," I directed my next words to the front of the room, "including the council, can find it in your hearts to do the same. Allow me and Manny to do right by this town and show the world that Ivy Falls is not only a place filled with important history, but a spot on the map that should not be missed."

My gaze drifted to Barb and Susan. Isabel. Even to Old Mrs. Vanderpool who sniffled into a tissue.

"When I came back to Ivy Falls, I took on the job of driving my mother to her treatments. Every time we passed the house on Huckleberry Lane, she gave me a wistful smile." I swallowed over the knot in my throat which grew tighter by the minute. "On her last day of chemo, she looked at me with a determined stare. Told me I needed to save the house because it was a critical part of the town's legacy. By letting Hearth and Home continue to film, we can all show the country, the world, the same thing my mother saw. That this town, its history, but most important of all, its people, are worth knowing."

Tessa swiped at her eyes and Manny gave her a gentle smile.

"Thank you for letting me say my piece. No matter what you decide, I want you all to know I won't stop fighting for Ivy Falls."

I sank down into my seat. The sea of faces before me a blurry haze as I blinked back my own tears.

The speech wasn't planned, but I knew Ivy Falls. That they'd never forget what I'd done, what I'd said, without some public act of contrition. They deserved it. My fit of anger had cost them so much, and they needed to see the regret on my face. Hear the pain in my voice and know I was truly sorry.

I didn't want to look at the council. Too afraid that my speech hadn't worked. That they'd rule against us in order to protect the town. If that happened, Lauren would walk away taking any chance we'd have to get things back to normal in town. To help tourism. To keep the stores on Main Street from going dark like that mysterious email predicted.

The council continued to quietly confer and I glanced at all the familiar faces. Ernie and Brad. "Fixer Ferris," Silvio, and Mrs. Vanderpool. I'd hoped when I'd mentioned the email sent to Hearth and Home that someone would speak up, confess they'd sent it, but there was nothing but silence. Whoever the author was, they'd remain a mystery for now.

Beck reached for my hand and gave it a squeeze. When he'd outbid me at the auction, I thought my world was coming to an end. That his return would bring nothing but misery. But each day he was proving he was worthy of my trust. That he wouldn't run when things got tough. I'd told him that this job was going to take everything we had, and he'd stood solidly by my side the entire time. Each day he was whittling his way into my heart and I no longer wanted to fight that warmth. Now I sought it out, craved it, in those quiet moments we found together.

My father stood with his chin jutted out, giving no sense of what the verdict would be. He knocked the gavel down and the audience went silent.

"We have made our decision." My father looked straight ahead, not a tick of emotion covering his face.

A sinking feeling of dread washed over me.

"After serious consideration, we have decided on a ruling of three to two that the stay on the permit for Hearth and Home Network should be lifted."

There was a mixed bag of response. Some people like Isabel and Barb and Susan cheered. Silvio, Brad, and Ernie grumbled their unhappiness with the decision. Manny leaned over and patted my knee. "Nice work, boss."

I let out a brittle laugh as he checked his watch.

"Now enough of this nonsense. Let's get back to work. We have a house waiting."

Everyone filed out of the meeting room and I hung back, waiting for Beck who was speaking with Miss Cheri. She practically glowed as she chatted with him, making me remember how perfectly he fit into this town.

After they said their goodbyes, Beck walked back my way. As soon as he reached me, his gaze turned apologetic. "Now I understand why you needed the house. Why you were bidding so damn hard for it. Why you treated me like I was an ass afterwards. Not that I hadn't already earned that kind of response." He reached out and tucked a loose hair behind my ear. "I'm sorry I didn't figure it out sooner."

"No one knew. Not even Tessa." I sank back into a chair on the aisle, the weight of the day finally taking its toll. "When my mother said the words to me, it felt like a final wish. That's why I was so angry when you outbid me. After the video, Huckleberry Lane was the last thing I could do to make things right. And when I lost it to you, it was like I was letting her down all over again."

He moved in and took the seat next to me. "I'm proud of what you did for Ivy Falls, for her, and for us, today."

"It felt good to get the truth out. To let people know that I mean every word about helping this town."

"I think they all know, they're just too stubborn to admit it. At least you won over Old Mrs. Vanderpool. She was sniffling up a storm in the back row."

"I'll take it," I laughed. "She's the toughest nut to crack in town."

His eyes darted to my mouth and then moved ever so slowly to hold my gaze. There was so much I wanted to say. That after we'd spent that night together, I'd allowed fear to take over and I'd pushed him away. But through it all he'd stayed firm. Honored what I'd asked and moved at my slow pace.

I leaned in and pressed my lips to his. The warmth of his mouth, the press of his firm hand against my back, released all the tension in my body.

I wanted him.

Wanted this.

With the permit issue behind us, and the house almost finished, I was ready to let him in. Allow myself to finally be happy again.

33

BECK

Homestyle Biscuits Better Than Your Grandmama's.

THE crashing sounds of my ringtone, the Cal Berkeley fight song, tore through the quiet office. I rushed toward it, hoping it was Piper. I'd called her twice this morning, and once yesterday, and still couldn't reach her. I'd been so busy with the permit mess in Ivy Falls, I'd neglected her in the final days before she returned to New York.

Before she got out of my car at the airport, she insisted she was fine. That she had a lot to do back in New York. Even so, it didn't assuage my guilt or the fact that I'd bought the house in hopes she'd live in Ivy Falls. That I'd never spilled that truth to her.

The growing thrum of a headache built in the back of my head.

"Holy shit, Beck. The whole office can hear that!" Pete stood in the doorway; arms crossed over his chest.

"Potential Spam" flashed across the screen and I silenced the noise. When I turned back to Pete, I double-blinked. Instead of his regular uniform of a button-down and slacks, he wore a full three-piece suit, complete with a silver-and-black-striped tie. His

206

hair was slicked back, and holy crap, were those cufflinks? I'd told him how important today was, but unless there was a funeral, Pete refused to wear a suit.

My own starched khakis and dark purple dress shirt felt too casual. I was the one who usually wore a suit to these meetings, but Teddy Ray was a no-bullshit kind of guy and I wanted it to seem like I wasn't trying too hard.

Pete caught me staring at his tie. "Don't worry. The suit's not for the presentation. I've got a meeting with the bank later."

He stepped inside my office, Bogie trotting up beside him. "What's going on? You look like you haven't slept in days."

I stayed quiet, not wanting to tell him about all the issues in Ivy Falls, which would only prove I wasn't keeping my word. Giving one hundred percent of my time to this pitch.

He picked up Bogie and sat in the chair near my desk. "Is it Piper? Are you worried she's using again?"

I eased down onto the edge of my desk. "No. We had a good visit while she was here. It's just that I keep calling her and she's not picking up."

Pete ran his hand over Bogie's head and the dog gave a little snort. "At some point you have to stop being her protector. She's a grown woman. You can't make choices for her."

"It's different with Piper, though. One bad night and…" I broke off, not being able to finish that horrific thought.

"I get it. I've had my own issues with my little brother, but we can't live their life for them, Beck. That's something you have to accept."

Deep in my gut I knew he was right. It was what my therapist said to me on repeat. But I was her only family, and it was my responsibility to keep her safe. To protect her from the cruelty of the world, even if she didn't want me to.

"About today." His mouth went firm. He knew I hadn't put in the time. "I've seen the entire pitch. Twice." His lips formed into a slow smile. "I was worried a few weeks ago about whether you had this under control, but it all looks good. The jingle alone is amazing. The last few months have been rough, but I feel like today is a turning point." He stood and crossed to the window, Bogie tucked under his arm. "Looks like our guest has arrived."

I moved up beside him and stared at the black SUV idling in front of the building.

"Don't let that good ol' boy intimidate you. You've done the work and it's better than anything Brinkley has ever had in their stores. Trust your team. Trust yourself and let's get this done."

He clasped my hand and I gave it a firm shake. My world felt like it was righting itself. That the tides were finally shifting in my favor.

※ ※ ※

"Second presentation today!" Teddy Ray Jones swept through the glass doors and into the conference room, the scent of heavy cologne trailing behind him. He took the seat at the head of the table, his tree-trunk arms settling over his potbelly. "This better be good. I'm wasting time and money by sitting here." He swung around in his chair, his eyes flitting over the room until they landed on me. "Mr. Townsend, the clock is ticking."

I still couldn't get over the fact that this bear of a man ran one of the biggest restaurant chains in the country. His hair was dyed shoe-polish black. The flannel shirt and jeans he wore said he was ready to milk a few cows, not listen to an advertising presentation.

He dressed down to throw people off, tired of everyone kissing up to him and his Wharton School business degree. Thanks to a few phone calls to his former staff, I knew all of this and planned on using it to my benefit.

"Today, we thought we'd start the presentation a little differently."

Sienna moved to the stool waiting for her in the center of the room. She picked up her guitar and slid the red-and-black woven strap over her head.

Teddy Ray tented his hands on the table in irritation. "Didn't come here for a concert."

Ignoring his comment, I gave Sienna a smile of encouragement. A single strand of magenta hair floated across her forehead. She strummed out the first chord and then a low plunk and a popping sound stopped her. The room stayed silent. Sienna froze.

Teddy Ray groaned and pointed to his watch. "Tick. Tick. Mr. Townsend."

I rushed toward a panicked Sienna. "What's wrong?"

"I broke a string," she whimpered.

"Do you have more?"

"Yes, in my case." The corner of her eyes watered, reminding me of Piper.

"It's all right. Go fix it. I'll take over until you're ready."

She jumped off the stool and rushed to the black case propped near the door.

This was one of those moments Torran talked about. Where all eyes were watching and what you chose to do next made all the difference. These past months I'd been torn between my job, Torran, my sister and all the memories of my parents. It had been a storm building in the distance waiting to come to a head.

My next move determined my future and I had to think fast. I nodded to Marissa who slid my laptop toward me.

"Our team has done a little research." I tapped at the keys and brought up the four-color rendering Torran had sent me. "This is a property in a small town called Ivy Falls which is about a forty-five-minute drive from here. We worked with a historic renovation firm to scout properties and put together a proposal for your company. This house was built in 1885. It still has good bones and a solid foundation. It would be the perfect site for Brinkley's next restaurant."

Teddy Ray pulled the screen forward. "1885, you say? Don't think we've worked on one that old before have we, Sam?"

One of Teddy Ray's suited minions shuffled to the table. "No, sir. That's the oldest, Mr. Jones."

"And this company can do it right, sir. They are also currently filming a TV pilot for the Hearth and Home Network. There's a possibility if the show gets picked up, they could feature this renovation, *your renovation*, in the future."

"Hearth and Home, you say? My wife Georgia loves those home shows!" He snapped his fingers and Sam took down the property's address and Torran's business information.

"Beck, uh, Mr. Townsend, I'm ready." Sienna's small voice forced me to step back from Teddy Ray, who continued to stare at the screen with interest.

Sienna strummed out the opening chord once again. "*Brinkley Foods brings you the best of Southern tradition,*" she sang in a wobbly voice. "*Hot wings, cold beer, and turkey pot pie, and you can never ever go wrong with a delicious side.*" Karl pressed a button on his computer and the sound of the recorded track flooded the room.

Teddy Ray cracked his neck from side to side and heaved out a long breath like the song was a waste of time. When the chorus rolled around, things changed. He began to bob his head as Sienna strummed out the jingle. By the time the third progression of lyrics started, the whole room was buzzing. Teddy Ray even managed to crack a smile at the line about the *homestyle biscuits being better than your mama's.*

As the final line faded out, Teddy Ray leaned back in the chair. His stare moved between my laptop and Sienna. The rest of the presentation hinged on the song. If Teddy Ray didn't like the restaurant idea, or the jingle, it was game over.

Teddy Ray tapped his fingers against the wide oak table. Marissa, the lead account executive, sat frozen in her seat. I wasn't sure Pete was breathing. No one in the room dared to move.

"Miss, what's your name?" Teddy Ray finally drawled out.

Sienna's big brown eyes went wide. Her mouth opened but no words came out.

"Her name is Sienna," I said.

Teddy Ray narrowed his eagle eyes at me. "I'm talking to the young lady." He focused his attention back on Sienna. "Did you write that jingle?"

She managed a small "yes."

He cracked his knuckles one by one like he wanted to torture every single person in the room. Finally, one side of his mouth twitched up into a grin.

"It's a mighty fine tune. I'd love for you to play it again. Except this time I'd like to hear it say 'homestyle biscuits being better than your grandmama's.' It'll remind folks that Brinkley's been around a good long time."

Pete's face broke into a wide smile as the entire room, including Teddy Ray's entourage, clapped along to the jingle one more time.

34

TORRAN

Bulldozed Into My Life And Flipped It Over.

EVEN though my nieces' laughs were loud enough to shake the birds from the trees, I couldn't keep my eyes open. I lay on the blanket spread across the grass in anticipation of today's Fourth of July festivities. The morning sun peeked through the bright green leaves and warmed my cheeks.

After the permit fiasco, work on the house was way behind. I'd been up all night adding finishing touches to the upstairs bathroom, adding new sconces and two gilded-frame mirrors which sat perfectly above the white porcelain pedestal sinks we'd installed. The bathroom was next on Lauren's filming list, and I wanted to make sure it was in tiptop condition before the production crew arrived on Monday.

An insulated cup brushed my fingers and I cracked open one eye to find Tessa standing over me.

"Large coffee with one squirt of that vanilla creamer you like and three sugars."

"Have I ever told you that you're my favorite sister?"

"I'm your *only* sister," she snorted.

I took a long sip, begging the caffeine to do its magic. My shoulders ached, and the knot in the back of my neck still throbbed, but a final dark caramel stain covered all the hardwood floors in the house.

A happy flutter filled my chest. We were so close to the end, and the house was better than I could have ever imagined.

In front of our blanket, Iris and Rose chased each other in circles. The red, white and blue hems of their dresses swirled out in wide circles. Miss Cheri and Mrs. Vanderpool played cards nearby with "Fixer Ferris." By the grim set of his mouth, the ladies were beating him at Hearts.

"Hey, you two," I said to my nieces, setting down my cup in the grass and pulling them into a hug. "Your bikes ready to go for the big parade?"

"Yes! Mommy let us put lots of ribbons on the handlebars," Iris crowed, her burnished copper hair shining in the sun.

"And Mr. Manny put patriotic lights on our spokes that sparkle and glow when we pedal. He did the same thing for Lou's bike too." Rose plopped into my lap; her curtain of blonde bangs plastered against her sweaty forehead.

I caught Tessa's eye. "Wasn't that nice of Mr. Manny? Isn't it great that he drops by so much?"

"Girls." Tessa quickly looked away from me. "I forgot napkins. Run to the ice-cream vendor near the fountain and grab some."

Iris took Rose's hand and they headed the hundred yards across the lawn in front of town hall.

"Please don't say those things about Manny in front of the girls," Tessa grumbled. "They're already too attached."

"Tessa, I see the way he looks at you."

"Stop. He's a friend. That's all. I can't handle any more than that right now."

The edges of her eyes watered and she sucked in a quick breath.

"Fine, not another word as long as you promise me a refill after I've finished this cup." I made a zipper motion over my lips and pretended to throw away an invisible key.

Tessa laughed as the girls raced back toward us and shoved a handful of crumpled napkins at her. "Speaking of deals, is Beck making an appearance today?"

"Yes. He's at the office waiting on a contract, but he promised he'd be here for dinner and fireworks."

I couldn't keep the smile from my face. When Beck had called to tell me they got the Brinkley account he had sounded like a child let loose in a candy store. He profusely thanked me and Manny for helping with the property idea, but in the end it was him and his team who put in all the work. I was so proud of him and I had to admit it was a great opportunity for our business too.

"Dad is planning on joining us for dinner." Her lips pinched together. "He'll give his regular speech on the steps of town hall and then come on over." She lowered her voice to a strained whisper. "Please try and keep things civil for the girls."

Lack of sleep and wanting to keep the day happy for my nieces had me vowing to play nice.

"Tell me more about the house." Tessa shifted her hands back on the blanket and kicked out her legs, settling the edges of her white sundress over her knees.

"I will but I have a question for you first." I set my cup down and settled my hands in my lap. "Are you having financial problems with the P&P?"

All the sun-kissed color drained from her cheeks. "Who told you that?"

"That anonymous email I talked about at the council meeting alluded to the fact that a lot of businesses in town are struggling." I kept my focus on her. "And I noticed that the shelves at the store look kind of empty."

She pushed the thick black sunglasses back up the bridge of her nose with a shaky hand like she thought she could hide from me.

"Please, Tessa. We don't keep secrets. Tell me what's going on."

"Since Mom passed, the shop has not met its monthly sales goals. People are buying more and more from online stores. Local authors are going to bigger cities to have their launch parties. As a result, I've barely made my last few payments to the bank." She grabbed a napkin and dabbed at her cheeks. "I've let Mom down and I don't know what to do."

I wrapped my arms around her and smoothed down her hair as she shook under the weight of all her responsibilities. "She'd be damn impressed by how hard you've been working, Tessa. How you'd do anything to keep the store going."

A quick thought hit me and I couldn't hold back my next question.

"Did you send the email to Hearth and Home? I'd understand it if you did."

"I wish I was the one who'd been smart enough to think of it, but it wasn't me."

I played with the edge of the blanket. "Do you think it was Dad?"

She leaned back and stared up at the trees. "As much as I'd like to say yes, I don't think it could be him."

"Me neither. Supposedly the email was sent from a computer at the library. If Dad was going to do something like this, he'd totally want to own it."

"True." She kept her eyes focused on the sky above. Several times she blinked like she was holding back more tears.

"Hey," I said, snuggling closer to her on the blanket. "We'll figure this out together. If anyone knows how to bring a business back from the brink, it's me. I mean, how many people can say 'fuck' several times on a home renovation show and still have a running business?"

"That's true." Tessa snorted out half a laugh in between her sobs. "The girls though, they'd be crushed if I lost the store. The P&P is like their second home and they've already been through so much."

I placed my hands on Tessa's shoulders forcing her to look at me. "The P&P will not go under. I'm doing the show and hopefully that'll bring people to town. If that doesn't work, we'll put together a plan, even if it means going to Dad for help. And you know how much it pains me to say that."

"Okay. A plan. That's good," she said, swiping at her cheeks again. "Enough crying for now. Please tell me more about the house. I need a good distraction."

"The kitchen is gorgeous. I managed to save the built-ins, and the refinished cabinets are perfection. After putting out some feelers to local antique dealers, I located some circa-1900 drawer pulls."

She gave me that knowing nod like she could picture everything I was saying. "Mom would be proud of what you're doing for Ivy Falls, Tor." Her eyes darted around the busy square. "She loved this town so much."

"I think that's why she wanted me to work on Huckleberry Lane. She knew if we could get it done it would be positive for the town. I just wish there was a way to prove to everyone that the restoration of the house, the production, it's all good for business."

As soon as I said the words an idea began to fill my head.

"What do you think about holding a community open house after it's finished? Invite the entire town to come and do a walk-through. Maybe then they'd all see how committed Manny and I are to the town."

"I think they already know that after your speech at the council meeting. But inviting everyone inside could certainly quiet the last of the complaints."

"I'll talk to Manny. See what he says."

"He admires you. Trusts your judgment. I'm sure he'll agree."

Iris and Rose continued to run around the park as the sun inched farther up into the sky.

"What happens now that the house is almost done?" she said casually. "Will you and Beck continue to see each other?"

I kicked at a small dirt clod with my flip-flop. "I'm not sure. Things have been busy with his work." I opened my mouth to say more but couldn't find the words.

"What are you holding back, Tor?"

"I can't ignore that when he's around it feels like the fractured pieces of my heart are suddenly whole. That the world feels brighter when we are together."

"That's good, right?"

"I'm scared. He cut me off once and I don't ever want to feel that kind of pain again. It nearly broke me last time, Tess."

She gripped my hand and gave me that unwavering stare. "From what you've told me, he's been through a lot since his parents' death. Maybe the two of you were meant to be. The house being the catalyst forcing you back together. But you'll never know until you fully open your heart to him again. Are you ready to do that?"

"He's spent these last weeks telling me about his life and the accident. All of his surgeries. What he's done to keep Piper sober. I think I love him more now than when we were kids."

The words spilled out before I could stop them.

Shit. I still loved Beck.

Tessa clapped her hands together and let out a small squeal. "Yes! I knew it." She threw her arms around me and tucked me into a warm hug. The girls, as if sensing something was happening, flew toward us until we all dissolved into a dogpile of hugs and kisses.

Beck had bulldozed into my life and flipped it over, but he'd also supported me, pushed me to take chances with the house. That day we sat in the council room, his steady gaze never wavering, I finally understood what I'd been missing these last years. I'd been holding on to the memory of him so tight and it'd made it impossible for me to open my heart to anyone else.

It was like something deep inside me had always been waiting for him to return. To prove to me that he was worthy of being a part of my life again. For better or worse, Ivy Falls was rooted in my blood just as my love for him was permanently stamped onto my heart.

"So after all that confession, what's your number today?"

The twinkle in Tessa's eyes said she already knew my answer.

"Definitely a solid seven," I replied.

Her beautiful laugh carried all the way up into the high branches shading us from the midday sun. Rose wrapped her little arms around my neck. "Piggyback to the car to get my bike?" she begged.

"Of course!" I hefted her up and moved in step with my sister, who led Iris through the maze of people who made Ivy Falls home.

35

BECK

You Can't Expect Me To Take You Seriously When You're Wearing That Shirt.

I tried not to panic when Piper's phone went straight to voicemail for the tenth time. She'd called and left a message during the Brinkley meeting. In her usual pissy tone, she insisted she was fine. Pete's words about not living her life for her bounced around like a ping-pong ball in my head. He was right, but it was hard to shake my need to check on her. Make sure she was doing okay.

"It's a holiday. Get your ass out of here." Pete stared at me from the doorway. Bogie sat beside him, panting with his little pink tongue hanging out. A red, white, and blue bow tie hung around his neck and matched the outrageous paint-splatter-style shirt Pete was wearing.

"I'm working on it. The Brinkley contract came in late yesterday and I wanted to look it over."

I slid the ringer to high and pushed the phone into my pocket. After Sienna promised to change the line about the biscuits, and we guaranteed he could see the Ivy Falls property in person, Teddy Ray gave us the account. I believed he'd honor our handshake, but I couldn't rest until I saw his signature on our contract in black and white.

Pete took two long strides toward my desk and shuffled the various papers into a small pile. "As your closest friend and partner, I'm ordering you to leave."

His attempt at being a hard-ass sucked. "You can't expect me to take you seriously when you're wearing that shirt."

"Hey, this is a tribute to Jackson Pollock. At least I'm being patriotic." He pointed to my white polo and khaki shorts. "Where are your stars and stripes?"

My worries about Piper were on the tip of my tongue, but he'd just tell me again that she had to live her own life. It was the truth but I still couldn't figure out that instinct to hover. To always want to protect her.

I grabbed my keys and wallet off the desk, ignoring his question about my wardrobe choices. "Fine. I'm leaving."

"Going to see that girl of yours?"

I couldn't keep the smile from my face. "Yes. Ivy Falls has a habit of turning Fourth of July into a spectacle. They have a parade down the center of town followed by a barbecue and fireworks show."

"Sounds like good, clean fun." Pete smoothed a hand over his mouth. That sad, faraway look colored his face again.

"What do you have planned for today?"

"Thought I'd take a ride on my Harley with Bogie in the sidecar. Maybe grab a burger and a beer in Leiper's Fork. Catch the fireworks along the Cumberland."

"Alone?"

Pete shrugged. "My brother is busy with his own life in Atlanta. And my mom." He rolled his eyes. "She's probably off on another one of those silver singles cruises." He slumped into the chair in front of my desk. "It's times like these I wish I had my own family. Not spent so much time working on my career. While I appreciate this business we've built, I'd love to have some other focuses in my life besides this agency and Bogie." He reached down and gave the dog a little head rub. "No offense, bud."

An idea quickly formed in my head. "Do you like berry cobbler?"

"That's a turn in the conversation," Pete joked.

"Answer the question."

"I'm pretty sure they'd revoke my 'good southern boy' card if I said no."

"Glad you said that." I snatched his keys out of his hands. "I think it's time I officially introduced you to Ivy Falls."

36

TORRAN

As Usual, My Father Has Crappy Timing.

SOUNDS of the twelve-piece band tuning up in the gazebo floated through the muggy air. The once empty lawn in front of town hall was now awash in colorful blankets, picnic baskets and squealing children sugared up on popsicles and cotton candy. The scent of barbecue from the Ivy Falls High School band fundraiser filled the air.

Tessa and Manny sat beside me on the blanket while Iris, Rose and Lou chased a butterfly they'd spotted. Their hair stayed matted to their sweet little foreheads after the long ride along the parade route.

Around us other families started to settle in for the afternoon, tossing around footballs and flying kites. I scanned the crowd for the one face I ached to see.

When we were alone after tonight's festivities, I was going to tell Beck I loved him. I'd been fighting it since I'd first seen his legs dangling from the ceiling, but now with the house nearly complete, I wasn't sure what would happen to us once it was done. All I could do was be honest about my feelings and hope he felt the same way.

"Looks like there's about to be a party around here." Beck hovered behind me. I jumped to my feet and quickly slid my arms around his waist.

"I was wondering when you'd appear."

He placed a warm kiss on top of what I was sure was a very sweaty head. He wound me in closer like he didn't care. "I kind of got kicked out of the office."

"Kicked out?" I said.

A man wearing a ridiculous paint-splattered shirt, a day's worth of dark stubble and a wide grin walked up to the blanket. Trotting alongside him was the cutest black-and-white dog I'd ever seen.

"Torran, this is my partner, Pete," he said.

We shook hands before I was pushed out of the way by Iris and Rose.

"Puppy!" they squealed, asking simultaneously if they could pet the dog.

"Of course." Pete smiled. "Bogie loves a good belly rub."

Once the girls were done fawning over the dog, Tessa stepped close to give the little mutt a small pat on the head.

"Pete, this is my younger sister, Tessa, and these are her two girls, Iris and Rose." I pointed to Manny. "That guy, and the beauty on his shoulders, are my partner, Manny, and his daughter, Lou."

He nodded in Tessa's and Manny's direction and then bent his long legs so he was eye-to-eye with Iris and Rose. He reached out a hand to each girl and gave them a firm shake.

"It's nice to meet you both." For the first time I could remember, both girls stayed perfectly quiet as they stared at him. "If I had to guess, I'd say both of you have had cotton candy today. Am I right?"

The girls swapped a surprised look.

"How could you tell?" Rose squinted her little eyes like she was trying to figure him out.

"Bright pink rings along the corners of your mouths," Pete teased.

"That's cheating," Iris said, finding her own voice.

Pete stood and his stare moved over the grass, to the gazebo, and then to the massive American flag hanging along the side of town hall. "Beck, you weren't kidding about this place. Teddy Ray is going to love the vibe." He turned to me. "When do you think we can bring him here?"

"We've got a lot going on right now with Beck's house. Maybe in a few weeks when we're done," I said.

"Yeah, Beck finally told me about it and the show too. Congratulations."

"We're not done yet," Manny grumbled, tucking his arms across his chest.

"I see a Frisbee on the corner of that blanket," Pete said. "Would you girls like to play?"

They squealed in delight. "Can we, Mommy?" they asked.

"Yes, but stay close."

Pete gave Tess a friendly smile and Manny glared at him like he was an uninvited guest. Manny wanted to give Tess her space but that didn't mean he wasn't going to stare down any good-looking guy who walked within ten feet of her.

The girls grabbed the Frisbee and yanked Pete and Beck toward an open patch of grass.

"Manny, why don't you and Lou go too?" I said.

"Fine," he grumbled. He took a step forward and then stopped. "Tor, did you tell the drywall guys to lock up last night?"

"Yes, their boss has a key. Why? Is there a problem?"

"Lou reminded me that I left my favorite hat at the house. When I went to grab it this morning, there were some windows open and the deadbolt on the back door wasn't latched."

"It's been hot lately and those guys worked late. I'm sure they just forgot."

"Yeah, guess you're right. I made sure everything was locked before I left." His gaze wavered back to where Lou stood with the girls.

"Go play with them." I shooed him in their direction and he mumbled something about "unwanted visitors."

After a half an hour, Beck wandered back to the blanket and sank down beside me. He pulled me in close and nuzzled his face into my hair. "Sitting here with you feels like a dream I never want to end," he whispered.

"A few months back it would have taken an army to force me to be in the center of town with practically every member of Ivy Falls. Or to sit here with you," I confessed. "But that's the crazy thing about life, you never know what's around the next corner. My mom always said if you had a bad day it was okay because when the sun rose again you got another chance."

He pressed a kiss to my forehead. "That's what this feels like—a second chance."

The tenderness in his eyes made my heart ache. I'd never expected for this beautiful man to return to my world. To flip all my plans upside down.

Beck leaned in and pressed a kiss to my lips. I couldn't get over the way his touch blasted heat through my veins. How the feel of his mouth caused every inch of my skin to hum. I tangled my fingers through the back of his hair and his kiss turned into a smile.

"While I'd love to lie you down on this blanket and do naughty things to you, I think the local ladies would not appreciate the show."

Old Mrs. Vanderpool sat on a nearby quilt and couldn't hide her look of horror. On the blanket beside her, Isabel wore a wide grin. She moved to her feet and approached us.

"Uh-oh, incoming," Beck said.

"Torran and Beck! It's good to see you." Isabel bounced toward us with a little too much glee in her step.

"Love the glasses. They're very patriotic," I teased.

She pressed a hand to the red, white, and blue star glasses perched on her face. "Got them from Minnie's Market. Have to dress the part, right?"

"Of course," I said.

"How is everything going with Huckleberry Lane?" She leaned in. "Word around town is it's a stunner!"

Beck and I swapped a smile. "It's coming along," I said.

"When will your sister move in? I know a lot of people in Ivy Falls will be glad to have her back," Isabel said.

"Well, I've been thinking—" Beck was interrupted by a jarring reverberation of microphone feedback.

"Welcome, Ivy Falls." My dad's gruff voice cracked through the air. "Please gather over by the town hall steps as we're ready to start our traditional singing of 'God Bless America.'"

I wanted to hear Beck finish his sentence but, as usual, my father had crappy timing.

Isabel raced back to her blanket as the crowd shifted toward the steps. Bright orange flares of the wavering sunset eased behind town hall. Fireflies zipped through the oncoming night with their hypnotic green glow. My father tapped at the microphone again and began his speech.

While I had many issues with Miles Wright the father, Miles Wright the mayor was a great steward for the town. His speeches were always filled with hope and created a sense of town pride that lifted up each citizen. I only wished he'd applied that same type of fervor to his own family.

Once the band finished the final bars of the song, Dad tapped the mic again. "Now, for the moment you've all been waiting for." He gave a dramatic pause. "The winner of this year's 'The Sign Says It All' contest is…"

The band came in on cue with a drum roll.

"Congratulations, Barb and Susan and all the folks over at the Sugar Rush Café. Their winning entry is… *What Do You Call A Sprinting Donut? A Sugar Rush.*"

Barb and Susan shared an excited hug and kiss as the entire crowd cheered.

"Bonus points to the ladies for working the name of their shop into their saying!" Dad added with a laugh.

After more applause for Barb and Susan, I chased the girls back to our spot on the grass. Glasses of lemonade and bottles of water made their way around our group as everyone ate and shared stories of past Fourth of Julys. Amos joined Isabel and Mrs. Vanderpool who sat next to Diego's family. They laughed and cheered as they all played cards.

Tessa and Manny sat further back on the blanket engaged in a deep conversation. I couldn't hide my smile. They could claim they were "just friends" all they wanted but there was something real between them.

Pete sat next to his dog in the grass and the little girls hovered close by. Earlier, Pete had talked my ear off about the sketches we'd sent for the Brinkley pitch and how Ivy Falls lived up to all of Beck's hype. He was intense but I liked how he and Beck worked as a team.

How he seemed to know about Beck's past, and Piper's issues, and supported Beck through it all.

Afternoon slowly morphed into evening and a bright bulbous moon rose over town. A smattering of stars shimmered like diamonds in the clear night sky. The first thud filled the air and a bright red blaze shot across the heavens. I reached back for Beck's hand but he was distracted by his phone. I didn't like the way his face twisted with worry.

"What's wrong?"

"I keep trying to get a hold of Piper but it goes straight to voicemail."

"She's probably out with friends. Having some fun." I pressed a hand to his cheek. "Let's enjoy this moment. We've earned it."

He leaned into my touch and everything felt right. Like we were meant to be together. Like nothing could ever keep us apart. I'd been so scared of what his returning meant to my life, but with every moment we spent together all I could see was a future filled with intimate touches and bright new memories.

I inched back between his legs and he wrapped his arms around my waist. The crowd ooohed and aaaahed as bright blue and white blasts punctured the night sky. Beck pressed a kiss to my ear, and I settled into his arms. The lull of his steady breaths brought me a kind of happiness I hadn't felt in a long time.

As I began to relax, movement in the crowd caught my eye. My father waded through a sea of blankets and picnic baskets. The haunted look he wore said something was wrong.

"I need a word with you both," he said once he reached us. Manny and Tessa moved to stand too, but Dad waved them off. "Not now."

Beck and I followed him through the maze of families, finally stopping at an open spot behind the town's gazebo.

"Minutes ago I got a call from Sheriff Brewer. It seems their dispatch received a call for a disturbance at 2227 Huckleberry Lane."

"That's not possible. There's no one there," I said.

My father hesitated, swiped a hand over his mouth as if he was trying to figure out what to say next.

"What else is going on?" I pushed.

"After the first call came in, a second one followed. This time it was a request for an ambulance."

"We have to get to the house," I said, gripping Beck's arm. "Dad, go back and tell Manny what's going on, please."

Beck was right behind me as I sprinted toward where Sally Mae was parked in front of the bank. Once we were buckled in, I sped through town.

"Whatever it is, Torran, we'll handle it," Beck said.

All I could do was focus on the road ahead and pray he was right.

37

BECK

Straight Into My Living Nightmare.

FLASHING red and blue lights greeted us when we turned on to Huckleberry Lane. Several police cars faced the house and an ambulance idled in the driveway. Along the curb, a half-dozen people sat with their hands zip-tied behind their backs.

"What the hell?" I said, quickly unlatching my seatbelt.

Torran made a sharp U-turn and pulled up to the opposite side of the street. Before she could put the truck in park, I jumped out the door. I didn't get twenty feet when a barrel-chested deputy blocked my path.

"Sir, you can't go inside."

"This is *my* house," I pushed back.

Torran rushed to my side. "Hi, Ben. Can you tell us what's going on?"

"Sorry, Torran. I'd forgotten you were working on this place." He rubbed a hand over his shock of black hair, the lines around his mouth turning grim. "We got a call from the neighbors about the front door being open and music blasting."

The radio strapped to his hip squawked and he turned it down. Several other officers shoved partiers past us and out on to the street.

"When we arrived we found several individuals trying to leave with items taken from the house. Once we got inside, we detained most of the suspects who we realized were very high. Deputies started searching rooms and discovered a female passed out on a bathroom floor upstairs. She had a faint pulse so we called 911. Paramedics are with her right now."

"Did you recognize the girl?" Torran asked.

"Nope," he replied. "My guess is none of these folks are from Ivy Falls."

"Can we go inside and look around?" she asked.

"No. It'd be best to stay out here until we get everyone cleared out."

A figure moved out of the shadows and walked in our direction. "Let them inside, Ben. They have a right to see what's going on. I'll take responsibility for the decision," Torran's dad said in his sternest mayoral voice. His gaze moved to Torran and she gave him a grateful nod.

"Of course, sir." Ben stepped aside and I sprinted toward the front door.

A nagging fear pounded in the back of my head. I had to see the damage. Take a look at the girl in the bathroom.

Several deputies stood in the entryway questioning and handcuffing two men and a woman. All of them swayed on their feet like they couldn't find the strength to hold up their own bodies. A painful breath crowded my chest as I jumped over broken beer and wine bottles littering the once immaculate hardwood floors.

Blue and green paint had been splashed across the soft cream walls. The antique light fixture was ripped from the ceiling and sat in pieces on the floor. Along the staircase railing a succession of sledgehammer gouges ruined Manny's beautiful work.

How was this happening? How had these people gotten in here?

A dozen other questions buzzed through my frenzied mind as I took the stairs two at a time. I raced toward the hallway bathroom. Before I could get inside, another deputy blocked my path.

"No one is allowed in," he said, rolling back his broad shoulders.

"This is my house!" I gritted out again.

The deputy waited a beat and then stepped aside. Two bright red equipment bags sat on the counter. Ripped gauze packaging and plastic tubing littered the floor. One dark-haired paramedic placed an IV line in a thin white arm.

I slowly inched forward. My heart practically vaulted out of my throat as I stepped over a smashed bottle of tequila.

"You can't be in here." The dark-haired paramedic waved me back.

Like a zombie, I took another step forward. My breaths came in strangled spurts. When I saw the beautiful face I loved, my knees gave way.

"Oh shit," Torran said from the doorway. "Is that Piper?"

A short black leather skirt sat high up on my sister's hips. Dried vomit covered her face. Her beautiful dark brown eyes rolled back in her head. The paramedic began shouting and started chest compressions.

"Is she not breathing?" My broken voice sounded odd to my own ears.

A young paramedic with short blonde hair raced into the room. "Get out. All of you!"

The deputy tried to pull me back to the door but I fought him off.

"No! That's my little sister. I need to be here for her."

I continued to struggle with the deputy. Torran grabbed the tail of my shirt and pulled me back into the hallway.

"This can't be happening. She's supposed to be in New York," I said, collapsing into her arms.

A loud, angry voice filled the entryway and boomed all the way up the stairs. Manny appeared at the end of the hallway, his eyes ablaze. Without saying a word, he started opening doors. His curses filled the air as he moved from room to room. He stopped at the bathroom and his swearing cut off.

"Is that who I think it is?" he said.

Manny took two steps toward us, and we all sank down onto the hallway floor. The scent of mahogany stain and fresh paint coated the air. The deputy backed out of the bathroom and the stretcher followed. The tinny grind of the wheels rattled in my head.

The dark-haired paramedic appeared and spoke into a walkie-talkie. "Pulse is back but thready. Could have been choking on her own vomit. It's alcohol poisoning or a possible drug overdose. We're on our way in for a full workup."

The blonde paramedic helped pushed the stretcher out of the bathroom. A thin breathing tube lined the area below Piper's nose. The men pushed the gurney forward and toward the stairs.

I jumped to my feet. "Can I come with her?"

The dark-haired paramedic gave me a long look. "Yes, but you need to sit where I tell you and do what I say if she flatlines again."

"Yes." I took a deep swallow. "Okay."

Once they reached the top of the landing, they lifted the gurney and collapsed the wheels. Step by step, the two men made a slow descent toward the front door.

"I'm coming with you," Torran said.

I held out a hand to stop her. "It's been Piper and me all along. My stupidity brought her to this point. To this fucking house. This is on me. I need to take care of her. Alone."

"Beck, *please* let me help you."

"Sir, are you ready?" the blonde paramedic called from the bottom of the stairs.

I turned away from Torran and walked straight into my living nightmare.

38

TORRAN

Look At The Full Board.

I didn't care what Beck said, I was going to the hospital. Only two steps from the stairs, Manny blocked my path.

"Move out of the way," I snapped.

"No. You have to respect Beck's wishes. His sister is very sick, and from his reaction this isn't the first time they've been here. Give them a chance to get her stabilized at the hospital before you go."

"But once I get there, he'll see he needs me."

"When this kind of shock happens, people need time to process. Sort out their feelings. Right now, Beck is nothing but adrenaline. His single line of thought is whether or not his sister is going to make it through the night." Manny's voice rattled like he spoke from experience. "He'll call for you when he's ready."

This was what I both loved and hated about Manny. In a crisis he was the voice of reason, even when I didn't want to think rationally. Most of my life when things didn't go my way, I lashed out. I wasn't sure if it was because of years of watching my father do the same thing, or if it was my need to control everything around me.

Working with Manny had taught me to slow down. To assess a situation and make a decision based on a realistic approach and sound numbers. For me, it was like trying to learn a confusing new game. All the directions were foreign at first, but if I let my mind go quiet, look at the full board, I could make a sound decision. It was just one more thing he'd taught me during our partnership.

The cops wrestled the last of the criminals out of the house. The frenzied chaos turned into mind-numbing silence except for a lone set of footsteps. My father appeared at the bottom of the stairs. I expected another look of disappointment but all that was shining back at me was sadness.

Deputy Ben came back into the entry like he wanted to talk to Manny and me, but my father ran interference again, steering him outside like he understood we couldn't deal with anything else tonight.

"I know you two have issues…" Manny tipped his chin toward the door. "But your dad has been really helpful tonight."

"I know." I struggled to talk over the sob jammed against the walls of my throat.

"Deputy Ben told me that this is a new wave of crime happening. People breaking into new builds and renovations to steal anything they can yank from the walls. It's especially popular with drug addicts. They take what they can carry and pawn it for whatever money they can get." Manny scrubbed a hand over the whiskers on his chin. "This may not be the best time to do this, but should we walk around and survey the damage?"

With a slow nod, I followed him down the long hallway of the second floor.

In the first two bedrooms hammer holes punctured most of the newly painted walls. Fast-food wrappers and empty whiskey bottles littered the floors. In the bathroom where they'd worked on Piper it was worse. The vanity mirror was ripped from the wall. Large chunks of porcelain were missing from the antique pedestal sink.

When we got to the master bedroom, I had to brace my arms against the threshold. In a drug-fueled frenzy, the partiers had gone at the walls with several different colors of paint. The spots they hadn't marked with graffiti they'd destroyed with sledgehammers.

Huge pieces of drywall covered the room leaving a fine layer of white dust on the dark hardwood floors.

Manny scratched a hand through his hair. "A lot of this is cosmetic. We can fix it quickly."

"What about the walls?" I moved slowly into the room. "There's at least two weeks' worth of work here."

He slung a thick, muscled arm around my shoulder. "It's not a problem. I'll call the guys back in and we'll take care of it."

While the bedroom was bad, nothing could prepare me for the horror in the master bathroom.

Used needles and crushed beer cans covered the white tile floor. The only things remaining of the antique cabinets were their dented chrome hinges. They'd even managed to steal the turn-of-the-century silver sconces I'd found at an estate sale outside of Chattanooga.

The sight was too much and I sprinted from the room. When I got to the top of the staircase, I collapsed.

"Hearth and Home is supposed to be here Monday to shoot. The entire future of our business, the livelihood of Ivy Falls, it all hangs on us getting the show finished." I was holding on by a thread. "And we still haven't sold Parkview. Everything is crumbling around us and there's nothing we can do."

Manny bent down and curled his massive arms around me. I melted into his side, not wanting to think about how the entire town was supposed to see the beauty of the house. The way we'd worked our fingers to the bone to bring a part of Ivy Falls' history back to life and how it'd all been destroyed in a single night.

39

BECK

A Devastating New Record.

THE monotonous beat of the bedside monitor was driving me fucking insane. I was glad Piper's heart had a steady rhythm, but every pulse was like an electrical shock reminding me where I was and why I was here.

She'd been unconscious for over twenty-four hours and remained very still in the bed. I'd overheard a few nurses whispering about how her heart had stopped and how long it would take for her recovery.

A new doctor moved into the room clutching a black tablet. His short brown hair was a stark contrast to his long white coat. A mint-green and pink striped tie poked out from under his collar. We'd seen a couple of older doctors in the emergency room, but this guy looked like he was barely out of college.

"I'm Doctor Foster." He shot his hand out toward me.

"I'm Beck. Piper's older brother." I was so exhausted I could barely get the words out.

"I'm filling in for the attending physician who is out today," he offered in a gentle voice. "I was just going over your sister's preliminary lab work." His finger scrolled across the screen. "Things are looking better."

"Oh, good. Thank you for letting me know," I managed to say over the gravel-like knot in my throat.

"Talk to her," he said in a smooth Southern drawl. "Family is often the best medicine in these cases."

"She can hear me?"

"Of course. Her body may be resting but her brain is still firing normally."

I turned and raised a brow like I wasn't too sure he knew what he was talking about.

"For two years I worked in different war-torn cities with Doctors In Service. Had quite a few patients who were unconscious due to bombings, caught in the crossfire during military uprisings. When they woke, they knew their family, or friends, were there. Piper will be the same."

The fervor in his voice said he spoke from experience.

"What's next? When can I take her home?"

"We need to make sure her vitals remain stable for a while." His lips thinned as he closed her chart. "I'm told that we can't release her until police have spoken with her."

In all the hazy moments of the last day I'd forgotten about the house. From the little bits I could remember, it was in bad shape. I couldn't imagine what Manny and Torran were thinking right now. How my sister's actions had destroyed what we'd all been working toward.

Piper murmured quietly in her sleep and I reached out for her hand, her fingers icy to the touch. So many times she'd accused me of treating her like a fragile doll, but that's exactly how she looked now, lying so still in the bed. Her dyed hair fanned out across the pillow while faint traces of her favorite red lipstick stained the corners of her mouth.

How the hell had she gotten this way?

She'd regained consciousness briefly in the ambulance. Once they'd moved her out of the ER, I'd overheard one of the doctors say her blood alcohol content level was 0.27—a devastating new record for Piper.

"I'll take your advice. Try to talk to her."

"She's lucky you're here. Too many times we have patients who come in and have no one looking out for their best interests. No one who cares if they live or die. She already has a fighting chance because of you."

Or she was here because of me.

"I have to finish my rounds. Let the nurse know if you need anything." He flashed me a professional-looking smile and left the room.

The machines continued to hum and beep as a dozen questions spun through my head. Why wasn't she in New York? Who were all those people in the house? Why did they pick it as the spot to throw their party?

None of those questions could be answered until Piper woke up. I couldn't dwell on how or why things had happened. Instead, I needed to figure out what to do next.

My job. The house. Even Torran. They all had to be pushed to the side.

Piper could be my only focus. Bidding on the house, digging up the past, had sent her right back to that dark place it'd taken years of therapy to fix. For all my moaning and worrying, *I* was the reason Piper was unconscious and paler than the sheets covering her body.

Ten years and I still hadn't learned a damn thing. The past was a malevolent bitch, and obviously, she wasn't done with Piper and me yet.

I dropped my head in my hands and swallowed back the ache threatening to burst from my chest. In this moment I needed our parents so much. They'd know what to do. What to say to make Piper think straight. To make better decisions. Pete was right, the oldest was always the caretaker, but that didn't mean we could handle the weight of being a parent. Making the tough decisions for a sibling that we should never have to make.

The plastic chair squeaked beneath my weight as I leaned in and set my head on the bed.

The damage was done. My only task now had to be helping her. Once she was discharged, she had to go back to rehab. I worried she'd fight me and then I'd have to consider a court order. Could you commit your twenty-four-year-old sister when she was clearly a danger to herself?

My thoughts began to spiral. If the police charged her with a crime, she'd need a lawyer.

From the day she was born, I'd always looked out for Piper. Protected her from the monsters she swore were under her bed or hiding in the closet. In elementary school, I hovered near her classroom until she made it safely inside. My parents told us that it was our job to look out for each other. That one day they'd be gone and all we'd have was each other. We both knew they meant when they were old and gray so neither of us were prepared when that fact became a reality too soon.

"Beck?" Piper's childlike voice shot a chill across my skin. I pulled the white plastic chair closer to the edge of her bed. "Where am I?" she asked.

"Memorial Springs Hospital."

With bloodshot eyes, she glanced at the stark bed sheets and the tubes spiraling out of her arms. A beat later the tears followed. "I'm so, so sorry."

Her heart rate clicked up a notch and I squeezed her hand. "It's all right."

"But the house—" She started to sob.

"Don't worry. It all can be fixed."

Her shoulders shook as tears coated her cheeks. "Torran must hate me."

"No. All she wants is for you to get better."

She took a shuddering breath. "You have to believe me, Beck, I tried to stop them from coming in, but Alex told me I had to pay off my debt."

"Who's Alex?" I asked.

"He's a guy I met in a club in downtown Nashville." The tears flowed freely down her cheeks and onto the paper-thin sheets. "When I was high, I told him all about the house. How we were making it beautiful to honor Mom and Dad's memory. He forced me to take him there, then his friends showed up and they started tearing things from the walls saying they could sell it all…"

Her entire body shook and her heart rate climbed higher. I moved onto the bed and pulled her into my arms. "We can't go back, Piper. All we can do now is get you help. The rest will sort itself out later."

I wanted to ask about what happened after I dropped her at the airport. The job she supposedly had waiting. But all those questions stayed jammed in my throat as she swiped away her tears.

"Am I going to jail?"

"I don't know. A cop has been here off and on waiting to question you. He needs to know how you got into the house and any details you can provide about that Alex guy and his friends."

"He wasn't arrested?"

"I'm not sure. We were told a bunch of people scattered when the police showed up."

The door creaked open and Torran stepped inside the room. Her blonde ponytail flopped to the side and purple hollows colored the area below her beautiful green eyes.

"Is it all right if I come in?" she asked.

While I ached to touch her, I wanted to finish my conversation with Piper in private.

"Can you give us a minute?" I heard my voice and knew it was too rough.

Hurt rippled across her face but she backed out of the room.

"Wait," Piper called. "Beck, I need to talk to Torran alone."

I reached out and gripped her hand. "You sure?"

"Yes. I need to start making amends again." The words tumbled out of her mouth in a way that made me want to wrap her in my arms and protect her from the cruelty of the world.

I pushed back from the bed and headed for the door. "I'll be right outside." I gave Torran a brief smile which she barely returned.

Once out in the hallway, I was greeted by a pacing Tessa. Pete stood a few feet away looking at his phone.

"How is she?" Tessa asked.

"Groggy and very sad. But she's coherent and talking so I don't think there's any permanent damage."

"We're all here for you. Whatever you need," Pete said.

"I'm going to take a leave of absence," I said to him, guilt knotting in my gut. "I know we just landed the Brinkley account, and I hate to let you down, but Piper is a mess. All I can think about right now is getting her back into rehab."

Pete gave me a weighted look that warned I wouldn't get away easily with my decision.

"Listen, Beck, I'm not letting you walk away from what we've built. I'm your friend first. Partner second. Take all the time you need. Get Piper settled and healthy again. Teddy Ray and I can get to know each other until you're ready to return."

"Thanks." I barely choked out the word. He gave my shoulder a firm squeeze and then disappeared down the hall, checking his phone again.

Tessa's gaze stayed on the door as if she was waiting for Torran to reappear.

"She's talking to Piper. It may be a little while."

"Okay. Tell her I'll be in the waiting area."

"I will," I breathed out.

She stepped in close. "She's a strong girl. You'll all get through this. It'll just take time."

Time.

I wished it could be that simple but I knew better. Because of my thoughtless choices, I'd stirred up the past and sent my sister back to a world where drugs and alcohol were her only comfort. I had to own that decision and accept that it would cost me any future I had with Torran.

40

TORRAN

Figure Out A Way To Be Whole Again.

PIPER poked at one of the many bruises coloring her arms. Tubing sprouted from her wrists like she was a tree growing extra limbs. She focused on her injuries, refusing to look at me.

"Beck said you don't hate me, but I can't see how that's possible after what I've done," she whispered.

I sat in the chair next to the bed, the seat still warm from Beck. "I'm confused. Worried about you. But your brother is right. Hate is not an emotion I'm feeling right now."

"Why not? You worked night and day on the house and my stupidity ruined it," she gulped. "I begged them to leave, to not take anything, but they wouldn't listen. And then someone offered me another shot." She stopped and shook her head. "I knew then I'd messed up and all I wanted was to disappear."

"How did you get in the house in the first place?"

She thumbed the edge of the white cotton blanket on the bed. "There was never an audition or waitressing job in New York. My landlord kicked me out for having too many parties. The last

240

money Beck sent me covered a few debts I had and my plane ticket to Nashville."

A single tear tumbled down her pale cheek.

"I thought if I got away from that life I could have a fresh start here. Seeing the house being restored, it felt like a new beginning. But the more I watched you and Beck together, the more I was reminded of my parents and what I'd lost." Her voice rattled and she gripped the blanket tightly to her chest. "The world started to get dark around the edges, and that aching need I tried to extinguish in rehab resurfaced. I stole Beck's key and made a copy."

Piper's small body trembled in the bed. A part of me wanted to say she didn't have to relive the night, but deep down I needed to know what happened.

"After he dropped me off at the airport, I waited a few minutes and then took a bus downtown. For over an hour I walked along the river until I couldn't fight it anymore." She shook her head like she didn't want to recall the memory. "I went into the first bar I could find. When they kicked me out after last call, I took a ride-share to the house. My plan was to hide out for a while until I could figure out my next move."

"How did those people know about the house?"

"My third night of drinking, I met Alex." She choked on the name. "He fronted me a bunch of money to drink and eat. When I couldn't pay him back, he said I owed him. After a few more shots, I mentioned the house and it all went to hell from there." Piper reached out for my hand. "I'll do whatever I can to fix this. Work three jobs to pay for the repairs. I usually only screw up my own life but now I've destroyed your beautiful work."

My heart ached to see her in so much pain. I wanted to be angry. Scream at her. Tell her she'd caused thousands of dollars' worth of damage, but it was the last thing she needed.

If the tables were turned and it was Tessa in that bed, I'd clear everything from my life to make sure she was safe. I loved Beck and I was willing to do whatever it took to support him as he helped Piper through the next several months. I'd work on the house while he found a local rehab facility for her. Each night I'd be waiting for him, arms open wide, as he returned from helping Piper rebuild her life. Together, there wasn't anything we couldn't face. Working on the house these past few months had proved that fact.

"You can repay me by getting better, Piper. Go back to rehab. Figure out a way to be whole again. If anyone knows how difficult that can be it's me, but you have something special on your side."

"Beck," she said through a rough sob.

"He loves you more than the world. Let him help you get better."

Piper blinked back a few more tears and squeezed my hand as if vowing a silent promise. A promise I hoped she could keep this time.

41

BECK

I Opened Pandora's Fucking Box.

THE last twenty-four hours were a blur. I couldn't remember the last time I'd eaten or gone to the bathroom. All my attention was focused on Piper and the next steps to get her out of this hospital and into a rehab facility where she could learn not to harm herself anymore.

My throat was sandpaper and my eyes burned. I dropped my head into my hands and took two gasping breaths. Air still refused to come like a giant inflated balloon pressed against the walls of my chest. It was the same wave of pain and anxiety that always manifested when Piper had a downward spiral.

I stood and stretched my legs, hoping I could get at least one good breath. The constant whir and hum of machines in the other rooms didn't help the steady rise of my blood pressure. With each step I took, the tighter my chest became. I'd been avoiding the thought for hours, but as soon as Torran left Piper's room, I had to tell her we were leaving. Knowing her, it was not going to be an easy conversation. She'd slowly opened her heart to me over the past weeks, and I was going to crush it again.

Now the cramp in my chest was a solid squeeze.

Holding on to the wall I tried to calm my breathing, slowly taking in air through my nose and letting it out through my mouth.

The door to Piper's room creaked open and Torran slid out into the hallway. She glanced down the sterile corridor, her gaze sweeping back and forth.

"Tessa went to the waiting room."

She nodded and quietly said, "Okay."

I ached to see her so ashen. So rocked by what my sister had done to our beautiful house.

"Are you all right?" I reached out for her and then let my hand drop to my side. She wouldn't want me touching her once I confessed what I had to do next.

"I'm a little tired but I'll make it."

"About the house." I stopped, trying to find the right words. "I'd like for you and Manny to go back and repair it. I'll give you whatever money you need to make it right. When Hearth and Home is done filming and you feel like the house is ready, I've decided I'm going to sell it."

"What? Why?" Her screech ping-ponged around the barren white hallway.

"The house has done nothing but bring back terrible memories. I was wrong to think enough time had passed. That I could waltz back into Ivy Falls, restore my childhood home, and suddenly that would make my world right again."

I tore a hand through my hair and sank back against the wall.

"For some reason I believed I could recapture the past. Will my memories back into some positive light. But my parents' deaths will always haunt both my and Piper's lives. I was an idiot to think any different."

"I get that everything is messy as shit right now, but don't give up on what we were starting to rebuild."

"No. Piper and I have to get the hell out of here. We're going back to San Francisco. I have a friend who runs a rehab facility outside of the city. I'm hoping he can find Piper a bed."

"Don't do this," she pleaded. "We can get through this if we stick together."

The words I needed to say became jumbled in my head. With each desperate look she gave me, I was splitting in two. Part of me wanted to stay here with her. Build the life I thought I wanted. The other part urged me to take Piper far away from the place that had caused all this destruction. My parents would want me to take care of her. Make sure she was safe. It was what I'd done most of my life, and it was the only thing I could do now.

"I can't pretend everything is fine. There are too many memories here," I said. "With you. With the house. By coming back to Ivy Falls, buying the house for Piper, I opened Pandora's fucking box and it almost cost my little sister her life." My voice shook and it took all my strength to stay upright. "She's all I have left in this world," I whispered.

"You're wrong." Torran's warm, beautiful fingers slid along my chin and forced me to look in her direction. "You have me and Pete and Diego. Hell, you have all of Ivy Falls who will support you if you agree to stay and put down roots." She pulled in a rough breath. "The day you outbid me on the house, you asked why I wanted it. I said it was to help the town. In part that was true, but I was also desperate not to lose my last link to you. Please, for the first time in your life, stop running and stay with me."

I wanted so much to pull her into my arms. Let the sweet smell of her wash over me, but the reality of the last hours had sunk in. As long as I acted broken, she wouldn't step away, so I did the only thing I could to make her leave.

"I am not running. This isn't about me anymore. And it certainly isn't about you, Torran." My volume rose with each word. "Stop being so damn selfish and see what's right in front of your eyes. I can't be here for you. My sister needs me. She's the only thing in my life that matters."

The rawest kind of pain etched into the lines around her eyes and mouth and it almost brought me to my knees.

"You can lie to yourself all you want, Beck, but you're scared." Her voice trembled. "After my mother died, it would have been easy to go back to Phoenix. Hide from the memories of her. I didn't realize it back then, but I wanted to be here to help Ivy Falls because it was the place she loved. The place that for better or worse knows me best."

Torran closed the space between us. I should have known she wasn't going to make this easy.

"Forget about me. Forget about the house," she said, her voice barely a whisper. "But Ivy Falls is your home. People here know you. Care about you. They'd do everything in their power to help, but you've gone it alone for so long you can't see that anymore."

"No," I spit out, taking a full step back. "Ivy Falls stopped being my home a long time ago. You'll never get it, Tor. You haven't been through what Piper and I have. Lost your parents in such a brutal way. Even now, if I close my eyes, I can still hear their screams."

I gulped down the fear, anger, and regret that crowded my already tight throat.

"Those flames that took my parents also peeled away the layers of the person I used to be. Destroyed me beyond words. The Beck you knew before no longer exists." I placed that firm mask of indifference on my face. "It was a mistake to come back to Ivy Falls. For these last few months, I've kidded myself into thinking I could have a normal life with you. But this episode with Piper, it's taught me that will never happen. It's always been the two of us, and I won't let anyone else stand in the way."

The tense set of her shoulders returned. "You begged me to be a part of your life. Said this felt like a second chance. Was that all bullshit?"

I did the one thing she hated; I shrugged like none of this mattered. That *she* didn't matter. Just the small movement sent a sharp and excruciating pain through me, but I knew it would bring back that armor I'd tried so hard these last months to peel away.

"You are a quitter and a liar, Beck Townsend!" Her shrill voice bounced against the pale walls, making more than one nurse glance in our direction. "What you told me that night you first showed me your scars, those were promises you never intended on keeping. One sign of trouble and you shut down. It's like with that fake picture you took years ago with that girl. You'd rather lie and hide from the people who care about you than deal with the struggle of facing your own fears. That's a sad and shitty way to live your life."

Deputy Ben appeared at the end of the hall. His eyes darted between me and Torran as he approached. "My apologies for interrupting but I need to speak to Miss Townsend if she's awake."

Torran stared at me for one long moment like I was nothing and it cut all the way to my soul.

"It's fine, Ben. Beck and I are done." She spun on her heel and stalked toward the elevator.

I closed my eyes, unable to watch her walk out of my life for good this time.

42

TORRAN

Grief Is An Unpredictable Animal.

FOUR days later the house still resembled a disaster zone. Deep blue paint soaked into the once beautiful dark caramel stain coating the floors. Hammer gouges took out large swaths of drywall. It was hard to stare at it all and not be physically ill.

Manny and I had managed to hold off Lauren as long as possible, but when she walked inside an hour ago all the color drained from her rouged cheeks.

"How quickly do you think you can fix it?" Lauren said, tapping the pointed toe of her bright red stiletto.

"It's going to take at least two to three weeks for labor and another two for new appliances to be ordered and installed," Manny replied. "But we *can* get it done. Think that will still work with the production schedule?"

Once again, Manny was saving us. I could barely form coherent sentences because I'd slept about five hours in the last few days. Every time I closed my eyes, my argument with Beck in the hospital replayed in my head. What he was going through with Piper was heartbreaking. I wanted to do everything right, comfort him in the way he needed, but I couldn't. All of it was too reminiscent of what had happened ten years ago. Back then he hadn't given me a choice, or let me support him, and it felt like the same thing was happening all over again.

Lauren swept a dark curl from her eyes and checked her phone. "Let me make a call and see what I can do." The grim set of her lips said we were screwed.

"They're never going to give us the time," I said.

Manny sank down next to me on the stairs. "Don't give up. If they want the show, they'll work with us."

I couldn't help the caustic laugh that burst from my lips. "There's no way we can fix this house in five weeks, Manny. You know that. We don't have a crew and the kitchen…" I couldn't finish the sentence. Couldn't think about all the work I'd done to the beautiful cabinets which were mangled and hanging off their hinges now.

"Hang in there. If we're going to do this, we need to be a team."

Like I'd seen him do a hundred times before, he reached for the brim of his baseball cap and clutched it with his thick fingers.

"When Gina died, I thought for sure I would never be happy again. After her funeral, I knew I had to be strong for Lou. That I'd have to be both her parents now." His usually strong voice went thin as he took a deep gulp. "Partnering with you, focusing on these houses, has made me a new man. Given Lou back her father. I need you to stay strong for me so we can get through this dark moment together. You hear me?"

I wasn't sure what would happen with Beck, but Manny's speech tore another hole in my heart. This job, our work, was about so much more than this house. It was about building a future for both of us. I couldn't give up now. Not after all we'd done to build this business from the ground up.

I squeezed Manny's hand as Lauren walked back in.

"You've got five weeks. Get it done and we still have a deal." She stalked back toward the door.

"Too bad I don't have a cute little saying like one of those signs in town to make this all feel better, but we will pull this off. We always do," Manny said on a heavy breath.

249

Lauren stopped and whipped back to face us. "What did you just say?"

"I was trying to put a positive spin on things," he offered.

Lauren flipped her hair from her shoulders and began to pace across the paint-splattered floor. "Torran, can you introduce me to your father?"

"Why?" I said, not liking the way she bounced on her toes like an idea was about to explode from her head.

"Just make the call. I'll explain it all later."

"Yes, of course."

"Good. Now I'm off to make some more calls." She flew out of the house and Manny and I swapped a confused look.

"What was that all about?" he said.

"I don't know but that gleam in her eye kind of scared me."

Manny laughed and pulled me to my feet. I forced myself to look at the damaged floors and paint-splattered walls.

"How are we going to fix all this, Manny?" I said, unable to keep the defeat from my voice.

"We're going to do what we always do. Dust ourselves off and get back to work."

"How? Our crew left to work on a job in East Nashville. It'll be weeks before we can get them back."

The lump grew in my throat as I surveyed the destruction around us.

"Why would Piper do this?" I should have been raging mad at her, but all I felt was sad after seeing her so sick and pale in the hospital. "We spent hours working together. She seemed happy. I thought she loved being here. It makes no sense that she'd allow this to happen."

"Grief is an unpredictable animal. Some people can go through all the steps and be fine. Others hold on to the pain and it slowly eats them alive." Manny slid his hands down over his face, looking so much older than his thirty-one years. "You can dig yourself a hole so damn deep it's hard to climb out unless you're willing to accept a hand to help you."

He didn't often talk about losing his wife, but in moments like these Manny's pain felt as raw as if he'd lost Gina only a day ago.

"You remember how dark those months were after your mom passed?"

"Yes, it was like trying to swim through a thick, black sea."

"You muddle through day after day and eventually with time the pain lessens." Manny let out a shaky breath. "I never told you this, but after Gina died I went to a dark place. Her parents came and stayed for a while to watch Lou. It got so bad that they threatened to take her from me if I didn't seek counseling. It took a moment like that to wake me up."

He skimmed his hand over my head.

"That girl on the floor the other night was in her lowest moment. Luckily enough, there were people here to make sure she'd come out the other side."

Manny's gaze moved to the rough hammer gouges that spread across the once pristine wood floors in the dining room.

"This house is simply drywall, brick and paint, Tor. The stolen fixtures and appliances can be replaced. But Piper, she's in pain. Without family and friends, she'll never be able to claw her way out of her misery. Let's hope this incident shows her it's time to get help and move on."

"I should have pushed back at the hospital. Forced Beck to listen to me."

Even though I didn't want to tell him, Manny had pulled the story about our fight out of me.

"Dammit, Torran, stop it. Just because you're hurting doesn't mean you get to tell other people how to grieve!"

"What the hell, Manny? I thought you were on my side!"

"I am but you have to stop expecting people to act like you want them to when they're in the depths of sorrow. If Beck tells you he needs to take care of his sister, respect that. When Tessa explains she's not ready to date again, be kind enough to heed her words." His voice wavered. "And your dad..."

"My dad?" I recoiled. "What does he have to do with this?"

He scrubbed at the back of his neck. "I know you're still pissed about what happened the day your mom died, but have you ever stopped to think about how hard that must have been for him? To not be with the love of his life when she took her last breath on this earth?"

He kept his focus on a small hole in his jeans like he couldn't bear to look at me. "You're so angry, full of grief, you can't even sit down and have a civil conversation with the man. Your sister sees his anguish. Why the hell can't you?"

His words punched all the air from my lungs and I sank back down onto the step. I'd never seen Manny this worked up before.

"I don't mean to make this any harder than it already is, but sometimes you need to step back and look at the world a little wider. If you do, maybe you can give a small inch of compassion to those around you who are in as much pain as you are."

If anyone else had said those words to me I would have fought back, but Manny was the most honest person I knew. He wore his grief quietly, like a heavy blanket weighing on his shoulders. Gina had been taken from him and Lou much too soon. Instead of cursing at the world, holding his anger in at his loss like I'd done this entire last year, he thought about his daughter. About me. How that fury would crush the relationships in his life that meant so much to him.

My sister had been begging me for months to hear my dad out, and I'd callously refused, not even considering the kind of pain that must be causing.

A hole widened in my chest.

If my mother was here right now, she'd be so disappointed in me.

"I'm sorry about the tough love, but you need it," he said, sitting down beside me again.

I leaned into his thick shoulder and he tugged me in close.

"The good thing is that you have time. Time to work things out with Beck. Time to talk to your dad. Promise me you won't waste another minute."

"I promise. Thank you for putting up with me. I know it's not easy."

The settling creaks of the walls and the cloying scent of spray paint made the house close in around us. It would take every ounce of strength I had to get through this, but I knew it was possible with Manny by my side.

We sat quietly for another minute until he shook his head. "Of all the things they had to destroy, why my beautiful staircase? It was some of my best work." He poked at a broken spindle.

"Aren't you the one who just said it all could be fixed?"

Manny huffed out a small laugh. "Should we start making a list of what we need to tackle in this mess?"

"No," I said halfheartedly.

He pulled me to my feet again and dragged me toward the disaster area that used to be our beautiful kitchen.

43

TORRAN

Coming Out Swinging.

A beautiful magnolia tree with bright white blooms shaded Mom's final resting place at the Ivy Falls cemetery. A recent bouquet of wildflowers—daisies, black-eyed Susans, and forget-me-nots—lay on the marble pedestal in front of her grave. For years, Dad brought her these exact flowers on birthdays and anniversaries. I set my own bouquet of stargazer lilies next to them.

"Bet you didn't expect me back so soon," I said to the marker.

For most of my life we'd attended the Ivy Falls Community Church, but I'd never given much thought to religion until my mom was in her final days. If I really believed in what the Bible said about the afterlife, then I knew Mom was probably up in heaven telling God about all the good books he needed to add to his TBR pile.

I closed my eyes and let the summer sun warm my face. Cemeteries freaked most people out, but I found them comforting. They were always quiet, peaceful, and for the brief moments I was here I felt closer to Mom.

"Things have turned out miserably."

I wasn't sure who I was talking to—her or the universe. I guess it didn't matter because, either way, I needed someone or something to listen.

"Beck is back in Ivy Falls and he's going through some real shit right now. I want to be there for him but he keeps pushing me away. The truth is I don't think my heart can take it again if he disappears."

The tears came freely and I didn't bother to swipe them away. Mom always said a good cry was soul cleansing.

"And the house on Huckleberry Lane." Just saying the words released a heartbreaking ache. "The one you not so subtly told me I should work on is a mess. Part of me feels like it's my fault that it's such a wreck. From the first day I saw Beck so out of place at the auction, I knew he had no clue what he was doing. I should've been more forceful. Made him see it'd be easier if he'd just sell the house back to me, especially since he had no intention of telling his sister the truth or how she'd react when she saw it. But he refused to listen."

"Sounds sort of familiar."

My heart nearly burst out of my chest as Tessa shuffled up next to me on the grass.

"Jeez! You scared the crap out of me."

"Sorry, I thought for sure you'd hear my footsteps."

"No. I was kind of having a moment here with Mom."

She laid her own bouquet of irises down next to mine and eyed the ones left by Dad.

"Hi, Mama," she said quietly before taking the place next to me on the grass. "I'm not even going to ask your number because by the bags under your eyes, and the fact that those overalls look like they haven't been laundered in days, I'd guess you were about a two."

"After the last two weeks, I'd say it was more like a one."

She kicked out her legs, smoothing out the lines of her yellow cotton skirt. "Well, you're in the right spot. I come here a lot to talk to her."

"Does it help?"

"It did last week when Billy never bothered to show for the girls."

A swirl of nausea rocked my stomach. "Tessa, I'm the worst sister ever. I totally forgot."

"It's fine," she said more to the air than me.

"I hate the word fine. It's what you say when you're hurting but you won't admit it to yourself or anyone else."

She blew out a long breath. "I was furious at first. The girls cried in their rooms. Dad showed up a little while after, like he knew Billy was going to bail out. He took the girls to Sugar Rush and Barb and Susan stuffed them with so many donuts I was sure they were going to be sick."

"I'm glad…" I took a thick gulp and offered her a smile. "I'm happy he helped out when I couldn't."

"Listen, Tor. You've got a lot going on between the house and Beck. There are times when you can't be there and I understand."

"I still feel bad that I didn't know. Did he ever call? Say why he didn't show?"

She gave me a sad shrug. "Yes. He fed me some nonsense about car trouble. Promised he'd come next weekend. I told him not to bother. That he'd be receiving divorce papers, and I'm asking for full custody. I'm done messing around with that shithead."

Her cheeks went deep pink but she stuck out her chin like her mind was made up.

"Whoa, Tessa. Way to go!"

"I'm tired of waiting on him to be a good father." She let out a bitter laugh. "He's never cared about me and the girls. Always put his needs before ours. I'm done being his doormat. Getting walked all over just because I'm nice. I deserve a man who is going to believe in me. Love me for who I am. I'm never settling for anything less again."

"Oh my God. Who are you and what have you done with the real Tessa?"

She fixed a steady stare on me. "I'm serious. Things are about to change. I'm not sitting back and letting the store die without putting up a fight. Dad and I have a meeting set up for next week. We're going to talk about simplifying my purchasing habits. Other streams of revenue I can research to bring in more money."

I tugged her in close. "That's my girl. I love that you're coming out swinging."

She put on a determined face but I could still feel her trembling.

"That's enough about me and my problems." She tipped her chin to the marker. "Were you getting any good advice from Mom?"

"I wish. I'd do anything to have just a few more minutes with her. Tell her how lost and broken I've been without her." I plucked a piece of grass and twirled it between my fingers. "If she was here, I know she'd tell me what to do about the house. How to handle things with Beck."

Tessa went quiet. Her eyes focused on the birth and death dates carved into the solid black marker Dad had insisted on. I'd wanted a muted gray. It was like Mom. Much more subtle. But, as usual, he did whatever he wanted.

"She would have liked it here. All the magnolias. The way the gardeners carefully clip all the grass around each headstone."

"True, even though she would have never chosen the one Dad picked."

Her brows pulled together. "What are you talking about?"

"The headstone. We told Dad she'd want gray."

"I never said that. In fact, it was Mom who told Dad this is the one she wanted."

"Are you sure?"

"Yes. You were right there when she spoke about it." She paused and pulled in a heavy breath. "This is the problem, Tor. You have tunnel vision when it comes to Dad. You want to blame him for everything without even knowing or remembering the truth."

"I think I remember everything he's done quite clearly, Tessa," I bit out.

"Really? Did you know that he almost resigned as mayor over the permit incident?"

I blanched. "What are you talking about?"

"He and Amos had nothing to do with it. It was the rest of the council who went behind his back and got the permit held up. Did you even bother to ask how he voted at the council meeting?"

"No. I just assumed he voted against me."

I didn't like the exasperated way she looked at me. "I love you but there are times I want to shake some sense into you."

"Okay." I gave in. "He helped a bit. That still doesn't take away from what happened at the hospital."

She turned to me, her mouth a thin, angry line. "How many times has he asked you to make time for dinner? Or to talk? If you'd get out of your own way, open your eyes for once, you'd see that he's been trying to explain what happened."

"Do you know the truth?"

She dipped her chin down. "We had coffee at Sugar Rush after the council meeting. I pushed him to tell me the truth. We went round and round about it until he finally gave in."

I kept my face emotionless, but I had to admit that it hurt that he'd spoken to her without me there.

"Tell me what he said."

"Mom asked him to stay away. Not to say a word about it to us."

"No," I snapped. "She'd never do that."

She reached out and squeezed my hand. "In those last days, she made it clear that all she wanted was quiet moments with us." Her gaze returned to the marker. "When she set her mind to something, you know she couldn't be swayed. She asked Dad to give that last day to us. She wanted to say goodbye to him alone. In private. The same way she wanted to do with us."

"That's not right. It can't be," I argued.

"Think about it. Was there ever a time in our lives that she asked for something from him and he balked?"

That ache in my throat swelled. She'd always wanted to protect us. Love us with everything in her soul. It didn't make sense that she wouldn't want us all at her bedside when she passed.

"I understand it may be hard to accept. But if you talk to Dad, he'll tell you the truth. When you hear it from him, you'll understand."

"I can't believe it."

Her mouth went firm again. "See, this is what I mean. There's a part of you that's closed off your heart. That's certainly caused by the way Dad has behaved over the years, but it's also caused blind spots for you." A sad smile crossed her lips. "Beck hurt you and you've been carrying around the pain for years. That's made you put up your walls to keep yourself protected. But," she sighed, "it also keeps you from connecting with people. I think that's why you're not fighting for Beck. It's too easy to keep your heart closed. Not be vulnerable with him again."

"He walked away from me, Tess," I ground out. "*Again.*"

258

"Yes, but you know he's wounded. That he's spent most of his life grieving." She took in a low breath like she was ready to deliver a truth I didn't want to hear. "Did you tell him you loved him?"

I shook my head.

"If you can't imagine your life without him, then you need to let go of that part of you that's scared. Track him down and tell him how you feel. Leave it up to him to choose. If he walks away, it'll hurt like hell but at least you can move on knowing you did everything in your power to make it work. Don't let your own grief and anger ruin your chance at love."

She was right. There were so many things in my life I was fighting. My grief for Mom. Anger over the house. Resentment toward my dad. Beck's instinct to run away. Worry that the town would never forgive me. I was so tired. Every part of me felt broken, but even with that knowledge I still believed I was putting up a brave front.

"Hey, I'm supposed to be the strong older sister doling out the good advice," I said.

"Strong? What does that even mean anymore? I read dozens of book blurbs every month that portray the heroine as this fierce soul who's usually brandishing a sword or a dagger. But there is more than one interpretation of the word. For me, being strong is standing your ground in the face of almost unbeatable odds." She looked at me pointedly. "Or forgiving someone who's hurt you, even if you don't think they deserve it."

"When did you get so damn wise?"

"It's all the self-help books I read," she joked. "But seriously, I've been in awe watching you build your own business, battle for what you want, it's inspired me. Made me want to do the same in my own life."

"How can that be? All I've done is screw up."

"There are people in this world who have had everything handed to them. They've never seen a rocky day. Fought against pain and sorrow. But you've had things in your life upended over and over and you still don't give up. It's like you're more committed than ever to succeed. It's inspiring not only to me, but I think to everyone in Ivy Falls."

This time I let out a full laugh. "I'm sorry. Did you see all the people sneering at me at the council meeting? That wasn't inspired. That was an angry mob."

"Why can't you see things even when they're right in front of you?" she grumbled. "After you gave that speech at the council meeting, there wasn't a dry eye in the house. At the Fourth of July picnic, people looked at you with a sense of pride. Like they knew deep down that you were fighting for the town in your own way."

My mind flitted back to the way Isabel and Amos had waved to us from their blanket on Fourth of July. How Barb and Susan had treated Manny and me like we were some kind of heroes when we came in to get coffee and donuts.

"I didn't notice any of it," I confessed.

"I know. That's why I'm here to force you to see the truth." She gave my hand a loving pat. "Now that I've talked some sense into you, what are you going to do?"

"First, I'm going to see Dad. Then I'm going to hunt down Beck wherever he is and tell him how I feel."

She gazed back at the marker. "She'd be proud of you if she was here."

I slung an arm over Tessa's shoulder. "She'd be proud of us both."

44

BECK

Stuck In A Time Loop.

WE'D been driving for twenty minutes and Piper hadn't uttered a single word. I tried not to stare at the baggy T-shirt and thin cotton skirt hanging off her bony frame. Without makeup, she looked ten years younger.

"Stop staring," she said, keeping her gaze pinned to the rolling hills and lush green landscape bordering both sides of the highway.

"I'm not staring, I'm looking for the turnoff. GPS says it should be somewhere around here."

Piper grabbed my phone and I couldn't help but shiver at the bandage on her hand where her IV had been.

"Is that it?" She pointed to a bright yellow sign with the words *Changing Attitudes* in block blue lettering. I slowed the car and made a turn on to an unmarked street. White wood fences lined both sides of the dirt road. In the distance, two brown horses grazed in knee-high grass.

At the end of the long drive an old white farmhouse loomed ahead. According to the doctor at the hospital, the property had been converted to a private rehab facility five years ago.

"I think you're going to like this place. They have a lot of group and individual sessions, and there are horses for equine therapy."

She stayed quiet until I pulled the car into an open space near the front door. I grabbed her suitcase from the trunk and followed her up a short set of steps. Rocking in the wind was a restored porch swing.

Piper glanced at her phone while I set down her suitcase.

"We have a few minutes before I have to check in. Want to sit with me?"

"Sure." I pointed to the swing. "Should we give it a try?"

Her answer was to move to one side and take a seat along the painted white wood.

"Thanks for looking after me these last couple of weeks while we waited for a bed to open. And for not taking me to San Francisco," she said quietly, her gaze moving around the property. "I think this is a better spot for me. Less temptation to run away. And you need to stay here for your work and Torran."

"This is a good place," I agreed. "I can come and visit whenever you need me."

I hadn't broached the subject of Torran with her. She'd asked too many questions, and I couldn't tell her what an ass I'd been when I'd broken things off. How the pain in her eyes nearly brought me to my knees. But it had to be done. My life could only have a single focus now: getting my little sister sober.

"I know I've already said this before, but I'm really sorry about the house. Being there, remembering the past, it shook something loose inside me. And when those guys started stealing and slamming those hammers into the walls, each blow felt like they were harming our parents." She gripped the edges of her skirt, her chin dipping down. "The memories of the house, our past life there was what drove me back to alcohol and drugs, but my time in Ivy Falls was also what forced me to recognize I need more help. Because, believe it or not, I do want to get better."

"I understand. We'll get through this together."

"Will I have to answer more questions for the police?"

Her voice was so small, childlike, it ripped me apart.

"Deputy Ben said he'd call if he needed more information."

"I can't believe Manny and Torran didn't press charges. It's what I deserved."

"Hey," I said, squeezing her hand. "They care about you. Want you to get better."

She bobbed her head and a single tear slid down her cheek. I pulled her into my side, trying to avoid her seeing the pain on my own face.

"When are you going to patch things up with Torran?" She shuffled her feet until the swing stopped moving.

"What do you mean?"

She narrowed her gaze. "Are you a complete idiot? I heard you two screaming at each other outside my room at the hospital."

"I'm sorry. You weren't supposed to hear any of that."

"Why? Because you didn't want me to point out what a total jackass you're being? Or that you've been lying about the fact that you bought the house for me?"

"Can we please not do this now," I said, rubbing at my tired eyes. My sleep habits were even worse. Every time I closed my eyes now all I saw was her laying lifeless on the floor.

"Yes, we will do this *now*. I've screwed up my own life, and I will not drag you down with me."

I was happy to hear the fire in her voice but this was not the time to have this conversation. "That's not what's happening here. I'm shifting my priorities to help you."

"Enough!" she whipped back at me. "You are my brother. Not my savior. Not my keeper. And certainly not my damn parent."

Her shaky hands twisted in her lap. The nurse at the hospital reminded her that her body would continue to rebel as the urge to drink messed with her system. Even though I'd seen Piper like this before, it still felt like a knife twisting in my gut as I watched her struggle.

"You fucking bought me our childhood home thinking somehow it would fix me." She shook her head. "Ten years you've spent caring for me. That's long enough, Beck." Her voice trembled but her lower lip jutted out like she needed me to hear her. "It's not that I don't love and appreciate what you've done. What you've sacrificed. But you can't save me." She leaned forward and clasped her hands in her lap. "Every single choice I've made is because I'm in so much pain I can't see straight. I think about all the things I'll never have with Mom. Watching me get married or holding her grandchildren."

Her voice wavered and she turned her face toward the calm of the countryside.

"The first time I took a drink was after a guy I had a crush on told me it was never going to happen with us. In that minute, all I wanted was Mom. For her to tell me that he was a loser who couldn't see how perfect I was for him." She tugged at a hair that escaped her loose braid. "She wasn't there so I chose the only thing that would numb the pain—first alcohol and then pills. It's a vicious cycle I've depended on for most of my life and it won't end until *I* want it to stop."

Piper rubbed her palms over the thin skirt covering her legs.

"Lying on the floor before I passed out, I focused on that beautiful chandelier Torran hung in the bathroom. In the glass droplets hanging from the iron frame, I saw my own reflection. Gaunt. Pale. Way older than my twenty-four years. I also saw Mom," she said so quietly I barely heard her. "How she'd spent so much time hanging over the edge of the tub during our baths. The way she'd always made sure we had a ton of bubbles. It hit me then how angry she'd be if she could see what I'd done to my life."

She swiped at her cheeks before rolling back her shoulders and sitting up straight.

"Trembling against that cold tile, I swore if I survived it would be the end of my addiction." Her gaze returned to her hands now clenched in her lap. "That I'd try with all my strength to clean up and figure out how to make my life something they'd both be proud of."

"That sounds like a good plan. And I'll help in any way I can."

"No!" Piper jumped up from the swing. "I have to do this on my own. It's time you started living your own life, and that life has to be with Torran. Stop torturing yourself over me. Over Mom and Dad. You're not responsible for their deaths no matter what choices you made."

Her tears came in a flood now.

"It was all an accident. A fucking horrible accident."

I dropped my head into my hands, trying to ignore the raw ache filling my chest. "That moment at the campground still haunts me," I said as a solid wall of pain hit me. "I've replayed it over in my head at least a thousand times and it never changes. I should have done more to get them out. Helped Mom with dinner when she asked. I'm so sorry, Pipe."

She returned to the swing and placed her head on my shoulder. "All these years we've both been hurting because we want to change the past. It's like we're stuck in a time loop, reliving that moment over and over. But if we're going to have any semblance of a life, we need to break that cycle and move on. For me, that means facing my addiction for real this time. And for you, it starts with forgiving yourself and making things right with Torran because, let's be honest, you've never stopped loving her."

"I don't know if she'll take me back. She's too angry. Too hurt. Not that I can blame her after crushing her heart. Twice."

Piper's eyes focused on me with a clarity I hadn't seen in years. "She should be pissed after the shit you've pulled. Ever since Tahoe, you've been running. After college, it was travel. Then all over the place for work. You were only in Atlanta that short time before coming here. It's like you're terrified to settle down. Make a connection with anyone."

She huffed out a breath and ran her hand over the braid running down her back.

"Torran has a right to be angry at me too for what I did to the house. Together we've wreaked havoc on her life. We need to acknowledge that fact and set things right."

"Torran accused me of the same thing. Of always running when things get tough. What if too much has happened for her to forgive me? She has the new show, and once the house is done, people will be falling all over themselves to hire her. I bring too much pain to her life." I shook my head. "She's better off without me."

"I've seen the way she looks at you, Beck. There's a tenderness there that can never be stripped away no matter how badly you've screwed things up."

"I wish I could believe you,"I said over the dry scratch in my throat.

"Do you remember how at Christmas Dad would hide one special present under the tree for Mom? He'd tuck it into a back, low-hanging branch, and pull it out after all the other gifts were open?"

"I can't think about that, about them, right now."

"Do you remember?" she pressed.

"Yes. It was always something handmade like a piece of jewelry or art."

"When Dad gave it to her, Mom would look at him as if he was the only human being on the planet. There isn't a word for how much they loved one another. It was almost eternal. That's the way Torran looks at you."

She placed her pale fingers over the top of my hand.

"Go to the house and tell her how much you love her. Say it over and over until she believes it's true. The two of you are like Mom and Dad." A sad smile lifted her thin, chapped lips. "You were meant to be together. Don't ruin that because you're too afraid your happiness will be wrenched away again because, dammit, that's no way to live."

It was both painful and freeing to hear Piper talk about our parents. For the first time in years, she didn't flinch when she said their names. It gave me hope that she was making the first steps toward recovery.

From the second I'd seen her laid out like a corpse on that bathroom floor, I'd moved back into my guardian role. Shoving everything, and everyone, aside—including Torran.

Her words in the hospital rang through my head. I did turn away from people, refuse to let them help me. It was a pattern woven into the fabric of my existence like the scars etched into my chest and arms.

My mind was empty.

Hell, my chest was a cavern. Like someone had hacked inside me and removed my heart with a dull spoon, ripping and tearing until nothing was left. Without Torran, my future was nothing but a long, barren road. She'd become a steady force in my life. Each moment we'd spent together reminded me that coming back to face my past was the right thing to do. She made me a better person. A better man. But in my fear, my stupidity, I'd thrown it all away.

266

A woman with long brown hair and scrubs covered in the Wonder Woman logo stepped out onto the porch. "Are you Miss Townsend?"

Piper nodded and it struck me again how young and fragile she looked.

"We need you to come inside to check in. There will be a group session right after."

Piper moved to her feet and gave me a tight hug. "Thank you for never giving up on me. I don't think I'd be standing here, living and breathing, if it wasn't for you. But it's time for you to get the hell out of here and work on your own life," she said firmly. "Tell Torran the truth. Apologize. Get down on your knees and beg for a third chance. Don't give up until she forgives your stupid ass and admits she feels the same way." She patted my cheek. "I love you, Beck, but don't come back until she's with you."

I wanted to reach for her again, protect her, but this time I stayed in place, feet planted on the porch as she clutched her suitcase and disappeared inside.

45

TORRAN

Make It Right, Torran.

THE musty scent of dust and my father's pungent aftershave hit me when the door to his office swung open. As a child, I was afraid of his dark-paneled space. The way he sat like an overlord in his stuffed high-back chair, telling people whether he'd lend them money to send their kids to college, open a business. Even then I understood the incredible power he wielded over the people of Ivy Falls.

His phone was pressed to his ear as usual. With a thick finger, he pointed to the wooden chair in front of his desk. He grumbled a few more words into the phone and hung up.

"Do you want anything to drink? A bottle of water?" he asked, like I was a customer.

"No. I'm okay."

His mouth softened and he punched a finger onto his phone intercom. "Isabel, please let everyone know I don't want to be disturbed for the next hour."

"That's not necessary," I insisted.

He waved me off. "Since you've been back in Ivy Falls, you've gone out of your way to avoid both me and this office. Now that I've got you here, I want this time to be uninterrupted."

An uncomfortable beat of silence passed. I smoothed out the wrinkles in my overalls. "Thanks for your help the night of Fourth of July. Manny and I appreciated you handling the police, and, well, all the chaos."

"Of course. You know that's all I want to do. Help." He sat back in his chair with his hands tented in front of him. "Since that night, quite a few people have reached out to me on your behalf." A hint of a smile ticked at his lips. "Several of them have sat in that same chair and expressed how worried they are about you and the future of your business. How this town is better because of all your hard work."

"Yeah, Tessa mentioned that to me."

The creases next to his eyes were deep caverns, and the skin around his once iron-tight jaw now sagged. It'd been a long time since I'd really looked at him.

Manny's comments about accepting how people grieved hit me like I'd struck a brick wall.

"I was at the cemetery yesterday. Tessa showed up and told me the truth about the day Mom died."

He pushed back from the desk and rose to his full six-foot-two height. He might have been gaining in age, but he still carried himself with a strength I had to admit I admired.

"I've been trying to find a way to tell you, but our conversations always turn into arguments. Your mother would have been disappointed about that."

"Our relationship has always been strained," I said quietly.

"Not always. When you were little, you used to love coming here. The tellers would let you count out the checking and deposit slips. They'd give you small bits of change to sort out: pennies, nickels, dimes. It wasn't until I started traveling more that our relationship changed."

"Maybe that's because you were never home. Missing all my track meets and Tessa's dance recitals."

"I was traveling to support our family," he insisted. "That's what a good father does."

"We didn't need more money, Dad. We needed you." I hadn't expected to get choked up, but I began to think about how broken our relationship was. How much Mom had been that bridge between us.

He rubbed the back of his neck. "As a father, you feel a duty to care for your family. It consumes your every thought. You worry about setting a good example. Showing your children what can be achieved through hard work. I was tough on you and your sister because I wanted you to be strong."

"Strong?" I gripped the edges of the chair, trying not to let my temper rise. "You pushed us away. Belittled us. You claim you were working to support us, but we felt abandoned."

"That was never my intention. My first thought was always of you, your sister." He gulped, his face going ashen. "And, of course, your mother."

"Tell me what she said to make you stay away that last day." I paused, softening my voice. "Please, I need to know."

All the blood drained from his face and he took two small steps before sinking back into his chair.

"When your mother accepted the treatment wasn't working, she forced me to make her a promise." He blinked several times and I recognized the pain in his eyes. "We'd been in love since we were in high school. In fact, we were a lot like you and Beck—practically attached at the hip. Together we built a life. She wanted hers to end with me thinking about all the happy moments we'd shared, not watching her take her final gasp of air. She asked that I not be in the room when she passed. That I keep her request quiet so it wouldn't upset you girls."

He ran a hand over his head, disturbing his perfect white helmet.

"By then she was so ill, agreeing to her request was the only thing I could do to ease her pain. She wanted her last memory to be of you two girls. She said she'd carry the image of your faces all the way to heaven."

For the first time in my life, I watched my father's perfectly curated façade crumble. He closed his eyes and pressed his hands to his face. A slow, choked breath hissed through his teeth.

"I loved your mother but I know now it was wrong for me to agree. You girls needed me and I wasn't there. It's a moment I will regret for the rest of my life. You, Tessa, the girls—you are my world. I'm so sorry that I let all of you down."

The heartbreaking pain in his voice sent me back to those moments when Mom had begged me to come home, spend time with him, forgive his past mistakes. Tessa had accused me of having tunnel vision when it came to him and she was right. I'd been so angry and heartbroken over losing Mom that it was easier to take my grief out on him rather than let him explain what happened.

Make it right, Torran.

The words beat out like a drum in my head. The way she looked at me with such intensity that last day. How she gripped my hands like she wanted me to understand. Her final request wasn't about the house or the town. It was about *him*.

I moved around the desk and knelt in front of him, taking his shaky hands in mine. "I'm sorry too. I know how persuasive she could be. How much she loved you. If she'd asked the same thing of me, I wouldn't have been able to say no."

He reached out and pulled me into a hug.

"I shouldn't have shut you out. Expected you to grieve like me. But most of all, I was wrong not to let you explain the truth," I whispered into his chest.

"I hope you never have to make the kind of choice I had to make with your mother." He held on to me like he'd do anything to make the years of our estrangement disappear.

The sound of his strong heart thumped in my ear. When I was a little girl and scared of the shadows in the night, monsters under the bed, Dad would be there. He'd sit on the edge of my bed and whisper words of comfort. Pull me close like this and swear he'd never let anything hurt me. I'd forgotten how much I'd missed that part of him. The vulnerable side he never really showed.

As he clutched me tighter, my gaze swept around the office. The surfaces that weren't littered with paperwork and books were covered with pictures of Tessa and me as kids. There were some more recent photos we'd taken with Mom before the chemo made her lose all her hair. Of Iris and Rose at the park. When I'd imagined his office, I pictured it to be as stiff and uptight as he was, but he'd made it a tribute to our family.

271

"Was it you?" I said so quietly I wasn't sure he heard me.

He pulled away and swiped at his wet cheeks. "What do you mean?"

"Did you send the anonymous email to Hearth and Home about the work we were doing on Huckleberry Lane?"

"No." He focused on me with steady eyes. He was telling the truth.

"In the email, it said that Ivy Falls was in dire financial straits. Is that true?"

"This town has been struggling for a long time," he said with a heavy sigh. "The signage contest was the first way I tried to create some buzz. Bring people in. As you may have guessed, it's not working the way I'd hoped. People aren't interested in coming to places like Ivy Falls anymore. Too much to do and see in the big cities."

"Is that why the town council is so keen on selling to developers? Why they keep throwing up barriers when Manny and I try and renovate these houses?"

He gave me a sad nod. "As time goes by, they get more afraid of what will happen if we don't start generating enough revenue. Or even worse, if Ivy Falls goes bankrupt."

"So this has been happening for a while?"

"Yes."

"And you still ran for mayor?"

"At first I didn't want to, but—"

"Mom talked you into it."

Again, another sad nod.

"Why didn't you tell me?"

"I thought with my finance background I could whip the town into shape. Unfortunately, I let your mother down there too." He turned his gaze away like he hated to admit defeat.

"No, you didn't. You've tried," I said.

"There is one good thing about that dang contest."

"What is that?"

"Your producer, Lauren. She asked me to talk to the store owners. To ask permission for the film crew to shoot all the storefronts and outdoor signs as part of what she called 'The Open' for your show. She thinks it'll create interest. Bring people here out of curiosity."

That explained her need for an introduction.

"If there even is a show." I let out a rough exhale and moved back to the chair in front of his desk.

"What do you mean?"

"Manny and I want it to happen but the timing is tight. She's given us five weeks to make the repairs. We have ten days left and there's still so much to do. I don't know if we'll make it."

There was a tick in his cheek I didn't understand. Was there another problem with the town? Before I could plunge down that spiral he said, "I should have told you this a while ago, but there are no words to express how beautiful you've made that house, Torran."

I held on to his praise like it was a precious gift. They were words I'd wanted to hear for so long but believed would never come.

"How do you know what it looked like? You've only seen it in total ruin."

"Not true. In late June, when you and Manny were out doing errands, I talked one of the workers into letting me inside." His shiny eyes stayed pinned on me. "The hardwood floors. The refurbished staircase. As I walked around, I saw all the small nods to your mother. The antique chandelier in the entry. How you'd painted her favorite shade of robin's egg blue in one of the upstairs bedrooms."

His eyes shuttered closed.

"For years she went on about how talented you were. How you had a knack for seeing beauty under all the rubble. I wasn't willing to accept any of it, until it hit me what a gift you have for restoration."

"Thank you." I took a thick gulp, unsure how to handle this new, kinder side of my father.

"What about Beck? Is he helping with the repairs—considering it was his sister who was involved?"

"His sister is very sick, Dad. She didn't mean to cause us any harm."

"Yes." His voice went softer. "Sadly I'd heard that via town gossip. Is he getting her the care she needs?"

"He's taking her to a facility out of state. He's helping with the financial side of things, but once the house is done, he's selling it."

"How do you feel about that? I know you two were getting close again."

He had the decency not to blush even though I was sure the memory of the two of us kissing in the bathroom was seared into his frontal lobe.

"I had a long talk with Tessa about it. She's helped me see that he's worth fighting for so I'm not giving up on him. He means too much to me."

He smiled. "I'd expect nothing less from you."

"I should be heading back. Manny's probably waiting on me."

"Torran." His quiet yet tense voice made me stop before I reached the door. "There's one more thing I want to discuss. Can you meet me at the house tomorrow around five?"

"What is it about?"

"A concerned citizen came to me. Wants me to check things over."

Now I understood that tick in his cheek. Of course someone in town was complaining again.

"I promised Tessa I'd pick the girls up from soccer practice. Is it okay if I bring them?"

"Yes. I'll see you at five sharp."

He gave a firm nod but there was something in the way he looked at me. It was a quiet, almost stoic, warning that our meeting tomorrow was going to be about much more than a simple complaint.

46

TORRAN

On My Own Terms.

THE girls talked nonstop all the way from soccer practice about Rose's recent attempt at playing goalie. It was hard to watch her tiny body moving in front of the net. Her jaw set like she was a lioness protecting her pride even with her little legs trembling. When she'd flung her body out and caught a ball midair, it took everything within me not to jump to my feet and do a little cheer.

"Why are we going to Mr. Beck's house today?" Iris asked as she turned the vent toward her, my old truck sputtering out the faintest bit of cool air.

"Grandpa said there was something he wanted to talk to me about."

The girls swapped worried glances. I'd tried so hard to keep the animosity between my dad and me hidden, but children did not miss a thing.

After our talk yesterday, I hoped things would get better on that front. It'd be nice to spend more time around the dinner table with Dad, Tessa, and the girls and not have to constantly bite my tongue.

"It's a good thing Mama will be there." Iris dragged a hand over the sweaty hair matted to her forehead. "She promised to have drinks for Rosie and me."

"No. Sorry, girls. Your mama is at the P&P today. I'll take you over there when I'm done at the house. I promise it won't take too long."

At least I hoped it wouldn't take too long, but my dad's words about meeting today made my stomach roll.

"But Mommy said—" Rose started, but Iris tapped her knee. Shook her head.

What was that all about?

We made the turn on to Danbury Lane and a puff of gray smoke floated out of the engine. The more I pressed the gas pedal, the darker the smoke grew.

"Oh no!" Rose cried. "What's wrong with Sally Mae?"

When the smoke billowed out into a larger plume, I pulled over to the curb only four blocks from the house.

"You two stay in the car."

I jumped out and grabbed the step stool from the back. Once the hood was cranked open I saw the issue. A crack in the water pump.

Great. One more thing in my life I had to fix.

I shoved the hood down and tossed the step stool into the truck bed.

"Sorry, girlies. Looks like we'll have to walk to the house."

Once I unloaded them and promised we'd come back for their soccer gear, we started in the direction of the house.

When we reached the first corner, a flash of black caught my eye.

"It's Mr. Beck!" Iris cheered as the sleek Mercedes pulled up.

What the hell was he doing here?

The window inched down and I was not prepared for the chaotic crash of my heart when he smiled in my direction.

"Sally Mae giving you trouble again?"

There were many words flying through my head. Some were gushy like *I've missed you*. And *God, you're beautiful*. Others were more of the sailor-type variety which I'd never say in front of the girls.

"Mr. Beck, we're going to your house to see our grandpa," Rose exclaimed.

"Will you take us there? My feet hurt after soccer practice," Iris added.

"Of course. Climb in." He beamed at them and I hated the way my ovaries did a little dance.

No. I was still confused and angry. He couldn't pull up, flash that panty-dropping smile, and think he could save us.

Before I could protest, Rose and Iris scrambled into the back seat.

"You go ahead and take them," I grumbled. "I'll meet you there."

"Tor, come on." He gave me a pleading look.

"I need the walk to clear my head," I insisted.

"Torran." His voice went firm. "Get in the car. Please. I'm headed in that direction anyway."

"Why?" The hairs rose on my neck.

"As soon as we get to the house, I'll explain everything."

Those whiskey-brown eyes went soft. The girls waited for me in anticipation. I yanked open the door cursing the fact that Sally Mae had put me in this incredibly awkward position. I'd wanted to talk to him on my own terms. Set the time and place. Not have to climb into his shiny and expensive car for a damn ride.

After I ordered the girls to put on their seatbelts, we drove in silence. Only a block from the house, cars lined both sides of the street. The drywallers had finished the last of the patch work yesterday. Manny talked to the painters and they weren't scheduled until next week, which gave us just enough time before the production crew for Hearth and Home returned. So why was the street jammed like there was some kind of block party going on?

"Why are there so many people in the house?" I breathed out as we pulled into the driveway behind Manny's truck.

Beck turned in his seat and flashed a smile at the girls. "Hey, will you run inside and tell your grandpa we're here? I need to talk to your Aunt Torran for a second."

"Sure," the girls chirped together.

"No," I spit out.

I wasn't ready for this. My mind was still spinning from my conversation with Tessa yesterday, and I wasn't sure how I was going to explain to Beck all my fear, anger and frustration over what was happening between us. How I wanted him to stay despite all the things he'd said in the hospital. That I knew my heart would shatter into ten thousand pieces if I lost him again.

"The girls can't go inside alone. There are too many dangerous tools and pieces of equipment out." I undid my seatbelt and waved them out of the car.

The closer I got to the house, the more anxiety crammed into the corners of my chest. Voices I recognized—Barb and Susan, Isabel, even Miss Cheri and Old Mrs. Vanderpool—floated out the open windows.

I swung back to Beck, and the grin he gave me said he was responsible for whatever chaos I was about to find inside.

47

BECK

So Much For A Sneak Attack

THE hunch to Torran's shoulders warned this might not have been the best decision, but I was all in now and couldn't turn back.

"You need to start explaining right now, Beck." The fire in her voice was not at total boiling because of the girls.

"Please, let's go inside and then we'll talk."

She mumbled out "jackass" under her breath before following the girls up the restored steps. I dragged in a full breath and prayed this was going to work.

In the last week, I'd made over a dozen calls to the people in Ivy Falls I thought might agree to my plan. I wasn't sure anyone would want to help the guy who broke Torran Wright's heart again, but I had to try. Luckily, they loved her more than they hated me.

Once inside the front door, we were greeted by several people working in the living room. The scent of turpentine and fresh paint clung to the damp August air.

Torran looked at me with a combination of shock and irritation.

In the formal dining room, Barb, Susan and Miss Cheri were surrounded by another ten people on their hands and knees scrubbing at what was left of the stains on the paint-covered floor. Even old Mrs. Vanderpool, with her little dog tucked into what looked like a baby carrier, was laying a coat of primer on the walls.

"Beck," Torran huffed out. "You said you'd explain."

"I know, but go upstairs first. Your dad is waiting for you and the girls." She started to shake her head but I stepped in close. "I need you to trust me right now."

"Trust you?" she said, her voice low and haunted. "How do you expect me to do that after everything…"

She stopped and glanced at the girls who watched us with wide eyes.

"Fine, I will see you upstairs."

She mounted the steps with the girls darting up and around her to reach the landing first.

I followed voices into the kitchen. Manny, Diego, Pete, Deputy Ben, and Silvio from the hardware store all worked on yanking out what was left of the damaged appliances.

Manny and I locked eyes. He tipped his chin to the corner of the kitchen. Once we had a bit of privacy, he said, "They're waiting for you upstairs in the master bedroom. Torran's dad told her to be here by five."

"Yeah, about that." I scratched at the whiskers on my chin. "Her truck broke down and I picked her and the girls up as they were walking here."

"So much for a sneak attack," Manny said.

All I could do was shrug. "She's here. That's what matters."

"True, but I need you to promise me you won't screw it up again."

"I swear I'm done making mistakes."

"Good, because you know what will happen if you make Torran anything but blissfully happy."

Manny tried to act all gruff but couldn't hide the light in his eyes as he watched the town help restore his and Torran's dream. Mine and Piper's too.

"I'm sure you're not the only one who will run me out of the city limits if that happens."

"You've got that damn right!" Old Mrs. Vanderpool yelled from the entryway. Her little dog barked along like he agreed.

The men all laughed before returning their focus to the double ovens, which were beat to hell.

I turned and walked up the stairs, observing all the people working to clean up the house. I was sure a thank you wasn't enough for Manny and Mr. Wright. When I'd first reached out, they were hesitant about my plan, of what Torran would do, but they still helped me rally the people of Ivy Falls and I was very grateful.

At the hospital, Torran railed at me for running. For not wanting to put down roots. Today, I was going to show her that I was done being scared to let people help me. That I was willing to put all my fears aside and make connections with the people I loved again, even if I was deathly afraid of how easy it'd be for any one of them to be ripped away from my life.

Inside the master bedroom, Tessa worked side by side with Mr. Wright repainting the walls. Isabel from the bank dumped paint into waiting pans. They were all laughing at some joke Mr. Wright was in the middle of telling.

Torran wasn't there.

"She took the girls to the bathroom," Mr. Wright said, dropping his roller into a pan. "I held up my end of the bargain, now you need to hold up yours."

"Yes, sir. My plan is get her alone. Tell her the truth about what's going on."

"She's going to give you a hard time. Push you away. Don't let her," he said.

"I have no intention of backing down. She can curse at me. Shout at me for my stupidity. All of which I deserve. But I'm not walking away ever again."

"Good. Now grab a roller and help us out. That dark blue spray paint is hard to cover."

I dropped my keys on the floor near the door and walked toward Tessa. Before I could say a word, she handed me a roller dripping with cream-colored paint.

"It's a good thing you've done here, Beck. Bringing the town together," she said.

"Something tells me there is a 'but' coming."

Tessa stopped mid-roll and turned to me. "But if you ever hurt my sister again, I will kidnap you, tie you to a tree naked in the middle of the summer and let the mosquitos make a meal out of you. I will then make it my mission to ensure that no store in a fifty-mile radius sells you any calamine lotion or Benadryl. Do I make myself clear?"

"Crystal clear." She would absolutely follow through on that plan if I screwed up again.

"Good," she huffed. "Now get to work. The best way to get my sister to soften up is for her to find you here working."

"Don't count on it." Torran stood outside the door with Rose and Iris at her side. "What the hell is going on here? Why is half the town downstairs acting like they're our cleaning crew?"

The girls let out a giggle.

"Auntie Torran, that's a sweary word," Iris said.

"Sorry, girls, but some instances call for a potty mouth." Her fiery gaze turned to me. "And why are you even here, Beck?"

"That's enough," Mr. Wright said. "There is an explanation for why everyone is in the house."

"Dad," Torran said in a warning voice. "Is Beck the 'concerned citizen'?"

He exhaled a low breath and dropped his paint roller into the pan. "Let's go outside and talk calmly about all of this."

Torran turned for the stairs but Isabel's voice stopped her.

"Please wait a moment. I have a confession to make, and I hope after hearing it you won't be too upset with me."

"What is it, Isabel?" Mr. Wright gave her a look of concern.

She gave him a small smile and tucked a silver hair behind her ear. "It's nothing bad, Miles. Well, I hope you don't think it's bad."

Iris and Rose giggled at the sound of their grandfather's name and Tessa quickly shushed them.

"I'm the one who sent the email. Brought Hearth and Home back here." She twisted her hands in front of her, heat coloring her warm brown cheeks. "This town is hurting and I wanted to help. Torran and Manny are incredibly talented and I wanted to showcase their work." Her gaze turned to Torran. "I'm sorry I didn't speak up at the town council meeting. Perhaps I should have, but you made such an eloquent speech that I didn't want to interfere." Her eyes fluttered in Mr. Wright's direction. "I know you've been doing everything possible to change things, make them better as mayor. I saw you struggling and I couldn't stand by and watch all the work you've done be for nothing." Her voice broke. "I only hope you all will forgive me for butting in."

Mr. Wright stepped forward and patted her shoulder. "You did the right thing, Isabel."

Now he was blushing too.

Torran pulled Isabel into a hug. "Even after all the rotten things I said about Ivy Falls, you still had faith in me. Thank you."

Like all the people downstairs, Isabel believed in this town. Wanted to save it. Nobody could be angry at her for that.

"Are Auntie Torran and Mr. Beck still in trouble, Grandpa?" Iris asked.

"Not if they have any sense in their heads," Mr. Wright grumbled as Isabel helped Tessa corral the girls to a corner of the room.

"After you," Mr. Wright barked in my direction.

Torran's face stayed an emotionless mask.

I'd forgotten how much it hurt to have her look at me like I didn't matter in her life anymore. That armor of hers was firmly back in place, and I wasn't sure I could ever strip it away again.

48

TORRAN

Fight For What You Want.

NOT two steps outside the front door, my dad started in.

"Please pardon my brazenness, but both of you are acting like complete assholes."

I barked out a laugh. "Well, hell, tell us how you really feel, Dad."

He dragged a hand across his tight mouth, but there was an ease to his body I hadn't seen in years. It was going to take me a while to get used to this new side of him.

"Torran's mother and I had thirty incredible years together," he started. "Sure, we fought, but I never ran away." He shot a dark, accusatory look at Beck. "And while there may be problems"—his steady stare moved to me—"a relationship as strong as yours is worth fighting for and…"

"Sir, I appreciate what you're doing, but this is between your daughter and me," Beck interrupted.

"Fine, but I want you both to admit that your lives are better together. A moment like this only comes along once in a lifetime. Don't be stubborn. Fight for what you want. I wish I'd done that with

284

Torran's mother. For both my girls." He flashed a sad smile. "Talk things out right now or, believe me, you will spend the rest of your life regretting it." He turned on his heel and strode back into the house.

Neither of us moved. Hammers and saws continued to pound and whir inside.

"Why did you bring my father into this?" I turned and pointed to the crowd working inside. "And why are Barb and Susan learning how to use a table saw? How did you even get Old Mrs. Vanderpool here, especially since this place is still a mess?"

The moment I walked into the house my heart clenched. This was not how I wanted any of them to see the place, but the sight of them working side by side, scrubbing away the last of the paint, sweeping up debris, made my throat go as dry as sandpaper. I thought of the community open house I'd wanted. This was sure as hell not it, but I was grateful for their presence anyway.

"I was getting to that, Tor. Just give me a chance."

The plea in his voice made me bite back all my other questions. I'd promised Tessa that I'd listen. That I wouldn't close my heart again.

"Fine, but make it quick," I said over the steady whir of that damn table saw.

"With Manny's and your father's help, I reached out to everyone in Ivy Falls and asked them to come here today. Manny let it slip that you only have a week left to get the house back into good condition before Hearth and Home films again. I figured more hands would help."

"Why does it matter to you? You said you were done with Ivy Falls." I wanted to say "and me" but couldn't push the words out.

"Piper is at Changing Attitudes. It's a rehab facility a short trip away from Ivy Falls. They have a great program with a lot of intensive therapy. It's a good place for her."

"I thought you said you were taking her to San Francisco?"

"She wouldn't let me and she was right," he said in a rush. "I'm sorry for being scared. Blind to what's in front of me. I thought fixing this house would help erase some of the pain of my parents' tragic deaths. Restore my sister's sobriety. I know now that the house is nothing more than paint and wood. What pulled me back to Ivy Falls was the sense that a vital piece of my life was missing."

He took a step closer, the scent of him washing over me.

"That missing piece was *you*, Torran. While I love this house, you are my home."

"But you insisted Piper was the only one who mattered in your life. That the Beck I'd loved no longer existed."

"I was wrong. The truth is when it comes to my sister, hell, even my own life, I make bad decisions because I'm too damn afraid to get close to anyone only to lose them again. It's become my default to use Piper's problems as an excuse to push people away." He dragged shaky hands through his hair. "I'm tired of running from what might be. What my life could become if I finally accepted my parents are gone and what happened to them was a terrible accident."

"I want to believe you. Trust you again. And I'll admit that I've built a wall around my heart, but how do I let that wall crumble if I'm afraid that you'll just take off when things get hard between us?"

"Everything you accused me of in the hospital was true." He scrubbed a hand over his face, his fingers trembling. "The night I told you about how my parents died I didn't give you all the details. When we got back to the campsite after snowboarding, my mom asked me to help with dinner. I was all ready to go inside the RV when Piper started pleading for me to have a snowball fight."

The grief in his voice was the same as Piper's the day she talked about being too frightened to move after the explosion.

"Piper quickly built her arsenal while my dad worked on turning on the propane tank outside. Watching her build those snowballs, my competitive side kicked in." Shame rippled over every line in his face. "I convinced my dad to cut up the carrots for the stew so I could show Piper how a snowball was really made. If I hadn't been so selfish, childish, I would have been inside when the RV caught fire. Maybe I could have pulled my mom out. My dad, he would have been outside with Piper. Alive. One choice and it changed my life forever."

"Beck, it's not your fault. You need to forgive yourself."

"I know but it's not that easy. Since they died, I've had this sense that my life is no longer my own. That I'm responsible for Piper because my parents aren't around to watch out for her. It's an obligation I take seriously, and it's ruled every part of my life: my job, my heart, my future." He heaved in a huge breath. "It wasn't until I drove past the Ivy Falls sign on the day of the auction that I began to realize I'd let so much of my life be ruled by fear. Fear of not taking care of my sister. Fear that I'd failed my parents. Fear that I was being punished for my selfish choice that day."

Every part of Beck shook. I ached to reach out but I was so tired of him pushing me away. All I could do now was keep my eyes focused on him so he knew I was truly listening.

"I thought I was doing the right thing by protecting my sister. Giving everything up to keep her sober, but I've learned that my hovering only makes things worse. If Piper's going to recover, she has to do it on her own."

He slid his hand over mine and I welcomed its warmth.

"It's taken me too long to find my way back to Ivy Falls." His stare moved along the new hand-carved railing Manny had made for the porch. "This house doesn't bring me pain. It's a reminder that the past can help you heal."

"But it caused Piper to go back to drinking, to drugs," I argued. "How do you know that won't happen again when she returns?"

"When those criminals were hammering at the walls, stealing the antiques, she said it felt like it was tearing our parents' memory away again. But now, she realizes how much she wants to honor and protect that memory. It's what she's holding onto in recovery."

He shifted his steady gaze back to me.

"This house might actually save her. Save us both." He tucked his chin down. "Maybe save us all," he whispered.

A long beat of silence passed. Inside, the people of Ivy Falls worked to bring the house back to life. They were giving it, giving us, another chance.

"I love you, Torran. I have loved you since that day your mom guided me down that sunlit aisle at the P&P and you moved aside to make a spot for me next to the window. I know I've hurt you, but I'm not running away this time. You're stuck with me, and I swear if you give me this one last chance, I'll spend the rest of my life proving I'm worthy of you."

"I've made some wrong choices too, Beck. Grief, fear, and anger have ruled too much of my life. I want to fight for this. For us, but

I'm scared that when the house is done, this bubble will burst. You'll have to go back to Nashville and I'll pick a new project here. How do we make us work in that picture?"

"We make it work because we fight for it."

He must have sensed my panic because he edged in closer.

"Do you love me?" he whispered.

I dragged in a long breath and tried to look anywhere but at him. He caught my chin in his hand and I stared into his warm brown eyes.

"Torran, do you love me?" he repeated.

He was a stubborn and infuriating man, but if I was going to love him I had to love every single part of him. Deep down I knew that no matter what had happened in the past, what challenges we faced in the future, I couldn't bear to live another day without him.

"Yes," I stuttered. "I've never stopped."

He wrapped me in his arms and hung on. All the small hums of his body reminded me how perfectly we fit together. That the day my mother had walked him down that aisle in the bookstore, his wide brown eyes and funny smirk landing on me, I'd fallen in love with him too.

"For so long I'd fought the pull back to Ivy Falls. I'd convinced myself that after being gone for so many years, you would never want me. That this house would only be a reminder of everything I'd lost. But time and circumstances, and maybe a sign I'd denied months ago, brought me home." Beck slid his hands through my hair. "Back to the town who still accepts, and loves, both me and my sister. To the girl who's haunted my dreams all my life and carved an indelible mark into my soul."

His tight embrace felt like a promise that he'd never let me go again. I sank into the heat of him. He'd said I was his home, but he was my safe harbor too. Neither of us could predict the future. What would happen with the show. How his sister would do in rehab. The one thing we could count on was each other. Were things going to go wrong? Of course. Was it possible that the show wouldn't get picked up? Yes. But whatever happened, at least we'd be together now. In the end, that was all that mattered to me.

"There is one final issue we need to discuss." He stepped back, his gaze sweeping over the house. "I've decided I'm going to move in once it's done."

"But what about your condo in Nashville?"

"My place is here. I want to ensure that the house stays in our historic care."

"Our care?" I stuttered.

"Yes." He clutched my hands tighter. "When you're ready, I'd love for this to be *our* home. My parents built some gorgeous memories here. One day I'd love for us to continue that legacy."

Tears burned the corners of my eyes. I moved in close and placed a gentle kiss on the edge of his neck. "Legacy," I whispered against the hollow of his throat. "One of my favorite words."

I wound my fingers through his silky hair. He pressed his hard body against mine and I melted into him. He was here with me. We were keeping the house. Continuing a dream his parents would have loved.

As our kiss deepened, a steady tap on the second-floor window forced me to pull away from him. Iris and Rose pressed their faces against the glass and waved to us.

"They've both been slightly out of control since I told them they could be part of the final taping for Hearth and Home." I glanced up at the house. "I have to hand it to Lauren, she was pretty cool about getting us extra time."

"She's like me, Isabel, Barb, and Susan—practically the whole damn town. We all know how amazing and talented you and Manny are."

Seeing everyone at work inside made my heavy heart light. This community always showed up for the people they loved. For the first time, I let myself believe that maybe I was finally forgiven. That all of Ivy Falls could see how much this town meant to me.

Beck pressed a kiss to my forehead. "Once the show goes on the air, it's going to be a total hit. We all know it."

The house, his sister, the video, they were trials that had pushed us to the edge. Each one a test to see if we could make it through. And here we were, hand in hand, finally standing in front of a dream we'd built together.

49

BECK

Not Even A Flicker Of Armor.

Eight months later...

THE little red dress was absolutely killing me.

Torran stood in front of the mirror in the master bathroom turning left and then right. She huffed out a loud breath and climbed on top of the toilet seat. "Finally," she grumbled, being able to get a full view of the dress. When Tessa came to the house yesterday with her girls, she had handed a garment bag to Torran and demanded she wear the dress inside to the sneak preview of the show tonight.

Ever since the executives at Hearth and Home had seen the rough edits of Torran and Manny's show, they were sure it was going to be a hit and urged Lauren and her team to amp up the promo. That meant she'd been here every day for the last week ordering marketing assistants to take dozens of pictures of each room and giving us zero privacy.

She was the reason I was currently hiding in the bathroom which, if I was being honest, I didn't mind because I was getting a full-on show of Torran in a silk dress that slid easily over her shoulders and dove into a deep V down her chest.

"Don't you think it's a little over the top?" She yanked up the front like somehow she could hide her beauty.

I moved in and wrapped my arms around her waist, pulling her down from the toilet seat. "It's sexy and perfect for tonight," I whispered against her beautiful neck.

Everyone was gathering in the center of town tonight to watch the first episode of *Meet Me in Ivy Falls*. Manny and I balked at the folksy title at first, but when word got out, the entire community was abuzz and we couldn't deny that it would bring a lot of attention to the town.

Mr. Wright had given permission to erect a giant screen on the lawn in front of town hall, and Barb and Susan had worked their magic to get all the local Ivy Falls restaurants to serve food and drinks.

The tap of heels against the stairs made me press my finger to Torran's lips. "If we stay quiet, maybe she'll go away."

Torran stifled a laugh. "Have you met Lauren? She's more tenacious than Pete's little dog looking for table scraps."

I brushed a hand over a piece of spindly pink insulation stuck to the hairs at the nape of her neck. I loved that she wore every house like a badge of honor. Proof that she was willing to do the work to make a property shine.

After my house was finally finished, she and Manny, at the request of the town council, agreed to renovate the Old Thomas Place at the edge of town. It was a special request as it'd just made Tennessee's Register of Historic Places and was the first home ever built in Ivy Falls.

"Did you know you have insulation in your hair?"

She checked herself in the mirror. "That must have come from the inspection we did today."

"How's that coming along?"

"Slowly. We've been studying all the old blueprints, but the place is a cesspool of rot and rodents. The whole subfloor has to be replaced and the plumbing is older than Mrs. Vanderpool. It's going to take a lot of work to make it historically accurate."

"If anyone can do it, it's you and Manny."

"He's been in a real mood lately," she said, trying to rub away the bits of fluff still clinging to her hair.

"Is it because of Teddy Ray?"

Ever since we'd won the Brinkley account, he'd been relentless about wanting to see the property Manny and Torran suggested for the future site of his restaurant in Ivy Falls.

"No. Manny pretty much told him and his minions that we wouldn't be able to talk about plans for the new restaurant for at least a few more months."

I gulped. "How'd he take it?"

"I'm pretty sure he's met his match in Manny."

"Then why is Manny in such a funk?"

She gave me that knowing gaze.

"Still in the friend zone with Tessa?"

"Yep. She's been quite clear that she wants to focus on the store and the girls. That she has no room in her life for a relationship."

"That makes sense but I also know what a great guy Manny is. I think Tessa will let him know when she's ready."

"Maybe after the divorce is final, she'll finally let herself be happy."

I reached out and squeezed her hand. "We can always hope."

She leaned in and pressed her forehead to mine. I held her close. Pushed the corner of the dress off her shoulder and marked her collarbone with my warm mouth. She leaned her head back, giving me more access until the sharp click of heels moved down the hall toward us.

We both held our breath until Lauren's footsteps faded. I leaned back against the counter and glanced around the room. Torran had outdone herself. The antique pieces that were originally on the wall above the sinks had been destroyed during the party. She'd been scouring antique shops within a hundred-mile radius of Ivy Falls to find replacements but had come up empty until Piper found a gorgeous pair of turn-of-the-century pieces on Etsy.

"Your sister did a good job finding the sconces," Torran said, meeting my gaze.

"Thank you for letting her help out as part of making amends."

"I see her fighting every day, Beck. She's really strong."

"Yeah, she's like my mom. A fighter."

Torran reached up to make sure one of the sconces was level. "How are things working out for her at Sugar Rush?"

"Barb and Susan have been good to her. The other day she was so excited to tell me about how she'd learned to make her first latte."

"One day at a time," she said, snuggling into my side.

"That's right." I bent down to press a kiss into her hair but froze when the footsteps returned. I slid a finger over her lips again. Her right eyebrow arched in annoyance and she licked my finger.

A flash of heat went through me and I spun her around so her back was pressed against the sink. I leaned in close, my mouth brushing over the shell of her ear. "This room is where it all started."

"Yep." She grinned. "This is where I almost took your head off."

I played with a loose hair that danced near her face. "That's not what I remember about that day."

In one quick move, I lifted her up onto the counter and spread her legs apart. I stepped in between them and circled my arms around her waist. She sucked in a cute little gasp when I slid my hands up the hem of her dress, first caressing her calves and then inching up toward her thighs.

With mischief sparking behind her eyes, she leaned in and pressed a kiss to my neck.

I loved that not even a flicker of her armor remained.

When I woke up with her in bed next to me every morning I had to take a minute, a deep breath, to remember she was real. That I wasn't just dreaming her into existence. For so long I'd pictured her being in my life again, but a big part of me had lost the ability to hope and dream after my parents died. Slowly, I was seeing that allowing myself to be vulnerable with her, letting her see both the light and dark in me, was not something I should be ashamed of. That while I'd been through hell, and I was still walking a rocky path with Piper, I could focus on the future. A future with her that held so many possibilities.

"How quiet can you be if we do a re-enactment without any in-terruptions this time?" she taunted.

My answer was to kiss her long and deep until her phone started blaring with some cartoon song about bumblebees.

"How have those little girls changed my ringtone *again?*" she said more with amusement than frustration.

She turned the screen toward me.

"Yeah. It's like he has a sixth sense or something."

She laughed and hopped off the counter. "Hey, Dad, you're on speaker."

"Where are you?" he asked in his "Mr. Mayor" voice.

"At home," she said, tugging her dress back up over her shoulders.

Home. I couldn't help the wide grin that covered my face every time she said that word.

"Everyone is already in the square. Lauren's been calling and texting me for the last thirty minutes about everything from extra chairs to a working PA system. Could you get a hold of her and tell her to cool her jets? Isabel and I have everything handled."

She smiled at how gently he said Isabel's name. We'd had several family dinners over the last few months and Isabel had been a guest on more than one occasion. Last week when he came over to help with the sod we were laying in the backyard, he finally admitted he liked her and both Tessa and Torran gave their approval.

"Lauren is actually here," Torran said. "Beck and I will talk to her, confiscate her phone if need be."

"I can hear you," she called from outside the door. "Don't think I don't know what you're doing in there." She went silent before adding in her shrillest tone, "I'm leaving right now, and please, for the love of God, don't break anything before I get pictures!"

"What is she talking about?" Dad grumbled.

"Nothing." Torran put her hand over my mouth to stop my laughter.

This time I returned the favor and licked her hand which earned me another little squeak.

"We'll be there soon, I promise," she said, biting back her own giggle.

"Do not be late, Torran."

"Yes, Dad." She ended the call and pulled me back in for another hot kiss.

The sound of the front door closing meant Lauren was on her way to the square to pester Mr. Wright some more.

"We should go too," I said, reluctantly pulling away.

"Only if you promise we can continue what we were just doing later tonight," she whispered against my neck.

I kissed her back and said, "Oh, that's a promise I plan to keep."

"For forever?" She held my gaze. "Through thick and thin? Good or bad?"

"Yes, even through issues with permits and green paint," I teased.

"And dumbasses who fall through rotten ceilings?" She winked. "Whatever the world throws at us, we can get through it if we're together."

I tugged Torran in close, loving the distinct thrum of her heart against mine. "Are you ready to go face all of Ivy Falls?"

"No." A teasing smile that lit up her face said this was no longer about redemption. It was about a future where she could restore the beauty of the town. Show the world its distinct and meaningful history.

Though she resisted at first, she finally let me pull her out into the hall. I still couldn't believe this was my house. The floors were restored to their deep caramel hue. It had taken weeks, but Manny had fixed the banister and the steps that led us down to the first floor. The entry felt fresh with its cream-colored walls and antique chandelier that Torran discovered on a weekend away in Louisville after the trespassers destroyed the original.

In the living room sat two oversized brown leather couches, two matching armchairs, and a glass and steel cocktail table. The focal point of the room was the shiny black piano we'd placed in front of the bay window.

Music had re-entered Piper's life in rehab. After she moved in, and some weeks of negotiation, we used part of the money in her trust to buy the piano. Every time she played, it was like I could feel my parents' presence. Like they knew we were finally home.

I pecked another kiss on Torran's cheek, inhaling everything about her. I'd been so terrified to return here. To face a past that forced me to remember a life that no longer existed. But with her by my side, I understood that I could build a new life and memories. A life that would make my parents beam with pride. For too long I'd been running from my fears, and I was grateful that winding path finally led me back to Torran, and Ivy Falls.

A LETTER FROM AMY

DEAR READER,

I'm thrilled you've found the first book in the *Ivy Falls* series. This story has been living in some form or another on my laptop for over seven years. It started as my "palate cleanser" book. My little escape when research for whatever historical book I was writing became too overwhelming. It's been through more revisions and beta readers than I can count, and I'm grateful to every kind soul who ever said "yes" to reading this story for me.

Ivy Falls was inspired by Franklin, Tennessee, a place I fell in love with when I lived in Nashville for six years. From the moment I drove through Franklin's town limits, I was captivated by its history and charm. How the community seemed to have a living, breathing heartbeat every single time I visited. As a girl who was born and raised on the west coast, I'd never lived anywhere with seasons, much less a place with a small town community feel. I guess that's what drew me in. Inspired me to create Ivy Falls. The kindness of the people and how they always seemed so happy to meet you. I will also admit that the wide cast of characters in the book was inspired by one of my favorite shows, *Gilmore Girls*. There is one scene in particular that has a very "Stars Hollow" feel. If you're a fan of the show too, you can probably guess which scene it is!

When I started to draft this book, I knew I wanted to center the story on a couple who deserved a second-chance romance. A couple who had a ton of history and were carrying deep-seated wounds. As the story began to build in my head, I heard the Taylor Swift song "Haunted" and instantly pictured ex high school sweethearts who meet again but as totally different people. People nursing heartache and hiding secrets they never intended to share until time and circumstances (hello, falling through an attic ceiling) forced them to form an uneasy alliance. As the series continues, I hope you'll follow along and fall in love with this little southern town and its community as much as I have.

One of the greatest things about being an author is hearing from readers. If you'd like to get in touch, you can find me here:

Website: amytruebloodauthor.com
Instagram: @atruebooks
Threads: atruebooks
TikTok: @atruebooks
Goodreads:
https://www.goodreads.com/user/show/172303447-amy-true

I also have a newsletter, True Writing, where you can sign up to get bonus content and future book updates.

ACKNOWLEDGEMENTS

Music has always been a big part of my life. Since the time of burning CDs and then the invention of the first iPod Shuffle (yes, I know I'm dating myself), I've created playlists. Every single book I've ever written has a corresponding playlist, so I might have done a little dance when I was told I could include the one I made for this novel. Each song holds a special memory of this book. The scenes where my characters were in their darkest despair. The moments when they felt the most joy. It's a similar parallel to the highs and lows of writing a book. Some days when the words flow, you feel like dancing to Paramore. On the days when you're fighting for a single sentence or a paragraph, you slip into the mood of an M83 song. The journey of writing a book has these same ups and downs, and I'm overjoyed that this special story has finally found its way out into the world.

Getting a book into the hands of readers is a Herculean task, and I have many people to thank. First, I am very grateful for my agent Kristina Perez, who immediately fell in love with Beck and Torran and became their greatest champion. To editor extraordinaire, Jennie Ayres, thank you for your incredible eye for continuity and for encouraging me to make every scene that much sweeter. Thank you Diane Meacham for designing an incredible cover and setting such a beautiful tone for this series.

One of the things that keeps me writing (even on days when I don't feel inspired) is the loving support I get from my family who allow me to live inside my head for long periods of time. Olivia, I love how you've become such a voracious reader and are always willing to let me toss character names and story ideas your way. Ryan, you continue to make me proud with your big heart and kind soul. David, none of this would be possible without your unwavering love. Thank you for always listening to my medical questions, and for the hours you've let me disappear into my make-believe worlds. To my sisters Wendy and Julie (who were the inspiration for Torran and Tessa), you constantly show me what true courage and love looks like. I am better because you are such a big part of my life.

To my AZ writing community, a big shout-out for your wonderful advice and for letting me commiserate with you when things haven't always gone right. Huge thanks also to my CP, Kelly deVos, who has such a great eye for pacing and for making sure my plotting is tight. Even when I was in my darkest hours with this job, you made me believe this book would sell. That is a gift I'll never forget. To Joanna Meyer, my publishing buddy, you are the best at making me see the silver lining in things. Thanks for letting me vent about the ups and downs of the writing world. For my beta readers over the years: Laura Heffernan, Marty Mayberry, Jen Blackwood, Riki Cleveland, and Jody Holford, your notes buoyed my confidence in this book and made me never give up on it. Massive hugs to you all!

One final message to readers… You are the beating heart of the book community. Thank you for your kindness and enthusiasm when it comes to my novels. The romance world is better because of you and your continuous belief in the Happily Ever After.

AMY'S PLAYLIST FOR

Meet Me In Ivy Falls

- ❧ "Your Biggest Mistake"—Ellie Goulding
- ❧ "Run Right Back"—Moon Taxi
- ❧ "Bad Blood"—Bastille
- ❧ "Spiralling"—Keane
- ❧ "Still Into You"—Paramore
- ❧ "IDGAF"—Dua Lipa
- ❧ "Don't Let Me Down"—The Chainsmokers ft. Daya
- ❧ "Reckless Driving"—Lizzy McAlpine ft. Ben Kessler
- ❧ "Talk Too Much"—COIN
- ❧ "Look After You"—The Fray
- ❧ "Daisy"—Goodbye June
- ❧ "Beautiful War"—Kings of Leon
- ❧ "New Person, Same Old Mistakes"—Tame Impala
- ❧ "Haunted (Taylor's Version)"—Taylor Swift
- ❧ "Hurts Like Hell"—Tommee Profitt ft. Fleurie
- ❧ "Wait"—M83
- ❧ "Perfect"—Ed Sheeran